I0692091

RED STAR
THE HUNTER TRIALS

ISBN 978-1-59433-738-3
eISBN: 978-1-59433-737-6
Library of Congress Catalog Card Number: 2018932773

RED STAR
THE HUNTER TRIALS

MARY FLINT

PUBLICATION CONSULTANTS
We Believe In The Power Of Authors

PO Box 221974 Anchorage, Alaska 99522-1974
books@publicationconsultants.com—www.publicationconsultants.com

Prologue

Iris was still trying to get over the initial shock of what had just happened as she gazed down on the charred, blackened ruins of what had been the first place she had ever been able to call home.

She barely noticed her best friend, Tasha, standing behind her in what had been a small plaza. Iris stood in the middle of it, fighting to keep herself under control. A few renegade tears rolled down her cheeks.

Tasha suddenly started to run.

Iris grabbed her arm. "What do you think you're doing?" she shouted, her voice gravelly from all the screaming earlier. "We don't know if he left soldiers behind. They could be anywhere!"

"I know that Iris," Tasha said, "but I have to …" She trailed off and looked down at her shoes for a moment, a tear sliding down her cheek. Then she looked back up. "I have to see home."

She shook off Iris's grip and took off running towards the outskirts of the village.

Iris couldn't take it anymore. She let her knees buckle beneath her and began to sob uncontrollably, not because her hands were bloody and sore, or because her face was stinging. It was because she had lost everything she cared about except for Tasha.

Iris clung to the pendant that hung around her neck on a black cord, her teeth clenched as her sobs became silent tears. Was it possible to die of a broken heart? Was that why he'd come and razed her home to the ground? She wiped her eyes as she heard footsteps behind her. Expecting to see Tasha, she stood and turned around.

"Did you …" She stopped mid-sentence. Tasha was not behind her. Instead, there was a figure in a red, hooded cloak that flapped in the wind. The cowl of the cloak hid the figure's face.

5

Iris took a step back. "Who are you?" She asked warily.

"I'm surprised you've forgotten me so quickly," the figure replied. Iris knew that voice. It was *her* voice! Iris's grief was rapidly replaced with anger.

"Forget? How could I have forgotten you? I've thought about you every day since you left!" Her voice was thick with contempt.

The figure sighed. *So much anger for one so young*, she thought.

"Iris, please! We've talked about this!"

Iris gave a short bark of mocking laughter. "Really? I don't remember that. We never *talked* about anything! All you ever did was give an excuse and change the subject!"

The figure winced at the stinging words Iris had said. But amid all the anger and contempt in Iris's voice, she detected another emotion: hurt. Deep, deep, hurt.

The figure sighed and held up her hands.

"You were young, Iris. You wouldn't have understood!"

Iris knit her eyebrows. "Young? You think that's an excuse I'm going to buy? You forget how much I *understood* when I was 'too young'! You forget how much I can remember!"

The figure began to say something, but Iris didn't let her. "If you were here, you could have saved everyone!" Iris motioned to the burnt rubble around them. "You could have saved *him*!" Iris's voice broke. More tears rolled down her cheeks.

The figure cocked her head. "Him?' Do you mean—"

"You know who I mean." "Oh, him. Iris, it wasn't possible. He was—"

Iris held up her hand angrily. "Don't say it! He wasn't an outsider so don't you *dare* say it!"

The figure took a small step back. "Iris, he didn't know about your gifts!"

Iris scowled. "That's where you're wrong."

The figure cocked her head again. "About what?"

Iris clenched her fists. "Everything! I can't see how you call them gifts," she yelled. "They're more like curses." She added bitterly.

The figure shook her head. "Iris, don't be like that!"

6

Iris scowled. "Why shouldn't I? All these *gifts*, as you call them, have caused me nothing but pain! You don't know what it's like!"

The figure nodded. "It's true that we are all different, but we also have similarities."

Iris rolled her eyes. "Could you *please* say *something* without it being a riddle for once?"

The figure paused, studying Iris. "I found him, Iris, just like I promised I would. That's where I've been all these years."

Iris felt her rage and hurt boil over. "So, he's more important to you, is that it?" The figure took a step back.

"Iris?"

Iris took another step toward the figure. "He was so important that you left us to fend for ourselves, running from planet to planet."

The figure sighed. "Iris, you misunderstand. You had guidance, he doesn't."

Iris held up her hands. "And I suppose you've been teaching him all about his 'gifts'?" The figure hesitated, and then said, "Not exactly."

Iris laughed harshly again. "All the *guidance* I ever got was being told to never show anyone my powers."

The figure was about to reply when she stopped abruptly. "What's this?" She asked quietly. She lightly touched Iris's cheek. There was a deep cut in the shape of a crescent moon. It would most certainly scar.

"Here," the figure said, reaching to touch the cut.

"NO!" Iris yelled, slapping her hand away. "I have had enough!" Iris growled.

The figure put out her hand to Iris. "Iris, please!"

Iris shook her head. "If you can heal this," Iris motioned to her cut, "I don't see why you couldn't have helped me! I don't see why you couldn't have saved all these people! I will *never* forgive you for that, *sister!*" She spat out the title as if it were acid.

Fresh fires sprung to life around the two sisters. The figure looked down at the ground for a moment, then looked back up at Iris. Iris's hair was the color of the fire, her eyes reflecting the flames.

It's fitting, the figure thought, then she said, "I'm sorry you feel that way, sister. *Re cacoma nee tri has,* Iris, *uvar megat vhar.*"

Iris said scornfully, "You know I don't speak the old tongue."

The figure nodded. "I know." Then she shimmered like a mirage, and vanished.

Iris wept bitterly until Tasha came back. A hard rain put out all the fires around them except for one:

The fire of hate and anger that burned in Iris's heart.

I will never forgive you!

Part One

Whispers and Shadows

1

(Edrix)

Rendaria isn't your ordinary planet. Just like a person has one face, but beneath that face, there's different emotions, thoughts, layers. Rendaria is the same way.

There's only one city, but it has levels.

There are ten levels, and another being constructed. Certain people live on certain levels. At the top, there's the bright beautiful buildings, where the important people, like The Chairman, our leader, and his officials, the other ten Chair Members that each administrate over one level, live.

As you go down, the levels get darker, and dirtier. At the bottom, there's almost no power. It's mostly where criminals and Hunters go to hide.

The kind of career you had, depended on what level you lived on. At the top, you became someone important. At the bottom, you're lucky to have an identity.

I came from the middle, Level Five. There, you mostly have artists, musicians, novelists, and other arts. The wages aren't great, but the living conditions aren't terrible. I was lucky to have the job I had.

When I was eight, my older brother, Jai, had caught the attention of the head of the REGS force on Five, Tiren Joice, a tall man with dark hair who didn't laugh much. He'd been a family friend for several years. REGS was what most people called our police. The real name is The Rendarian Enforcement of Global Security, but the acronym, REGS, is usually used.

Anyway, Joice entered Jai into the Higher Program at REGS.

Those that graduate from the program become Higher Ones. The term came from the fact that those who went into the Higher Program had specialized training. They were better at, well, everything, but each Higher One had their focus, like diplomacy, infiltration, knife combat, hand-to-hand, the list goes on.

10

After Jai graduated, he moved up through the ranks pretty fast. He was able to get me in when I was fifteen. I was the youngest initiate ever accepted into the Program, and the fastest to graduate.

Now, at the age of seventeen, I'd been graduated for seven months. I hadn't really been interested in a particular field, so I'd specialized in the thing I was worst at: knife combat.

Truthfully, REGS wasn't what I really wanted to be doing. I *had* looked up to my brother, I still did, but I didn't really think that REGS was for me. Part of me hoped I would fail the Program and be sent home. Instead I had graduated faster and earned higher scores then the rest of the initiates.

I guess I kind of felt duty bound to stay. My dad had been in line for Grand Commandant, the REGS head. He'd died in a hover car accident when I was twelve. I guess I wanted to make up for that.

On the bright side, it paid well. Jai and I each sent half of our paychecks home. I earned sixty credits a month, and Jai got a full hundred. The combined sum of eighty was enough to keep our mother, dark haired and blue eyed, and my little brother, Zaren, who shared the same traits, fed and living for the month. They wouldn't be able to live glamorously, but my mother would never have spent it that way even she could. Having lost both her parents at a young age, she'd grown up being frugal, and continued to do so. Anything she could spare she gave away.

I wish I got to see them more, but even when I did, it didn't feel the same. Jai and I each got to go home once a month, but our rotations were different. We were never there at the same time.

I wanted a mission. When Jai had first graduated, he'd gone on his first mission in a matter of rotations. The only mission I'd gotten was to deliver a report to the next floor up. Higher Ones were supposed to have important jobs, like guarding special convoys, escorting diplomats and—if they were lucky—the Chairman himself.

Jai keeps telling me to be patient. I suppose it's technically a good thing that I don't have an assignment. That means that there's not a lot going on.

But there have been whispers, things Jai has said when he thinks I can't hear him. Whispers of a group that's spreading a message, a message that Jai and his superiors don't want the rest of us to hear.

A message of hope.

2

(Edrix)

"Edrix!" I looked up from my hover bike as Jai approached me. It was hard to hear him over the sound of mechanics working and ships coming and going in the REGS hangar bay. The scent of fuel was strong in my nostrils.

"How can I help you, Agent Solan?" I asked him. Since I was in the Higher Order, I got the privilege of calling him either "agent," or "sir."

He nodded to my bike with his chin. "You going somewhere?" He asked.

I shook my head. "No, I was just putting something away."

Jai and I really didn't look similar at all. Jai had blue eyes and light brown hair with a lighter skin tone. I had black hair and medium skin, with bright green eyes. Actually, everyone in my family looked like Jai.

"Well," he said, "you have a transmission from Mila Solan. Take it when you can."

"Will do," I said. He nodded and went to talk to the pilot of a returned Sky Sailor. Mila Solan was my mother though why she was calling me was a mystery. Since Jai and I were both on duty, we had to use her name, just like I couldn't call him Jai. He could call me Edrix because he was higher up in the line. I locked the control console on my hover-bike and left the hangar.

The hallway was silent as the door closed behind me, closing out the sound of engines and the scent of fuel. I headed towards a terminal where I could take my transmission.

REGS isn't exactly picturesque. The walls, floor and ceiling are a dull gray with plain white lights on the ceilings and walls.

I found a terminal and scanned my personnel card. The transmission popped up with an option.

Accept or decline? I tapped *accept* on the touch screen. The picture fizzled for a moment while the connection was made. The screen cleared and I was looking at a young woman with glossy black hair and sparkling brown eyes.

"Jess?" I asked in disbelief. She smiled.

"Hello, Edrix. Sorry if I confused you. I stopped by to see your family and used their comm system."

I hadn't seen Jess in four years since she was moved to another district. She was like an adopted sister, and my best friend, even though she was five years older than me.

"What brought you back home?" I asked laughing a little.

"I got transferred back so I came by for a visit. I'll admit, I was a little disappointed you and your brother aren't here." She brushed her hair behind her ear. Most people that knew the both of us said we looked a lot alike. I couldn't see it, but I guess we did look similar. My mother said that we had the same determined look when we were told we couldn't do something.

"Sorry about that. If we'd known you were coming we could have waited to use our home rotations."

She made a brushing off motion. "Don't worry about it. You're both big kids now. Can't take a rotation off for me."

I laughed.

"How are things there?" She asked.

I shrugged. "Pretty quiet. I haven't gotten an assignment yet."

Jess's smile lessened a bit. "Don't worry about it too much. I know a lot of people have already told you that."

I shrugged. "I guess I'll just have to be patient."

She smiled again. "That's the spirit." There was a beeping noise from her side of the transmission.

"I have to go, the call time's about to run out." She gently touched the screen. "It was good to see you again."

"You too."

We said our goodbyes, and the screen went back to its usual display. I stood there for a minute thinking about our conversation. Jess had almost looked … disappointed when I'd said nothing was going on. And then relieved when I told her I hadn't gotten an assignment? I shrugged it off. She would have been worried if I said I did have one. I turned to leave the console when my communicator beeped. I pressed the control on my wrist.

"This is Higher One Solan," I said.

"Supreme Authority Fisk would like to speak with you."

I recognized Commander Tara's voice. She wasn't a Higher One, she was just a Lower Agent; Fisk's equivalent in her Order.

"I'll be right there," I said. I turned off the cuff on my wrist and headed for the lift.

"Supreme Authority's office," I said. The lift began to hum as soft, strobing lights went up the walls. I wondered what he wanted to see me for. Only a small part of me dared to hope it was an assignment. I sighed. It was probably just the usual questionnaire about work shifts and what not.

The lift came to a stop. The doors opened as the female computer voice droned,

"Lift 778 has arrived at the Supreme Authority's office."

Most of the time, we just say "S. A." It saves time. I walked past the front desk that was attended by a female officer. I waved my ID badge over a scanning panel by a door to the left of the desk. A light above the panel flashed green and the door opened.

S. A. Fisk was a tall man with graying red hair and a temper to match. He had piercing blue eyes and cheekbones sharp enough to cut paper. The orange Supreme Authority emblem was emblazoned on his lapels. He looked up from his data pad as I came in.

"Mr. Solan," he said. His voice was robotic and deep from his artificial larynx. There were about fourteen other agents in the room. Four Higher Ones and ten Peace Keeper class. I stood next to the other Higher Ones. Jai stood quietly behind Fisk. Fisk rose from his desk, hands clasped behind his back. My heart started to beat faster. This was it. I was getting an assignment!

"Agents, we have a riot on Eight," Fisk said, his robotic voice echoing around the room. Everyone was completely silent as we stood at attention. I was listening to Fisk, but I kept glancing at Jai, still standing behind the desk. That meant that he was Fisk's assistant. I knew he was important, but I didn't think he was *that* important. Fisk was saying something. I focused back on him.

"Higher One Sanders will be in charge." He went over to a tall agent with blonde hair that stuck up in spikes. Sanders had been in REGS almost as long as Jai had, about seven years. Sanders had a lot of scars on his face, and a prosthetic eye. He had mostly been on assignment to apprehend Hunters. It was one of the most dangerous missions, but it was what he specialized in. I didn't like him much. He was a bully. My first rotation in training, he had picked on all the smaller cadets, giving them the hardest jobs, rigging training courses, and making sure everything they did was wrong. Myself being six feet tall—and inch taller than him—didn't have a lot to worry about, but it still made me mad.

Fisk continued. "Your goal is to help the REGS force on Eight to control, or if possible, end the riot." He paused. "Use any force necessary." His voice made his last statement echo around the silent room ominously.

"Dismissed."

We all turned to leave. I felt excited. My first real assignment. Sure, it was nothing huge, but it was a start. I felt like I was floating. I glanced at Jai. He slowly slid his eyelid down in a wink. My elated feeling disappeared. Fisk hadn't chosen me, Jai had pulled strings. I didn't want to have a pity mission. I wanted a mission because I was good enough for it, not because my older brother felt sorry for me. That's what I had seen in his eyes. Pity.

3

(Andresha)

I typed the password in again slowly, double checking each letter and number.

The clearance light came on red again and the console made an angry beeping sound at me. I reached for my braid to tug in frustration, only to remember that it was coiled on the back of my head. I glanced around. No one had noticed me yet. I was in one of the highest security buildings on the planet, the Core. It was where all the planet's information was stored. Everything from what the Chairman said in his speech this morning (which was not that noteworthy) to which shoe you put on first before you left for work.

I was trying to hack said Core. Now, before you start wondering what I'm doing, probably breaking the law, I'll save you the trouble. I am. I'm committing crimes punishable by life in prison, or sanitation on Ten. Now I bet you're wondering if I do this sort of thing a lot. I do, and before you ask, I rarely get caught.

Rarely.

Call me what you will, hacker mercenary, criminal, con. I've heard and been called them all. I've been called rebel, vigilante, insurgent, renegade, and rogue as well. I preferred the word *patriot*, but insurgent sounded cool too.

I rubbed my forehead. I had the wrong password. How was it the wrong password? My contact had given it to me along with all the other passcodes and security measures I'd gotten through so far. I bent over the console.

"Happy," I whispered, "I've got a problem."

I could almost hear Jim sigh. He *hates* his code name.

"What is it Water Bird?" I liked my code name.

"The password's wrong."

"*Wrong?*" He hissed. I glanced around again, only moving my eyes. The floors, walls, and ceiling were polished and white. All the bright lights reflected off of them, hurting my eyes. People went

17

around the room, giving or taking data pads, working the consoles, or watching others do those things. Everything here was white. Even the uniform I wore was white with bright blue piping.

"What do we do?" Jim asked. I wasn't sure what to do. I was suddenly aware that every eye in the room was watching me. I pretended not to notice. I heard the door open on the other end of the room. Then guards poured in as an alarm started to blare.

A REGS Higher One with red hair and a long scar across his left eyebrow, pointed to me. He looked familiar.

"Andresha Kanway, we finally see each other face to face again." He said. Great. They knew my name. I straightened up. I remembered the Higher One, where he had gotten my name. I grabbed his name from the sea of memories in my mind and shut the rest out. I didn't have time for those.

"It has been a while, Agent Jarome Lars." I bit my tongue as Lar's face turned crimson. *Keep it together* I told myself.

"That's *Higher One* to you!" he said through gritted teeth. I shrugged, making him angrier. He shook his head.

"I didn't believe it at first, you know. That you'd joined them." I glanced up to the ventilation duct above the console I had chosen as my escape route.

"Well you always did have *impossibly* high hopes for me," I said back. I wished my comm was still on. Then Jim would be hearing this and know to start the extraction plan. Lars tightened his grip on his Buzz Stick, a long baton with enough electricity to knock you out for six hours.

"I had faith in you, Andresha," he said quietly. I took the pins out of my bun and let my tightly braided black hair fall down my back. One section, with a dyed red streak, fell loose over my forehead.

"Don't tell me you're actually feeling sorry for me," I said. When I'd taken my hair down, I'd managed to activate my ear comm. Now Jim would *hopefully* hear what was going on. Lars shook his head.

"I wish you'd had the same faith in me," he said.

I raised my eyebrow. "That would imply there was something to have faith in."

I guess I should mention that I had a quick and impeccably sharp wit. Lars winced a little from my barb. Then he just shook his head.

"Oh how the mighty have fallen," he said bitterly. I looked at the scar on his eyebrow, knowing I'd caused it. Another voice sounded in my ear. It was Jim's.

"Extraction is ready, Water Bird," he said. I resisted the urge to sigh in relief. I could get out of here.

"I'd love to reminisce down Memory Lane," I said to Lars, "but I really don't have the time." I threw my data pad at him. He caught it without even flinching, but I used the momentary distraction to slam my fists onto the console, sending sparks flying everywhere. Then I was up on the console and jumping to the ventilation shaft. The cover was already loose, so my arms went right through the opening. I pulled myself into the shaft and shut the grate behind me. Only now did I let myself shudder. Lars hadn't changed a bit since that day three years ago, when—

No! I stopped myself from thinking about it. It would only distract me. I tapped my ear again.

"Happy, you there?" I asked. There was silence for a moment, then a burst of static.

"I hear you. I'm almost to the Break-Out point." I paused for a moment. I was on the twentieth floor. The break-out point was five floors down. I rounded a corner and found a shaft that went down.

"I'll be there in seven minutes," I said. I shut the comm off again and slid down the shaft. My mind returned to the password. Why would he give me all the right answers to get in and then the wrong password? It didn't make any sense. I racked my brain, but nothing came. Maybe my contact had been given false information as well? I made a mental note to ask Chief for permission to investigate.

I made my way to floor fifteen and dropped down out of the shaft. I glanced around, but no one was in sight. I quickly got my bearings. According to the number on the wall, I was in section C-17. Break-Out was in D-04. I needed to go left. Everything was still white and shiny, giving me a headache. I ran down the hall, turning another left, and then right. I was now in D-10. There were three hallways branching off in front of me: straight, left, and right. The numbers went higher going right, so I went left.

And ran straight into a guard.

"Hi!" I said brightly. Then I shoved him so hard, his head banged against the wall. He slumped unconscious to the floor. I quickly took his communicator and smashed it under my boot, then continued to D-04.

I was the first one to arrive at the window. I didn't bother looking out, knowing it would make me sick. I waited for Jim to show up. Five minutes and still no sign of him. I tapped my communicator.

"Happy, are you there?" I asked. There was no response. I tried again. "Happy, do you copy?" All I got was a burst of static. That meant his communicator was either being jammed, or it was offline. I pressed a hidden control on my wrist, switching my comm channel.

"Command, this is Water Bird. Can you hear me?"

There was a brief silence, then I sighed with relief as I heard a voice on the other end of the transmission.

"This is Command, Water Bird. What's your status?"

I looked for Jim down the hallways again. Still no sign of him.

"I can't reach Happy. Can you still detect his Pill?"

The 'Pills' were small chips that were placed in one of our teeth before a mission. If captured, we could compress it with our tongue, and the heavy sedative inside would effectively place us in a coma. If the antidote was not received in ten hours, the sedative would, in short, kill us. Every Pill can be triggered by remote if an operative cannot activate it. The relevance of this is that Command would be able to track Jim from his Pill's signal.

"Yes," the operative on the other side of the transmission said. "He's—"

Gunfire cut her off. It was coming from my left, echoing off the walls.

"Cancel that, Command," I said, "I've found him." I shut off my communicator and ran towards the gunshots. Not the best idea you say? I whole heartedly agree with you, but I did it anyway. I was well away from D-04 when Jim came racing past me.

"Come on!" he yelled. I slid to a stop and caught a glance at the REGS agents following him. One of them was Lars. Joy and happiness. I spun around and took off running again, catching up with Jim. He was breathing heavily, and he had a wide cut on his cheek that was bleeding heavily. He pulled his hand gun from his concealed shoulder holster and snapped a few shots off at our pursuers. I didn't stop to see if he'd had any success. I saw evidence of Jim's close calls. His sleeve was torn, and a bullet had shaved a track through his sandy colored hair.

"You've looked better," I said to him. He flashed me a smile.

"That's probably true," he said. We arrived back at the window in D-04.

"Call Sunrise," Jim told me, his gray eyes watching for REGS, "my comm's useless."

"I noticed," I said. He threw me a mock scowl. I switched my communicator's channel again. A REGS boot appeared around the corner. Jim immediately shot at it. When he's standing still, he never misses. There was a yelp of pain, and the boot disappeared. I turned on my communicator.

"Sunrise, we're ready for Break-Out!" I said. Bullets whipped past me.

"Get down!" Jim yelled and pushed me to the floor. He returned fire with deadly accuracy. I'm not a terrible shot myself, but I didn't have a gun. I wasn't *supposed* to need one. I reminded myself for the zillionth time not to take weapons advice from my contact.

"I hear you, Water Bird." Sunrise's voice sounded in my ear. "Proceed to extraction coordinates." I tapped Jim's shoulder. He dipped his shoulder to let me know I had his attention, not taking his eyes off the corner for a second.

"He's ready!" I yelled. He nodded. We both went to the window. Upon examination, we discovered a serious problem.

"It doesn't open," Jim said. Another mistake our contact made. Then everything started to fall apart. I realized that the alarm has been ringing this whole time, and heard the sound of many boots coming this way. Then Lars appeared, seemingly out of nowhere, and grabbed my sleeve. I tried to grab his collar, but he kept my arm still. I heard Jim's gun fire. Lars screamed and clutched his shoulder, releasing me. I pushed back into him, sending him into the wall. The boots were louder now, as well as shouts from their owners. We couldn't go back the way we came.

"Water Bird, are you ready?" Sunrise said.

I looked at Jim, then back at the window. Maybe...

"Yes, we're ready," I said.

Jim raised his eyebrows in surprise. "Did you perchance miss the fact that the window *does not* open?" He shouted.

I held out my hand for his gun. He gave it to me. He knew better than to waste time and ask me what I was doing.

"I saw that it didn't have hinges, if that's what you mean."

I emptied the rest of the mag into the glass, leaving a web of cracks. Then we ran towards the window top speed. I pushed off the floor at the last second, kicking out the glass. Then Jim and I were falling towards the ground.

4

(Andresha)

The wind whistled in my ears as we fell. I quickly changed my fall into a dive and Jim followed suit.

"Sunrise," I yelled, "any time now!"

Jim looked at me. It must be weird to only hear one side of the conversation.

As if it was waiting for me to say something, a Sky Sailor de-cloaked underneath us. It was a small craft, but it could carry about five people comfortably, a few more if necessary, and had a small storage unit in the back. From this angle, it looked like a bird. A hatch in the roof slid open, and Jim and I shot into it. As soon as our feet cleared the threshold, a confinement field activated, absorbing our momentum. Little by little, it lowered us to the ground. The hatch closed, and the sailor cloaked.

A tall man with greying hair came out of the cockpit.

"Everybody okay?" Short asked. He was wearing a REGS uniform and his blue eyes were full of worry. I sat Jim in a chair and pulled a med-pack out of a cupboard. I heard the blinking of monitors in the cockpit.

"Except for this cut," I said, "and a bruised rib or two, we're fine."

I opened the med-pack and found a sterilizing pad and dabbed Jim's cheek with it. He grimaced and inhaled sharply.

I wrinkled my nose. "It can't hurt that bad!" I protested.

Jim gave me a half smile. "It *usually* gets me sympathy," he said.

Short had disappeared into the cockpit while I cleaned Jim's cut. He came back in with two bottles of water and handed one to each of us. Short was one of the nicest people I knew. He was probably the closest thing to a father I'd had since I had met him a year ago. I was fourteen, then. It felt like forever.

I made Jim drink his water, but I set mine aside. I found a small tube-like tool in the pack. A cauterizer. I'm sure it had a fancy long name that meant the same thing, but I couldn't remember it.

I activated its violet beam and ran it over Jim's cut. In a moment, it had stopped bleeding. I placed a flesh colored adhesive bandage over it. Then I found a syringe of painkillers in the box. I peeled off the stero-wrap and injected them into Jim's arm. After a moment, he relaxed.

"Thanks," he said.

I packed up the med-pack and put it back in the cupboard. Short picked up my water and handed it to me as we walked into the cockpit.

"Are you hurt?" He asked.

I shook my head as we sat in the chairs facing the view port.

"A couple of bruises and scrapes, plus some hurt feelings," I said. I took a sip of my water. It was cold and refreshing. I caught a glimpse of myself in a blank monitor. My hair flew out in all different directions. I wasn't really surprised, seeing as I'd just been in a fire fight and then jumped out a window. I quickly undid my braid and combed through my hair with my fingers. It came down to the middle of my back when it wasn't braided.

"Do you want to talk about the last part?" Short asked. He was pretending to fly, his hands on the controls and his gaze fixed straight ahead. I looked at his REGS uniform again.

"Did they pull you out of cover for this?" I asked.

He shook his head. "No, my mission was already over. Besides, you're just avoiding the question."

He was right. I didn't really want to talk about it. I leaned back in my seat as the Sailor drifted down through the levels. I sighed.

"Lars was there," I said finally. Short nodded in understanding. He was one of three people that knew about my past.

"And that rattled you?" he asked.

I nodded. "Every time I see that scar on his face…"

Short put a comforting hand on my shoulder. "It wasn't your fault, Andresha," he said kindly.

It actually was, but I didn't protest the fact. I redid my hair in a side braid and wrapped the end around my finger in thought.

"I know it isn't," I lied, "I just wish …" I wish my brother would start acting like my brother again. I didn't voice the thought.

Short waited patiently for me to finish. Fortunately, I was spared from having to do so when the comm fizzled on.

"Sunrise, what's your status?" a man's voice said.

I recognized that voice. It was the Chief himself. I sat up straighter, even though he couldn't see me.

"The Happy Bird has been recovered, Chief," Short said.

"What's its condition?"

Short and I both looked back at Jim.

He set his jaw. "I'm fine," he said crisply.

Short looked at me. I shrugged. What he told Chief was up to him. Short sighed. He muttered something about hoping Jim didn't kill him or something and replied.

"One wing's fine, the other's got some bad scrapes, a couple feathers are bent."

"Happy Bird" was the code phrase for Jim and me. Each of us was a wing. "Feathers" referred to ribs.

There was silence on the other end of the transmission for a moment. Then Chief asked, "Is it up for another flight?"

My breath caught. Another mission? Now? I brushed a stray strand of hair from my face as I looked back at Jim. We had barely gotten out of the Core! I told myself to hear Chief out. I raised a quizzical eyebrow at Jim, a gesture meaning, *are you?* He nodded, then came into the cockpit.

"Yes, Chief, it is," I said.

"Right then," Chief said. "Here's the thing. We've got a mob in a square on Eight. District Seventeen. I take it you know what that means."

It wasn't a question. All three of us knew.

Chief continued, "It's gonna be the standard two passes. Once with the package, one more to leave a note. Got it?"

"Yes, sir!" Jim and I spoke in unison. We'd both known what Chief had meant by standard, but it never hurt to be reminded.

Short sat back in his chair, his arms crossed. "With bird or plates?" he asked.

"Plates if you have them," Chief answered. "Just get in there fast. The REGS detachment there just asked Headquarters for more troops, especially Higher Ones. Get in there, make the passes, and get home."

Funny how we called an abandoned bunker full of death-penalty criminals home. Funny *I* called it home.

Short nodded once. "Understood, sir. Sunrise out."

He closed the channel and looked at me, flipping switches on his console and grabbing the steering yolk.

"Both of you, get ready to fly!" he said. I got out of my chair and followed Jim to the back of the Sky-Sailor. Jim opened the small cargo hold. He handed me a jacket with a red line pattern and matching helmet. The ship suddenly rumbled. I stumbled over to the comm panel next to the door.

"Short!" I yelled over the rumbling outside, "What's going on?"

"Just some turbulence in the Transit Stream," he explained.

The Transit Stream was large tube-like structure that allowed ships like the Sky-Sailor to travel from level to level. It was hardly used, however, seeing as REGS were the only people with ships, and they were usually kept on site. I looked over at Jim who had pulled on his helmet. I followed suit and zipped up my jacket. I pulled on the gloves and closed the helmet's face shield. Jim handed me a G-plate and a large bundle wrapped in white canvas. The package. Jim took another bundle, then reached into a small bin and pulled a small round disk out of it. He handed the disk to me.

"You can leave the note," he said.

I took the disk and slipped it into my pocket.

We strapped our feet to the G-plates and stood in front of the Sailor's exit hatch.

"These don't have retaining fields," Jim said.

I nodded. I had already known this, but again, it never hurt to be reminded. I held my bundle tightly in my arms and crouched as low as I could to the G-plate's surface. The Sky-Sailor rumbled again.

"Good luck!" Short called. The doors opened and Jim and I raced into open air.

5

(Edrix)

I gripped my rifle as I glanced over the dark buildings. This was my first time on Eight. The agents around me put on their helmets and loaded their rifles. The streets were dusty, with bits of trash and rubble strewn around. Most of the windows in the buildings were broken, or missing all together.

"It's not all like this." I looked to my right. An older agent, Burnes, I think, motioned to the buildings. "This is just the bad district, that's all."

I didn't say anything. Technically, being a Lower Agent, he shouldn't be talking to me without permission. I knew he didn't mean any harm by it. Of course, Sanders didn't see it that way.

"Agent, that is your superior!" he shouted, storming over to us. Burnes ducked his head.

"I'm sorry, Higher One."

"Did I give you permission speak?" He shouted. "You don't speak Unless I say so!" Sanders' blow hit him in the jaw. Burnes fell.

"I gave him permission!" I shouted. Sanders' attention switched to me, his fist still raised for another blow. That wasn't necessarily a good thing. It was never a good idea to get in the way of a senior officer, but I couldn't stand for this.

"What did you say, Solan?" Sanders sneered. I could hear the anger in his voice. He liked to make sure everyone knew who was in charge.

"I said, 'I gave him permission.'" I spoke calmly, with just a hint of steel in my voice.

"Why?"

I wasn't expecting that. I took a deep breath, thinking fast. "He's been to Eight before. I wanted to know what to expect."

Sanders stared at me for a moment. "Move along then," he said, then moved away from us.

I helped Burnes to his feet.

"You shouldn't have done that," he said quietly.

"Sanders is just a bully," I replied. Burnes didn't say anything. I couldn't take my eyes off the red mark Sanders' punch had left on his cheek. Then Sanders called for helmets on. I slipped my helmet over my head and secured the strap. Then I slid the visor down. Burnes did the same, blocking the mark from view.

Our assault uniforms were light grey, almost white. Everything, boots, cargo pants, and jackets with padding and bullet resistant plates over them were the same color. Even the gloves and the helmets. Each one had a blue Star of Rendaria on the shoulders.

The large ramp leading down from the Lifts extended, and we all walked towards the troop transports that were waiting for us. Most of the Sun lights, the enormous lights that provided light on the Levels, were broken or switched off, and the few remaining ones starting to dim.

It was extremely cold, cold enough I could have seen my breath if my visor had been up. A few lights twinkled eerily in the windows of the dark buildings. I couldn't suppress a shiver.

A small dot of color on one of the buildings across from me caught my eye. I focused my visor on the spot and zoomed in. It was roughly star shaped, with six lopsided points, crudely drawn with red paint. That was odd ...

Sanders went to the front of the squad. I refocused my visor on him.

"All right. Commander Toraldo has asked for reinforcements. That's us." I glanced around. Being a Higher One, I stood in the front. Burnes now stood behind me, silent. Sanders continued.

"We are to help contain the rioters in the main square until she either reaches an agreement with the rioters, or gives the signal for us to move in." I wasn't sure what he meant by that.

"You'll be in groups. I will assign you to your teams upon arrival. Any questions?" A hesitant hand went up towards the back. Sanders nodded towards them.

"Why are they rioting?" An agent toward the back asked.

People around me murmured in agreement, or repeated the question to themselves.

"That information is not vital to the mission," Sanders said. "What's your name, Agent?"

"Kahar, sir."

Sanders nodded once and tapped something on a data pad. He then quickly ordered all of us into the transports. There was some very quiet conversation as the transports started up. Sanders was hiding something. I could tell, and I had a feeling it was important. An uneasy feeling settled in the pit of my stomach. The back of my neck tingled. Something was not right.

It didn't take long for the transports to get us to the riot. You could hear them before you saw them. Yelling, clanging. There was so much noise, you didn't know what was what. The transports deposited us behind a large building. The noise was intensely loud here, even with our helmets filtering the sound.

Sanders instructed myself, Burnes, two more Lower Agents, and another Higher One, Jenkins, to go around to the right of the building close to the platform where Commander Toraldo was stationed. We were to wait for instruction, but to stop any violence we saw. We all went to our assigned positions.

The noise was deafening now. I turned around the building and saw them. Men, women, and even children, all shouting, waving hands, fists, arms, and scraps of fabric. Why were they here? I tried to make out what some of them were saying, but it was all an incoherent roar.

Over the course of an hour, my group had to stop five fights, mostly because the rioters were targeting us. I heard the sound of a Buzz stick being used. I looked to my left to see a bloodied agent being dragged away with an unconscious rioter. People were going berserk. What kind of riot was this?

I looked up at the front of the building, where the head of Eight's REGS force, Toraldo, was trying to be heard over the rioter's shouts. She'd been doing this since we got here. Agents with rifles stood behind her, their visors hiding their faces. She was a diplomacy specialist. My eyes searched above her for some kind of answer. I had been listening to her as much as I could, but she never directly addressed the cause of this riot.

There! My eyes found it. A sign over the front door reading, FOOD RATION DISTRIBUTION.

Why were they rioting here? Food rations ...

Suddenly, the deafening shouts of anger changed. There were still those who were angry, yes, but there were other cries as well. They were pleas. Cries of the hungry and desperate. I looked over the crowd. Everyone was too thin, their cheeks sunken and eyes hollow. Some were so thin I could see their ribs through their shirts. I was speechless. This was no riot. It was a crowd of people desperate for food. I gave all my attention to what Toraldo was saying.

"Until the output of the factories meets the requirements of the Chairman, all food shipments will be blocked ..." I stared at her, horrified at what she was saying. My head was pounding. Why? Why? WHY? The thought echoed around in my head over and over again. I was feeling dizzy.

Jenkins suddenly pointed overhead. "Up there!"

I forced myself to fight my nausea and follow his pointing finger. G-plates. There were two of them coming towards us.

G-plates, or Gravity Platforms, were small boards made of metal about fourteen inches wide and thirty inches in length. The rider's feet were strapped to the board so the rider's side would be facing forward. G-plates could reach higher velocities then a hover car, making them extremely difficult to control. A rider either had to have a retention field, or crouch as close to the board as possible. They were fairly simple to build if you had the right components, but were usually banned from street use.

The G-platers were good. They were almost touching the boards with their knees, their arms and heads tucked close to their bodies. They wove around the taller buildings with ease, though one was a little sluggish. As they got closer, I could see that the sluggish one had a leather jacket with a black and green pattern. The other had a red and black pattern. They had matching helmets and held large, white bundles.

The people had noticed them now. There were pointing fingers and whispered questions. Toraldo and her guards had also noticed them. I saw Sanders speaking into his comm. The G-platers circled around the crowd.

Everything went completely silent. It was deafening. I could hear my heart beating inside my chest. The red G-plater flipped up its visor. I could tell she was a woman. There was a lock of hair that hung in her face with a streak of red dye. Both riders dropped something—their bundles—over the crowd. As I watched, the bundles split open, and small white parcels rained down. Children eagerly reached towards the sky. Parcels landed in their hands, and on the ground. Some of them opened as people scrambled to grab them. I saw packages of emergency rations, with a piece of fresh fruit in each one; some of them even had a few pieces of candy. Probably more than what these people got in a rotation, I thought. I kept watching. They didn't grab as much as they could and hurry away. Everyone was making sure everyone had at least one of the parcels. I stared in awe. It's hard to describe what I felt right then. There was the sound of a G-plate again. The rider with a red jacket swooped over the crowd, dropping a small, disc-like object.

Bomb. That was my first thought. I dropped my rifle and crouched to the ground, covering my head with my arms.

Silence. There was no explosion, then I heard a gasp.

"Look!" A little girl with blonde hair plaited in two braids down her back was pointing to the sky. I followed her pointing finger.

There was a holographic Rendarian Star, the symbol on the Rendarian flag, turning slowly in the air. Instead of blue, however, this star was blood red.

"Red Star!" The cry came from the back of crowd, then there were two, then three, then five, ten, eleven, the whole crowd took up the chant. They waved their hands, fabric, even scraps of paper in the air.

"Red Star! Red Star! Red Star!"

I stared. As far as knew, nothing like this had ever happened before. I felt a pang of nausea. I didn't know that there were food riots, or starving people either. Sure, things could be tough on Five sometimes, but I'd never assumed that it got this bad. Commander

Toraldo and her guards stared. Sanders hand was on his ear. Someone must be talking to him.

The G-platers made one more pass over the crowd. This time, the red one said one phrase in a clear voice that carried to everyone.

"There is hope!"

The phrase sent a chill down my spine, and sweat beaded on my forehead.

"Shut that thing down!" Toraldo shouted, pointing to the star.

I was still feeling dizzy. I felt a hand on my shoulder. I turned to see Burnes. I couldn't see his face, but when he spoke his voice was full of concern. "Are you all right?"

I tried to answer, but I couldn't. I sank to one knee, and Burnes crouched with me, then pulled my helmet off. He was about to ask me again when he stopped. I felt my helmet vibrate slightly. Sanders must be giving an order. Everyone around me raised their rifles. I realized what they were about to do.

"No!" I yelled, shooting to my feet. I grabbed Jenkins rifle and twisted it out of his hands. Everything happened so fast. Sanders yelled something, and two Peacekeepers grabbed my arms, pinning them behind my grasp. I kicked and fought.

"NO!" I screamed. I screamed it over and over again. The Peacekeepers dragged me towards the transports. Gunfire started. Screams echoed around me. A bomber uncloaked in the sky.

The Peacekeepers dragged me around the corner and shoved me into the prisoner's cell in the back of a transport. I surged forward, but they slammed the door shut and locked it. I kicked and hit, all whilst screaming at the top of my lungs. I didn't know how much time passed, but my voice went hoarse, and my screams turned to sobs. I never stopped kicking the door, even when the transport started moving. I knew what had happened.

There was no one left alive in that square now.

6

(Edrix)

The ride back to REGS Headquarters seemed like an eternity. I was sitting on the floor, unmoving. I felt numb and cold as I stared at the door. My throat was raw from screaming and crying, my eyes were red and swollen, and my head was pounding. I didn't feel like fighting, even when I heard voices coming towards me. My chest felt cramped, like someone was squeezing my heart as hard as they could.

When the doors opened, I couldn't move. The pain in my chest made it so I could barely breathe. There were two guards, one tall and thin, the other slightly shorter and heavily muscled. They pulled me out of the transport. They had to drag me towards the hangar exit. The smell of fuel burned my nostrils. I hung my head. This was where it had all started this morning, when Jai had told me I had a transmission.

This morning seemed like years ago. Just a few feet to my left, my hover bike was parked where I'd left it. Then, when I thought things couldn't get worse, I heard him.

"Edrix!" Jai's voice hit me with a wave of guilt. I'd let him down. I looked behind me. He was running towards me now. He must have been waiting for me to come back with the other agents. I couldn't find my voice to answer him. I doubted I'd be allowed to anyways.

"Stop!" he shouted. To my surprise, the guards obeyed.

"What is going on?" Jai almost shouted, his voice full of anger. I didn't look up. I didn't want to look at him.

"We're escorting him to the Detention level, sir," one of the guards said.

"I can see that, Peacekeeper, but I want to know *why!*" Jai shouted, his voice cutting like a whip. The guards actually recoiled from his startling anger.

"It's classified, sir," the tall one said carefully.

"On whose authority?" Jai snapped back. The guards looked between each other for a moment.

"The Grand Commandant," the shorter one said.

I felt my heart sink. This was bad. The Grand Commandant had heard about this and ordered me to be detained. I didn't get it. REGS was supposed to be the good guys, the people that kept things in order. The phrase that once gave me comfort now caused me to shudder. I was beginning to wonder just what 'kept in order' meant.

"We'll see," Jai said, his voice ominously low.

The guards dragged me to a lift that took us to the Detention level. Everything was steel gray. Everything, even the lights were a grayish hue, or maybe it was just the reflection. The guards abruptly shoved me into a small cell, activating the blue force-field behind me. In the event of a power disruption, or failure, metal bars would slide down over the opening, keeping prisoners contained. I picked myself up and looked around the cell. There was a small cot along the back wall, nothing else. There wasn't even a blanket.

I didn't get up for a long time. My heart hurt too much. Finally, I got up and sat on the cot, my head in my shaking hands.

"Different being on this side of the bars, huh?" a voice mocked.

My head snapped up as I looked for the speaker. In the cell across from me, there was a man sitting on a cot similar to mine. I judged him to be in his mid-thirties. He was sitting with his knees drawn up on the cot, his right side turned away from me.

"I'm sorry?" I said, the first words I'd said since the riot. My voice was low and raspy. The man laughed.

"You, a REGS, on that side of a force-field. It must be different." He spoke as if he were explaining something to a young child.

I folded my arms. "A little," I said shortly.

The man laughed again. I wondered if he did that a lot.

"How did you know I was REGS?" I asked quietly.

He motioned towards me with his head. "Your uniform," he said.

I looked down. I was still wearing the Incursion uniform, minus my weapons belt. I took off the jacket and draped it across the foot of the cot, leaving me with a gray undershirt. I noticed how cold it was, but I didn't replace the jacket. I leaned back against the wall.

"What about you?" I asked the man.

He raised his eyebrows. "What about me?" he replied.

I shrugged, "Who were you, before you came here?" My voice echoed off the walls.

The man smiled sadly. "Someone who would see a change in the world," he said softly.

"Quiet!" a guard snapped.

The man shrugged. I didn't know what else to do. I held my head in my hands; unable to think of anything except for the screams I had heard in the transport. The face of the blonde girl haunted me, the one that had pointed out the red star hologram in the air. My stomach tightened at the thought.

Footsteps brought me back to reality. Two Lower Agents stopped at the cell across from me.

"Get up!" One of them commanded.

I heard the man's soft voice, "And if I say no?"

The guards responded by grabbing his arms and pulling him out of the cell. They then marched him towards the lift. I rose to my feet and tried to look after them, but they were hidden from my view. I looked at the now empty cell. My gaze fixed on the wall the man had previously hidden from my view. There was a small, six-pointed star a few inches above the thin mattress. Just like the on one the building on Eight, just like the hologram in the sky. *Someone who would see a change in the world.* The man's voice echoed through my head.

Two agents that patrolled the aisle of cells walked past.

"Did you hear about that riot on Eight?" one of them said.

The other shook her head, "No, what about it?"

"They were worried about something in one of the factories, I guess there was an explosion," the first said.

The second inhaled sharply. "Do we know why?" she asked softly.

The first agent shook his head. "No, but S.A. thinks it was sabotage."

They passed my cell and went out of earshot. I was angry now. Fisk was lying to everyone else about this. Sanders' reply to Agent Kahar's question sounded in my ears.

"That information isn't necessary," I muttered. It had been a secret all along. But why? Why would the Chairman even *do* that? I ran my hands through my hair and put my head against the wall.

More footsteps came my way. I looked up and Jai was coming through the door, force-field activating behind him. I could tell from his rushed movements that he was in a hurry.

"I can't stay long." He said, confirming my thoughts. He thrust something into my hands. I looked down. It was my sketchbook and drawing kit, both well-worn from years of use. Jai put his lips next to my ear and whispered,

"Draw it for me."

I pursed my lips and nodded. It was something we'd done for years. I'd always had a talent for sketching. Living on Five, I had no shortage of opportunities to develop that talent. Jai had never shown an interest in it, but whenever I couldn't explain something, or words just couldn't convey what I wanted, he'd have me draw it. Jess and my mom did it, too.

Jai quickly squeezed my shoulder, then left the cell, the force-field activating behind him.

I stared at my sketchbook's worn cover. How was I supposed to draw this? How in the world was I supposed to convey the horror of it all? The disgust I had felt? I supposed I would just have to start with drawing what I'd seen and hope I did those people some sort of justice.

I drew everything in five hours, not wanting to miss a detail. Hands reaching for the parcels of food, reaching for Agent Toraldo, and the blonde girl, pointing at the red star projected in the sky. Those were just a few. My hand ached by the time I was finished, but I felt better. Now I waited for Jai to return.

He never came. Instead, five Peacekeepers arrived at my cell. I quickly slipped the sketchbook into one of my larger pockets. They instructed me to follow them. I didn't resist. I think one of them looked a little disappointed when I let him cuff my hands behind my back. They marched me to the lift. I was itching with curiosity, but knew asking questions would get me nowhere. The lift took seven and a half minutes, longer than usual. The doors opened to a spacious hallway in the usual dull-grey colors. The Peacekeepers marched me down the hall to the last door. I was more than surprised when the uncuffed my hands and opened the door. Inside, the walls were white, and the reflection of the lights made them look like they glowed. The floor was still light gray. IBright lights covered the ceiling. I couldn't tell who or what was in there. One of the guards waved me through the door. I hesitated for a moment, then walked through.

There were six people in the room. Two of them were Higher Ones. They stood on either side of the doorway, hands on their weapons. In the back corner, two doctors stood with data-pads. That couldn't be good. In the middle of the room, I noticed one empty, straight backed, metal chair.

I started to feel sick as I realized that it was for me.

To one side, was Supreme Authority Fisk. If it weren't for the chair, I might have glared at him. Jai was nowhere in sight. The last person really caught my attention.

"Higher One Solan," Nero Jackal said, "please have a seat."

I swallowed and did what the Grand Commandant ordered.

7

(Edrix)

I studied the Commandant as I sat ramrod straight in the chair. He was tall, about an inch taller than myself, and had dark hair shaved close to his head. Naturally, he wore a REGS uniform, with numerous medals pinned to his lapel, and his face seemed to be contorted in a permanent scowl. His eyes were grim and gray, like the floor. He had his hands clasped behind his back, and was pacing across the small room. He stopped and motioned to a tray of food on a small table next to me.

"Hungry?" He asked. The smell of the food made me feel sick. I turned my head away, and one of the Higher Ones took the plate away.

"What happened on Eight, Solan?" He asked me. His voice was almost too soft to hear, like a cat's purr.

"I'm not exactly sure, sir," I said. As a Higher One, I had the privilege of calling him 'sir.'

"You're not sure?" He repeated. I really wasn't sure at all. I was still trying to piece things together. I didn't reply to his question. He stopped pacing. He turned to look at me, then cocked his head to one side.

"Why did you attack your fellow Higher One then?" Nero asked.

I clasped my hands together to hide that they were shaking. What was I supposed to say to this? My thoughts raced. I could tell the truth, but then what? Things were starting to come together. Why we weren't told the reason for the riot. I had a feeling if I told the truth, it would be treason. Why did I care so much about this? Why couldn't I just shrug it off and get on with my life? Because it's wrong, I told myself. Because I wasn't like Sanders and Fisk. I took a deep breath and looked into Nero's eyes.

"Because they were going to kill innocent people," I said.

I waited for Nero to tell the guards to shoot me, or drag me back to my cell. A bit dramatic maybe, but I was on edge. Instead, Nero just smiled.

"That may have been true at first." He turned his back to me.

"That is, until until those terrorists showed up."

I knit my eyebrows for a moment in surprise.

"The people on the Gravity Platforms?" I asked. Nero raised his eyebrows a little. Then he pursed his lips and nodded once.

"Yes. They tried to hack the Core earlier. They've been causing quite a stir," he said.

I vaguely remembered a few reports about a raid on a REGS convoy between levels Three and Four a few weeks ago. These must have been the same duo.

I scowled. "I don't see what this has to do with those people."

Nero wheeled around to face me.

"They chose to turn away from their Chairman, and support these ... criminals," he purred.

"I was under the impression that criminals had the right to a trial," I said.

Nero smirked coldly. "Trials, in this case, would be a formality." He glanced at the doctors in the back. They were furiously tapping on their data-pads.

"Those people had obviously committed treason," Nero said calmly. I glanced at Fisk for a moment, wondering why he hadn't spoken. I was struggling to control my anger.

"They were showing gratitude!" I said tensely. Nero cocked his head, an expression of disbelief and puzzled wonder on his face.

"They disregarded the assistance of their Chairman!" He spoke as though I was a small child. I was really angry now. He was brushing all this off as if it were a minor *inconvenience* to him.

"The Chairman was going to let them starve! What was there to show gratitude for?" I dared to raise my voice.

Nero turned away and walked towards the door. I held a vague hope that he was going to leave. Instead, he stopped between the two Higher Ones. He straightened. Without looking at me, he asked,

"Would you do it again, Higher One?"

"Do what?" I returned.

"What you did?"

I didn't know what to say at first. Then, I thought about something Jess said once:

Sometimes, the best answer is simply yes, or no. It keeps things from getting complicated.

I squared my shoulders. Keep it simple, I reminded myself.

"Yes," I said.

Nero spun around to face me. I locked eyes with him. Those dead, cold eyes. I leaned forward, just a bit. My heart pounded as a thousand doubts raced through my head, but those eyes dispelled them as quickly as they came. I felt the weight of the sketchbook burning in my pocket. Those eyes would give that order again, and he wouldn't feel anything.

"I'd do it every time!" I said. My voice was tense, on the verge of shouting. And then in Nero's eyes, I saw anger.

"You would rebel against your Order, then?" He asked, his voice as soft as ever with just a hint of conceit. I hesitated as I considered his words. So what I had done was considered rebellion. It took everything I had to keep my voice steady as I answered him. *Keep it simple.*

"Yes, I would."

Nero looked at me in disbelief. "You would repeat an entirely futile attempt to stop justice?" He purred. His use of the word 'justice' made me sick.

I looked him in the eyes and held his gaze.

"Yes."

The Grand Commandant's face turned a shade darker as his anger rose. The doctors were whispering now, and something was beeping crazily. Fisk was as pale as the walls.

"Do you know, what the punishment for this is?" Nero asked, struggling to keep his voice calm. I decided to take a guess.

"Public execution?"

Nero sneered. "Nothing so dramatic."

"Banishment to the Surface is the sentence for treason," Fisk said, devoid of expression. The first words he'd spoken to me.

My blood ran cold and I couldn't suppress a shiver. The Surface was inhospitable. A desert wasteland in some places, in others freezing glaciers. There was constant wind causing sandstorms and blizzards. To be sent there was the same as being executed—but much longer. The words I uttered next were a surprise to everyone in the room … including myself.

"I'll take it." I growled the words in a defiant challenge. Nero's face twisted into an expression of utter contempt. His voice seethed with anger when he spoke.

"So be it." He hissed, enunciating the words to the extreme. The Higher Ones stepped forward.

"Take him to the Central Lift," Nero said. He turned back to me.

"What a waste," he said simply, then left the room, followed by Fisk. I stood and the Higher Ones grabbed my arms. They started to cuff my hands, and I counted silently to five. Nero should be in the lift by now.

Just as the Higher Ones started to fasten the cuffs, I let my legs buckle, collapsing to the ground. Just as I'd hoped, the Higher One's went with me. As we hit the floor, I felt their grips loosen. I rolled away from them, and came up in a crouch.

I didn't need to worry about the doctors. I slipped my hand into my right boot.

One thing a knife specialist always had was a hidden knife. I changed the position every rotation to a different sheath. Even Jai didn't know where I kept it. Today, it was in my boot.

I pulled it out now, staying in a crouching stance, holding the blade down to get more leverage behind my strikes.

It was a simple weapon. A black textured handle, and a six inch long blade. It was weighted for throwing as well.

The Higher Ones were on their feet now and running towards me. I slashed the first Higher One's leg, disabling him. I straightened and slammed the hilt of my knife into the other's temple. I quickly cut all their radio cables and cuffed their wrists to the chair. The doctors had disappeared out a door in the back of the room. I grabbed one of the Higher One's guns as an alarm began to wail.

The Peacekeepers were gone from the hallway. I started towards the lift, then stopped. Nero would know I was gone by now, and would be directing those. I quickly entered the maintenance tubes

41

that went from floor to floor. They were hot, stuffy, and loud. All the components in the walls buzzed like hundreds of insects.

The hangar was my goal. My hover-bike should still be there. I briefly thought of finding Jai, then discarded it. Things would be better for him if he didn't know I was gone. Better if someone had to tell him. I checked the marking on the wall of the tube. A-3. No wonder it had taken so long for the lift to get here. I was on the second floor! I'd never been past the tenth. I'd have to go down seventeen floors to get to the hangar. I found a ladder and quickly began to descend.

I was two floors down when they started sending Agents into the tubes to find me. I heard the clatter of boots on the ladder above me. When I stopped, I heard that they were also coming from below. I quickly climbed down the last rungs to solid ground. There were four tunnels that branched off my position. One in every direction. I quickly thought of the layout in my head. Taking the tunnel behind me would get me closer to the hangar. I quietly made my way to the next ladder and continued downwards.

I had to take five more detours before I finally arrived at Q-46, about seven sections from the hangar. The tubes were like an insect nest now, swarming with agents. Luckily, I didn't have a Trigger, or wouldn't have made this far. Triggers were only assigned when an agent left REGS headquarters. This way, if needs be, the Trigger could be activated by remote, ensuring that the agent would not disclose any vital information. Permanently. I could hear the shouts and clatter of boots all around me. I was trapped. I bit my lip as I stepped off the ladder, holding my gun ready. I heard a foot step behind me, and I spun around, bringing my weapon up to meet the threat. I found myself pointing the barrel of my gun at Agent Burnes' forehead. He put his hands up slowly.

"Put your gun down!" I ordered. Burnes obeyed, slowly setting his weapon on the ground. I motioned for him to slide it to me. He did so with his foot. Without taking my eyes off him, I stooped and picked it up. He kept his hands above his head in plain view

"You know you won't make it to the hangar," he said. I knit my eyebrows together.

"What makes you say that?" I asked. He pursed his lips for a moment.

"Because there's about twenty-five agents coming in each direction." He said. I paused and listened past the buzzing of the tubes. He wasn't lying. I'd already heard them.

"So your friends are coming to save you, is that what you're saying?" I asked him. He slowly lowered his hands just a little.

"I can hold them off for you," he said. I stared at him in disbelief. Hold them off for me? I didn't even know this man, not well anyways. The most I'd done for him was say I'd given him permission to speak.

"Why should I trust you?" I asked. He had been at the square. He'd followed his orders. I looked at his cheek, where Sanders had punched him. It was now an ugly black and blue.

Burnes took a deep breath. "Because I'm with them," he said. He had reached his hand into his pocket, and now he withdrew it, holding a small, silver disk. He pressed a button in the middle, and a small hologram appeared.

A red Rendarian Star.

I'd now seen that star four times in one rotation. Twice on eight, in my adjacent cell, and now here in Burne's hand. *Because I'm with them*, echoed in my mind. The G-platers. He was with them, but Nero had called them terrorists. *Do you really believe what he says now?* I asked myself. *They were saving those people. They didn't hurt anyone.* My head started to hurt. Everything was twisted in a complicated web! I began to understand just what Jess meant.

The boots were getting closer. I could hear their voices now, checking in with other groups as the jaws of the trap started to close. I looked at Burnes again.

"You can't possibly hope to get away." I said. He smiled sadly.

"No, not really," he whispered. He looked away for a moment, then back at me, a new conviction in his eyes.

"But this would be worth it." He murmured. He held out his hand, and before I really knew what I was doing, I gave him his weapon. I looked at Burnes with a new respect.

"Thank you." I said quietly. Burnes gave me a wry smile.

"Could you just do me a favor?" he asked, and I nodded. That would be the least I could do for someone who was about to die for me.

"Name it."

Burnes thought for a moment, looking down at his shoes. Then he said,

"When you find them, find Klein for me," he said softly. "Tell him what I did."

I wasn't sure what 'them' he was talking about, but I could hardly refuse his last request.

"I will," I said, and I meant it. I was going to find this Klein. Burnes gave me one last smile. Then he turned towards the tunnel, where those voices were coming from. I opened the grate that would lead me out of the tubes. Burnes suddenly turned back to me.

"One more thing!" He called. I stopped myself before I dropped through the opening and looked back at him.

"What?" I asked. He smiled that wry grin again.

"Tell Water Bird that I'm sorry about the Core," he said. Then he raced down the hallway and disappeared from sight. I heard gunshots and yelling from the corridor.

"Thank you, Agent Burnes," I whispered. I dropped down the grate and into the hallway. I had faced one of two obstacles on my escape. Little did I know that the second would break what little of my heart was still intact.

8

(Andresha)

"I don't believe this!" I growled and slammed my helmet onto the desk in front of me. "They killed almost an entire district because we fed them!" The other three people in the room looked on with mixed expressions. One mirrored my anger and grief, another had a look of sadness. The other was blank.

"Are you done taking it out on my desk, Agent Kanway?" Chief asked me. I pressed my lips into a thin line and nodded stiffly. Chief was an impressive figure. Tall, burly, but handsome in a roguish, commando sort of way. I stared down those intense blue eyes. Satisfied that I wasn't going to yell anymore, he nodded. He ran a hand through his short black hair.

"How many?" He asked quietly.

Short picked at his jacket. "About a three hundred ... maybe more," he said quietly. He'd changed out of his REGS clothes and was now wearing his uniform. Black shirt with our symbol on the right sleeve, black pants and boots, with his utility belt around his waist. No one here went anywhere without their gun.

Chief sighed. "Do you have anything to add, Agent Hummer?" He said.

Jim folded his arms angrily. We were just wrapping up our debriefing. Chief had asked to see us as soon as our Sky Sailor had touched the landing pad.

"They're saying we did it. That we sabotaged one of the factories." Jim said. Chief pursed his lips.

"That is important. Thank you, Agents. Dismissed."

I spun on my heel and left the small office off to the side of the Command Center. Jim and Short were right behind me. I tugged my braid in frustration. Why would REGS do something like that? Why? It didn't make sense. If anything, what we did would have helped "increase the output of their factories," I shook my head in disgust.

45

As if he could read my thoughts, Short said, "Because they started cheering."

I stopped walking and turned to face him. The Command Center was brightly lit with consoles and lights that blinked in different colors. The room was huge, with plenty of room to move around. This was so if an intruder made it this far into the base, defenders wouldn't be in a cramped space with lots of potential tripping points. Honestly, if an intruder got this far, we'd have more to worry about than just being able to move around. Right now, there were only a few agents monitoring comm channels and REGS reports, or making sure things in the base were running smoothly. I looked at Short now, still angry.

"When you cheer for a team at a sporting event, the other team doesn't go in and kill you!" I protested.

Short nodded once. "That could be argued, but this isn't sports, it's politics," he said.

I tugged my braid again. "And we all know how much I hate politics," I said. The two men nodded. Only Short really knew why. My brother wasn't like that. He actually followed politics, and understood what was going on. In fact, I think he actually *liked* them. Jim now chimed into the conversation.

"What do you mean it's politics, Short?" He asked.

Short folded his arms. "Well," he began, "it's like this. The Chairman rules with fear, and the belief that no one can go up against his authority. When you came in, and contested that, and the people went our way, he had to stop it before it spread. He knows if we have the support of the people, this movement will be unstoppable, so he's trying to make them fear us instead."

I shrugged. "Well he just might if these rumors keep going around that we're blowing up factories," I said.

All three of us jumped when an agent called Chief to the Command Center, then, not realizing that we were there, called myself and Jim to come as well.

"We're right behind you, Jinx," Jim said.

Jinx twisted around in his chair. "Sorry," he said.

I didn't know Jinx very well. He was in his thirties, and didn't talk to people much. He was rather intimidating, being six-and-a-half feet tall. He kept his head shaved, giving him a skull like appearance. Then of course, there was his face. About three months ago, Jinx had come back from a mission with horrific injuries to his face. As a result of the severity of the injuries, and our lack of equipment at the time, Jinx now had a long scar that began at his hairline, down through his right eye, across his lips and ended at his jaw. His right eye had been replaced with a cybernetic, but instead of brown, this eye didn't look like an eye at all. It was more of a metal sphere with a red laser in the center. It gave him the look of cyborg. It didn't bother me, but most of the agents had started calling him Redeye. Instead of getting upset, Jinx had just adopted it as his codename.

"It's what I am," he'd said.

I stopped my reminiscing as Chief came out of his office.

"What is it?" He asked.

Jinx tapped a control on his console. "REGS just sent out an apprehension order," he said.

I folded my arms. "Maybe someone escaped today's massacre?" I asked.

Jinx shook his head. "I don't think so," he said. "This one's a bit unusual." He tapped another control and a REGS Personnel file was projected into the air.

"Agent Edrix Solan," Jim read the name.

I cocked my head at the file picture. He was young, that's for sure. Black military haircut, tan skin, tall. I glanced at the age on the file. Seventeen. Two years older than myself. His eyes were the brightest green I'd ever seen.

"What's his position?" I asked, but no one heard me. They were still talking.

"He was on Eight today," Jinx was saying.

"He did something to get himself taken into custody. Reports say he just escaped out their main hangar on a hover bike. They lost him in the stream."

Jim peered at the file.

"It says here that he's mentally unstable."

I glanced over at him and raised an eyebrow. "And in REGS that usually means 'aware.'"

Jim nodded. "True." He agreed. Chief repeated the question I had asked two minutes before.

"What's his rank and position?"

Jinx flipped through some more files on his console, muttering to himself occasionally. Finally, he shook his head.

"I can't find his rank, but looks like this was his first mission off base. His brother, Jai, is higher up."

"How high?" Short asked. Jinx shrugged.

"I'd have to do some digging." He said. Chief motioned to the holo-file floating in the air with his chin.

"Get on it. Try to find something about his background too."

Jinx nodded. "Yes sir."

Chief walked over to the middle of the Command Center. Jim and I followed him. I folded my arms and shifted my weight to one foot. Short stayed further back. Chief flipped through files on a console. His mouth was drawn in a tight line. His eyebrows furrowed as he studied something.

"What do we do now?" I asked.

Chief tapped a control. "Make a call," he said. There was a short burst of static, then the transmission stabilized. Chief quickly motioned to an agent in the corner of the vast room. The agent nodded back and turned to his station. He would rotate the frequency of the transmission to ensure it wasn't being listened to by an outside party.

"This is Blizzard. What is it?" A woman's voice came over the channel.

"Where are you?" Chief asked.

"I'm on my way back." She replied.

Chief tapped another control, his scowl deepening. "Do you know an Edrix Solan in REGS?" He said.

There was a brief silence, then Blizzard answered him again.

"Yes, I know him. What's happened?"

There was a slight strain to her voice. It was barely there, like she was trying to conceal it. I glanced at Jim. He didn't seem to notice it. Chief didn't either.

"REGS just sent out an apprehension order for him. I was wondering if you might have heard anything up there," Chief said. There was another pause, then an answer.

"I've heard nothing. Do we know why?"

Another agent turned around in his chair. "Sir, update on the REGS Agent."

Chief looked up from his console. "What is it?"

The agent consulted his station monitor for a moment, then replied, "REGS command has just placed a substantial bounty on Solan, sir. Dead or alive."

I swallowed nervously. A bounty hadn't been issued from REGS command since, well, since my bounty of sixty-five-thousand credits. I was wanted alive. Now this agent was wanted either way. I bit my lip and tugged my braid again.

Blizzard spoke again. "How substantial are we talking?'"

The agent consulted his monitor.

"Sixty-seven thousand dead and …" He again consulted his monitor.

"Two-hundred-and-fifty-eight-thousand credits alive."

There were gasps of amazement all over the room. My heart literally skipped a beat. That was *a lot of money*. Both ways. I glanced up at Jim. He was shocked, I could tell. Rendarians were empathic. Where we couldn't read minds, we could read emotions. Only a few, however, could really read them clearly. Most, like myself, only caught small glimpses unless an emotion was incredibly strong, like the surprise in the room.

We all looked at Jinx as he spoke.

"Confirmed, sir. Seven Hunters on Ten have accepted the bounty."

Chief ran a hand through his hair. I watched him anxiously, wondering what he was thinking.

"Blizzard, change of plans. Hold your position and await another agent to meet you."

I didn't know why, but he looked at me before continuing.

"Find Solan and bring him here. Top priority to all agents."

"*What?*" The word was out of my mouth before I could stop myself. What in the universe was he thinking? Bringing a REGS agent here? Not just any REGS, but one that had the largest bounty in the history of Rendaria on his head, as well as potential mental issues, here. To our secret base. Chief shot me a stern look.

"Understood," Blizzard said, and she ended the transmission.

"I'm going!" I said to Chief.

He sighed. "I knew you were going to say that."

Hope rose in my chest. I knew I couldn't change his mind about this REGS person, but I could at least see this guy before we brought him here. Besides, I knew Blizzard would listen to me, and Chief would listen to her. She was his Second in Command, after all.

Chief ran a hand through his hair. "No, you're not," he said. quietly. I took a step back. Not go? Not go?!

"Why?" I voiced my next thought out loud.

Chief looked at me, folding his arms. "Because I need you here, and I need someone out there who's gonna keep their head."

Anger rose in my chest. He was doing it again.

"Keep their head?" I repeated through gritted teeth. "Are you saying I won't *keep my head?*"

Chief did not mince words with me.

"Yes."

If there hadn't been other people around, and if I happened to not be on duty, I would have either yelled or cried. Whichever one worked, but I kept myself in check.

"Have I ever acted rashly out in the field?" I said evenly, remembering all my diplomacy lessons from years back. Raised tones will only raise a war. It had been drilled into my head.

"Yes," Chief said flatly. I bit my lip, containing my anger. Was he really going to bring that up? To his credit, Chief didn't go into detail. He stepped closer and lowered his voice so only I could hear.

"I know you're upset, but I need another agent up there who's been in REGS and knows how this guy thinks," he said. I bit my lip harder and tasted blood.

"If he's 'mentally unstable,' then no one is going to know how he thinks," I almost hissed.

"You're not going," he persisted.

I pursed my lips and furrowed my brow. "Yes, sir," I muttered.

He bit his lip and stepped back. "Agent Short, rendezvous with Blizzard at her position. We'll see if we can get a location on the REGS agent."

Short glanced at me, then nodded. "Yes, Chief." Then he left the room.

Chief turned to Jinx. "Jinx, while you're digging around REGS files, see if you can find what this guy did on Eight," he said heading for his office again.

"Yes, Chief," Jinx said.

I stood in the middle of command, staring at the floating file of Edrix Solan. There was something in those eyes. I didn't know what it was, but I wasn't sure I liked it. The only person who'd ever come here from REGS was Short, and he'd been looking for us. I cocked my head and glanced at the file again as I got an idea. Maybe I couldn't find him in person, but ...

"Let me help you with that digging, Jinx," I said. "It will go faster that way."

He shrugged. I went to the station next to him and sat down. Jim gave me a half smile as I powered it up.

"I guess I'll just go get something to eat," he said.

"Do that," I replied.

9

(Edrix)

I wiped the tears from my eyes as the multicolored lights closed around me in the Stream. My hand desperately went to my pocket, hoping this was all just an awful dream. Disappointment crashed over me as I found it empty. The sketchbook was gone. I'd barely gotten out of the hangar with my hover bike and into the stream before REGS got their hovercraft organized.

The grate where I'd dropped out of the Tubes was three sections from the hangar. I had replaced the grate above me, willing myself to shut out the shouts and yells from the other side. I had run down the hallway, reaching the door. I'd had to hurry, I knew. Burne's distraction wouldn't last forever. The door was locked, but I had quickly tried to bypass it with my security code. I crossed my fingers, hoping beyond all hope that it would open. A heartbeat later, it had. I had let myself breathe a small sigh of relief. They hadn't recalled my clearance yet, but I had known that I couldn't count on my codes again.

The hangar had been buzzing with activity. After a moment's hesitation, I had quickly located my hover-bike. It had been in a quiet area, by an open bay door. There were some Sky-sailors getting ready to take off. When they were gone, the door would close, and I would have lost my chance. I'd walked calmly through the crowd, keeping my head down and my mouth shut. I had forced myself from breaking out in a run every time someone said my name. I'd had no doubt that they were all under orders to apprehend me. At one point, an officer spotted me.

"You there!" she had shouted. I had known better than to stop, but I had. She had then pointed to a box of tools to my left.

"Hand me a hydro-wrench please!" she had said, then looked back down at the piece of machinery she was repairing. I had sighed inwardly with relief, then moved to the tool box. I had found the tool the officer had asked for, then carefully walked over to her. I had pretended to look at my non-existent wrist communicator as if it were something important and handed her the wrench.

"Thank you," she'd said absently. I had walked away as quickly as I could without becoming suspicious.

I had finally gotten away from all the people, the Sky-sailors were closed and preparing for takeoff, and I had just touched my hover-bike's handle when a cold, commanding voice had stopped me cold.

"Put your hands on your head and turn around."

I had complied with the speaker's wishes. When I then faced him, however, my heart had skipped a beat.

"Jai?" I had whispered. There he had stood, his gun in his hands and pointed at my chest. One glance at it, and I had known the safety was off.

"What are you doing?" I had asked him. He had pressed his lips in a thin, angry line and answered.

"I was about to ask you the same thing."

My mind had raced.

"I can't stay, Jai. They're going to send me to the Surface!" I had cried. I had expected Jai's gun to lower as he realized the gravity of what I had said. It hadn't.

"And this is the best way you could think of to avoid it? Run off by yourself and become a fugitive from the Higher Order?" He had said tersely. I'd knit my eye brows in confusion. What was he doing?

"Yes," I said uncertainly.

Jai's grip had tightened on his gun. "I have a better one," he had said. Hope had begun to rise in my chest. Maybe he was going to come with me, help me escape! I'd thought. His next words had crushed that small hope.

"Apologize to the Grand Commandant, cleanse of your mistake!" he said loudly, not quite a shout. I took a step back in surprise and disbelief. My hands lowered to my shoulders. I had gotten a sudden, stabbing pain in my head that had made me double over. It was like my thoughts were arguing with themselves. One part of me had

53

screamed the logic of Jai's argument, The other had brought up all those hungry faces, gun barrels rising.

I had put my hands to my forehead with my eyes squeezed shut. For just a moment, a flicker of concern had crossed Jai's face. Then his tone had softened a little.

"Edrix, you swore an oath, just like I did," he'd said. I opened my eyes, the pain in my head had subsided a little. That's right. I had. The pain had lessoned a little more. I needed to keep it. Jai had lowered his gun and continued.

"That's right, we swore to protect the innocent, to protect Order!"

And suddenly, my mind had felt like it had been shattered. Jagged pieces of this conversation had rattled around in my head. Jai's words had echoed in my head. *To protect the innocent, to protect Order!* What little part of my mind that had sided with Jai, no—with REGS—had sunk into the back of my mind. I had scowled then with new determination. I had known that I was right.

"Then I'm the one who kept my oath down there, Jai," I had said with tears in my eyes.

"That's what I did. I tried to protect those people, and I was arrested for it!"

Jai had scowled, anger and disappointment in his eyes.

"Traitor," he had said bitterly. I had tried to swallow past the lump that had formed in my throat as tears had spilled onto my cheeks. I had then reached my hand into my pocket, stepping close to him.

"I'm sorry you can't see why," I had said softly. Then I had placed my sketchbook in his hands.

"But maybe this will help you know." I had choked back a sob as I heard the clatter of boots. They had found me. Jai had just stared at the book in his hands. I had raised my right hand with my thumb and my first and second fingers extended to the center of my forehead. The REGS salute. Then I was on my bike and out the bay door, just as the Sky-sailors took off.

So now here I was, in the Stream and running for my life, and trying to figure out which brother had betrayed the other.

54

10

(Edrix)

Four rotations. That's how long I had been on the run from REGS. Now I was on Level Seven, where the planet's refineries were located. It smelled horrible, and there was always a black haze in the air.

After I had replaced my REGS gear with an old refinery uniform, I'd spent the last three rotations looking for anything about the star I'd seen. I had gone to Level Six first. Not a lot of security, but I still had to be careful. I hadn't been able to find anything. I soon realized that to find what I wanted, I'd have to go deeper—literally.

I hadn't been ready to go to Ten, not yet. I had gone to Four first. That was where the planet's food was grown. There I had been able to find some references to a group that was rebelling against the Chairman. I had heard a shopkeeper discussing how REGS agents had ransacked his neighbor's home. Three people wearing street cloths had chased them off, but had left a hologram of the star I had seen behind.

I didn't talk to anyone directly, knowing they wouldn't discuss something like this with a stranger. I kept my distance and just listened. Next I had heard some farmers saying that REGS transports had been hijacked or disabled over the past few weeks. Each time, a red Rendarian Star had been left behind.

I had decided that the red star had to be significant. Why else would they leave it behind? They wanted it to be noticed. Then it had hit me. Red Star. The group must call themselves Red Star.

With a surge of confidence, I had then approached a shop merchant. I had noticed that he put some of his wares away when certain people approached. I had decided that he must have been a part of the local black-market. Every Level had one, except maybe One and Two. Ten was practically one large black-market in and of itself.

55

Anyway, I had approached the shopkeeper, who did his usual routine of quickly stashing choice items away behind the counter when he thought I wasn't watching. He had been shorter than I was, and had thinning brown hair. He had been slightly overweight, and had worn a long robe that I think was supposed to look regal, but instead looked cheap and overdone.

"Can I help you?" the man had asked a little too cheerfully. I had shrugged and pretended to look at the small display of items on the counter in front of him.

"Not yet," I had said. This had assured him that I was not his usual customer. There had been three more people at the shop as well. I had not wanted to say anything before they had left. I had picked up a small brooch and pretended to examine it. I did so for about thirty seconds, but it had taken me much less than that to determine that it had been fake. A quick glance at the rest of the jewelry for sale was all I needed to see that everything else was fraudulent as well. Except for the pieces behind the counter of course. Those were the real goods.

Finally, the other browsers had drifted away, and I was the only customer left at the shop.

"Anything catch your eye?" he had asked hopefully.

I had shrugged. "Not really. I was hoping for something more..." I had glanced around, then leaned my elbow onto the counter and whispered, "valuable."

The man had grinned mischievously. He had reached under the counter and revealed a long necklace made of thousands of tiny diamonds. He had then gently laid it on the counter for my inspection.

"Something like this?" he had asked in a whisper. I had lifted the necklace in my hand and hefted it a little. It had been heavy. How someone could wear that, I didn't know, but that wasn't my problem.

The necklace had definitely been real. There had been a seal of verification of its authenticity on the back of the necklace.

I had set the piece of jewelry down on the counter. I should probably call command and—

Stop! I had told myself. You're not a REGS agent anymore. I had realized that the shopkeeper had been looking at me expectantly. I had shrugged and set the necklace on the counter.

"Maybe," I had said, "but I'm looking for something even more valuable."

The man's eyes had widened a little in anticipation.

"I want information," I had said quietly. The man had pretended to be insulted.

"Does this look like a tourist kiosk?" he had asked indignantly, motioning to his shop with his arms.

I had straightened and folded my arms. I had stared at the man, meeting his gaze.

After a moment, I had said, "No, it doesn't, but I do know that you have about three thousand credits worth of stolen jewelry behind that counter."

I had leaned forward a little, just enough to slightly over shadow the man with my hands on the counter. "Give me one good reason not to report you to REGS?" I had said ominously low.

The man had swallowed and tried to hide his shaking hands in the voluminous sleeves of his robe.

"Very well," he had said quietly. "What do you wish to know?"

I leaned back, but I hadn't stopped staring at him. "Red Star. I want to know where I can find Red Star."

The man had laughed. "Do you really want to get mixed in with that treasonous lot?" he had asked.

I had raised an eyebrow. "Says the man who runs a black-market," I had said without expression.

The man had sighed. "Fair enough." He had held up his hands. "I don't know where they are exactly, but they've been most active on levels Seven, Eight and Nine."

I had known he was telling the truth in that regard. I had read enough reports to know that.

"Go on," I had pressed.

"If you want to find them, I suggest you go to Seven. I have a friend there that might be able to help you … for a price," the man had said slyly.

I had put a trinket on the counter. A trinket was worth half as much as a credit.

"Ten credits for a name," I had said flatly. The man had sniffed and put his nose in the air.

"It's dangerous to be discussing these things. Twenty credits."

I had known he was going to haggle. I'd had forty credits with me. I had allowed twenty credits for the shopkeeper, no more.

I had scoffed. "Twenty credits to tell me a name? Thirteen, or I walk away."

The man had considered this for a moment. "Eighteen?" He asked.

"Sixteen," I had returned.

"Deal."

The man picked up the trinket I had given him, then I had given him eight credits.

"Tell me the name and I'll give you the rest," I said. The man considered for a few more moments, then, after looking both ways, whispered, "Remlon Trake."

I had nodded and tossed him the other eight credits, plus one more.

"To keep your mouth shut," I had said. The man had nodded and hurried to the back of his shop.

I had taken his advice and come to Seven. I still had a gun, I kept it hidden in one of my uniform pockets, but I only had six shots left. Of course I had my knife, but that would be a big clue as to who I was, unless I restricted myself to fighting like a street thug.

I coughed as I walked through a black cloud of fumes from a nearby refinery. I had visited the shopkeeper one last time before I'd left Six to arrange a meeting place. He had told me to go to the steel refinery on Fifthday.

Now, Fifthday had come. I was waiting behind the steel refinery. The shopkeeper hadn't given me a specific time so I had been waiting here all day.

"You wanted to speak with me?"

I turned around. There was a man standing behind me. He also wore a refinery uniform, and his face was streaked with grime and sweat.

"That's right," I said, stepping towards him.

"That's far enough, I think," the man said, holding up a hand to stop me. I did as he asked.

"Why did you come here?" He asked me. We slowly walked in a circle, moving at the exact same speed.

"I was told you could help me find something I'm looking for," I said.

"That depends on what you're looking for." He replied.

I was silent for a moment, then I said, "I'm looking for Red Star."

The man—I assumed he was Remlon Trake—stopped walking. I stopped as well.

"What do you want with Red Star?" He asked. I hesitated again. I hadn't thought this far. What did I want with Red Star?

"I want to join them," I said. The man raised his eyebrows and continued his slow walk. I followed suit.

"I see," he said simply. We walked around each other in silence. I could hear my heart beating in my ears. Would he tell me where they were? Something wasn't right. He was too excited. Then I noticed him slip his hand into his pocket.

We drew our guns at the exact same time.

"What are you doing?" I asked.

Remlon grinned. "Getting rich."

He kept his gun trained on me as he pulled a communicator from a zippered pocket in his sleeve with his other hand. He tapped a control.

"This is REGS Command," a voice crackled over to me from the communicator.

"This is Remlon Trake. I have your wanted Agent in custody. Come get him and bring the money."

He switched off the communicator and replaced it in his pocket.

"Money?" I asked.

He laughed. "You have no idea, do you, kid?" He said.

"You know," I said briskly. "It was pretty bold of you to say you had me in custody when I have a gun pointed at your head."

He shrugged. "And I have one pointed at yours."

I glanced around me. I was outwardly calm, but inside I was close to panic. This was an experienced Hunter. REGS would always have teams ready to leave. One could be here in eight minutes after receiving a report.

It had already been three.

The area behind the refinery was pretty much empty. I could see anything that could help me. I could try and run, but I knew that would be pointless. Trake would shoot me before I could take three steps. I could shoot first, but if I missed I would be dead. It's not that I didn't have confidence in my abilities. I had great aim, but I always had to plan for the worst. My best bet would be to disable Trake and get out of here. I had five and a half minutes to do so. Already I could hear the hum of REGS vehicles coming this way.

Trake suddenly grinned at me.

"Looks like your friends are here," he said. His finger tapped the gun trigger. I glanced up and could make out the silhouettes of the REGS party now. Two cars, five bikes and a sky sailor.

It was now or never, I decided. I aimed slightly above Trake's left shoulder and fired.

The instant after I pulled the trigger, I rolled forwards. Trake flinched to the right as he heard the gunshot, just as I had hoped. His finger reflexively pulled the trigger on his weapon, but the shot went above my head. I came up out of a crouch and grabbed Trake's gun arm and twisted it left.

He cried out in pain and dropped his gun. I kicked it farther away with my foot. Then I pulled Trake forward, kicking his legs out from under him at the same time. He hit the ground hard and didn't move. All this happened in less than ten seconds.

I quickly checked Trake's pulse. It was strong and steady, I had only knocked him out. I was preparing to stand when a glint on his neck caught my eye.

He had a fine gold chain around his neck with a small square on it, like a tag. I flipped the tag over and read it. I recognized it immediately; it was a Hunter verification.

Hunters were a strange organization. They searched for people or objects in exchange for payment. Hunter licenses were illegal on Rendaria; they had to be obtained off-world. Usually, Hunters were only seen on Ten, unless they were hunting.

Regs must have put a bounty out on me, and it must have been a big one.

I glanced up. The REGS team would be here in two minutes, maybe less.

Trake groaned and opened his eyes. Before he could get up, I had my knife out of its sheath and the tip pointed under his chin.

"Where's Red Star?" I demanded.

Trake laughed. "Why should I tell you?" He asked. I pushed my knife a little closer to his neck. He stiffened.

"Alright! They're on level Nine," he said. "Look for an old mechanical warehouse about two miles from Lift Twenty-three."

I raised my eyebrow. "And that's where they are?"

He smiled grimly. "If you make that far, kid. They'll find you."

I sheathed my knife and ran. I heard the REGS team landing behind the refinery, but I didn't look back. I had a destination now, and I was going to find it.

* * *

The Lifts were huge. There were several placed around the planet. Four of the biggest were stationed around the Central Lift, but they were dwarfed in comparison. The Central Lift was massive. It was circular, about two miles in diameter, twice the size of the other lifts.

It had taken me three hours to reach Lift Twenty-three. I gotten there mostly on foot, but had managed to catch a bus for an hour of the journey. There weren't a lot of people around, which was the most dangerous part.

Everyone going on and off of the Lifts were REGS agents.

I kept my head down and headed for the Lift as nonchalantly as I could. I didn't doubt that the REGS party Trake had summoned had reported my escape by now, and every REGS agent was probably on the lookout for me.

The last two times, I had been able to hide in cargo containers to board the Lifts, but I didn't have time to do anything like that this time. I reached the energy gate around the lift, staying in the shadows. There was a group of transports coming out. That would be my chance to get in. The large gate creaked open. I dashed inside between the transports, keeping low until I reached a stack of crates. I took a moment to steady my breathing and heart rate, then I walked towards the Lift. I didn't duck my head, or look from side to side. I walked normally, looking straight ahead. I was halfway there when someone called out.

"Hey, you!"

I didn't stop; I kept walking. There were plenty of other people around so I pretended to think they were talking to someone else.

"Stop!" they called again. To the everlasting gratitude of a person to my left, he stopped.

"Me, sir?" He asked. I didn't listen to the other man. I moved into a crowd of agents. I had to get to the Lift before someone sounded the alarm. Otherwise, I was surrounded.

I reached the Lift door. Now I just needed to get on the Lift and get it to start without an access code, ID, or DNA scan. Easy, right?

Wrong.

I stepped into the lift, and alarms went off like crazy. That DNA scan I mentioned? It's automatic. If your DNA isn't on file, or flagged—as mine most likely was—then it would deny entry and alert security.

The Lift doors were starting to close. I dashed inside. A high pitched shrieking noise began as the doors slammed shut. I covered my ears and knelt next to the keypad. I took a deep breath, then uncovered my ears and ripped off the panel covering. I studied the innards for a moment, then repositioned some choice wires. The Lift started to move. Now to get this shrieking noise to stop.

I ripped out every wire I could get my hands on the led to the audio systems. Finally, the shrieking stopped. I sat back against the wall, exhausted. My head hurt, and my ears were ringing. Lights gently strobed up the walls of the Lift, my breathing echoing in the empty space. I had the Lift all to myself. Now I just had to get out.

The Lift stopped five minutes later. When the doors opened, I could still hear alarms everywhere. I would just have to make a run for it. I drew my knife from the sheath in my sleeve and ran out of the Lift.

I almost ran straight into an agent. I kicked him in the chest and sent him sprawling, but I didn't waste time looking after him. I could see the gate closing ahead. I ran towards it as fast as I could. Somewhere behind me, I heard the sound of a hover craft taking off. I wasn't going to make it on foot. I looked around.

There! Hover bikes to my left. I ran to them and started one up. I heard the sounds of gunshots behind me. No time to lose. I raced the bike to the gate. I made it out with centimeters to spare. Two miles on foot would be impossible, but on hover bike? I could make it.

Nine had even fewer Sun-lights than Eight had, making visibility difficult. To my surprise, it was cold. Very cold. I shivered and noticed that my breath made puffs of steam in the air.

A bullet narrowly missed my head. I glanced behind me and saw three more hover bikes. There was a Sky-sailor above them, steadily gaining on me.

I glanced around me, desperate to find this mechanical warehouse Trake had told me about.

I never made it that far. Burning pain erupted in my arm as a bullet struck home. I yelled in pain and my bike flipped, dumping me in the street. I landed heavily on my shoulder and heard something snap. More pain.

I fought the reflexive tears that swarmed my eyes. I needed to keep going! I looked at my arm and my head started to spin from the sight of blood. I tore my sleeve and pressed the fabric to the wound. I gasped as the action caused another spike of pain to shoot up my arm. I turned around. The bikes were nearly here now. I slumped my shoulders in defeat. It was all over.

Then I saw it, the warehouse, or at least what I *thought* was the warehouse. I pushed the doubt out of my head. It *had* to be the warehouse. The building was made of steel sheets and was leaning heavily to one side. One wall was beginning to peel off. There were no Sun-lights on in that area, so I couldn't see more than that. Not my first choice, but a necessary one. I limped towards it, pain flaring in my shoulder and arm. My make-shift bandage was soaked in blood, and I was getting dizzy. I thought I saw something moving inside the warehouse, but I couldn't be sure.

"Help!" I called. I wasn't sure if I even uttered it aloud. I started to fall, then strong arms caught me.

"I gotcha," a man's voice said.

Then a woman spoke. "Get down! They're coming!" she said. Her voice sounded familiar. The man pulled me behind a building. Someone crouched down beside us. We scarcely breathed as the sound of hover-bikes and the Sky Sailor passed us. After a moment, the woman said, "Clear."

We all relaxed. The woman turned to me and gently took my face in her hands.

"Edrix?" She asked urgently. "Edrix, can you hear me?"

I recognized that face.

"Jess?" I whispered. She smiled and nodded.

"That's right."

The man spoke again. "Looks like he came to us."

Came to them? What was that supposed to mean? Then it clicked.

I had been looking for Red Star. I had found them.

11

(Andresha)

I woke to the beeping of my communicator. I lifted my head off my arms. I must have fallen asleep at my desk. I rubbed my eyes and looked around.

My room wasn't anything fancy. It had a bed in one corner with a small table. A dresser in the other, and a small bathroom. My desk was next to the dresser, where I had fallen asleep. I grabbed my communicator now from the drawer I'd placed it in.

"Commander Kanway," I said. The voice that came over the transmission belonged to Short.

"We're back. Chief wants you in the med-bay," he said.

They'd finally found him. This mysterious REGS agent that had been the talk of our senior agents for four rotations now.

"I'll be right there," I said. I ended the transmission and pocketed the device, then I grabbed my jacket from where I'd draped it across my bed. I swung it on as I exited my room and caught a lift up to the med-bay. I tugged my braid in impatience. Why was it so slow today? I wondered. I had spent the last four rotations pouring over every REGS report I could get my hands on looking for a reference to this Solan guy. About six-hundred reports later, I had not found a single one. Not his name, not his rank, not even his favorite breakfast food. It was like he'd been erased from history. That didn't happen to a lot of people. I should know, it had happened to me.

Why did I have keep finding common aspects between us? It was really quite annoying.

Finally, the doors slid open and I entered the white walls of the med-center. I walked over to a nurse that was transferring data from a console to her data-pad.

"Excuse me," I said. The nurse looked up.

"Where's Chief?" I asked.

The nurse tapped her pad a few times, "Number thirteen to your left."

65

I nodded. "Thank you."

I followed her directions to a room numbered thirteen. I knocked briskly.

"Come in," I heard Blizzard say. I took her invitation.

The REGS agent looked different up close. He was wearing a grubby refinery uniform with a bloody make-shift bandage on his upper right arm. He sat quietly on a cot. Short and Chief stood across the small room, but Blizzard—a.k.a. Jess—stood next to said REGS agent.

Chief looked up as I came in. "There you are."

I motioned to the REGS guy with my head. "Has he said anything?"

Jess raised her eyebrows. "We didn't want him to have to say everything twice."

Fair enough, I thought. I was ready to get this settled. This guy had been all anybody had talked about. I wanted to see if he was worth all the fuss. If he was worth getting erased from history. I wasn't optimistic.

My mood brightened when Patrisha came in. She was a petite blonde girl with brown eyes. It seemed like she never spoke above a whisper, she was so shy. But all that shyness melted away when she was given a patient. She was one of the best doctors we had.

She smiled pleasantly at the REGS agent. I searched my mind for his name... Edrix! That was it.

"I'm just going to give you a quick scan," she said. He smiled back at her a little. But I noticed it didn't reach his eyes. Almost, but not quite.

Chief finally said something. "Edrix, can you start at the beginning please? We know REGS took you into custody, but we don't know why."

Edrix looked down at his hands while Patrisha waved her scanner-wand around him.

"I'm not sure I know myself," he said quietly. "This was my first mission off base, going to Eight to contain a riot."

Ah-ha! So he *had* been on Eight that rotation. He was talking again. Talking about the riot, how he figured out what it was about.

66

"Then you guys showed up." Edrix said. "The G-platers. You dropped the food."

Patrisha had finished her scans by then, and was tapping her scanner, the wand placed neatly in its slot on the side. Then she gently removed the crude bandage and cut his sleeve away from the wound. She ran a tool over it, stopping the bleeding and covering it with a clean white bandage.

"After the star appeared, everyone started cheering," Edrix said, almost in a whisper. He folded his arms tightly.

"When Sanders gave the order to fire, I ... I tried to stop them, but they locked me in the transport. Then they locked me in a cell for a few hours, back at Command. After that they took me to Nero— the Grand Commandant. He said I was being sent to the surface. Then I ran away."

I raised my eyebrow. "They were going to banish you to the Surface because you disobeyed an order?"

Edrix shrugged. "It didn't make a lot of sense to me, either."

Patrisha ran another tool over his shoulder in small, circular motions.

Short tapped his chin in thought. "How did you get away?" He asked. "REGS would have been on lockdown before you made it past the door."

Edrix rubbed his arms. "Burnes held the agents off for me," he said quietly. Then he looked up.

"Is there someone called 'Water Bird' here?" He asked. His question caught me off guard a little. How did he know my code name? I realized that everyone was staring at me, waiting for me to speak up.

"That's my code name," I said. Edrix looked at me for the first time since I'd come in. His eyes were so green, they almost glowed, but they had a haunted look in them. I sighed to myself. He just saw almost three hundred people murdered. Didn't I see that same look in the mirror every morning?

"He said to tell you ... that he was sorry about the Core?" Edrix said hesitantly. I bit my lip. Agent Burnes ... my contact. Edrix picked up on my hesitation.

"Does that mean anything to you?" He asked.

I nodded stiffly. "Yes," I said shortly. Chief looked over at me. I nodded, confirming his thought. Patrisha looked between all of us for a moment, then broke the silence.

"Well, Chief, he's fine. I've taken care of his arm, and his shoulder. The bullet just grazed him, and the shoulder was sprained, but," She turned to Edrix and smiled, "You should be fine in no time." She said quietly, her usual tone of voice. Chief nodded, his brow knit in thought. Patrisha began to gather her things.

"Thank you," Chief said as she left, then turned to Jess. "Jess, give Short and I some time please. Get Andresha up to speed."

Get me up to speed? Up to speed on what? This Edrix guy had been our main concern for four rotations. Everything else seemed to have been forgotten. Jess only nodded, then beckoned to me with a finger to follow her out of the room. I followed her. The door had barely closed when I said, "Do you know him?"

Jess smiled and laughed a little. "You're still not shy about asking questions," she observed.

Jess had joined Red Star around the same time I did. In fact, I'd known her before I even knew Red Star existed. I made a 'go on' gesture with my hand. Jess bit her lip.

"Yes, I know him. I'm a family friend. We grew up together," she said.

So this guy had known Jess a lot longer than I had. We walked in silence for a while, then I asked, "What do you need to get me up to speed on?"

Jess sighed. "The Core problem."

In any other situation, I might have laughed, but I knew this wasn't funny. The wellbeing of our movement—maybe even the planet—was at stake.

"What about it?" I asked.

Jess pursed her lips. "The new Level that's being built?" she began. I stared at her intently. She hesitated. I motioned for her to continue.

"Go on," I prompted. Jess folded her arms and tapped her chin thoughtfully.

"It could mean nothing..." she began again. I stopped walking, touching her arm to signal her to do the same. She sighed and stopped beside me.

"They haven't asked for any new equipment," she said.

I knit my brows in puzzled thought. "Didn't they start construction over five years ago?" I asked.

Jess nodded. "Exactly. After this long, they should be constructing homes, businesses." She put a hand to her forehead.

"Forget that, they should be populating it by now." I bit my lip.

"It's good they aren't though, isn't it?" I asked. Jess knit her brow.

"That depends on your definition of 'good,'" she said.

"Granted," I replied. Jess bit her lip.

"We need that information. Chief and I are both getting bad feelings about this, but ..."

"The info you need is still locked up in the Core," I finished. Jess nodded, looking grim. I decided to change the subject.

"Speaking of bad feelings," I said, "I'm not sure I like this Solan fellow."

Jess folded her arms as we started to walk again. "Why not?"

I shrugged. "Something about him doesn't seem right. I mean, why would they tell him about us? Why reveal what they've been working so hard to keep secret to *him*?"

Jess cocked her head. "Perhaps because he already knew."

"Still," I protested, "maybe we shouldn't be too eager to welcome him with open arms."

Jess scowled, something she rarely ever did. "Why, because he's a REGS agent? Your brother was one too, you know. Probably a lot higher up in the ranks. So was Short. Red Star welcomed them," she said. Now I bit my lip. She was right, of course. She always was.

"And they came looking for us, too," she added, effectively cutting off my only retort.

I held my hands up in surrender. "I know that, and I'm not saying we should kick him out or lock him up," I said. My negotiation professor would be having a fit if she saw me right now, rambling like this.

69

"I just mean," I pursed my lips, "That there's something ... strange going on."

Jess nodded. "I have to agree."

I breathed an internal sigh of relief. At least she didn't still think I was crazy.

"What's he like? Solan, I mean," I asked. Jess glanced at me. I knew what she was thinking. One minute you don't want anything to do with him, and now you want to know all about him. I shrugged.

"I've been looking for information on this guy for four rotations, and I couldn't find a thing. All I know is that REGS thinks he's going crazy."

Jess gave a wry smile. "That would describe all of us, I think." I laughed. Wow. I hadn't laughed in a while. It felt good. I raised my eyebrow. Jess took the hint.

"Well," she hesitated, "I could tell you."

I raised both eyebrows now and leaned my head towards her as I said, "But?" I let the word stretch out. Jess cocked her head and looked at me.

"Maybe you should just get to know him," she said simply. Then she turned and walked back the way we'd come, leaving me standing in the hallway.

12

(Edrix)

I watched Jess leave with Water Bird. That's all I knew her as. The man they called Chief ran a hand through his hair.

"I'm not sure what to tell you, Edrix," he said. I studied him more carefully. He had jet black hair, and would probably be as tall as myself. He had an athletic build, and intelligent blue eyes. He was probably in his mid-twenties. But right now he looked as if he had the weight of the world on his shoulders. I had seen Jai look like that, my dad too. It was the look of someone in charge.

"Could you maybe explain who Burnes was?" I asked. The girl with the braid—I recognized her as one of the G-platers—had looked shocked when I'd given her his message. Chief looked at Short, who nodded once. Chief looked back at me.

"Burnes was a contact we had inside of REGS. He couldn't leave REGS without detection because of his low rank. He didn't want to endanger his family. Instead, he decided to give us as much information he could find from the inside."

"That's how you infiltrated the Core," I said quietly.

Chief nodded. "Unfortunately, it was a trap. REGS knew someone was tipping us off, so they filled their database with false security systems and passcodes to find who it was. Burnes was the only one who accessed it," he said.

I looked down at my hands. "Do you think he's dead?" I whispered.

It was Short who replied. "I hope he is," he said. "It would have been better than being captured."

He was right. The room was silent for a long time.

Then Chief said, "We'll talk again later." He turned to Short. "Give him a room."

Then he stood and left the room.

* * *

The room Short gave me was small and simple. A bed on one side of the room. A small closet and a small table with two chairs on the other. After I had showered and changed into clean clothes, I sat on the bed, exhausted from today's events. I'd given up on trying to understand them. I jumped at every small sound. In my mind, I was still on the run. In my mind, I was still on the run. I wished for a window, but I knew there would have been no point to it. There would be nothing to look at.

I jumped to my feet when there was a knock on the door, immediately at attention. Then I caught myself and relaxed a little. Old habits die hard.

"Come in," I called. The door opened and Jess entered the room.

"How are you feeling?" She asked softly, sitting next to me.

I shrugged. "It's been a crazy week, that's for sure," I replied.

We were silent for a moment, then Jess said, "I'm sorry about Jai."

I bit my lip and ordered myself not to cry. I'd done enough of that.

"It was weird," I said softly. "Just a few hours before, he was willing to listen to me. He brought me my sketchbook. Then, it was like he didn't remember anything about that."

Jess put a hand on my shoulder. "I'm not sure what to say," she said. "What you've just been through, well, it's why Red Star was created. To try and stop these things from happening."

I stared at my hands as I held them in my lap. I wondered which event she was referring to. The riot on Eight, or amnesiac older brothers. It was most likely the former. Jess thought for a moment, then she said, "How about a tour?"

I looked up. "A what, now?" I asked her.

She grinned. "A tour of the base," she said. I shrugged. I was ready for something different, and this place did seem pretty interesting.

"Sure," I said and she led the way out of the room.

* * *

The base was impressive. It wasn't huge, but still impressive. It was roughly oval shaped, with three floors. The colors were much more tasteful than REGS. Instead of dull greys covering everything, the walls were a soft white, and The floors were a rich blue color. The hallways and rooms were well lit, and everyone we passed seemed friendly enough. There were a few consoles placed at even intervals throughout the hallways.

We started at the bottom and worked our way up. Jess showed me the arboretum where they grew fruits and vegetables, as well as medicinal herbs. There was a gym down there, too, as well as a shooting range with multiple holo-targets that could move around the room. The remainder of that floor consisted of weapons lockers and a large hangar. Jess didn't show them to me, just told me they were there.

"It's not that I don't trust you," she said, "but we have some strict rules here."

I didn't mind. If our positions were reversed, I would likely have done the same.

The second level contained rooms like mine, where the residents of Red Star lived. The interesting part came towards the end of the tour.

"Don't let the door scare you," Jess told me as we walked. "He just likes to make sure his space is respected."

I didn't know who she was talking about, but I was glad she had warned me.

We soon came to a thick metal door three feet taller than me. The border was painted in faded yellow and black stripes, and covered in warning labels. One read: **DO NOT COME IN WHILE ORANGE LIGHT IS FLASHING WITHOUT PROPER CONTAINMENT SUITS!**

Then, in smaller text, it continued:

(IF YOU DO NOT DO THIS, THEN YOUR SKIN WILL TURN PINK, YOU WILL GLOW IN THE DARK, AND IT WILL *NOT* BE MY FAULT!)

Another, in even larger print said:

DO NOT KNOCK ON THIS DOOR WHEN THE *TEST* LIGHT IS FLASHING. IF YOU DO, YOU WILL BE RESPONSIBLE FOR THE DESTRUCTION OF THIS BASE AND EVERY STRUCTURE WITHIN THE NEXT SEVEN HUNDRED KILOMETERS!!!

I raised my eyebrows at the door. More signs were plastered all over it, all of them containing warnings of some sort.

"Is this a … lab?" I asked Jess. She smiled a little.

"It's pretty obvious, huh?" She replied. I studied the door, an amused smile working its way onto my face. Then my eyes found a small sticker at the very center of the door with tiny print reading:

"Today is Love Your Pet Day. Be sure to tell your pet that you love it."

I blinked to make sure I was reading it correctly. I was. I looked over at Jess and noticed her studying a panel of lights above the door. There were twelve in all, each a different color. One was bright blue with the word TEST underneath it. It was flashing at quick intervals.

"Well," Jess said, "we might have to come back later."

I tried to hide my disappointment. I was wondering what was on the other side of that door. I began to follow Jess as she started towards a lift. To my surprise, it opened and Water Bird stepped out.

"Pardon," she said and walked past us. She walked right up to the door and tapped controls on a huge keypad next to the door.

"Um, I don't think—" I began, but she wasn't listening to me. She folded her arms as the key pad emitted a high pitched chirp. Then there was a loud *hiss!* of escaping air and the door began to open.

I glanced at Jess, who shrugged. A fowl smelling grey-ish fog was rolling out of the doorway. Water Bird was already inside. Without a word, Jess and I followed her.

"Hey!" Water Bird shouted. Just visible in the fog, I could make out a figure wearing large black goggles and a lab coat holding a large flask of something green, large black rubber gloves on his hands. The grey fog was spewing from the mouth of the flask. When Water Bird shouted, the figure emitted a startled cry and the flask fell from its hands and shattered on the ground. An alarm immediately began to blare.

"WARNING!" called an automated voice. "End of the thirty-fourth reality! This reality will be neutralized it ten, nine, eight …"

I covered my ears. The fog really smelled awful, and a sizzling sound was coming from the ground where the flask had broken.

"No, no, no!" the figure, who I assumed was a scientist, cried. He grabbed a red can off a counter nearby and emptied the contents onto the ground by his feet. The alarm stopped and the sizzling sound increased.

"Computer!" a man's voice called. "Activate filter protocol seven-R!"

There was an affirmative beeping, then the sound of a large fan filled the room. Within seconds, the fog had dissipated. My eyes widened as I took in the sights around me.

The lab had to be the biggest room I had seen so far. There were tables covered with beakers, microscopes, consoles projecting holograms into the air, and several other gadgets I couldn't name. At first glance, it seemed that everything was a chaotic mess, but as I looked more carefully, I could tell that everything was organized on each table or desk. A data pad of notes was placed beside each project. A stairway in the back led upwards, where I could see the tips of green leaves. Plants.

I directed my attention to the scientist. It was a young man now, I could see, about my age. He pulled his goggles off, unleashing a head of reddish curls and hazel eyes. His face was covered in soot except for where his goggles had been. He was furious.

"Really, Dresha?" He said, barely below a shout. He grabbed a large cylinder off a table and ran it over the bubbling green goo by his shoes.

"The sign says 'No knocking!'" he continued. "That includes opening the door *without* knocking!"

Water Bird, or "Dresha," as he'd called her, shrugged. "Yes, well maybe you should have put that on the door too, but I doubt there's room seeing as you have an entire instruction manual on it!"

The scientist muttered something under his breath as the tool emitted a laser beam and disintegrated the bubbly spill.

"And what," the scientist said, a dangerously pleasant tone in his voice, "can I do for you, *Commander*?"

Another name for this girl. I wasn't even sure which one to call her.

Commander Dresha (I guess) brushed off the sleeve of her jacket.

75

"I needed the report on—" She stopped midsentence.

"You didn't!" she gasped in a mixture of horror and rage. She stormed past the startled scientist towards a desk near the back of the vast room. The scientist's face changed from angry to annoyed.

"Don't touch it!" he shouted and raced after her. I followed them.

The girl was standing in front of a large tank filled with colorful reptiles the size of my finger. Several were curled up and unmoving.

"What did you do to them?" Dresha yelled. The scientist let out an exasperated sigh.

"For the last time, Dresha! They are not real reptilian lifeforms! They are holographic representations of them! Besides, even if they were real, they're not dead. They're Rogathan Cresteds. This is the time of year they go into hibernation. I'm trying to study the synaptic patterns their brains go into," he said in a tone that he might use while explaining something to a small child.

Dresha rolled her eyes. "I'm not stupid, and stop calling me 'Dresha.' It's not my name!" she said angrily.

The scientist raised his hands in the air. "I don't see what your problem is!" he replied in an equally fierce tone.

So 'Dresha' wasn't this person's name. This conversation was confusing me.

"Jim uses it *all* the time!" the scientist continued.

Not-Dresha took a step towards the scientist, who jutted his chin out towards her.

Jess now cleared her throat, the sound carrying over all the other noise in the lab. Both scientist and commander stopped in their tracks.

Jess stepped up next to me. "I think that's enough," she said evenly. I looked between the three of them. It looked as though the situation was about to come to blows between the two younger people, but Jess had stopped them without raising her voice at all. It was a talent of hers. Not-Dresha and Scientist-person stepped away from each other and turned to face Jess. Now that I had a closer look at them, the scientist was quite tall, only about an inch-and-a-half shorter than myself. His limbs were wiry, and he had a mischievous grin.

Not-Dresha was about two inches shorter than him. She had an athletic figure and her black hair was parted to one side and braided over her shoulder. One lock was free on the side of her forehead with a streak of red dye. She carried herself like a commander, I thought, her arms folded over chest and her dark brows in a scowl. It was her eyes that caught me off guard. They were a deep purple color and gleamed with intelligence.

Jess folded her arms and glanced between the two of them. "This is, quite frankly, childish of both of you," she said, her voice still a normal volume. She reached over to a table and picked up a data-pad.

"I think this is what you needed," Jess said to the girl, who was scowling slightly, and pursing her lips. She took the pad.

Jess continued, "I don't think the lizards are in any danger, and next time, please heed the signs on the door. This is a heavily populated area, after all."

"Yes, ma'am," was all the girl said, a slight edge in her voice.

Jess raised an eyebrow, but turned to the scientist. "I don't think panic was necessary," she said.

The scientist hung his head a little. "I'm sorry I over reacted, Jess," he said sheepishly. He turned to Not-Dresha (I really needed to know her real name). "I'm sorry my lizards scared you," he said.

She stared at him for a moment. "They aren't really holograms, are they?" She asked. The scientist grinned, giving him a slightly crazed look.

"Nah, these ones aren't anyways, but they really are just in hibernation," he replied. She raised her eyebrow at him and shook her head.

I was studying the tank. "Why aren't they all asleep?" I asked. They both jumped in surprise.

"Pardon?" the scientist responded. I motioned to the tank as I leaned down to get a closer look.

"You said this was the time of year they went into hibernation, but only a few of them are asleep," I said. The scientist's eyes lit up.

"You noticed that did you? Did you notice that there are different colors of lizards as well?" He said.

77

I got a feeling he liked to lecture about these things. I must have impressed him with my observation.

I nodded a little. "Now that you mention it, but not before."

The scientist folded his arms and looked at Not-Dresha.

"Look, he's observant, but he's also honest! A true rarity nowadays." He gestured to me while he spoke. He turned back to the tank.

"If you take a closer look," he said leaning down next to me, "Only the lizards with a green and yellow pattern are asleep." He gestured to the leafy foliage around the tank. "They need to have an environment with vegetation. This gives their brains the signal that it's safe to hibernate now that they're hidden. Now," He motioned to a group of lizards with a pink and white pattern. "These little guys need to have flowers, because that's where their camouflage works best, and the fragrance of the blossoms disguises their scents from predators."

He opened a large jar to one side of the tank and lifted out a group of large pink and white blossoms. He carefully opened the tank and set them in a small hole that had been dug near the pink lizards. He smoothed dirt over the flowers, then replaced the lid of the tank. I watched as the pink lizards all slowly curled up in the flowers, and promptly shut their eyes and disappeared into the petals. I shook my head in amazement.

"That's amazing," I said, and I meant it.

The scientist waved my praise away with one hand, his eyes still fixed on the lizards in the tank.

"Yes, yes it is." He folded his arms and tapped his chin in thought.

"I'm still trying to figure theses ones out," he said pointing to the remaining lizards. "These blue ones need something that has to do with water, I'm sure," he said distractedly. "And these orange and yellow ones have me baffled."

Jess cleared her throat again. "Edrix," she said, "this is Nelvin, the head of our science division."

Nelvin grinned and shook my hand. "You must be the Edrix guy we've been hearing about. Nice to meet you!" he said, still pumping my hand enthusiastically. I liked this Nelvin.

"The same to you," I said.

Not-Dresha now spoke. "You're going to make his arm fall off," she said, her face expressionless. Nelvin released my hand, then swept his hand towards her, as if presenting a guest.

"Edrix," he said, "this is Commander Andresha Kanway of Red Star," he said grandly and rolling his r's, as if he was announcing the presence of the Chairman.

Thank goodness! I finally knew what her name was! Kanway … It sounded familiar. I searched my memory, but I had never seen this person before. Coincidence, I guess. Andresha stared at me for a moment, then turned and walked away. Nelvin looked at me and shrugged.

"She's always like that at first," he said.

I shrugged. I didn't expect to be friends with everyone right away, or possibly ever. After all, I was from the enemy side.

Nelvin looked back at Jess. "Have you given him a tour yet?" He asked her. Jess gave him an amused smile.

"I showed him this far," she replied. Nelvin spread out his hands.

"What do you think?" He asked me.

I looked around the enormous room again. "It's … impressive," I said. Nelvin grinned, that slightly crazed look coming back into his eyes.

"It's kinda the only word for it," he said. I nodded in agreement.

Jess opened her mouth to say something, then Andresha was back.

"Chief wants us," she said to Jess, who looked at me apologetically.

"I guess I'll have to cut out tour short," she said.

"That's all right," I said nonchalantly. I would have been content to spend the rest of the day just exploring the lab.

"I'll finish it!" Nelvin said, like a kid volunteering in class. Jess raised her eyebrows and glanced at me.

I grinned. "Sounds good to me."

Jess glanced back at where Andresha was tapping her fingers on the doorway.

"I'd better get going," she said. "I'll talk to you later." She followed Andresha out of the room, the door shutting behind them with a loud *bang*!

Nelvin grimaced. "Does she always have to slam it behind her?" He muttered to himself, then said to me, "Feel free to look around. "I'm gonna clean up a bit. Just don't touch the terathite compound, it might explode." He disappeared through a door hidden by a large leafy plant. I wandered around the lab, occasionally tinkering with something, but I didn't touch anything that was bubbly, liquid, or spewing smoke.

"Does that happen a lot?" I asked.

"Does what happen a lot?" came Nelvin's muffled replied.

"What just happened a few minutes ago."

"Ohhhh," he said. "You mean the whole ignoring-the-light, coming in and scaring the daylights out of me, then rushing to the defense of sleepy lizards, and turning the whole thing into a debate, what just happened?" I blinked a few times.

"Yeah," I said simply.

"*All* the time!" he called.

A beaker to my left suddenly spouted a ring of smoke and made a hissing sound. Then something ran across my foot just as I heard a call of "loose rat!" from somewhere else in the lab. I turned around as Nelvin came out of the door and walked into the plant.

"Oh, drat!" he exclaimed. He struggled in vain for a moment, but it seemed as if the plant had grabbed him, its stems and leaves wrapping around his wrists and coat. I went to his aid, but the plant had a vice grip.

"I could cut you out of there?" I offered, but he shook his head.

"No, no! Don't do that!" He grunted as the plant pulled his hair. "Took me years to get it this big. Cut it and I'll have to start over." He turned his head towards the back of the lab.

"TRISHA!" he called. A few minutes later, a blonde woman bustled into view. It was the doctor that had examined me when I'd first gotten here. She clucked her tongue as she saw Nelvin.

"I told you we should have moved it," she said, but not unkindly. It seemed as though she never spoke above a whisper.

Nelvin swatted a leaf away from his face. "This is the only spot in the whole lab where it's not in the way!" he protested. "And the temperature is perfect."

Trisha shook her head again and began carefully pulling the stems away from him.

Finally, Nelvin was free from the grip of the plant. He brushed a few stray leaves off his arms, though one was still stuck in his hair.

"Thank you, Trisha," he said, then turning to me he added, "This is Patrisha, my assistant in keeping me sane, and one of the best doctors we have."

I shook Patrisha's hand. "We've met." I said. She smiled shyly at me. Nelvin hung his lab coat on a hook.

"That's good," he said. He turned to Patrisha. "I'm going to finish his tour, wanna come?"

She shrugged. "Sounds fun. I got all my work done." Nelvin grinned.

"Wondrous! Hungry?" He asked me. I shrugged. I was actually starving, but I didn't want them to feel bad.

"A little," I said.

Nelvin clapped his hands once. "Great! I'll show you the mess hall!" he said excitedly.

Patrisha nodded her head enthusiastically. "We don't have much, but Chef makes it taste prime!" she said.

Maybe this place wasn't going to be so bad.

13

Jess stood in back of the mess hall with the man known to everyone as Chief. Everyone but her, that is, but she did not use his name. They were watching a group at a table towards the back of the brightly lit, crowded room. Two boys, one girl. It was impossible to make out what they were saying amid the chatter floating around the room. Suddenly, all three burst out laughing.

"He's making friends," Chief said quietly. Jess nodded distractedly. Edrix, one of the boys, was telling a story. He made a motion with his spoon to illustrate something. The table burst into laughter again.

"It's good," Jess replied. Chief leaned back against the wall, his arms crossed.

"What do you think?" He asked. Jess's eyes left the table and looked at Chief.

"About what?"

"My idea."

She took a deep breath and looked at the small group again in the rapidly filling room. It was like this at mid-hour. Everyone who could was coming in to get something to eat before returning to work.

"I don't know," she whispered. "I'm worried about him. Seeing his brother like that ..." She trailed off.

Chief nodded. "Which is also just another piece in our ever growing puzzle," he said grimly. Jess nodded absently.

"You told Andresha?" Chief asked.

Jess pursed her lips. "Most of it. I told her about Eleven, but I haven't told her the real reason yet."

"Why not?"

Jess gazed over the room again. There were only two chairs left in the room, at Edrix's table. She looked back at Chief, considering her words carefully.

"I thought it might be best if you told her," she said. Chief almost laughed.

82

"Me?" He asked. "I'd be the worst person. You should have seen what happened after I told her she couldn't go look for him." He jerked his head in Edrix's direction. "Besides, we can't get in the Core anyways. We're going to have to tell everyone eventually."

Jess folded her own arms now and turned to him.

"First of all, you're going to have to do something about that," she said, referring to his first statement. "Second, well, Edrix might be able to help us get in."

Chief perked up, but ignored the first part of her answer.

"How?" He asked.

She shrugged. "He's been in REGS for almost a year, he might know something."

Chief drained the remainder of the liquid from his cup.

"Just give him my offer," he said, but she shook her head.

"Not yet. Give him a few rotations to settle down. He's already overwhelmed, and I want to see how he gets along with everyone," she said.

Chief raised his eyebrow. "He did come to us, and besides, I think they like him," he said nodding to the group they had been observing. Now Jess raised her eyebrow.

"They do, but there's something … I don't know. I want to wait a little longer," she said.

Chief shrugged. "Fine, but if we don't get into the Core soon, this whole movement is going to go up in flames."

14

(Andresha)

The mess hall was packed with people. Jim and I could see exactly two chairs left in the room. We surged towards them before someone else could take them. Upon reaching them, however, I had to suppress a groan. Nelvin and the new guy were sitting there, Nelvin recounting some kind of laboratory disaster. The one bright spot at the table was Patrisha, who politely added input when invited. I was ready to eat in the hallway, but Jim had other ideas.

"Mind if we join you?" He asked. All conversation at the table stopped.

Nelvin grinned. "Sure! Have a seat."

Jim pulled my chair out for me, then sat down himself. Joy and happiness, I was sitting across from Edrix. Stop that! I told myself. I didn't know anything about him, I shouldn't be judging him like that! But at the same time, there was something inside me that screamed danger, something from memories I swore I'd never look at.

I realized I was staring and quickly looked down at my bowl of soup. It was just a simple broth, but it was hot. I also had a plate of fruit. I stirred the soup around with my spoon, one elbow on the table and resting my cheek on my fist. My mother would probably have a fit if she'd seen me now.

That thought hurt my heart. I pushed her memory down in my mind, buried it under others. I didn't have time for tears right now.

Nelvin had introduced Jim to Edrix, who were now engaged in a conversation about how well Edrix liked the base and so on. I swallowed a spoonful of soup, even though it was still piping hot. Jim got along with everyone so well. I listened to them for a while, Jim once asked me about how I liked the targets on the range. I told him that I liked them very much and explained to Edrix that they were new. He shrugged.

84

I glanced at Nelvin, who was talking again. His dishes were set to the side, empty. Patrisha's were the same. Jim and I had just started eating, but Edrix's food was barely touched. He sat now, his spoon in his hand, gripping it so tightly his knuckles were white. He stared at the soup as if it were some kind of ravenous beast.

I swallowed the piece of fruit I had been chewing and said, "It's food. You're supposed to eat it."

His head snapped up. He swallowed. "I know that," he said quietly.

"Is there something wrong with it?" I asked, keeping any accusing tone out of my voice.

Edrix shook his head. "No, I'm sure it's great, I just ..." he trailed off.

Patrisha, always a gentle soul, immediately took notice. "You don't have to eat it," she said gently.

Edrix swallowed hard. "No, it's all right, I " He hesitated, looking rather pale. "It's just been a while since I've eaten, that's all," he said tightly. No one at the table said anything, so naturally, I had to open my mouth.

"I would think that REGS would treat its agents better than that."

Edrix's head snapped up. "What?" He asked.

I shrugged. *Why did I say that?* I thought to myself.

He scowled a little. "They give us food, if that's what you're asking," he said.

I told myself to shut my mouth and leave the room, but of course, I didn't. "So you run away and suddenly you can't get food to eat?" I said. "Or are you just used to a wonderful feast and can't stand the sight of *civilian* food?"

I saw the muscles in his hands tighten as he looked away. We were both on our feet at the same moment, our faces inches from each other.

"So you think I'm stuck up, is that it?" Edrix demanded, hands leaning on the table.

"Pretty much," I said. Nelvin tried to calm the waters.

"Look, Dresha. You didn't have to sit here," he said.

85

"Except that it was the only seat left in the room, Nelvin!" I snapped. I noticed that the whole room had gone silent and was staring at us. I pushed my tray away.

"I'm not hungry either," I said and stormed out of the room, but not before I saw Jess standing in the back of the room, shaking her head. I knew she would side with him. They grew up together, after all.

15

(Andresha)

A week passed by relatively quickly. I had been busy trying to intercept anything about Eleven, and meeting with countless contacts so far, leaving me with little time to think about Edrix. I hadn't learned anything about Eleven, but I had learned that the food crisis on Eight was worsening. After reporting this to Chief, he had agreed that something had to be done, and ordered another parcel run.

So there I was, sitting in in the back of the arboretum, carefully filling the small boxes and attaching parachutes. I'd asked Patrisha to come help. She said she wouldn't be able to right away, due to an outbreak of a virus, but would be there when she could. She would never pass up an opportunity to help someone. The only person helping me at the moment was Jim. He placed a large piece of fruit in a box and sealed it up, then reached for a parachute from the stack between us.

We sat in the middle of the fruit trees that grew in the room. They were big, gnarly things, but this way we could pick the fruit fresh and sit on the soft patches of grass that surrounded the trees. I liked sitting here whenever I had the time. It reminded me of the good parts of home, the parts I could think about. I picked up a piece of fruit from the ground next to me. It was round with a purplish pink skin. I studied it as Jim continued to fill boxes.

"I noticed you've been avoiding Edrix," he said evenly. I scowled at the fruit. I *had* been avoiding him ever since the scene in the mess hall, but I figured that he probably wouldn't be staying long. REGS would give up eventually and cancel the apprehension order and bounty. If he was *really* that important, they could say he was dead. They had done it before.

"And if I have?" I asked Jim, a slight edge in my voice.

He shrugged. "I just don't see why you don't like him, that's all."

I placed the fruit into a box and sealed it shut. "You were there."

87

Jim attached a parachute to his box and set it aside, replacing it with an empty one.

"So you got in a fight. If I remember correctly, you and I argued quite a bit before we became friends," he said. I growled softly to myself. Right again.

I could still remember. I had been fourteen then, and we'd fought whenever we were in the same room together. Over almost anything.

It had started when Jim had first come here. He had seen me in the command center and said, "Is this *really* a place for a little girl?" In response, I had walked over and punched him the face.

"Am I still a little girl?" I had demanded.

Jim had touched his rapidly blackening eye, then sneered, "Yeah, 'cause that's what little girls do."

At this, I had tilted up my chin and said with utmost dignity, "If that's the case, then there's only one 'little girl' in here, and they have a black eye!"

Then I had stormed out of the command center before Chief could say anything. It had continued like this for months. Finally, we'd gotten stuck on an assignment together. Jim had apologized for calling me a little girl that day, and asked if we could be friends. "After all," he had said with a chuckle, "We do a pretty good job of tearing each other down when we argue, think about what we could build when we work together."

I smiled at the memory. A little corny, perhaps, but he'd meant it. I realized Jim was waiting for an answer.

"That was different," I said.

"And that means it's the same," he said. I rolled my eyes as I sealed up the last box.

"Come on," I grumbled. "Let's get these boxes on their way."

We put the now filled boxes into a crate and pushed them out of the arboretum. I was a little disappointed that Patrisha hadn't shown up, but there would be other opportunities. We pushed the crate into a lift.

"It was different, because you weren't a REGS Agent," I said.

Jim looked over at me, an amused expression on his face. "What if I had been?" He asked. I looked over at him, a laugh on my lips, but his expression stopped it. He no longer looked amused, but genuinely curious. I shrugged.

"I don't know," I said quietly, "because you weren't."

A strange look crossed his face that I couldn't read. What was that all about?

The lift doors opened and Jim pushed the crate out. He looked normal now, no trace of that weird look. I shook my head a little and followed him into the hangar.

Jess and Chief were waiting for us. I could see Short inside the cockpit of a small plane, ready for the boxes to be loaded.

Jim pushed the crate over to them. "We've got about three hundred in here," he announced.

Chief nodded. "Good. Someone from medical will be here in a minute with more filled with medical supplies," he said. I didn't look at either of them. I knew they were disappointed about last week. Frankly, so was I. I should have just kept my mouth shut and eaten my soup.

I should *probably* apologize …

My thinking was cut short as the door opened behind me. I turned around and let myself grin. Patrisha was walking towards us with … The smile faded from my face.

It was Edrix. He was pushing a crate similar to the one next to me. This one had a lid on top. They came up level to us.

"Here's the medicine you asked for," Patrisha said. Jess nodded.

"Thank you, Dr. Jones." Another agent came over and placed the crate onto a loading arm. It would load the crate into the plane so Short could drop them.

I nodded a greeting to Edrix while everyone else was talking. If I was going to apologize, now was my chance.

We stood facing each other awkwardly. I couldn't think of a single thing to say. He nodded at me. I returned it. Then he nodded again. I caught myself before I could repeat the action. If we weren't careful we'd be nodding to each other all day. We had taken the first step, though. We had acknowledged each other.

The agent placed the crate of food boxes next to the other crate, then pulled the lid off the one filled with medical supplies. Edrix seemed to notice them for the first time.

"Those are like the boxes you dropped at the riot," he said.

Jess nodded distractedly. She was looking at a data pad and frowning.

"In fact, that's where these ones are heading," she said.

Edrix bit his lip. "Are you sure that's a good idea?" He asked. I glanced at Chief, who had just given Short the signal to take off.

"What do you mean?" Jim asked good naturedly. Edrix folded his arms.

"Well, last time you did it, almost three hundred people were killed," he said. Jess glanced at us and Patrisha bit her lip.

"We didn't mean for that to happen. We just wanted to help them," Patrisha whispered.

Edrix shrugged. "I still don't think it's a good idea to drop those boxes again. REGS will be watching for you there." Chief handed a data pad to an agent who hurried off.

"We aren't leaving a symbol this time," Chief said. "Short has orders to drop the supplies, then return here. Nothing else." He whispered something to Jess, then left the hangar.

Edrix didn't look convinced, but he didn't say anything. His first statement echoed around in my head. *Well, last time almost three-hundred people got killed.* It sounded like he was blaming us. I chose my words carefully as I spoke, not wanting to be misunderstood.

"We were just trying to help them, you know," I said quietly. Edrix swung his gaze to me. I was shocked at how much anger and pain he had in his eyes.

"And that went great, didn't it?" He said bitterly. Now I felt my own anger rising. I scowled.

"We didn't kill them—You did!" I retorted. Edrix turned to face me now.

"REGS killed them! I tried to stop them!" he said tensely.

"And you're all just one in the same, aren't you? 'A world united in order?'" I quoted REGS' ridiculous slogan, my voice practically

90

dripping in sarcasm. I glanced around the room. Jess was on the other side of the hangar, and Patrisha was gone. The only other person in the room was Jim, who tried to intercede.

"We know you tried to stop it," he said. "And that's good. We just don't want them to starve, that's all."

"Well, we wouldn't need to worry about that if REGS hadn't stopped their food supply," I snapped.

Edrix—of course—immediately went to REGS defense. "REGS isn't all bad," he insisted.

I stepped forward, my face close to his.

"Really? I hadn't noticed past the Peacekeepers lining streets, agents making unjust arrests, and Higher Ones thinking that they're greater beings than us," I growled. Jim started to say something, but I didn't hear him. I was too upset.

"I hadn't noticed past the starving people, the executions, and the rest of REGS who just sit by and watch it happen!"

Edrix had turned away from me and was walking towards the door. I called after him.

"Just. Like. You!"

Something in me had snapped. I don't know why I said that last part. I was angry, yes. Angry at REGS and the Chairman. But why was I so angry at Edrix? It didn't make sense.

Edrix turned back towards me. His emotions were strong enough, I wouldn't be surprised if every Rendarian in the hangar could read them. Anger, sorrow, and guilt. Guilt was the strongest of all.

He was ready to retort when the hangar alarms started to blare. I looked up in surprise at the blue lights flashing on the walls. There was a damaged ship coming in.

Chief was suddenly in the room. "Kanway, I want you in my office in ten minutes." He walked past me to Edrix.

"You come with me now!" he said. Jim hurried over to him.

"What happened?" he asked. Chief turned to him, handing a pad to Jess as he did so.

"Short's been hit. The mission failed." He turned back to Edrix.

"You were right."

16

(Edrix)

The doors closed behind me as I entered Chief's office. He hadn't said anything else in the hangar. What did he mean I was right? That REGS had been waiting for Short? He hadn't explained. Chief now stood behind his desk.

"Jess said to give you time to adjust. I think it's been long enough," he said. I knit my eyebrows in thought. I was still fuming over Andresha's accusation. What did she know about REGS? There were lots of good people there, I mean, Jai was a good person, wasn't he?

But I was beginning to doubt even that.

"Long enough for what, sir?" I asked him. Chief studied me.

"You knew REGS would be waiting for Short," he said. "How?"

I hesitated. I still felt reluctant to share a lot about REGS security. I shook myself out of it. REGS was over for me. They hated me. REGS wanted me dead, and that was that. I'd never be able to go back. I took a deep breath.

"It's standard procedure," I told Chief. "When there's been hostile activity on a Level, they always double the REGS force on the Level in question for a minimum of a month."

Chief nodded a little to himself. "They were there all right. Landed a solid hit on Short's craft," he said.

"Was he able to drop the supplies?" I asked.

Chief raised an eyebrow. He looked like someone else when he did it, but I couldn't place who.

"I thought you said it was a bad idea," he said.

I shrugged. "Just because it was a bad idea doesn't mean I didn't want it to succeed," I said. Chief smiled for half a second.

"You sound like Jess," he said. I decided to take that as a compliment. Chief sighed.

"He didn't drop the supplies," he said. He held up a hand to forestall the question I was about to ask.

"There was no one to receive them. Level Eight is empty."

I stood there shocked. Empty? Eight was huge! Everyone couldn't have simply disappeared.

I hung my head. "Are they …?" I didn't finish the question. I couldn't. All those faces flashed before my eyes. Chief shrugged.

"We don't know. I'm hoping they were just relocated." He was silent for a moment, as if he was considering something. Then he spoke again.

"Now, Edrix, you have a choice to make."

I looked up. "A choice, sir?" I asked.

He nodded and clasped his hands behind his back and paced behind the desk.

"You have two options. One, you can stay here and hope that REGS will eventually lift its bounty and apprehension order. You would be welcome here for however long that may take. Or,"

He paused again, looking at me intently, then continued. "You can become a part of our movement. An agent of the Red Star."

I was stunned, to say the least. Join their movement? That would be treason of the highest kind. Worse than the crimes I'd already committed in REGS eyes. But on the other hand …

I looked down at my shoes, embarrassed. "You mean, you're still offering this to me, even after what happened in the mess hall last week, and just now, in the hangar?" I asked timidly. Chief stared at me hard, his arms folded.

"That's not my problem, but I expect you to work it out before it *needs* to be my problem," he said sharply. "This isn't Basic School, so don't act like it."

I flinched a little at his tone, but I knew I deserved it.

"I have a question," I said. Chief raised an eyebrow.

"And that would be?"

I took a deep breath. "Why don't you tell anyone your name?"

Chief stared at me for a full minute.

"Think about it this way, Edrix," he said. "If captured, anyone who knew my identity could be made to reveal it, thus endangering Red Star and all its agents. They would become a valuable target for

REGS, and they would have to constantly guard their tongues so that they didn't reveal it to others. I don't want *anyone* to carry that responsibility other than myself."

I considered his words. From a tactical perspective, it made sense. Keeping knowledge to a minimum would decrease the likelihood that someone would slip up—or betray you—but from a personal standpoint, it would be incredibly lonely, being unable to get close to *anyone*.

"You make a valid point," I said finally, "but I have to admit, it makes me more curious, I mean, REGS can't do more then look up your background."

Chief ran a hand through his hair. "They could also look up if I had any family and where they were, as well as any colleagues and friends. Besides, *my* background would be enough to get the majority of REGS forces combing Nine."

I smiled a little. He had obviously examined all the angles.

"That just makes my curiosity increase," I said.

Chief's mouth twitched in what *could* have been a smile, just a hint of one. "You wouldn't be the only one," he said, his voice light, but his eyes blank.

I grew serious again. This was a huge step I was taking. If I wasn't accused of treason yet, this would assure that I was. I would be labeled an insurgent and known as a disturber of Order.

I looked over at the chair beside me and saw her sitting there, the blonde girl from Eight. She was staring at me with her sunken eyes and hollowed cheeks, asking me a silent question:

Are you going to let me die again?

REGS would kill again, regardless of the number, if they decided they had disobeyed the Chairman. Red Star would be the one to stop them.

I looked Chief in the eye. "I'm in," I said.

He reached over the desk and we shook hands. "Very good, Agent Solan," he said. "Welcome to Red Star."

17

(Andresha)

"You didn't!" I protested. Chief looked up at the ceiling and let out an exasperated sigh.

"Yes, I did, Andresha," he said. Oh, it looks like we were on first-name basis today. I wasn't going to go along with it.

Chief folded his arms.

"Give me one *really* good reason why he shouldn't join," he challenged me. I bit my lip and thought hard.

"He's a REGS agent," I tried.

"Not good enough," he said. I thought again.

"Because … because …" I trailed off. Chief was looking at me expectantly.

"Because there's something in him that reminds me of dad!" I blurted.

Chief's gaze softened. I sat down in a chair in front of the desk and stared at my hands in my lap. There, I'd said it.

Chief sat down across from me. "I don't think he's anything like that," he said softly. I looked up at him, forcing tears back from my eyes. I couldn't do this right now.

"Why did you want to talk to me?" I asked, changing the subject. Chief pursed his lips for a moment, then sat back in his chair.

"We got a message earlier today from a contact. Someone has information for us, but will only talk to a direct representative." I calmed down a little. I was still slightly in shock from what had happened on Eight, and I felt bad about what I'd said to Edrix. Again.

"Do we know who this 'someone' is?" I asked. Chief shook his head.

"No, but I want you to check it out with Jim." I nodded. It sounded fine to me. I was ready for something to do. "When do we leave?" I asked. Chief stood up and moved behind the desk.

"Tomorrow morning," he said. He slid a pad over to me. "That's all the information you need. The location, and this 'someone's' demands for talking." I nodded as I glanced quickly at the pad. Nothing I couldn't handle. I stood and turned to leave.

"Andresha," Chief said. I bit my lip. Just a little bit of his professional tone had left his voice, just a hint.

"Yes?" I asked. He was silent for a moment.

"Jess trusts him. It's going to be fine. Work it out."

I bit my lip and glanced behind me. Funny how that seemed to make everything fine.

"Yes, sir." I said. I saw his face fall a little.

"Dismissed," he whispered, and I left the office.

* * *

I walked into the gym and almost got impaled. The knife flew by my head and stuck itself into a humanoid shaped holo-target next to the door. The target didn't look realistic in anyway. It had no facial features, just two arms and legs and a head made out of orange-yellow squares. The target disintegrated, leaving the knife stuck in the wall. Usually, the holo-targets were only used in the shooting range, but we had some in the gym for hand-to-hand and, obviously, knife combat.

"Sorry!" came a distracted shout. I turned towards the sound. I raised my eyebrows at the scene before me.

Edrix was surrounded by several holo-targets like the one I'd just seen. Ten at the most. It was one of the combat simulations programed into the computer. The holograms would "attack" you, and you would have to defend yourself. If you got hit, you would only be momentarily immobilized. A hit to a critical area would let you feel a slightly larger shock, effectively knocking you to the ground.

But I didn't think Edrix needed to worry about that, even though he was facing them with only a knife in his hands. It was mesmerizing to watch him, almost like a dance.

He was good. I watched as he swept a hologram's legs from beneath it, then stabbed it with his blade. The hologram disintegrated into orange energy blocks and disappeared. Three more went down with three slashing motions. One hologram grabbed him in a head lock with one arm, the other holding his knife hand. I watched as Edrix quickly reached into his left boot and pulled out another knife, this one a few centimeters longer than the other he held in his right hand. He reared his head back into the hologram, then thrust his knife behind him. The hologram disintegrated.

There were five left. He tossed one knife in the air briefly and caught it by the blade, then in a smooth motion, threw the knife across the room. It caught another hologram in the chest, and its energy cubes scattered across the room.

Edrix sprinted across the room and retrieved his knife, then stood before the remaining four holograms, simply standing for a moment, knives at the ready. As one, the holograms started forward. Edrix grunted and ran to meet them, but he angled to one side. The holograms were running at him in a line. Edrix was now abreast with them. He growled and dived over to the first hologram, driving his knife into its back, then he pivoted on his foot and did the same with the next. He continued this action for the last two. Then he stopped his remaining momentum by dropping to the ground into a roll. He came up in a crouch, knives ready.

The computer beeped, and the cubes scattered across the floor disappeared. I couldn't help myself. I clapped. He was better than good. He was amazing! I wish I knew how to knife fight like that. I knew a few basics, but I knew I couldn't stand up to someone with that much skill.

Edrix stood up, replacing the knives in their sheaths. One in his boot, the other in a scabbard that was strapped to his left forearm. I noticed he had a similar sheath on his right forearm as well. He walked over to me and pulled the knife that had almost hit me out of one of the thick mats that lined the wall.

"Thanks," he said. I now noticed a few more people in the gym, mostly in the exercise area on treadmills or the weight benches.

"You're pretty good with those knives of yours," I said. "How many do you have?"

Edrix shrugged. "It depends on the objective, but the most I've ever had on me at one time was ..." He paused for a moment. "Twelve."

I raised my eyebrow. "That's a lot of knives."

He shrugged. "If it saves your life."

I nodded a little. "Are they all weighted for throwing?" I asked and he nodded.

"How does that work?"

He raised an eyebrow, then showed me the knife he'd just retrieved. "The handle is heavier than your standard knife. That ensures that there's enough weight to drive the knife into its target. The blade is then counter balanced so that the knife will spin through the air."

I nodded. An idea began to form in my head. Maybe a way to get over my differences with Edrix Solan.

"Will you teach me?" I asked. Edrix slid the knife into the scabbard on his right forearm.

"Teach you what?"

"How to knife fight."

He folded his arms and I folded mine. "Why?"

I shrugged. "Because I'm not good at it. I know enough to live through an attack with a petty thief, but against someone like you, I'll only survive if there's a gun in my hands. That's all anyone here's ever been able to teach. Shoot them first," I replied.

Edrix rubbed the back of his neck. "And in exchange for this you will …?" He left the question hanging.

I considered the question. "Well, what do you want to know?" I asked him.

He cocked his head to one side. The movement reminded me of Jess.

"Well, what are you good at?" He asked. I thought for a moment.

"Staying out of sight and improvising?" I suggested. He shrugged.

"I'm afraid I already know that," he said.

"Hand-to-hand?"

"Got that too."

We were silent for a moment. What was I supposed to know that a Higher One didn't? He would have had *way* more professional training then I ever had.

"How about Red Star protocols?" Edrix asked.

I knit my eyebrows in confusion. "What now?" I replied.

He shrugged. "You know, like rules."

I tapped my chin, then counted off my fingers as I spoke. "Umm, obey your commanders, don't steal anything, and don't kill anyone. That's about it," I said.

He looked unconvinced. "Really?"

I nodded. "Really, that's it. I *could* get down to nit-picky details, but that's what they all boil down to."

He shrugged. "Well, we can work it out later, Commander," he said. "We'll start tomorrow."

"I want to start today," I said.

He raised his eyebrows.

"If that's all right with you," I added hastily.

"Sure," he said shortly. He walked over to a wall with rows of equipment. In the middle there was a rack of blunted knives.

"Pick one," he said. I glanced over the section. They all looked the same. Black hilts, some bound with leather, most without. The blades were silver, but many different shapes. I selected a knife with a leather bound handle and a six-inch blade. It felt heavy. Edrix held out a hand, and I gave him the knife. He examined it briefly.

"This one isn't for throwing," he said handing the knife back to me. "Just stabbing and cutting."

I shrugged. "Sounds like a good place to start," I said.

"Right you are. Pick a spot," he said and motioned to the different matted sections on the floor around the room. I chose the one closest to the wall. I had noticed a first aid kit nearby, and I might need it later. Edrix selected another knife from the wall and came over to me.

"Why don't you just use one of those?" I asked, motioning to one of the knives strapped to his arm.

He gave me a wry smile. "Because those aren't blunted."

I blinked twice. "That's a good reason."

He showed me a basic stance: holding the knife blade down in my right hand and slightly crouched.

"Alright," he said. "Come at me." I hesitated, then lunged forward with my knife. Edrix easily swayed to one side. My thrust met no resistance so I stumbled off balance. Edrix stepped forward, tripping me. I fell to the ground, twisting so I landed on my back. Then Edrix's knife was pointed under my chin. This all happened in less than ten seconds. Edrix stepped back and offered me a hand to get up. I resolutely ignored him and got up myself. Edrix shrugged.

"I guess we'll start with balance," he said.

He had me practice making lunges and cuts by myself, and how to compensate for a miss. I did this for an hour, then he had me start practicing with a throwing knife.

"You have to be able to judge how many rotations the knife needs to reach its target either blade or hilt first," he said, then showed me how to hold the blade, and demonstrated the basic arm movement for throwing.

I did this for another hour. He would give me pointers on how to improve my throws, though I personally thought I just needed to hit the indicated area on the wall. I was a dead shot with a hand gun, but I couldn't hit a three-foot wide target with a knife.

I finally stopped, my arms tired from throwing the knife and my pride sore from missing the target every. Single. Time.

Edrix nodded. "You're pretty good."

I looked at him in disbelief. "'Pretty good?'" I echoed. "How in the world was that good?"

Edrix replaced my knife back on the wall. "What, you mean missing the target?"

I looked down at my feet. "Yeah," I said biting my lip. "I mean, I never miss with a gun, I don't see why I can't hit with a substantially larger projectile."

He had the nerve to laugh. "Sorry," he said, "but throwing a knife and shooting a gun are two very different things. When you shoot, the gun does the throwing for you, figuratively speaking. All you have to do is aim and pull the trigger. When you throw, you have to think of which way to move your arm, how many times you want the knife to spin, so on and so forth. Make sense?"

I nodded a little. "I guess."

He headed towards the door. "Hitting your target will come later," he said. "Right now, you just need to get you're technique down." Then he left.

I looked back at the unscathed target on the wall. I wasn't ready to call him a friend yet, but we had made a good start.

100

18

(Edrix)

There was no sound other than that of our breathing. I was on lookout with two other agents, Jinx and Tompson. Jinx had a large scar on his face and a cybernetic eye that glowed red. Tompson was tall with dark hair that fell to her shoulders and dark skin. According to Nelvin, she was one of the oldest members of Red Star.

We didn't talk, simply watched the dark streets. We were sitting outside the rundown warehouse over the base. It was strange, but this place was already starting to feel like home.

Nelvin and Patrisha were delighted that I'd joined, of course, and Nelvin had wasted no time getting me up to speed on how things worked here. It was much simpler than REGS had been. It was just what Andresha had said in the gym yesterday.

She was an interesting character. She had gotten the basics of knife throwing pretty quickly, and her fighting technique wasn't far behind.

She had met me again this morning for practice tips, but I'd only had about five minutes before I had to go on duty. I had told her what I could in such a short time, but mostly just to keep practicing. After a certain point, that was all you could say.

I looked down at my new jacket. It was simple black leather with the Red Star symbol emblazoned on the lapel. It felt good to wear it; I actually felt good about what I was doing. It was a new feeling, to be honest.

I glanced over at Jinx.

"Why is it called Red Star?" I asked him. He turned to look back at me. He shrugged.

"No one really knows. Red Star was founded before either of us joined," he said motioning to Tompson.

I looked at them in confusion. "I thought ... I thought Chief started it," I said. Jinx laughed.

"No. We've had two Chiefs before him," he replied. Two? How could there have been two? How long had Red Star been organized? I voiced this thought aloud to Jinx. He thought for a moment.

"Ten years or so?" he said finally. I reeled back a little in surprise. Ten years! REGS had only started paying attention to this group a year ago.

"So REGS never paid you any attention until last year?" I asked. Tompson shook her head.

"No, we just didn't really do anything ... big. We were pretty active five years ago, but our first Chief was killed shortly after that, so we went back to the shadows. Our second Chief left two years ago and never came back. Once the current Chief got everything organized, we were able to start doing more then Whispers."

"Whispers?" I repeated. "What are those?"

"Basically it's just anti-REGS or anti-Chairman propaganda," Jinx said. "Hacking news channels, graffiti, mercy missions. Sometimes, Nelvin even manages to hack the Chairman's speeches."

I held up a hand to stop the conversation, my first two fingers raised in a signal for *listen*. I had heard a sound to my left and I wanted them to hear it if it was repeated. It came had come from farther down an alley, from the direction of Lift Twenty-Three.

There it was again! Barely audible, but because we were quiet, we could hear it.

Jinx signaled for me to move with him towards the sound, but for Tompson to stay behind in case it was a ruse to lure us away. We were as silent as shadows as we crept into the alleyway. We were about halfway up the alley when we found the source of the sounds.

She stepped out from behind a pile of crates. A gun was in her hand and pointed at me. I raised my rifle to my shoulder, my finger close to the trigger.

"Stop where you are!" the woman said. Out of the corner of my eye, I saw Jinx raise his rifle as well.

"What do want?" He asked her. She was on the shorter side, with matted blonde hair and brown eyes. Her face and hands were streaked with dirt and she had dried blood on the side of her face.

Her clothes were dirty and torn. One sleeve looked like it had been burned. Her hand shook as she held the gun.

"You're from Red Star right?" She said, her voice shaking. I didn't answer. Jinx was in command. He spoke now.

"Why would that matter to you?" He asked her.

"I want you to take me to the one you call Chief," she said. Jinx carefully took a step forward.

"Why?"

She shook her head and tightened her grip on the gun. "Take me to him!" she demanded.

I watched her carefully. Her eyes weren't steady. They flicked between Jinx and me and the rest of the dark alleyway, like she was afraid something was going to come out of the wall. They lacked the conviction of someone ready shoot.

"You're not going to shoot." I said. Both Jinx and the woman looked at me. I gestured with my head.

"The safety's still on," I said. "If you wanted your threat to be valid, you would have switched it off."

The woman slumped her shoulders in defeat and lowered her weapon. Jinx held out his hand for it, and she bit her lip, then handed the gun to him. He examined the weapon, then stepped back and raised his rifle again.

"There's no mag," he said. "It's empty."

The woman put her hands up. "I don't want to cause trouble," she said. "I have information for your Chief about the Core."

This news didn't mean anything to me, but it must have to Jinx. He gave an involuntary start of surprise.

"And why should we trust you?" He asked, his grip tightening on his rifle. The woman swayed a little, and I noticed now how pale she was.

"Because I need your help," she said. "I can give this information in return. I know how you can get inside."

Jinx and I glanced at each other. I shrugged ever so slightly. It was his decision. Jinx turned back to the woman. "What kind of 'help' do you want?" He asked.

She swayed again, but fought to stay on her feet. "I want a Haven," she said. I looked over at Jinx. Asking for a Haven was asking for protection. Maybe she was running from something?

"That's not up to me," Jinx said. "That's up to Chief.

I glanced behind me. Tompson had come back from the warehouse.

"It's clear," she said, meaning there was no threat to the warehouse.

Jinx thought for a moment, then nodded.

"Alright. We'll take you to Chief," he said. He turned to Tompson. "Cuff her hands and blindfold her," he whispered. Tompson nodded and did what he said. The woman didn't resist, allowing her hands to be restrained and the blindfold tied without complaint.

We led the woman back to the warehouse and helped her down the ladder. After the door closed above us, Tompson removed the blindfold, but left the cuffs on. The woman looked around, bewildered. Tompson and Jinx walked over to a comm unit, leaving me with her.

"What's your name?" I asked her.

She bit her lip and hesitated. "Tasha," she said finally. "What's yours?"

"Edrix," I replied.

Her eyes went wide. "*Edrix Solan?*" She gasped.

I knit my brows. "Yes," I said warily.

Tasha looked at me, her mouth open in surprise. "I don't believe it," she whispered.

I was about to ask her what the big deal was, but Jinx came back before I could say anything.

"Chief's agreed to talk to you," he said to Tasha.

She nodded. "Thank you. May I have these hand cuffs off, please?" She asked.

"No," Jinx said shortly, "but we will have a medic take care of your injuries."

Suddenly, Jess came sprinting around the corner.

"Jinx, Solan, get back up there," she said. We all turned towards her.

"What's wrong?" I asked.

104

Jess handed Jinx a data pad. "Andresha and Jim were meeting a contact. We lost communication with them an hour ago, and REGS is swarming the location with bombers. We need you to verify their location and status, and get them back here," she said.

Jinx glanced at me. "Do you really want me taking a rookie up there?" He asked. "Tompson and I could go after Hummer and Kanway."

Though it sounded spiteful, Jinx had only been asking out of concern for my safety.

Tompson nodded to Tasha. "And what about her?"

Jess waved them both aside. "You and I can take care of her, and as for Edrix," she paused, then said, "he's got more field experience than most. Now get up there!"

I'd only had one non-training field mission, but I kept my mouth shut.

We both nodded and scrambled back up the ladder.

Jinx quickly looked at the data pad. "I've got their location. Let's go," he said and I followed him into Nine's dark streets.

19

(Andresha)

I coughed as smoke surrounded me. There was pain in my left arm, and I couldn't move my feet. I slowly raised my head and looked around. Thick, black smoke swirled around me, and I could feel the heat from the fire. There was a beam lying on my ankles, and my arm was bleeding. I sat up and pulled my feet out from underneath the beam. Thankfully, I didn't feel like anything was broken.

I felt a hand on my shoulder and I started and spun around. Then I breathed a sigh of relief when I saw who it was.

"Jim, don't do that!" I exclaimed. He held up his hands in surrender.

"I didn't mean to startle you," he said. "Are you all right?" I nodded.

"You?" I asked. He nodded in response.

The bombers had come out of nowhere. Jim and I had been here by this abandoned building about two miles away from Base to meet the contact Chief had told me about. He had been there, but not what I had expected.

I had expected his worn clothes and slight frame from lack of food and money. That's what he had asked for in exchange for his information. I had expected the unkempt hair and beard, the shifty eyes, the dirt caked on his face and hands, and the wary gaze he had given us.

What I hadn't expected was for the clothes to be a work uniform. The dirt to be soot and ash. The cuts on his hands.

"And who might you be?" he had called out to us. His voice had been low and coarse. Jim had left the talking to me. I was better at it than he was.

"The people interested in your information," I had said. The man had pretended to be confused.

"I don't have any information," he had said. I had raised my eyebrows.

"Not even about ... Level Eleven?" I had said. A bit dramatic, maybe, but it had worked. The man had given a guilty start. I had then pulled out a small pouch from under my jacket and tossed to him. It had landed at the man's feet.

"Go ahead and open it," I had said. He had done so slowly, opening the mouth of the bag. It had been filled with food.

"There's money too, if you tell us what you know," Jim had said. The man had straightened, squirreling the bag away into his pocket.

"Why should I trust you?" he had asked, his voice still full of suspicion.

"Larson sent us," I had said, referring to the agent who had contacted him in the first place. "He told us to meet you here."

The man glanced between us, then relaxed slightly.

"Alright then," he'd said. "What do you want to know?"

I didn't say anything for a moment, I had just looked at him, letting him wonder.

"I want to know what's happening on Level Eleven," I had said. "Why isn't it complete yet?" I had felt a small balloon of apprehension in my chest. I had hoped beyond all hope it was nothing to worry about, that it wasn't something else to put on Chief's plate.

The man had laughed. "It's not complete because they aren't building anything there!" he'd said, still laughing. I had lifted my chin a little higher into the air and folded my arms.

"Then what are 'they' doing?" I had asked him. The man turned serious now. He stepped closer to me. I had seen Jim casually drop his hand to his pocket where his gun was hidden. The man had glanced around him.

"It's a mine!" he'd hissed. I had kept any emotion I was feeling off my face.

"A mine for what?" I had asked. The man had stepped even closer. I could then smell his rank breath and unwashed clothes.

"That's far enough," Jim had said. The man hadn't acknowledged him, but he had stopped.

"Magic!" he had whispered.

I kept myself under control. I kept my face blank, but my heart was racing as fast as my thoughts. A mine? What did he mean by 'magic'? I had spoken again, keeping my voice even.

"It's against the law to mine on Rendaria," I had said, but the man had laughed before I had finished speaking.

"The laws don't apply to him!" The man had exclaimed. A cold hand of fear had clutched my heart.

"Who's 'him?'" I had asked. The man had opened his mouth to speak, but no words had come. He had suddenly stiffened. He had put a hand to his head, then fallen to the ground. I had dropped to crouch beside him and searched for a pulse, but there was none.

"He's dead!" I'd exclaimed. Then the bombers had come.

Jim and I had dashed into the building to keep from being seen, but we'd played right into their hands. REGS had bombed the building with us inside.

* * *

Jim helped me stand, then he examined the cut on my arm.

"It's superficial," he said, "but it needs to be cleaned."

We both coughed. I crouched down on all fours and motioned for him to do the same. The air was cleaner down here. I looked over at Jim.

"We need to get out of here," I said. He nodded.

"I know, but we have a problem," he said. "All the exits are blocked with debris."

I looked around the room. I didn't even know where the exits were anymore.

"Options," I said. Jim looked around.

"The comms are useless. Dig our way out?" He asked. I shook my head.

"We'd have no hands left before we even got half-way." I swallowed and looked him in the eye.

"We're trapped."

20

(Edrix)

We saw the smoke before we reached the building. Jinx and I rushed towards the source.

"Redeye to base, are we clear?" Jinx said into his comm. My earpiece clicked as Jess responded.

"Affirmative. REGS is no longer in the area."

We cautiously approached the burning building. Fire and thick, black smoke poured from the windows. Jinx shook his head a little. I could feel the fire's heat from three feet back.

"Command, the building's on fire," Jinx said into his communicator. "We can't get in."

"You've got a bigger problem," I heard Jess's voice in my ear. "REGS bombers are on their way to your location. ETA of five minutes. They're probably heading for the building again."

Jinx and I looked at each other. Five minutes. Five minutes to locate Andresha and Jim, dig them out, and leave the scene before REGS arrived.

I ran towards the building.

"Edrix, stop!" Jinx shouted.

"If they're in there for another hit, they won't make it!" I shouted back.

I rushed to the building and leapt through a broken window, pulling my collar up to cover my nose. The smoke was so thick inside, you could have cut it with a knife, and the heat was brutal.

"Water Bird? Happy?" I called. There was no answer.

"Commander?" I tried again. I forced my way through piles of burning debris.

"Over here!" I heard Andresha's voice from behind a wall in front of me. The doorway was blocked with a pile of collapsed roof.

"Dragon," Jinx said through my comm, using the code name I had been assigned, "I can see the bombers."

"Understood," I grunted. I started pulling debris from the door way. There was a loud groaning noise from the ceiling above me. I pulled a beam over and uncovered a small opening.

"Come on!" I shouted. A moment later, Andresha and Jim crawled through, coughing and covered in soot. Andresha had a cut on her arm, but for the most part, they looked fine.

I dropped the beam and helped them to their feet.

"Go!" I yelled. We had one minute before REGS dropped bombs on the building. I could hear the sound of the bomber's engines now. The three of us ran from the building to where Jinx was waiting. We all ran as fast as we could down the street as we heard bombs drop behind us, followed by the explosions. We stopped in the next block, taking shelter in a dark alley. Andresha and Jim both broke into a fit of coughing because of the smoke. It probably didn't help that we all smelled like the stuff. Jinx looked at me sternly.

"Just what were you thinking?" He demanded. "You're lucky you got out of there with all that smoke! I'm surprised you didn't suffocate without a mask."

I held up my hands to stop him. "I know, I know! I used my shirt."

Jim looked at me. "You didn't when we crawled out of there."

I turned to him. "What?"

"Your shirt," he said. "It wasn't over your face after you dug us out."

It had to have been! Otherwise I likely wouldn't have been able to breathe.

I was about to say so when Andresha swallowed.

"Umm, Edrix?" She said quietly.

"What?" I repeated. She was pale. She lifted a trembling hand and pointed to my arms. I looked down and my heart skipped a beat.

My arms were on fire. No, not just my arms, it was spreading to my shoulders, down my shirt.

"Edrix?" someone said, but I wasn't listening. Something was wrong. I heard sounds I couldn't comprehend. A swirl of voices, breathing, footsteps... It was like my brain was going to over load. I put my hands over my ears. I think I screamed, but I couldn't be sure.

My vision tunneled, and everything went black.

21

(Edrix)

The first thing I saw when I opened my eyes was the white walls of the Med-Center. I was lying on a gurney, a dozen wires attached to my head and chest under my medical gown. My throat was dry, and I had an IV needle in my arm. I moved my head and immediately regretted it. A sharp pain throbbed in my temples and I winced. Jess's anxious face appeared above me. She looked over at someone I couldn't see.

"He's awake!" she called, then looked back at me. She smiled a little.

"How are you?" She asked quietly. I groaned in reply as the headache came back.

"What—" I started, but my throat was too dry. Jess quietly shushed me.

Patrisha's face came into view now. "That's a relief," she said, looking at a console next to my head.

"Everything looks normal," she said, a small note of confusion in her voice. She looked at me.

"How do you feel? Does your head hurt?" She asked. I nodded, knowing my voice wouldn't work. Patrisha left for a moment, then returned with a glass of water and a straw. She pressed a button and my bed rose to a sitting position. Patrisha held the straw to my lips and I drank thirstily. I drained the cup and sighed.

"Thank you." My voice was still a little gravelly, but my throat felt better. Patrisha put the cup down and injected me with a syringe.

"That should help the headache in a few minutes," she said quietly. I looked over at Jess.

"What happened?" I asked.

Jess pursed her lips. "We're not exactly sure, Edrix," she said gently. "You grabbed your ears and screamed, then collapsed on the ground. Jim and Jinx were able to put you out before you were … hurt."

111

She had hesitated, but why? Being on fire was a serious thing, wasn't it?

Patrisha reached into her pocket and pulled out a small white card with letters and numbers on it, descending in size.

"What's the smallest line you can read?" She asked, holding it in front of me. I could easily read the smallest line of symbols. I repeated them aloud. Patrisha didn't say anything. She just put the chart back into her pocket and tapped a control on a console.

"All right, I want you to tell me when you can't hear the sound anymore," she said. She played a series of beeps in different volumes, gradually making them softer. I finally said,

"I can't hear it."

Then I paused. "Is something burning?" I asked. Jess glanced at Patrisha, then left my curtained off section of the room. A moment later, she came back in.

"Nelvin," was all she said.

Patrisha nodded. "Well, Edrix, there is not much I can tell you," she said. She pulled another chair up next to my bed. "I'll tell you what I do know. Your eyesight is more than twenty-twenty. We don't have a measurement for it. Your ears can hear better than anyone I've ever seen, and your sense of smell has improved by leaps and bounds." She held up a hand to forestall my questions.

"I just don't know why, Edrix. Nelvin's been working night and day to figure it out, but …"

Night *and* day?

"How long was I out?" I asked, my voice shaking a little.

Jess looked tired. She put an elbow on her armrest and rubbed her forehead.

"A week," she said quietly. I blinked in incomprehension. A week?

"Are you saying, that I'm an alien?" I whispered.

Patrisha shook her head quickly. "Oh, no. You're still Rendarian," she said. "Just a special one."

I froze. Someone had said that before. Who had it been? I searched my memories, but it came up blank. I shook the thought away. It had probably been when I was little, or something on an audio-novel or something. It was coincidence, that's all.

112

I looked up as Chief entered the room. "You're awake," he said. "How are you feeling?"

I shrugged, my gaze focused on my blanket. Chief turned to Patrisha.

"Does he need to stay here?" He asked.

She shook her head. "I don't see why. He's fine."

"What about the ..." Chief trailed off.

"Fire." I finished for him. "What about the fire that was on my hands?" Patrisha pursed her lips.

"I don't know about that either, Edrix," she said softly.

I glanced at Jess. "But it hasn't happened since I fell unconscious, right?" I asked.

Jess sighed. "Look at your hands, Edrix," she said.

I held one of them up and noticed the gloves for the first time. They were white, but they went all the way up my arms and over my hands. They were fingerless, but the finger holes were lined with a shimmery grey material. There were metal bands around my wrists as well. I reached for the top of a glove.

"Don't—" Jess warned, but I was already pulling the glove off my hand. Everyone was quiet, as if they were waiting. I looked at my hand. It looked normal. No flames, just my skin.

Then, as I watched, my entire arm erupted into flames. I simply stared at it, not sure what to do. There was no pain. The fire wasn't burning me. Then Jess put the glove back on my arm.

"Nelvin made these for you," she said. "They suppress the flames."

Chief folded his arms. "I guess that answers my question," he said. I bit my lip and looked down at my blankets to hide the tears gathering in my eyes. What was wrong with me? I remembered how I'd gone through the fire to get to Andresha and Jim. I had to have touched a dozen burning beams and other debris and inhaled tons of smoke, but I was perfectly fine. The fire on my arms and hands just now hadn't burned me. I'd only felt a slight tingling sensation.

Chief was saying something to Jess, but I wasn't listening. One tear escaped my eye and rolled down my cheek. Patrisha put a comforting hand on my shoulder.

Jess looked at me again. I kept my head down. She gently held my hand.

"We're going to figure this out," she said softly. I glanced up at her, then looked back at my hands. Jess smiled sadly and left the room with Chief.

Patrisha wrung her hands for a minute, then she said, "Do you want some time to yourself?"

I nodded, just slightly. She tapped a few buttons.

"You should get some rest anyway. It will do you good." She lowered my bed a little so I would be able to sleep, then she tucked my blankets under my chin. I didn't react. She gave a reassuring smile and lowered the lights. Then she left.

I stared at the curtain for an hour, as if it had the answers.

"Why?" I whispered to it. Naturally, it didn't answer.

Another tear rebelled and ran down my face. I angrily dashed it away. I listened to the babble of other doctors and nurses in the Med-Center. I could hear every word as clearly as if they had been speaking to me. Garris had a concussion and wouldn't be able to return to duty for a week. Lestra needed an IV for dehydration. Check the supply of syringes, we might be running low.

My thoughts drifted to the two doctors that had been in the back of the room back at REGS, when Nero had been questioning me. What had they been doing there? The more rebellious I'd become, the more frantic their note-taking had been.

I put my head in my hands, the glove material rough on my skin. Why had my life become such a mess? Why did I have to join REGS in the first place?

Because you thought it was the right thing, I thought.

Well, it wasn't, I replied to myself flatly.

I lowered my hands and leaned back against my pillow. Sleep seemed impossible, but I must have dozed off after a while.

When I woke up again, Patrisha and another nurse were quietly moving around me.

Patrisha smiled. "Just checking on you," she said. I nodded a little. Then my gaze caught something behind her.

On one of the consoles in front of my gurney, there was a small framed painting leaning on it. The scene depicted a large flower garden. It had to have been on Five. The flowers were all in bloom, and there was a large tree to one side of the scene. A swing hung from one of its branches. Grass surrounded everything. The technique was familiar to me. The way the paint was textured, the colors, the brush strokes. I couldn't remember where I'd seen it before, but its familiarity calmed me.

"Who brought that?" I asked softly. Patrisha turned around, startled.

"What? The painting?" She asked. I nodded, and she shrugged.

"I don't know. It was here when we came in."

I looked at the painting again. It had been a long time since I had painted. Almost a year. My eyelids got heavy, and I drifted to sleep. I dreamed of that garden, of the swing, as I often did. After all, it was my garden.

22

"I'm worried about him," Jess said as she left the Med-Center, Chief falling into step beside her.

"Do you think he'll be able to figure it out?" He asked. She shrugged.

"I honestly don't know," she said. "I want to help him, but—"

"But you don't want him to find out," Chief finished. Jess nodded. They stopped as they waited for a lift, then the doors opened and they walked inside.

"I was on my way to talk to our newest tenant," Chief said, thumbing a control on the panel by the door. "Want to come along?"

Jess shrugged. She could use a distraction. "Sure." He folded his arms and turned to look at her.

"It's not your fault. You know that, right?" Jess shrugged again.

"I don't know. I feel like … I don't know."

"Hey," Chief gently put a hand on her shoulder. "It was going to happen eventually."

Jess bit her lip. "I just don't know if he was ready," she said softly. Chief smiled.

"You were never going to know," he said, but not unkindly. "He'll just have to make himself ready."

"I suppose so," Jess replied.

23

(Andresha)

Note to self: Stop eating in the Mess Hall when you are irritated to the point of violence.

I walked into the Mess Hall and grabbed a plate of food and a cup of water. I wasn't really hungry, but if I didn't eat something, I knew Jim would ask for an explanation and/or force me to eat it. I sat down at a random table before Jim had even finished getting his plate and began to mechanically shovel food into my mouth. Everything tasted bland, even the fruit.

The Edrix situation had me feeling like a cornered cat. He'd had fire on his arms, and he was completely unscathed. It was not normal, and it was scary.

Jim sat down next to me and ate his food calmly. He didn't try to start a conversation, which I was thankful for. After a moment he stopped eating and put his elbows on the table and looked at me past his clasped hands. I stopped forcing food into my mouth long enough to ask, "Why are you staring at me?"

He didn't answer right away, just continued to look at me with a slightly amused expression.

"I'm afraid you're going to choke," he said. I shrugged, but I stopped eating. I stared at my plate and pushed food around with my fork. I noticed that the food on my plate consisted of a helping of a white mashed vegetable drizzled in gravy and a slice of meat. A small helping of purple fruit was in a small bowl to the side of the plate. Not something we got every day, and it had all been flavorless to me. Jim shrugged and started to eat again while simultaneously working on a report.

I went over the past week's events in my mind, trying to figure *something* out. I started with what I knew for sure. There was a mine on Eleven, an *illegal* mine, which was run by someone who was good at evading the law. Criminal master mind, perhaps? Ten was crawling with them, and that was right above Eleven.

117

Thinking about Edrix was the hard part, but I forced myself to do it.

He is fire proof, can hear some of the softest sounds, see better than the average humanoid, and could probably out-sniff a Rezzian bloodhound.

I shuddered a little. I'd never liked fire.

"Mind if we join you?"

I looked up, roused from my contemplation. A tired looking a Patrisha and a discouraged looking Nelvin were standing by the table. I realized that Patrisha was the one who had asked the question.

"Sure," I said.

They both sat down. Nelvin was typing on a data-pad, his brow furrowed in thought.

"You both look like you haven't slept in a week," I said. Nelvin glanced up for half a second, then went back to his data pad.

"One could say the same thing about you," he said. I didn't say anything. It was true, I hadn't really slept since the fire.

Jim looked up. "How is he?"

Nelvin shrugged. Patrisha sighed and said, "Physically, he's fine, as far as I can tell. But mentally, who knows. If he's feeling well enough, I'm going to release him."

I suppressed a shiver. I'd just started to get know him, when this happened. Now, I was terrified of him.

"Is that wise?" Jim asked.

Patrisha shrugged. "There's nothing else I can do for him. If he needs counseling then we'll work that out, but if I keep him cooped up in the Med-bay, he'll be bored out of his mind. There's no reason he can't return to duty as long as he wears the gloves."

I looked at my food, trying to keep down the stuff that I'd already eaten. Why was I so worried about this? No one else was. Not even Chief and he'd seen what I'd seen. It didn't bother him at all. *On the outside at least,* I reminded myself.

Patrisha had gotten a bowl of soup, but was just stirring it around with a spoon. Nelvin didn't have anything to eat, just his data-pad. Jim, trying to change the subject, asked Nelvin, "What are you working on?"

Nelvin didn't even look up. "I'm trying to discern the cause for Edrix's epidermal tissues to become fire resistant and if it is possible to reverse the process."

Jim and I looked at him blankly. I understood half of what he was saying, but not having a decent night's sleep for a week made it difficult. Nelvin looked up at the ceiling and sighed.

"I'm trying to figure out how he became fire proof, and how to reverse it."

Understanding dawned in Jim's eyes. "Any luck?"

Nelvin shook his head, but there was a determined look in his eye. "Not yet," he said.

Jim nodded. "That's a good way to think," he said.

We all sat in silence. Jim and Patrisha were the only ones who ate. I didn't have an appetite, and Nelvin was too busy.

I jumped when a voice asked, "Is anyone sitting here?"

My head snapped up. It was Tasha, the woman who'd asked for a Haven.

Patrisha smiled. "No. Please join us."

That was Patrisha for you. Always being nice and cheerful. I think I'd only seen her sad twice, and I had *never* seen her mad. I looked up from my cup of water just in time to catch a tiny glint of uncertainty in her eyes, but it was gone in an instant. Tasha sat down at the head of the table between Patrisha and me. I tapped my fingers on my plate, wishing Jim was done so we could leave. We had lookout together after this with Jinx. I was ready to get my mind off this mess.

"How do you like the base?" Jim asked. Tasha just shrugged. I studied her more closely. Most of her injuries had healed. There was one cut above her eyebrow that had required a few stitches that still looked fresh. Her hair was washed and brushed now. It barely brushed her shoulders. You could now see that it was a golden blonde color. Now that I saw the two of them together, Tasha and Patrisha looked very similar. They both had dark eyes and golden hair, and some of their facial features looked the same. I shrugged to myself. Coincidence, I decided.

Jim tried again. "How are you feeling?" Tasha didn't look up from her plate.

"Better," was all she said. Jim looked at me and raised his eyebrows a little. I shrugged my shoulders slightly. I didn't have the energy to try and work this out.

Tasha spoke again, but she didn't take her eyes off her plate.

"You know," she said in between bites of food, "this place really isn't what I thought it would be."

I didn't dare look at her. I stared at my plate and forced myself to eat a bite of my now cold food. It was a mistake. I almost gagged on it. Patrisha put down her spoon and turned to Tasha.

"How do you mean?" She asked nicely. Knowing her, she was probably determined to improve things for Tasha. I envied her sometimes, how easily she got along with people.

Tasha shrugged. She did that a lot.

"This is supposed to be a rebel insurgency. I haven't seen a whole lot of rebellion happening of late."

I glanced up at her now. She was scraping the last traces of food from her plate.

"There's just not a lot happening right *now*," I said quietly. Tasha seemed to not have heard me.

"It's a disappointment really. Your security is shabby, your base is in an obvious location, and your 'Chief' obviously has no experience keeping things organized. I had no trouble finding it, and I was almost unconscious."

And that's when my temper started to heat up. Chief and I may not have gotten along sometimes, but that didn't mean I didn't respect him.

I shot out of my seat.

"And what makes you think you can just waltz in here and start criticizing our organization?" I said. Tasha was on her feet now as well.

"REGS is going to find you sooner or later if you don't fix things up," she said defiantly.

I moved around my chair so that I stood before her. "If our base was really that easy to find, REGS would have already found us."

She turned to face me. "*Our* base?" She asked indignantly.

"Not again," Nelvin groaned, but I wasn't listening.

120

"You asked *us* for a Haven," I said. Tasha tilted her chin up. We were the same height.

"It was obviously a mistake, she said. I bit the inside of my cheek.

"Yes," I said acidly, "It was." I walked out of the room, Jim following behind me.

I tugged my braid in frustration. Now I wanted to cry.

"You really need to stop doing that," Jim said. I knew what he meant. I needed to stop getting into fights with people in the mess hall. I just needed to stop getting into fights, period. I stopped walking and put my head in my hands. I leaned my forehead against the wall.

"I know."

A few rebellious tears slipped down my cheeks. I thought I was done with things like Edrix. Things that scared me to death.

"I'm just not myself," I whispered. Jim didn't say anything, and I was glad for it. I bit my lip and wiped my face. I didn't have time to cry. Jim changed the subject.

"Have you seen Short since he got back from Eight?" He asked. I nodded, grateful for the change of topic.

"Yeah. He's fine. He wasn't hurt during his last mission, so he's back on duty."

We walked in silence as we rode a lift up to our lookout point. When the doors opened, we signed in on a panel, then settled down next to Jinx. He nodded in greeting, but otherwise he was quiet. I cleared my head and focused on my surroundings. I could worry about Edrix and Tasha later. If I thought about them anymore, I was probably either going to cry, scream, or both at once.

24

(Edrix)

Patrisha released me from the Med-Center the next day. As long as I wore the gloves, I was fine, so Chief let me return to my usual duties. Nelvin was still his cheerful self, and we still ate lunch with Patrisha. Sometimes Jim or Short would join us, but I never saw Andresha.

Before I had left, Patrisha had run a few more tests. Other than the fact that my arms were perpetually on fire without Nelvin's gloves and my improved senses, everything else *seemed* normal.

A week after I was released from the. Med-Center, Chief called me to a briefing. We met in a room off of the Command Center. There was a large white table in the center of the room with the Red Star in the middle of it. There were eight chairs around it, with one more at the head of the table. When I arrived all but one of the chairs were filled. Chief sat at the head of the table, Jess sat on his right, and Andresha on his left. Jim sat between Andresha and Tasha. Patrisha sat at the end of the table next to Nelvin. The seat next to Jess was empty.

"I saved you a spot," Nelvin said as I approached.

"Thanks, buddy," I told him. I sat down in the empty chair and glanced at Jess. She was staring at the table, her arms folded and a concerned expression on her face. I looked over at Andresha, but she wouldn't meet my gaze.

Chief put down his data pad and sat back in his chair.

"Alright, we have a problem," he said. "Andresha and Jim found some disturbing information concerning the construction of Level Eleven. It's not a Level at all, but a mine."

There was a ripple of unease throughout the room. Mining on Rendaria was a crime punishable by death.

"We don't know who's operating it, but it's not REGS," Jess said. Nelvin leaned forward.

"Do we know what they're mining?" Nelvin asked.

122

Andresha shook her head. "Not unless the description of 'magic" makes sense to you," She said. Magic? What was that supposed to mean?

"What do we do about it?" Patrisha asked. Andresha nodded.

"Exactly. What *do* we do now? We don't need to break into the Core do we? I mean, we have information about Eleven now," she said. Chief and Jess looked at each other. Jess nodded. Chief set his mouth in a grim line.

"What I am about to say now is Class Ten information," Chief said. I straightened in my chair. That meant that it was to be discussed with no one except for those that were in the room unless given Chief's permission. We all nodded in understanding. Chief took a deep breath.

"We didn't need to get in the Core for information about Eleven," he said.

Andresha sat forward in her seat. "What?" She asked. "You mean we went in there for *nothing*?" Jess shook her head.

"Not nothing. You were instructed to bring back a file block, not an individual file. This was to prevent information from being discovered in case you were captured, but that doesn't matter now," she said.

Chief took a deep breath. "Red Star didn't build this base. It was originally going to be the base for an Elite REGS Higher One unit," he said. "The project was abandoned, and Red Star's founder took the base over. We have a portion of the Core in this base."

I reeled back in surprise. A piece of the Core? Why? What did that have to do with breaking into the other one and stealing files?

As if he had read my mind, Chief said, "You're probably wondering why we have it. Like I said, this was going to be a REGS Base. They needed a database to keep surveillance on." He folded his arms.

"REGS didn't pay any attention to this base until now. Unfortunately, REGS did not erase the location of the base from the Core's Hub, even though they thought it had been demolished."

Nelvin spoke now. "Do they know we're using the base?" He asked.

Chief folded his arms. "I don't know, but it's safe to say they suspect it. Time has been on our side for a while. Since there's so much information in the Core, we figured it would take them awhile to find it, but after reading the reports we've intercepted, we believe they're getting closer to finding it."

No one said anything. Finding the base automatically meant finding us, and that would mean death one way or another.

Chief looked around the room grimly. "We're in a race against time. Based on the reports, we estimate we have about four weeks before the file is found. Our only chance is to either retrieve the file, or delete it before it's found." He turned to me. "Edrix, we're hoping you might have some insight on the Core and its security structure."

I folded my own arms and turned to Andresha and Jim. "How did you try to get in before?" I asked them.

Jim shrugged. "Infiltration," he said.

I shook my head. "No offense, but I'm not surprised it didn't work. Core personnel is always rotated. No one has the same shift twice. The passwords and security codes are changed every twelve hours. Since you escaped the last time, they've added DNA, fingerprint, voice, and retina scans at every check point, lift, and console."

I turned to Chief. "I'm afraid an assault won't work either. That's where most Higher Ones are stationed, along with about thirty-percent of REGS main force. We don't have the numbers, equipment, or knowledge to take it down."

Tasha spoke now. "I think this is where I come in." Chief nodded, and she turned to the rest of us.

"Before I came here, I worked with a Hunter," she started carefully. I could tell from her tone that she didn't want to go into it. "Before I left, we were invited to participate in a tournament."

Jim laced his fingers together and leaned his elbows on the table. "What kind of tournament?"

Tasha looked over at him. "A tournament to find the best Hunter or Hunters, if they work as a pair.

"It's a test, to find the Hunter good enough to get into the Rendarian Core," she said. Confused glances were exchanged.

124

Who else would want to get into the Core? Andresha voiced this question aloud. Tasha shrugged.

"I don't know. The contestants only know him as the Client."

"What does this have to do with us?" Short asked.

Tasha turned to him. "The winner will receive plans of the Core, along with the needed equipment to get inside. Code breakers, DNA simulators..." She looked over at me. "Everything to counteract what you mentioned.

"If some of your agents pose as Hunters and enter the tournament—and if they win—you get everything you need."

Jinx held up his hands. "Hold on just a minute! Why should we do anything you say? We don't know you, or the Hunter you were working with. What if this is a trap?"

I looked at Tasha, then at Chief. It was legitimate question. Tasha had come here just two rotations ago, bleeding and battered, and trying to threaten her way inside, then asking for a Haven.

"If it is a trap, it's a pretty expensive one," Jess said. "We tapped the news feed on Ten. Word about the tournament is out there. Each Hunter is being paid two-hundred Cols just to accept. That's doubled if you're a pair."

Jim gave a low whistle. Cols was the currency on Rezz. Each on was worth twice as much as a Rendarian credit.

"That *is* expensive." Nelvin agreed.

"Besides," Tasha said, "I came to give this information to you. It's supposed to be a secret—just between Hunters—so my partner didn't like it."

"Is that why you were in such bad shape when you showed up?" Patrisha asked.

Tasha nodded.

"How did you even know that we wanted to get inside?" Jim asked.

Tasha gave him a wry smile. "When the same pair of people try to break into the same place three times, it's pretty obvious that they're either desperate or have a death wish."

Jim nodded to himself. Everyone else was fixed on the table.

Chief looked around the table.

"I'm putting this up to a vote," he said. "Jess, Tasha, and I will abstain from voting. All who agree, raise your hand."

Everyone was silent for a moment while we thought. My mind raced. A tournament between Hunters was risky. Some would probably try to eliminate competition before the tournament even started.

But alternatively, it was what we needed. I didn't know a lot of people here very well, but I knew we all had the same purpose. And I couldn't bear the thought of REGS destroying it all, like they had on Eight.

I raised my hand along with everyone else at the table.

The vote was unanimous.

25

(Edrix)

"So now the question to be asked is who will go?" Jinx said. Chief looked over at Tasha. "You're the expert, who do you suggest?"

She thought for a moment. "No more than two, that's for sure," she said.

Jim folded his arms. "Only two? If we want to win this thing—"

Tasha cut him off. "More than two hunters together would draw suspicion. Occasionally, for a large mission, more than one Hunter will be hired, but they never willingly work in large groups on their own. There's a greater chance of being betrayed, and," she smiled wryly, "less money for everyone."

Jim nodded. "Makes sense," he muttered, mostly to himself.

Short rubbed his chin in thought. "Whoever goes needs to be good on their own then, and they need to make a good team."

Tasha nodded. "Yes, I agree," she said. She turned to Chief. "This is your organization, and I won't make decisions for you, but I have two suggestions," she said.

Chief nodded. "I'm listening."

I looked around the room. I couldn't help but wonder who she'd suggest. I didn't know anyone well enough to make my own prediction, but I had feeling that Jim would be going. I'd seen him practice, and he was good. Plus he'd survived the Core three times.

As for the other person, it would probably be Andresha, Short, or Jinx. Jinx had the look of a Hunter, but Short was more skilled. I'm not sure where he got his training, but it reminded me of the REGS style. As for Andresha, she'd been in the Core, too, and even though she professed to only be good when she had a gun in her hand, I knew that wasn't true.

Tasha laced her fingers together and rested her hands on the table.

"One would be Commander Kanway," she said. Andresha looked up in surprise. Tasha grinned.

127

"That's why I started that argument in the mess hall. I knew you had the combat skills, but I wanted to see if you had the attitude."

Andresha blinked a few times. I had heard about the incident from Nelvin a few rotations ago.

"…Thank you?" Andresha said hesitantly.

Jim shrugged. "If she goes, then I should go," he said. "Everyone knows how well we work together," he said.

Jinx and Short nodded. Jess and Chief were silent, but Tasha shook her head.

"That's exactly why you *shouldn't* go. You've been seen together too many times. If you go in as a team, every Hunter would recognize you in an instant," she said.

Jim wasn't to be swayed easily. "We're going to have to be in disguise anyways, right?" He protested.

Tasha nodded. "Yes, but it can't be terribly elaborate. We don't know what kind of tests this tournament consists of or how long it would take. They can—and most likely will—scan for cosmetic surgeries, and even if you dyed your hair, you might be there long enough for it to grow out," she shook her head again, "It's up to your Chief, but I strongly advise against it."

Chief nodded. "She's right Jim. It's too risky," he said.

Jim slumped back in his seat. I ran a hand through my hair. If not Jim, then whom? Andresha and he worked best together. Short maybe?

Nelvin spoke up. "Well if he's not going than who is? You're not going to send her in alone are you?"

Tasha smiled. "No, I don't think that would be wise."

Andresha scowled slightly at her words, and I felt a wave of defensive anger from her. *Only natural*, I thought. Nobody liked the suggestion that they weren't good enough, especially with her personality.

Tasha spoke again. "My other suggestion is Edrix."

My head snapped up in surprise.

"Me?" I asked.

"Him?" Andresha asked at the same time, a slightly shrill note in her voice. Tasha looked between us, trying to keep an amused smile under control.

"Yes, Edrix, you," she said.

I held up my hands. "First of all, I have the biggest bounty in Rendarian history on my head. I can't just walk into a crowd of Hunters! I'd be lucky if REGS got my body in one piece!"

Jess nodded. "Agreed."

Tasha held up a finger. "That's the *perfect* reason," she said. "It's not uncommon for skilled fugitives like yourself to become Hunters. In the Hunter Code, it forbids acquiring a bounty on another Hunter. You going would exempt you from the bounty," she said.

I looked around the table. Jinx and Jim both nodded. Even Jess looked convinced.

I knew Tasha was right about the code. We had been required to study it in the Program, but ...

"That's all well and good," I said quietly, "but I still can't go."

I put my hand on the table so everyone could see the glove that covered it. The entire room went silent. Tasha leaned across the table and felt the material.

"You can't take them off?" She asked. I nodded. She sat back down and shrugged.

"I wouldn't worry about that," she said. "The material is perfect. It's fire proof, so no one's going to question that in a Hunter's line of work."

I looked down at my hand, unsure how to answer.

Chief looked at me, then Andresha. "It's up to both of you, I won't make you go," he said quietly.

I looked over at Nelvin.

"Are the gloves durable enough for combat?" I asked him.

He nodded. "Easily."

Andresha leaned over and whispered something to Chief. He nodded a little and held up a hand.

"I don't want you to hurry this decision. Take some time and think about it. Tell when and what you have decided, and we'll reconvene then. Dismissed."

Everyone got up to leave.

Nelvin patted my shoulder. "Are we still on for lunch?" He asked and I nodded. As we reached the door, I realized that Chief and

Andresha hadn't left yet, they were just sitting there. I shrugged to myself. She probably wanted to talk to him about something, but she looked like she'd just been handed a ticking bomb.

* * *

Jess found me ten minutes later in the arboretum. I was sitting under one of the fruit trees. It reminded me of home.

"There you are," she said softly. I looked up as she approached. I had heard her come in five minutes ago and look around the rest of the room. I'd chosen a tree in the back wanting to be alone.

She sat down next to me, a data pad in her hand.

"I know you've already had a long day but ... I think you should see this," she said softly, handing me the data-pad. I clicked on the screen and looked it over. It was REGS report. It read:

"Mila and Zaren Solan taken into custody. Currently being held at REGS headquarters on the 5th Level" ...

I let the pad fall from my fingers. My family... they'd *arrested* my *family*! My hands shook and tears filled my eyes.

"Why?" I whispered. "Why?" My body began to shake with silent sobs and I covered my face with my hands. Jess took the pad off my lap and took me in her arms. I cried. She held me while I did. Why? It echoed in my head over and over again. It was me they wanted. Were they trying to bait me? Why didn't Jai do something?

"Zaren won't know what's going on," I whispered. "They'll probably separate them."

Jess stroked my hair. "I know, Edrix. I wish I could tell you everything was going to be all right."

I had stopped crying now, but my heart still ached. That ache slowly turned into a hard resolve.

"I have to go on this mission," I said quietly. "Red Star's the only way I can help them now."

Jess didn't say anything, but she squeezed me a little tighter and kissed the top of my head.

26

(Andresha)

I waited until everyone else had left the room. Now it was just Chief and myself sitting at the table. I was still kind of in shock over the whole thing. I was flattered by Tasha's suggestion, but I couldn't do the mission with Edrix. I needed someone I knew and trusted with me, someone I knew who had my back. Someone I wasn't *afraid* of.

Chief looked at me. "What is it?" He asked. I folded my arms and bit my lip.

"I want to do it ..." I started. Chief nodded.

I blinked a few times. "You're agreeing?" I asked. Chief nodded again.

I stared at him. "You're not going to give me the whole 'you're too young' speech?"

Chief smiled sadly. "Andresha, I don't like the idea of you going, I really don't, but I'm not going to stop you. That wouldn't work well with our situation," he said kindly. I smiled a little. It might sound cold to you, but it meant the world to me.

"Thanks," I muttered.

He shook his head. "Don't thank me," he said. "In five minutes I'm probably going to get my head examined."

I smiled again, but became serious once more. "I don't know if I can do it with Edrix," I said. Chief folded his arms.

"Because of the..." He trailed off. He didn't need to finish. I nodded.

"Yeah."

Chief sighed. "Like I told him, Andresha, I won't make you go. This has to be your decision."

I stood up and walked around the table, thinking. Edrix was fine with his gloves, I knew that. But what if he lost one? What if he lost them both? He almost lit the base on fire last time. I stopped walking and stared at the floor.

Chief got up and walked over to me.

"Do you trust him?" I asked. "Do you trust him as much as you trust Jess?."

I looked up and met his gaze. I knew Jess trusted Edrix, even Short did, but I needed to know if Chief did as well.

He nodded. "I trust him, Ana."

His old pet name for me. I took a deep breath. "Then I'll go," I said. He opened up his arms and I stepped into his embrace.

27

(Edrix)

An hour later, we all assembled again. I had informed Chief of my decision, and I guess Andresha had made hers as well. We all sat in the same spots, but this time, Andresha met my gaze. It was hesitant, but she did it. She still looked nervous, though. I smiled a little, and she returned it for just a moment. That was a relief. We'd just started to be friends, I didn't want that to disappear.

Plus it would be awkward to go on a mission with someone who didn't like you.

Chief spoke now, casting his gaze over all of us.

"Agents Kanway and Solan have accepted the mission," he said. Nelvin grinned and gave me a subtle thumbs up. Jess looked over at me. She was smiling, but she also looked worried. She nodded once.

"Now," Chief said clasping his hands on the table and looking at Tasha. "What's next?"

She looked up in surprise.

Chief nodded encouragingly. "You're the expert here," he said.

She nodded seriously. "Right." She tapped a set of controls on the table. A holographic screen came up.

"The tournament will take place in two weeks. I don't know what kind of tests you'll be put through, but I will brief you on the Hunter Code as well as some of the opponents you might face," she said.

"Where is this tournament going to take place?" Andresha asked. "What's the terrain going to be like?"

Tasha tapped another control and a hologram of a planet came up. It was almost completely white with a few bodies of water and patches of green.

"The tournament will be held on the planet Rezz. It's a world mostly made of ice and snow. A few places are warm enough to grow vegetation.

I don't know if the tournament itself will be there, though. I don't know locations or specifications, but the tournament will most likely

133

be held in an arena of sorts. I don't know what kind of terrain you'll have, or what you'll face."

I looked at the image of the planet hovering above the table. It looked cold. Short ran a hand through his hair. "If this tournament is on a different planet, how are they going to get there?" He asked. "We have two Sky Sailors and a few planes but nothing space worthy. Won't Hunters be expected to have ships of their own?"

Tasha nodded. "Excellent observation. True, they'll need a ship, but they can't get one here. I have a friend on Rezz you can meet with before the tournament begins. He can give you a ship," she said to Andresha and me.

"What will he expect in payment?" Jess asked.

Tasha waved her off. "He owes me a favor, and this will be the easiest way for him to pay me back."

Patrisha brushed imaginary dirt off the table's surface. "They still need to get to Rezz before that then," she said.

Jim leaned an elbow on the table. "The only space port on the planet is on Level One, and we can't get into the Lifts. They're screening anyone who comes within a mile radius of any of them."

Tasha smiled wryly. "That's why you won't go to One," she said.

Andresha shook her head. "I don't think you were listening. That's the *only*, emphasis, space port on the *entire*, emphasis again, planet," she said. "Plus, only the Chairman and those he authorizes can use it."

Tasha grinned wider. "That's what they want you to believe. There's one on Ten. You'll go out that way."

Part Two

The Anvil

28

(Andresha)

My knife hit the target's center and they computer made a satisfying *beep!* It was my fifteenth hit in fifteen throws. My best score yet.

Edrix nodded approvingly. "Good. You can hit it with either end of the knife."

A week and a half of guided practice had paid off. I went over to the target and pulled the knife out of the hologram. With a little help from Nelvin, Edrix had reprogramed the training computer to create targets as well as humanoid training holograms. For the last four rotations, I'd never missed a single target in a set.

Edrix had been right. Once I had gotten the basic throwing motion down, my accuracy had returned seemingly on its own.

Now, Edrix motioned me over to the knife wall. I walked over to him.

"Pick two knives and put the rest back," he said. Out of the four knives I'd been using, I picked a standard size and one that was a few centimeters longer. I put the other two back on the wall. Edrix handed me the sheaths for the knives I'd kept.

"Put one on your wrist and one on your ankle," he said. Since I was left-handed, I put one sheath on my right wrist and the other on my left ankle.

"All right, now what?" I asked. Edrix raised an eyebrow.

"You got them where you want them?" He asked. I knit my eyebrows together in thought. There was something in his tone that put alarm bells ringing in my head, like I'd forgotten something.

"Yes ?" I said cautiously.

He shrugged. "All right then. I'd thought we'd try something different."

He went over to the controls for the holo-targets and tapped a program.

136

"We'll start slow," he said. Four holo-targets appeared in the room around me, the same ones I had seen Edrix practicing with when he'd first gotten here. Two of them had knives of their own. I took my stance and drew my first knife, the one on my wrist. I held the blade down like Edrix had shown me. I nodded to him now, signaling that I was ready. He pressed a button and the holograms leapt into action.

I stabbed one hologram as soon as it came into range. Then one of the armed ones approached me. I ducked under its horizontal cut and slashed through it with my own knife. It disintegrated into a pile of cubes. Then, before I knew what was happening, one of the holograms had my knife hand in a vise grip, and wrapped its arm around my neck in a chokehold. I could still breathe, but if I didn't break the hold, I'd be given the 'kill-shock' as we called it, or the shock that meant I had lost. I struggled against the hologram for a moment, then remembered my other knife strapped to my ankle. I reached for it with my right hand and ... nothing! I couldn't reach it!

I brought my foot up and—with a bit of twisting—my hand grasped the knife. I stabbed backwards into the hologram. It disintegrated and released the choke-hold and my knife hand. I didn't have time to react to the last hologram. Its knife smacked into mine and sent it clattering across the floor. I cried out in pain as a burst of electricity knocked me to the ground. I couldn't move for a second, then the computer beeped and the hologram disappeared. I tested my limbs and found that I could move them again. I groaned and got to my feet. Edrix came over to me.

"You alright?"

"Yes," I muttered.

Edrix folded his arms. "What do you think?" He asked me.

I thought for a moment. "I couldn't reach my knife very well."

He nodded. "Cor-rect. If you hadn't been in that chokehold for so long you would have been fine, but the simulation sped up to compensate for the time you would have taken catching your breath."

He drew one his own knives. "If you were facing me, what you try to disable first?" He asked.

I answered automatically. "Your knife hand."

He nodded. "Exactly. So, if I want another knife, I want it in a place that my *right* hand can reach easily. That means putting it on my right ankle."

I nodded in understanding. It was a good point.

"Everything else was good. You just missed a small detail." Edrix said, "Keep working at it."

We both looked up as Short entered the gym. "How's it going?" He asked.

I shrugged, but Edrix said. "She's getting better." I smiled a little at the praise.

Short nodded. "That's good." He handed Edrix a data-pad. "This is for you, from Nelvin," he said.

Edrix took the pad. "Thanks," he said. Short nodded and left. Edrix held up the pad.

"Just let me look at this," he said. I nodded absently and started putting my knives away, hearing Nelvin's voice coming from the pad and Edrix answering him. I looked up as Edrix came back over.

"What did Nelvin want?" I asked. Edrix shrugged. Nelvin and Patrisha had been put in charge of prepping our disguises for the mission, checking everything with Tasha, of course.

"He wanted to know if I looked better in purple or green. Green apparently brings out my eyes better."

I couldn't help but laugh.

"I think he's enjoying this," I said.

Edrix raised his eyebrows. "I *know* he's enjoying it."

29

(Edrix)

The day had arrived. Andresha and I were assembled together at the entrance to the base with Chief and Tasha, along with our friends. Jess was there with Nelvin and Patrisha. Jim and Short were there too.

We were just getting ready to leave. Nelvin and Patrisha had given Andresha and me our wardrobes this morning and were now giving us the final touches.

Andresha had a simple dark green shirt with three-quarter sleeves and dark pants. She had brown boots with a small blade concealed in each heel. It would come in handy if her hands were tied behind her. As was to be expected, she had her gun with her, as well as two knives, one on her belt, the other on her wrist. She had a utility belt with a steel cable and spare ammo clips and navy poncho to wear to the space port and when we got to Rezz with its cold weather. Her hair-do was the same, but Tasha had added two more streaks of color. One purple, one teal-blue on either side of the red streak.

I also had a dark green shirt and dark pants, but my boots were black with knife sheaths in each one. I had two sheaths on each leg, and one on each wrist. I had a dark jacket to wear in the cold with two additional concealed knives. I also had my gun and utility belt.

Nelvin now handed me a pair of the gloves. These were all black, even the silvery material around my fingers. The only exception was the silver band around the wrists.

"Here you go. You can trade these out," he said.

I hesitated as I took them in my hands. I had grown so used to the gloves being on my hands that the thought of taking them off terrified me. I didn't have to worry when I had them on. I knew in the back of my head that the gloves worked, but my heart still began to pound. What if I dropped them? What if I tore them? What if they *stopped* working? What if I couldn't control it long enough to switch the gloves out? I pulled off the white gloves I had been wearing and handed them to Nelvin. I went as fast as I could, but I still I hesitated as I pulled on the black gloves. Tasha noticed.

"Don't worry," she said. "They're the same gloves as the other ones, and no one will question them. If they do, just give them a stern look and tell them to mind their own business."

I shrugged. "You're the expert." I finished pulling on the gloves.

Nelvin nodded his approval. "You look like a Hunter," he said. I raised an eyebrow.

"I'll take that as a compliment."

He grinned. "It was meant as one."

I shoved his shoulder a little and he held up his hands in surrender. "You win, all right! That hurts!"

Andresha and I both grinned as Nelvin pretended to pout and rub his shoulder.

Tasha hastily wiped the smile from her face and handed me a gold colored tag on a chain. She handed one to Andresha as well.

"These are your Hunter licenses," she said. I slipped the chain over my neck and slid the tag under my collar. Andresha did the same. The licenses would have our names and the dates the licenses were issued as well as when they were expired. Mine would specify that the bounty on me was void to any Hunter.

I was going as myself, but Andresha had asked for another identity.

"It's not common knowledge that he's with Red Star," she'd said. "I'm all over the place."

I had a feeling there was another reason, but she hadn't said anything. Her first name was the same, but on the tag, her family name was Kath.

I glanced around at everyone. "I think we're all set," I said. Short didn't say anything, he just shook my hand. Jim did as well. "Good luck," he said.

"Thanks."

Patrisha smiled at me. "Make me proud," she whispered. I smiled back. Nelvin hugged me, but just for a moment.

"Stay alive," he said. I assured him that I'd do my best. Andresha was making her goodbyes as well. She got hugs from everyone, even Jim and Short. When she got to Nelvin, he handed her a small box.

"Here," he said, "these may come in handy."

Andresha took the box and opened it. Inside were five hair pins. She raised her eyebrow.

"Hair pins?" She asked. Nelvin nodded.

"If you find you're self in a tight spot, just ask a pin for what you need. Don't do something like a space ship though, otherwise you'll be disappointed."

Andresha still looked a little confused, but she put the pins in her hair.

"Thanks, Nelvin," she said quietly. Everyone filed out of the room except for Chief, Jess and Tasha, who would be guiding us to Ten. I stopped in front of Jess. She put her hands on my shoulders.

"I'm proud of you," she said. I didn't know what to say, but my vision got blurry as my eyes filled with tears. She smiled kindly and pulled me into an embrace.

"I love you," she said.

"I love you too."

"Be careful."

"You know I will," I said when I could. She stepped back.

"Yes, I do." She wiped her eyes on her sleeve, then hugged Andresha as well. Then we both stepped over to Chief. He folded his arms.

"I was thinking." He said.

Andresha tossed hair out of her face. "What?"

Chief hesitated, then said. "Jade might be there."

I had no idea what he was talking about, but Andresha seemed to understand.

She nodded. "I didn't think of that. Do you think she would help us?"

Chief sighed. "I don't know. But it would be worth a try."

"But would she even recognize me?"

"You haven't changed that much. It was only two years ago."

"I've changed a lot since then!" Andresha protested.

"You know what I mean."

Andresha tugged her braid. I looked back and forth between them. I didn't understand. Who was this "Jade" they were talking about? They had obviously met her before.

Andresha bit her lip and pulled Chief aside.

"What if we get separated?" She said quietly. I think they'd forgotten I could hear them. *I* forgot I could hear them.

Chief glanced over at me, then said, "You'll have to tell him."

Andresha looked over at me as well. "You're sure?"

Chief looked grim, but he nodded. "I'm sure."

I was still confused, but decided that they weren't going to tell me. Tasha moved to the ladder. I was ready to follow her when Andresha surprised me.

She threw her arms around Chief's neck. He embraced her in return.

"You come back to me," he whispered, his voice slightly muffled.

"I will," she replied. She kissed his cheek and whispered, "I love you."

Chief didn't answer for moment, then he finally said, "I love you too."

Their embrace lingered for another moment, then Andresha finally stepped away and wiped her eyes. Both of them were crying. Tasha led the way up the ladder and we climbed in silence. When we exited the ladder, and Tasha had gone aways ahead I turned to Andresha.

"You know who he is?" I asked her.

She nodded, another tear glistening on her cheek.

"He's my brother."

30

(Andresha)

We followed Tasha through the dark streets of Nine and took one of the buses that ran on the level. I fingered one of the pins in my hair, wondering what Nelvin had meant. They were hair pins, after all, not fairies.

Then of course, there was my brother to think about.

I smiled a little to myself. A bit of sadness was in heart my though. I'd finally mended our relationship just in time to leave, possibly to never return.

Stop being such a pessimist! I said to myself. You need to focus. I straightened my shoulders and shoved all the sad thoughts to the back of my mind. I had work to do. I wondered if we would see Jade again. Was she even still alive? Being a Hunter wasn't exactly the safest business in the universe.

We got off the bus three hours later and walked for another twenty minutes until Tasha came to a stop.

"There it is," she said. I looked up in amazement.

"Is that an ... *abandoned* Lift shaft?" I gasped. Tasha nodded.

"REGS shut it down over twenty years ago due to mechanical failures. They couldn't tear down the shaft, so they just ripped out the components."

Edrix ran a hand through his hair. "Umm, if they ripped out the components, that means there's no *lift* in there. How are we supposed to get down there?"

Tasha turned around and gave us a mischievous grin. "I said REGS ripped out the components, yes, but I didn't say who put them back in." She waved us forward. "Come on!"

We approached the towering cylinder that reached from the ground to the Level's ceiling. We stopped in front of the Lift's doors. A quick inspection told me that the lift had received regular upkeep. No rust coated the doors, and all the power circuits in the entry console were new.

"This is where I leave you," Tasha said. Edrix looked at the Lift.

"Just tell me you're going to tell us how this works before you go."

Tasha smiled. "Of course I will."

She tapped a control on the pad next to the door and a scanning beam projected grid in the air.

"Put your Hunter tags in there," she instructed. Edrix and I did as she said. The panel made an affirmative beeping sound and turned green, then disappeared. Then the doors slid open, bathing the three of us in bright, white light. Tasha shrugged and lifted her arms.

"Ta-da!" she said in a sing-song voice. "There you have it."

She turned serious again. "Remember, on your way to the space port, do not talk to anyone. If you make eye contact with someone, look aggressive. Don't let yourself look lost, frightened, or inferior to them in anyway. You're Hunters. Act like it."

Edrix and I nodded in acknowledgement. I'd survived Ten once, I could do it again.

"Consider it done," I said. Tasha smiled.

Edrix and I walked into the Lift. The inside was entirely white and seemed to glow.

"One more thing!" Tasha called. We turned to look at her. She lifted her closed fist to her forehead, then down to her heart.

"That's the Hunter salute. It means that you'll complete the job, or die trying."

And with that happy news, the Lift doors closed and began to move.

* * *

The Lift had finally stopped moving. This one was faster than the lifts run by REGS. It had gotten us to Ten in three minutes.

I looked over at Edrix. "Ready?"

He shook his head. "I never will be so we'd better get going."

He pressed the control to open the door and we stepped out of the Lift, its doors shutting behind us.

Ten was dark. Even darker than Nine. There were a few Sunlights sprinkled around at random intervals, but they barely flickered with

144

power. The only sources of light came from lanterns hung on poles on the street side. I put my chin up and shoulders back. Edrix and I walked boldly down the street. There were hardly any people in sight, but that didn't mean they weren't watching. I shivered inwardly. Ten was warmer than Nine, but it sent shivers down my spine. My every instinct told me to bolt to cover. I noticed my hands were shaking, so I hid them under my poncho. I took a deep breath and forced myself to calm down. It had been years since I'd felt it this bad. Edrix glanced at me, then pulled me into a side alley.

"Are you all right?" He asked. I glanced around.

"How do you know there's not someone in here?" I whispered.

"I can't hear anyone breathing in here, it's empty," he said. "Now are you okay?"

I swallowed. He said it so casually. I was going to have to get used to his new hearing.

I nodded a little. "I just need a minute."

I took a deep breath and let my heart beat slow down. Then I nodded to Edrix. "Alright, I'm ready."

We came out of the alley way and followed the twisting streets. I was still feeling a little uneasy, so I rested my hand on my gun. I felt much better after that.

I breathed an inward sigh of relief as a tall building came into view.

"There it is," Edrix said. I nodded. It didn't look like much of a space port. The building that I assumed was the hangar had a sagging roof and the walls were peeling off. To the side of it was a smaller building that was in the same shape. There were a few people congregated around it.

"I think that's where we secure our ride," Edrix whispered. I agreed.

We made our way over to it, shoving our way through the small crowd assembled outside the building. When we reached the door, Edrix ignored the **APPOINTMENT ONLY** sign and went inside.

The inside was worse than the outside. Insects crawled over the walls and the furniture. Rust and grime coated the walls and it smelled like dead rodents. I fought the urge to revisit my breakfast.

There were two desks in the room attended by two burly men. The two had been talking to each other, but looked up in surprise as I let the door slam shut behind me.

"Morning, gentlemen," Edrix said evenly.

"What d'you want?" one of the men drawled. I wrinkled my nose at the smell of his breath.

Edrix folded his arms. "My associate and I need passage off world."

The other man waved his hand towards us. "Then go to the space port."

Edrix scowled. "I have an appointment," he said. The first man crossed his arms over his chest.

"Do you now?" He asked. In reply, Edrix brought out his hunter tag, which also revealed the knife, strapped to his wrist. The man gulped.

"Ah, yes! You wanted to go to Rezz, yes?" he said. Funny how the sight of a deadly weapon could jog one's memory. The man stood before we could answer and opened a drawer in the desk. He took out two holo-plastic tags on lanyards and handed them to us.

"There's your passes, sir. Good trip," he said quickly.

Edrix dipped his head as we took the passes and we exited the building.

I let myself gag. "Ugh!" I groaned. Edrix nodded and brushed an insect off his shoulder.

"I have to agree," he said as we walked towards the Hangar building. "Let's just get out of here."

31

(Andresha)

Thankfully, the ship wasn't as bad as the "space port." It was a large freighter type ship so there weren't any rooms for passengers. We were assigned a section of the cargo bay. There weren't even bunks to sleep on. We didn't have any sort of luggage, so we just sat on some boxes and waited for the rest of the passengers to board.

We kept to ourselves, since most of the other passengers were most likely either Hunters, or REGS spies.

We wore the lanyards around our necks. Once in a while, a guard would come by and ask to see your tag. It was after one had just left us that Edrix spoke to me.

"You sure you were okay back there?" he asked.

I nodded, looking down and my hands and fiddled with the hem of my poncho.

"Yeah. Sometimes, when I'm somewhere like that …" I stopped, then tried again.

"When I was younger, I would get panic attacks sometimes. They don't really happen anymore, but being someplace like that makes me nervous."

Edrix nodded. I brought my knees up to my chest and wrapped my arms around them. I looked over at him. He was sketching in a small sketchbook.

"What are you drawing?" I asked him. He glanced up, then tilted the book so I could see the drawing better. It was woman kneeling in a garden with a cat curled up beside her.

"It's my mom," Edrix clarified. I nodded slowly, awed. The drawing was so realistic, I felt like I could step into the picture.

Edrix must have thought my silence meant confusion because he dug into his pocket and pulled out a holo-disk. He pressed the button in the middle and an image sprang up. I could tell that it was the woman from the garden. She had blue eyes and brown hair.

"She's beautiful," I whispered.

147

"Thanks," he muttered. There were others in the image. I recognized a younger looking Edrix, a baby in his mother's arms, an older boy who I assumed was his older brother in REGS, and an older man.

"Is that your father?" I asked. Edrix nodded.

"Yeah. He died when I was twelve."

"I'm sorry."

He waved me off. "It's fine." He motioned to the baby. "That's my little brother, Zaren. He's five now."

Edrix was the only person in the picture with black, curly hair and green eyes. Everyone else had brown hair and blue eyes. Edrix switched off the disk and put it back in his pocket. I noticed he didn't mention the older boy. It must have been a painful subject so I didn't ask about him. Edrix started sketching again.

"Are you from Five?" I asked him. He nodded without looking up. It made sense, I thought.

"How long have you been drawing?"

He stopped sketching and thought for a moment. "I started getting serious about it when I was seven, but my mom taught me ever since I could hold a pencil."

"Is she an artist?"

Edrix nodded. "Yeah, a *really* good one. The Chairman actually ordered paintings from her."

His gaze grew distant. "We used to draw together a lot."

I wasn't sure what to say to that. "What about your father?" I asked him. "Was he an artist too?"

Edrix laughed. "Oh no! He grew up on Three and joined REGS when he was eighteen. He always said that it would be a miracle if he drew a stick-figure."

I laughed too. It felt good after being so glum and serious all day.

Edrix put his sketch book away. "What about you?" He asked. "What did your parents do?"

I hesitated. What was I going to say? I still wasn't sure about my trust in Edrix, so I decided that I would be as vague as possible.

"Well, my dad was a scientist," I said. "My mom was a nurse."

Edrix nodded. "So you grew up on Two?"

I hesitated again. I didn't want to *lie*, but I didn't want to tell him either.

I sighed. "I'm sorry, I … I don't really like to talk about it."

Edrix resumed his sketching. "That's all right," he said. I breathed in internal sigh of relief. That was easier than I'd thought it would be. We sat in silence for a minute.

"Do you think that REGS knows that this space port exists?" I asked.

Edrix didn't look up. "Wouldn't surprise me," he said simply.

I brushed hair out of my face. "Then why would they let it keep going?"

Edrix didn't answer right away. "Your guess is as good as mine," he said finally. "There's a lot about REGS that I don't know."

I wasn't sure how to answer that either, so I didn't.

The silence stretched on for a while. I didn't bother counting the minutes. Edrix glanced over at me.

"You can get some sleep if you want. I'll keep watch."

We'd both decided to keep a watch since we had no idea who was on board. I nodded.

"Thanks."

He shrugged. I curled up on the floor, my head on my arms. I shifted a little, trying to get comfortable. It was a little disconcerting, feeling the floor moving underneath you. Edrix glanced at me again, then took off his jacket and folded it up.

"Here," he said and handed it to me. I took the jacket.

"Thanks," I whispered. I curled up again, this time using the jacket as a pillow and listened to the hum of the ship's engine. I wasn't sure when, but I fell asleep.

32

(Edrix)

The ship landed twelve hours after we'd left Rendaria. Andresha and I walked off the ramp and were met by a wall of ice-cold air. I shivered as I looked around. There was nothing but white for miles. Andresha caught my gaze.

"It's snow," she said to me over the sound of the wind and ships coming and going. I'd never seen snow before in my life except for in paintings. I decided right then that none of them had accurately captured its brilliance, or the way it sparkled, even though the sky was over cast and grey. Living underground, we didn't get snow.

I took a deep breath. I was standing on an entirely different planet! As a Higher One in REGS, I might have been able to go off world one day if I had ever been assigned to guard a diplomate or ambassador. Usually, it would have been rare, but since Rendaria had applied for membership in the Galactic Counsel, ambassadors had been leaving and arriving almost constantly.

Andresha adjusted her poncho. "Quit gaping. Someone's going to notice."

I snapped out of my contemplation and started walking. She had a point.

This space port was much busier than then one on Redaria. The babble of a hundred conversations floated to us. There were about two hundred people milling around the port, either boarding ships or disembarking. Andresha scanned the crowd.

"There's our man," she said motioning to a food vendor. I followed her gaze to a tall man with flaming red hair buying something from the vendor. As he turned towards us, I could see his golden eyes.

"Just like Tasha's picture," I said. Andresha nodded.

"Let's go say hello."

We walked over as the man paid the vendor. Before I could say anything, the man turned around and smiled at us. "Ah, you must be Edrix and Andresha," he said. Up close, I could see a narrow scar above his eyebrow, and he had large, bird-like nose. He shook our hands. "Tasha told me you were coming! How was your trip?"

Andresha and I glanced at each other. "Um …well enough, I guess," I said.

The man laughed. "On that whale of a freighter? That's being a bit generous, I think!" He held up a hand.

"Where are my manners? Harris is my name, Mr. Harris, pleasure to meet you!" He handed us each a hot pastry wrapped in paper.

"Here, you must be hungry," he said. We accepted the food and I took a bite. It was warm and filled with a sweet red jam, and the pastry was flaky and crisp. Mr. Harris motioned to a hover car parked outside the space port.

"Come along. We best be getting you that ship."

I glanced at Andresha and she shrugged, then we followed him to the hover car and got in. He started it up and pulled away from the port.

"So, you two are entering into the tournament, eh?" He asked. I glanced at Andresha, not sure what to say. She answered for me.

"Yes, that's right." She said. Mr. Harris nodded.

"Tasha started being your tech support?"

Andresha pursed her lips. "Umm, she told us about the tournament, but she didn't say anything about 'tech support.'"

Mr. Harris laughed. "She wouldn't! Always embarrassed about it, she was." Andresha looked at me and shrugged. Neither of us knew what to say.

It turned out that Mr. Harris didn't live terribly far from the space port, only about five miles. I stared in amazement as the car came to a stop. There was a huge bunker in the middle of the snow with a small house was nestled to one side. Mr. Harris pulled up next to the house. We all climbed out and he locked the hover car.

"I can't tell you how glad I was when we finally got hover cars out here! The snow is *terrible* to drive in!"

He placed his keys in his pocket and laughed again.

"Now," he said. "Let's go find you a ship." He waved us to the bunker and started to trudge through the deep snow.

151

I shivered as an icy wind picked up. He certainly was an interesting character. I wondered how Tasha had met him.

Mr. Harris opened a panel and pressed a few buttons, then a red beam of light emerged and scanned his face. The panel emitted a high pitched chirp. There was suddenly a loud *boom!* of ice cracking as the doors began to open. They eased open and settled with an echoing *BANG!*

Mr. Harris dusted off his hands then waved us inside.

I'd never seen so many ships in one place that wasn't a REGS hangar. There were ten ships of all different shapes and sizes. I stared in awe.

Andresha glanced at me, then said flatly, "Close your mouth, or a ship might mistake it for a hangar and fly in."

I snapped my jaw shut. I was beginning to discover just how unpredictable she could be.

Mr. Harris clapped his hands and rubbed them together.

"Now, what kind of ship are we looking for?"

Andresha folded her arms and tossed hair out of her face. "A ship fit for a Hunter."

Mr. Harris snapped his fingers, then pointed at her. "I know just the one!" he said and headed for one of the smaller ships.

"I have one that's bigger of course," he said as he led us down the rows of ships, "but it handles only slightly better than a small moon so I think you'll like this one better."

Just as it had no sun, Rendaria didn't have a moon, either. The only ones I'd ever seen were in my astronomy studies in the Program about other worlds.

"It has a more impressive weapons system of course." Mr. Harris was saying.

Andresha said, "Let's just start with this one."

Mr. Harris nodded. We'd stopped in front of a ship just slightly bigger than a skysailor. Mr. Harris retrieved a remote from his pocket and pressed a button. A boarding ramp lowered down with a hiss of steam.

Mr. Harris led us aboard. "So, Tasha finally decided to call in her favor, did she?" He asked as Andresha and I followed him up the ramp.

"That's what she told us," I said.

Mr. Harris nodded. "Good. This is the easiest way for me to do it."

Andresha and I glanced at each other.

"That's what she said," I replied.

Mr. Harris laughed. "Oh, I'm sure she did. Thinks she can read me like a book she does."

He opened his arms as we entered the ship. "Here we are. The *Triumph*, I call her."

I looked around the ship. It had almost the same layout as a skysailor. A cockpit with two chairs in the front, and a storage compartment in the back. There were two bunks that slid out of one wall. The only differences were the controls for the weapons and the small brig next to the storage compartment. Andresha was looking over the controls in the cockpit.

"Can you drive this thing?" I asked her.

She nodded. "Easily."

Mr. Harris rattled off technical aspects of the ship. "She's got two J-class engines with a back-up stabilizer. A fully functional Photo-drive, and auto-adjusting gravity. You won't feel a bump while you fly."

I wished Nelvin was here to decode all this stuff. I knew the basics of a skysailor engine, enough that I could repair one, but space travel was beyond me. I had no idea what a J-class engine even was. To my surprise, Andresha knew more than I did.

"Auto-gravity, huh? I won't have to readjust it every time we go to a different system?" She asked.

Mr. Harris nodded enthusiastically. "That's correct."

I looked at Andresha and she nodded. "Sounds perfect."

I turned to Mr. Harris. "We'll take it. How much?"

I expected him to laugh, seeing as it was his favorite thing to do, but instead he got very serious. He shook his head.

"No, this is my payback to Tasha. It's better if I do it this way. Safer, for her." He bit his lip, then smiled again.

"I wish you luck. Where you're going, you will need it. Now, you best be off. The tournament is held on the other side of the planet. May victory find you easily," he said, then waved and exited the ship.

Andresha sat down in the pilot's seat, and I sat in the other one. She pressed a control and the ramp went up.

I looked out the cockpit and saw Mr. Harris standing to one side of the ship. He gave us two thumbs-up, then waved. I nodded to him. Andresha tapped another control and took hold of the steering yolk, then she carefully maneuvered the ship out of the bunker.

She took a deep breath. "You ready?" She asked, looking over at me. I raised my eyebrows and shook my head.

"I already gave you that answer on Ten."

She grinned and brought the *Triumph* into the air.

33

(Andresha)

I felt the knot in my stomach tighten as we flew in view of our destination. From above and in the rapidly darkening night, all I could see was a small building with twinkling lights in the windows. Next to it, was an ominous black mass that I couldn't make out. It was like a shadow. I glanced at Edrix. He didn't *look* nervous, but then, neither did I.

"Looks like a charming place," I said. Edrix turned towards me.

"In a scary sort of way," he said.

I flicked a switch above my head. "Do you remember where we're supposed to land?" I asked Edrix.

He pointed out the cockpit window. "I think they'll tell us," he said and I followed his gaze.

There were two ships coming towards us. Sure enough, the transmission light blinked. I tapped the control to turn it on.

"State your intentions," a harsh voice said.

"This is Andresha Kath on the *Triumph*. I'm here for the tournament," I said. "Where do I land?"

There was a short silence, then a burst of static followed by the same voice.

"You'll land in section four. Report to the Hub immediately after landing."

The transmission ended.

"Friendly people," I muttered.

Edrix chuckled.

I looked over at him. "What's so funny?"

He grinned. "We're at a tournament for Hunters and you expect them to be *friendly?*"

I knit my brows and sniffed the air indignantly.

"I didn't say I expected it, but it would have been a pleasant surprise."

Edrix just smiled and shook his head. If I hadn't been so nervous, I might have laughed too.

We found section four and I landed the ship.

"Make sure we have the invitation," I told Edrix.

He patted his pocket. "I've got it here."

I nodded and grabbed my poncho that I'd taken off and laid on one of the cots. I slipped it over my head then turned to Edrix.

"We're looking for a Hunter called Jade Hura," I told him. He nodded. "I know. Do you know what she looks like?"

I'd forgotten about his ears again. I shrugged. "I haven't seen her in two years, but last I saw her, she was, well, my height, and she had dark hair and blue eyes."

Edrix nodded. "I'll keep an eye out." Seeing as he could see better than the average Rendarian, I had no doubt that he would.

I lowered the ramp and followed Edrix off the ship. I inhaled sharply as the cold hit me and I shivered. Now that the sun had set, it was even colder.

"They didn't tell us where the Hub was," Edrix said. I motioned to the smaller building we'd noticed earlier.

"I'm betting that's it. If it isn't, they can probably tell us."

We walked over to the building, our feet crunching in the snow. When we reached the door, a scanning arm popped out of the wall. Its beam of light went over each of us, then it disappeared back into the wall. Then a panel by the door opened and an electronic voice said, "Your Hunter licenses, please."

Edrix and I scanned our tags. The panel made a beeping noise and the voice said. "Welcome. Please check in with Thanos upon entering."

The doors slid open. I glanced at Edrix once, then we both entered the Hub.

We were greeted with a rush of warm air. It made my face tingle a little after being in the numbing cold. Music played from speakers somewhere near the ceiling. The walls and floors were a polished amber color. You could use them for mirrors. Huge chandeliers hung from the ceiling. There were about fifteen people milling about the room, talking to one another. From their apparel, I didn't doubt that they were Hunters.

I leaned towards Edrix and muttered, "Are we in the right place?"

He rubbed his ear. "I don't know, but something smells delicious."

I couldn't smell anything, but that meant nothing to him.

"I wouldn't advertise that too loudly," I whispered. He nodded.

A man approached us from one of the groups of Hunters. He was wearing a long, robe-like garment in a deep blue color. It was accented by a thick gold chain that hung around his neck. A large golden disk encrusted with gems hung from the center of the chain. The man had a dark beard and hair that fell to his shoulders. He spread his arms in a welcome gesture, his dark eyes twinkling.

"Welcome friends!" he said brightly. "I assume you are here for the tournament?"

Edrix nodded, folding his arms. "That's right. The computer told us to speak to Thanos?"

The man smiled and bowed and spread his arms. "That would be me, my friend. Delilah told me the last two guests were here." I raised an eyebrow.

"Delilah?"

Thanos smiled. "That's the computer's name." He held out a hand. "May I see your invitation, please?"

Edrix dug the invitation out of his pocket and handed it to him. Thanos looked it over.

"Very well," he said and handed it back. He cleared his throat.

"Allow me to properly introduce myself." He drew himself to his full height, about two inches shorter than Edrix.

"I am Thanos, the head of ceremony for this tournament. I will be conducting the proceedings for tonight's banquet and for the tournament when it begins tomorrow." He bowed deeply again, then straightened.

"Your names?" He asked us. Edrix kept his arms folded.

"I'm Edrix Solan. This is my associate, Andresha Kath," he said, motioning to me. I raised an eyebrow in acknowledgement. Thanos bowed his head.

"A pleasure to meet you," he said. "Dinner will be served shortly. In the meantime, please feel free to mingle."

He moved over to another group of people. Edrix raised his eyebrows.

"Friendly enough for you?" He asked jokingly. I ignored the comment.

"So tomorrow, we could very well end up killing each other, and they want us to make friends? It doesn't make sense," I said. Edrix nodded.

"True, but they could be trying to keep us from killing each other at the first opportunity." He looked around the room. "Besides, this is the opportunity we need to see if Jade is here."

I nodded in agreement. "I say we split up."

He nodded back to me. "Alright, but be careful."

I rolled my eyes. "You're as bad as Chief."

Edrix made a face and walked away.

I looked around the room. I hadn't seen Jade for years. I wondered if I would even recognize her if she was here. I decided to try and find the friendliest-looking people in the room. I scanned the large hall and decided on a group towards the corner. There were two men and a woman talking together. I studied them as I walked over.

One of the men had a mohawk dyed neon green. Tattoos covered his muscular arms. The other man was also brawny, but his hair was blond and pulled back in a ponytail. The woman's hair was cobalt blue with streaks of pink and purple. All right, maybe not the friendliest looking people in the room, but it was too late to turn back now. They stopped talking as I approached.

"Well, well, well, what do we have here?" Mohawk man said.

The woman raised her eyebrow at me. "I've never seen you around before."

I shrugged. "Probably because I usually keep to myself."

The blond man turned to me now. "Then what brings you over here?"

I flicked imaginary dirt off my shoulder.

"Curiosity. I 've never seen so many Hunters in one place without a fight breaking out."

The woman laughed. "The fighting starts tomorrow, sweetheart."

Mohawk man held up his hands. "Hold on, you're saying you're a Hunter?" He said to me. "How old are you, twelve? I didn't know they gave licenses to little girls now."

I raised my eyebrow. Jim would be dying of laughter if he was here.

Instead of answering, I just walked away. Anything I said would have started a fight. Diplomacy tactics had *not*, emphasis, prepared me to talk to these people.

34

(Edrix)

Spending twenty minutes talking to Hunters was not my idea of a fun party. At first, I'd felt overwhelmed after seeing all the Hunters in the room. How were we supposed to have a chance against this many people? But after talking with a few of them, I found out that some of them were just passing through. The Hub was kind of like a hotel for Hunters. You could come and get your ship repaired or refueled as well as stay while such tasks were completed. I wasn't sure how many of them were only here for the food, but I guessed I would find out tomorrow.

Andresha came over to me. "That was terrible," she said. I looked at her.

"What happened?"

She tossed hair out of her face. "Every person I talked to just wanted to start a fight, much less make friends," she sighed. "Most of them treated me like a kid so ..." She trailed off.

I wasn't sure what to say. She was young for the average hunter. I guess Tasha either hadn't considered that, or didn't think it was a problem.

Just then, Thanos clapped his hands from across the room.

"Excuse me, but dinner is ready. If you will all follow me."

Andresha and I followed him and the rest of the group through a set of huge double doors. Inside was a long table the same amber color as the walls.

"Please have a seat," Thanos said, seating himself at the head of the table. Andresha and I started to get seats towards the end of the table, but Thanos called out, "Solan,"

I turned towards him and he beckoned us over.

"Come sit up here," he said.

I was instantly on alert. Why did he want to talk to me? I looked over at Andresha and met her gaze. Andresha pursed her lips for a moment, then gave a stiff, almost imperceptible nod. Proceed with caution.

160

We went over to the seats he motioned to. We were two seats away from him. Droids brought plates of food to each person. There were steamed vegetables, a helping of meat and gravy, a thick slice of bread, and bowls of fruit placed on the table.

I was hungry, so I began eating with vigor. Andresha ate, but not as enthusiastically. I caught her staring at me.

"What?" I asked. She shook her head.

"Men and their food," she said. as if it were an explanation.

I shrugged it off and continued eating.

Thanos looked up from his plate. "So, Edrix," he said. I looked up.

He took a sip of his drink and continued. "What made you decide to become a Hunter?"

I took a sip of water, then replied. "It pays well."

"Better than the Higher Order on Rendaria?"

I smirked. "Much better."

Thanos chuckled.

"What about you … Andresha was it?" he asked.

I glanced at Andresha, unsure of what she would say. *Please,* I thought, *don't let your tongue get away from you.* She calmly finished slicing a piece of fruit.

"I don't like people telling me what to do," she said finally. Thanos nodded.

"I see. Tell me then, what—"

He was cut off by an outburst of shouting from outside the dining room. I could hear the voices clearly, but they were speaking another language.

Andresha whispered to me, "What's going on?" No one else in the room could hear her, she spoke so softly, but I could. I shook my head slightly.

Thanos looked to the doors, a slightly concerned look on his face.

"I wonder what that could be about," he said.

Then the doors opened with a thunderous *CRASH!*

I looked in the door way and was struck the overwhelming feeling that I'd seen her before.

Standing in the door way was an athletic young woman, the crumpled body of a guard at her feet. She looked to be about my age, but her hair was as white as the snow outside and swept up into a high ponytail with some loose around her face. Her skin was incredibly pale. She wore a dark grey shirt and black pants with black boots. She had two belts around her waist that crossed over each other that carried two knives and several small pouches and ammunition. Two guns were holstered at her sides, and she had several bracelets around each wrist that looked to be made of common steel. Out of place with the rest of her gear, was a long black cord that hung around her neck. On the cord was a brass pendant. I think it was a Rendarian rune, but I couldn't tell.

What caught me off guard the most was her eyes. I couldn't describe them as a color. The only way I could describe them was that they looked like mirrors. They were cold eyes and sent an involuntary shiver down my spine.

"Thanos," she sneered, her voice cold and cutting like a whip. "I can't believe I wasn't invited." She put a hand to her forehead, closing her eyes in mock distress. "It hurt me so terribly when you revoked my invitation." She lowered her hand and walked forward, her boots making no sound on the polished floor.

She cocked her head to one side. "And then, it made me horribly angry." She stopped at the end of the table. "And you *know* what happens when I get angry."

Thanos had gone pale. He managed a thin smile, "I'm not in charge of the —"

The new comer let out a short bark of laughter before he'd even finished speaking.

"Ha! Excuses, Thanos, excuses. They always were your favorite form of communication." She strode over to a chair towards the center of the table. That chair was occupied by a man with a cybernetic arm. The new comer cleared her throat.

The man looked up. "What do you want?" He asked.

The woman smiled coldly. "You're in my seat," she sneered.

"Get lost, lady," the man said.

There was the sound of a gun firing, and the man slumped across the table. The woman grabbed him by the collar and pulled him out of the chair, dropping his lifeless body to the floor. The entire room

162

was completely silent. The woman sat in the now empty chair and a droid hurried over with another plate of food.

I glanced over at Andresha, not daring to say a word. She flicked her eyes towards me. If this was the kind of competition we were up against, I wondered—not for the first time—if we had any hope of coming out alive.

35

(Edrix)

I didn't sleep a wink. Thankfully, the rooms Andresha and I were given weren't nearly as extravagant as the dining hall and entryway. They were about the size of our rooms back at Red Star. But the mattress and the pillows were too soft, and I felt like I was drowning in the blankets. I'd tried sleeping on the floor, but it didn't come. Every small noise startled me. The woman who'd barged in on dinner quite honestly frightened me. How she'd killed that man for a chair without an apparent second thought. Where could I have seen her before? I was sure I'd never met her before in my life, but that feeling was there.

Sometime around midnight I finally fell asleep. Nightmares of Eight greeted me, like they always did. The gun shots, the bombs, Jai's disappointment.

I started awake to a loud knock on my door. I picked myself up off the floor and went to the door and answered it. A relieved Andresha was on the other side.

"Thank goodness," she said. "I heard a fight break out down here."

I yawned. "Aside from lack of sleep, I'm fine."

She smiled wryly. "Same here. Thanos said that breakfast is in ten minutes."

I nodded. "I don't think you should go out there alone, just in case our dinner guest is there."

She looked even more relieved. "I was hoping you were going to say that. I was about to offer to conduct reconnaissance."

I laughed. "I'll be out in five."

I closed the door and quickly gathered my things. After I'd cleaned my teeth I met Andresha outside.

"Anything happen?" I asked her. She pursed her lips and shook her head.

Breakfast was a buffet, which was quite a relief after the dinner incident. I kept looking over my shoulder the whole time. I didn't

164

have much of an appetite, so I ate only a small plate of food. Andresha was the same. We didn't talk the entire time we ate.

I'd just finished the last of my water when Thanos entered the room.

"Good morning, friends," he said grandly, sweeping his arms wide. "Those who have entered the tournament, please follow me. It is time to begin."

We gathered in front of the huge, black mass we'd seen from the air. The sun had only just begun to show over the peaks of the snowy mountains. Thanos instructed the contestants to line up. Andresha and I stood next to each other. Thanos stood on a floating platform above it.

"Hunters," he said, "Today marks the beginning of our long awaited tournament." His voice rang over us as it ran through an amplifier most likely attached to his collar. His robe was a deep green today, but the chain was the same.

"The winner of this tourney will be awarded with the honor of accepting the ultimate Hunt." Thanos continued. "May I present the sponsor of this event." He raised his arms and a huge screen flickered on behind him. There was nothing but a silhouette.

"The Client," Thanos said grandly.

"The Client" said nothing. He didn't move. He just … *was.*

Thanos continued. "Allow me to introduce our contestants."

He started at the beginning of the line. There was Gerris, a native of Rezz with the characteristic black hair and red eyes. Tasha had told us about him. He relied mostly on brute strength, but had a few grenades and a rifle in case that wasn't enough. Another duo Tasha told us about was Frenz Tip and Lyta Garrison. They were your basic Hunters. Both were extremely skilled in hand-to-hand combat and were formidable pilots. There was the group that Andresha had tried to talk to the night before. All the names blurred together. Thanos called our names, and a spotlight briefly illuminated us. It was most likely my imagination, but I thought I saw the silhouette move, just a little. I dismissed it. Thanos rattled on more names. Then he got to the end.

"Fara Emrick. Twelve Apprehension Orders in the Galactic Counsel, and twenty-four Death-marks."

The spotlight shone on the woman from last night. She didn't look any different, but under the bright light, her pale skin and hair almost seemed to glow. She stood with her arms folded, staring straight ahead.

Thanos took a deep breath. "Now, your arena!" he shouted.

The large screen shrunk to let us have an unobstructed view of the shadowy mass. I could see now that it was an enormous building.

"This," Thanos proclaimed, "is the Anvil."

Suddenly, lights near the ground illuminated the blackness of the mass. I could now make out a doorway directly ahead of us. There was also a large square tile on top of the building that glowed blue. As we watched, there was a sharp *snap!* of electricity that emanated at the tile and traveled across the whole building. Above the tile, there was a large, square platform-like structure on a track.

"The platform you see above the Anvil is what we call the Hammer. In the Anvil you will all face trials that will test your skills as Hunters. At the end of each trial, those that survived will be eligible for advancement to the next trial but," Thanos held up a finger, "the Hammer will strike the tile on top of the Anvil, and the Hunter with the least desirable performance, will be eliminated."

My heart was starting to beat faster. It took everything I had to keep my hands from shaking.

"The rules!" Thanos boomed. "Inside the Anvil, there is only one rule: You will leave with those you entered with. If you enter as a pair, you leave as a pair. If one of your team fails, you all fail. If you enter alone, that is how you leave."

Andresha and I looked at each other. What if I failed and she paid the price? She smiled a little at me. I forced myself to return it.

Thanos motioned to a hovering platform halfway to the door. It was filled with backpacks.

"On entering, you will each be allowed to grab *one* pack," he said. "Taking more than one will result in automatic elimination. Once inside the Anvil, that rule is void."

166

I whispered to Andresha, "Our first priority is to get inside. Just grab your pack and run in. We should try and stay close to each other."

She nodded.

Thanos held up his hands. "Hunters, your first trial!"

He paused dramatically. "Enter the Anvil. The tournament begins ... NOW!"

Andresha and I shot forward, running at top speed for the platform. Everything was in absolute chaos. I heard gunshots and shouts behind me, but I didn't dare stop to look. I reached the cart and grabbed a pack, Andresha doing the same. Gerris swept past us, a pack in his hands. We were twenty feet from the door. I heard something whistling behind me. I grabbed Andresha and pulled her to the side as a knife flew past where my head had just been. Someone suddenly pushed me violently from behind. I fell to the ground. I heard Andresha's gun fire. Then she pulled me up, the weapon still in her hand and her pack on one shoulder.

"Come on! Come on!" she screamed. We ran towards the door that was just twenty feet away. Almost the entire group had passed us. We couldn't be the last ones in. Ten feet, five feet. We raced through the door way and stopped.

It was a dead end. There was nowhere to go. The walls were made of a dark grey metal, and the room was dimly lit. The other Hunters were gone. I turned around, remembering that there had been someone just behind us, but I stopped.

The door way was gone. There was only a solid wall behind us.

Uneasiness crept over me. I slipped one of my backpack's straps over my shoulder and un-holstered my gun, holding it ready.

We were trapped inside, which I assumed was the point. There was a crackling sound, then Thanos's voice boomed down to us.

"Very good. The contestants have been narrowed by five. Now, we will have one last elimination."

A screen flickered to life on the wall. We saw the Hammer slam down onto the tile on the roof. At first nothing happened, then the screen switched to show one lone Hunter as electricity traveled down the walls. It converged on the Hunter who I assumed had come through last. He screamed and fell then was ominously still.

"Twenty-six of you remain," Thanos said. "Your next trial begins now."

A doorway slid open in the wall in front of us. I thought about the Hunter that had been "eliminated." That could have been Andresha and me. Not only did we have to keep ourselves from being killed, we had to impress the Client at the same time.

How were we going to survive?

36

Tasha woke with a start. She immediately looked at her hands. There were no cracks. She ran her hands up her arms and felt her face. Nothing, just her skin.

"Crazy dreams," she said to herself. It was time for her to get up anyways. She showered and dressed, then headed to the mess hall.

She didn't stay to eat, she simply grabbed a bowl of mush and ate as she walked to the lab. She stopped to examine the lights above the doorway. None of them were on, so she entered the code and the door opened, letting her in. She smiled and greeted a few of the other scientists in the lab, though there weren't many this early, and settled down at her work station.

As much as she attempted to tell herself otherwise, the nightmare had bothered her. She tried to put it in the back of her mind, but it kept coming back to her. She tried to focus on her work.

In case the Tournament didn't work, they still had to find a way to delete Red Star's location from the Core, but getting inside, probably wouldn't be an option. So Nelvin had come up with an alternative—a virus to delete all files in the Core pertaining to Red Star.

Even if Edrix and Andresha succeeded in winning the tournament Nelvin suggested that it would be the best way to keep the base hidden.

"Even if we delete the files, they could come up with other ways to find us," he had said. "This way, anything in the Core that has anything to do with references to the base, or anything that has to do with the organization, will be deleted. They can't find us if they can't collect data on us."

Chief had agreed. If Edrix and Andresha *didn't* succeed, it was going to be difficult to install the virus, but hopefully not impossible. Nelvin thought that it might be possible to trick REGS into uploading the file themselves, but it was still only a rough idea.

She looked up as the door opened and Nelvin came in whistling.

"Morning." he said to no one in particular, or maybe he was talking to the lab. He fed the remaining lizards in the tank, then used a watering can with a long spout to water the "Grabby Plant," as Tasha had named it.

He moved around the room, humming a soft tune to himself as he poured the contents of one beaker into another that was over a small flame. It erupted into a cloud of smoke. He tapped something on a data-pad by the beaker, then dropped a small marble into a flask on another table. The liquid immediately started to bubble. Nelvin tapped the pad again, then came over to where Tasha was working.

"Greetings and salutations," he said leaning over her shoulder to see her screen. "Whatcha workin' on?"

Tasha shrugged. "The virus."

Nelvin paused and looked at her. "You mean the computer one, right?" Tasha nodded.

"Good, because the *actual* viruses aren't allowed out from behind that door." He motioned to a thick metal door in the back of the lab and moving to another table behind her. Something started to hiss, followed by a loud popping sound. Tasha didn't ask. Sometimes it was best not to.

"I don't understand why people always put *glass* doors in front of something important," Nelvin continued. "Then all someone has to do to cause havoc and destruction—is break the glass." He paused, then looked over at the screen in front of Tasha.

"Which computer virus are you working on?" He asked.

She turned to look at him. "The one for the Core. What other computer virus *is* there to work on?"

Nelvin squinted as he looked at the lines of code more closely. "One for making all of the REGS monitor screens pink, apparently."

Tasha sighed and deleted the code. Nelvin pulled a chair from another desk and sat down.

"Are you okay?" He asked. She put her elbows on the desk and rested her head in her hands.

"It's this nightmare I had ... It keeps coming back to me."

"Want to talk about it?"

Tasha sighed. "Not really."

170

She was silent for a moment.

"Have you ever, felt like," she stopped, then tried again. "Have you ever felt like you aren't ... *real* anymore?"

Nelvin knit his brows. "What do mean?"

Tasha thought for a moment, then said, "Like, you walk around and you have thoughts and feelings, but there's just something *missing*."

Nelvin shook his head. "Can't say I have."

Tasha nodded in understanding. "Well, that's how I feel after this dream." She smiled a little. "My weird subconscious, huh?"

Nelvin nodded. "Probably. Sometimes, when our brains experience things they don't understand, they'll incorporate it into our dreams as an attempt to understand it. You have been working with a lot of computers lately."

He motioned to the screen. "Now, how about we get started on that code?"

Tasha nodded. "Sounds good."

If only you knew, Nelvin, she thought. *If only you knew.*

37

(Andresha)

We were immediately launched into the next "trial" as Thanos so *dramatically* put it.

When we entered the doorway, we found ourselves in a small alcove that led into a large room with all the other Hunters spread across the room in alcoves like ours. The walls were completely smooth, black metal. About forty feet up, the walls ended at a larger room above us.

"Is there something up there?" I asked Edrix, knowing that his eyes were better than mine. He looked for a moment, then said, "Yes, there's a doorway on the left side."

I nodded to myself. "That's probably our destination." I looked around the room. "The real question," I continued, "is why we all haven't started killing each other?"

Edrix looked up towards the ceiling, then down at the floor. He gingerly put out a hand and reached towards the middle of the room. There was a sharp snap of electricity and Edrix quickly drew his hand back and shook it a little.

"There's a force-field," he said unnecessarily. "We have to wait for them to say 'go.'"

I folded my arms and shifted the pack on my shoulders. Obviously, the goal was to get to the top of the walls, but how? Edrix and I had cables, but they were only twenty-five feet long. They wouldn't reach the top of the wall. We could launch them partway up, but they wouldn't have an anchor, and there wouldn't be a way for us to climb the last five feet. If we were lucky, one of us might be able to reach the floor above, but we were back to the issue of anchoring the cables.

Thanos would have to give us a way up. Of course he probably wouldn't *give* it to us. That would kind of ruin the whole *finding the best Hunter* thing. We'd have to *find* the way that Thanos gave us to get up the walls. Make sense to you? Me neither.

172

I was pulled out of my contemplation when Edrix suddenly pulled me away from the door. It slammed shut behind me. I was about to thank him, but he pointed to the ground.

"We have a problem," he said.

I looked down. Water was pouring into the room. It was already above my ankles. A buzzer went off, signaling the start of the trial, but the force-field stayed up.

The water started rising faster.

"We need to disable the force-field," Edrix said. That water was up to my knees now. I examined the wall. Nothing to indicate a force-field. I whipped out my scanner and ran it up the wall. My scanner made a high-pitched beeping sound.

"Here!" I shouted. There was something in the wall in front of us, about halfway up. It was a standard force-field projector. I tapped a control on my scanner. Nelvin had programmed our scanners to shut down some tech. I selected the proper setting and let it run. The scanner's beep got louder and higher. There was a burst of electricity from the other side of the room. I looked up. The woman from dinner, what was her name? Fara. That was it, Fara Emrick. She had her force-field down and was heading out of her alcove. As I watched, two more, then five more Hunters were out. I tapped another control on my scanner.

"Come on!" I muttered. Edrix was working on the other side.

Eleven Hunters were out now, and the water was up to my shoulders. The scanner made a final squawk, and the wall exploded in a shower of sparks. I could see the blue field flickering now, and the gaping hole in the wall that was still sparking. Then the other side exploded as well. The force-field was down. Edrix and I surged out of our alcove. Panels in the walls began to glow, and then shot out of the walls. That must be our way up!

"The panels!" I shouted to Edrix. He nodded. Water was pouring from somewhere on the ceiling now, filling the room faster. We'd be swimming soon. The water was up to my neck.

One of the Hunters, I didn't know what species she was, with blue skin and green hair was leaping from panel to panel. She had almost reached the top.

Fara climbed onto a panel, then reached down to the glowing propulsion orb underneath it. I watched in frightened amazement as she ripped it out, then threw it to the side. The panel stopped moving. Fara then drew one of her guns and aimed. I realized what she was going to do.

"Stop!" I shouted and surged towards her. She either didn't hear me, or ignored me. She pulled the trigger and the blue-skinned Hunter fell back into the water. She didn't come back up. Thanos' voice boomed down to us.

"Terra Relic has been eliminated."

I was so shocked I almost drowned.

"SWIM!" Edrix shouted. I quickly pushed off the ground and began to swim towards Fara's platform. Four more Hunters were fighting on another side of the room. Fara drew her other weapon and fired three more times. Three more Hunters went down. Thanos called out their names. Horant, Vicktla, and Rema, a trio, all eliminated. Ominous red ribbons floated on the water. I forced myself not to vomit.

Fara put her guns away and leapt onto another platform, then another, and another. I blinked twice and she was at the top. I met her eyes on accident. She smiled coldly, then took a small, round object out of one of the pouches on her belt. It began to blink. She dropped it down and laughed. The sound sent chills down my spine.

I realized what she had dropped.

I turned to Edrix, who had just fought off another Hunter. If we hadn't been in mortal danger, I would have congratulated him on doing so while swimming.

"Get to the platform!" I screamed. I swam as hard as I could, watching the falling, blinking object in my peripheral vision. It was going to be close ...

I grabbed the platforms edge and hauled myself up. Edrix was right beside me.

"What is—" he started, but the blinking metal ball hit the water. There was a powerful *BOOM!*

Edrix and I were knocked back into each other as the explosion rocked our platform. Water splashed at least ten feet into the air, spraying us with boiling water. I would have fallen off the platform if Edrix hadn't grabbed my arm and pulled me back on. He did it just in time. Electricity sparked across the water. There were two Hunters left swimming. They screamed and faded from view. I swallowed. My face and hands stung from where the boiling water had hit me, and I was completely soaked.

"What was that?" Edrix sputtered. I wiped water out of my eyes.

"It would seem to be an electro-concussion grenade," I said.

The chaos continued. The platforms that were moving began to crash violently into the walls, sometimes knocking their passengers off. Edrix shook his head.

"I don't think we're getting up that way," he said. I had to agree. I looked around, then I had it.

"The water's over eight feet now. We can use our cables!" I shouted to him over the roar of the water. Edrix looked hopeful for a moment, then his face fell.

"There's nothing up there to anchor them," he said. I looked around desperately. After the grenade, we'd been pushed over by another Hunter's alcove. The force-field generator was still smoldering. Edrix snapped his fingers.

"I've got it!" he exclaimed. He drew two of his knives. Then he inserted the blades into the smoldering hole in the wall. After a moment, he took them back out, glowing red hot.

"Quick!" he said. "Wrap your cable around one!" I had no idea what he was up to, but I didn't have any alternatives. I wrapped my cable end around one of the knife hilts, securing it with the small, tooth like clip. Edrix did the same, then he took a deep breath and put one knife in each hand, then held them by the tips of the blades. I gasped as his flesh came in contact with the hot metal, but he didn't even flinch. He threw the knives as hard as he could.

Our cable reels made soft *zzzzz!* sounds as the knives traveled upwards. Then we heard them hit the ground above us. I suddenly understood his plan. If we survived this, I was going to tell him how much of a genius he was. That is, *if* the knives were hot enough and *if* they held our weight. We didn't have time to wait, and I didn't look to see if there was anyone else left.

I pressed a button on my cable reel and pushed off the ground, making sure I still had my pack. In the chaos of our frantic swimming I'd forgotten that I had it. The reel carried me upwards. So far, the knives were doing what we'd hoped they'd do: That the hot blades would melt the metal above us and let the blades sink into the floor.

My cable pulled me all the way up the walls, stopping with my head and shoulders above the wall, my eyes level with the knife that had sunk hilt deep in the ground, which was not metal, but plastic. I grabbed the floor with my arms and pulled myself up. Edrix came up a minute later. I wanted to stop and catch my breath, but I couldn't. We had to keep moving. I detached my cable from the knife.

"It worked," I said. Edrix detached his cable and pulled the knives out of the ground.

"Come on." He sheathed the knives and I got to my feet. Then I realized that no one else was there. It was just us, with three more Hunters still coming up.

"They must already be in the door," Edrix said. We ran towards it now, a dark square in the wall. We raced through it to an empty room filled with square pillars placed evenly around the room. It was empty except for us. I turned around, but the door was gone. A screen appeared in its stead. It was Thanos, the image of the Client behind him.

"Well done, Hunters," he said. "The field was narrowed by six. Now, we will have our elimination." The video cut to the Hammer rising above the Anvil. I stood tensely, my fists clenched tightly by my sides. The Hammer came down and I screwed my eyes shut. There was the same *SNAP* of electricity as last time, but there was no sudden pain. We'd made it. I forced myself to open my eyes. Another Hunter was shown on the screen, this one with blue skin and black hair collapsed to the ground, wisps of smoke coming from his body.

"Hunter Terrick has been eliminated. There are nineteen contestants left," Thanos said, and the screen disappeared.

176

38

(Edrix)

In less than two hours, we'd gone from thirty-two Hunters to nineteen. It was awful.

Andresha and I huddled against two of the pillars, facing each other. I sat cross-legged, she hugged her knees to her chest. We were both exhausted, physically, mentally, and emotionally. I held out a hand.

"Let me see your pack. We should go through them while we can," I said.

She shrugged the backpack off her shoulders and handed it to me. I nodded in thanks and opened both packs. Each contained a canteen of water, and extra cable, five packages of food, a med-pac, and a blanket.

"Here." I handed her one of the blankets. "You can use that to towel off a little." I told her. She'd started to shiver.

"Thanks," she whispered. I dug through the packs some more, than sighed in triumph. Each pack also had a heating lantern. I got mine out and set it up, then activated the power. Soon, it was glowing with a warm, orange light. Andresha had taken off her poncho and laid it to dry.

"Is that wise?" She asked. "Someone could see it."

I shook my head. "Nobody around to see it. I checked the room. It's a dead end again, and there's no one else here."

Andresha nodded silently. I opened one of the food packages and handed it to her. She took it silently. It didn't have much. Just the white chalky sticks that were food in name alone. I handed her a canteen as well. She took a stick out of the package and took a bite. She chewed silently for a moment, then swallowed and said,

"It's not too bad, once you manage to chew it."

I laughed a little. She took another stick, then handed the bag to me.

"It'll make the food last longer," she explained. It was a smart move. I bit into a stick. It certainly wasn't Chef's food. It wasn't my mom's cooking either. The thought pained me. My bite of chalk became a powdery, gooey mush in my mouth and I had to choke it down. I quickly took a drink from my own canteen.

We didn't eat much. I rolled up the top of the bag and put it in my pack. Andresha took a long drink of water, then put her canteen down and wrapped the blanket around herself.

She sniffed and quickly wiped her eyes. Then she did it again, and then again. I got up and went over to her.

"What's wrong?" I asked.

She didn't speak at first, then she said,

"I just hate this whole thing!" She buried her face in her hands for a moment, then continued, "I'm tired of surviving a warzone, then having to sit and wait for that stupid Hammer to kill someone!"

I didn't know what to do for a moment. I put a hand on her shoulder. She wiped her eyes again.

"I'm sorry." I said.

She waved me off. "It's nothing."

She wrapped her blanket tightly around her and curled up on the floor.

"Andresha?" I asked.

"Yes?" She replied.

"How did you know what that grenade was called?"

She smiled a little. "I didn't. I made it up."

I chuckled to myself. I looked back at her and she was asleep.

* * *

I woke to Andresha shaking me. She'd slept for four hours, then she'd kept watch while I slept.

"How long was I asleep?" I asked her.

"Four hours, roughly. There's been a development." I sat up and ran my hands through my hair, instantly awake.

"What happened?"

178

She pointed across the room. "The wall opened up. I guess they want to test us again."

We quickly packed up our gear and stowed it away in the packs. Andresha had donned her poncho again, and we each shouldered a pack. I looked at her.

"Are you ready?" I asked. I was feeling better now that I had gotten some sleep.

Andresha nodded. "Let's get it over with."

I nodded and we walked through the doorway.

We were in a huge room, even bigger than the last. It was filled with tall walls. Not as tall as the other test, but taller than I could see over.

"A maze," Andresha whispered. I took a deep breath, then let it out slowly.

"Now what will they want?" I said. In response, another screen appeared before us. As usual, it was Thanos with the Client behind him.

"Good morning, Hunters. I hope you all got a chance to rest." Instead of his green robe, he was wearing one with a deep purple hue. The same chain hung around his neck.

"Today, your first trial."

Andresha groaned. "Please tell me he didn't say 'first.'"

I shushed her, but it was good to see her feisty attitude was back.

Thanos continued. "What you see before you, is a maze."

Andresha rolled her eyes. "I couldn't tell, could you?"

I grinned a little. I returned my attention to Thanos.

"If you reach the middle, you will find eight flares. You must take one of these flares and get out of the maze. Anyone who exits without a flare will be eliminated. That means those with flares are fair game. Your trial begins ... now."

The screen disappeared and Andresha and I raced towards the maze. As soon as we entered, the entrance was blocked. We stopped to look only for a moment. Then we continued. There was no time to worry about what we couldn't fix. As we ran through the maze, we quickly discovered that it was booby-trapped. Once, when we turned a corner, we were almost impaled by six-inch long spikes that shot out of the wall.

After an encounter with a trap door full of snakes, Andresha stopped me.

"I have an idea," she said. I wiped my forehead with my sleeve.

"I'm listening," I said. She motioned to the walls.

"Give me a boost. I can look over the walls and see what direction we need to go."

I considered it for a moment, then agreed. I made a step with my hands. Andresha stepped into it, and I lifted her into the air. She was silent. Then she jumped down.

"What did you see?" I asked her. She blew a piece of hair out of her face.

"Well, Fara's already reached the middle. She's headed back out. We need to take the next three lefts, and then a right and then straight. Then I'll need to look again."

We followed her directions, avoiding a barbed net that shot out of the wall. When we stopped, I lifted her again, then she would direct us through the next few turns. In ten minutes, we'd reached the middle. Three flares were gone. Andresha grabbed one.

"Now, where are we supposed to get out?" She asked. I examined the flare. Ours was orange. The other four were different colors; a green, a yellow, a purple, and a turquoise.

"I think we're looking for a door that has an orange light above it."

Our heads snapped up as we heard the sound of gunfire.

"Sounds good to me," Andresha said. She put the flare down and I lifted her again. A moment later she jumped down again. "I see it. This way."

We ran away from the sounds of gun fire. Thanos' voice echoed down to us. "Hunters Joelean and Eric Warrin have been eliminated."

We rounded a corner and almost got decapitated by a giant of a man wielding an axe. He was taller than I was, with tattoos all over his body. He roared. I guessed he wanted our flare. He swung at us again. I pulled knife from a sheath in my jacket and threw it underhand. The man stopped mid-strike and collapsed.

180

"C'mon!" I said to Andresha. We were able to get out of the maze when something wrapped around my ankle and pulled my feet out from underneath me. I fell forwards and hit the floor hard and felt something warm run down my face. I began to be pulled backwards by whatever had a grip on my ankle. I twisted myself so I could see my foot. My ankle had a cable wrapped around it. Somewhere to my right, I heard Andresha cry out, and then the sound of a gun.

I tried to find where she was, but I couldn't see. She couldn't be dead. She couldn't.

The cable released my leg and I slid to a stop. Before I could get to my feet, a gun barrel was pressed to my head. I looked up. The gun was held by an older woman. She wore a full face helmet and a black tank-top. One gun holster was strapped to her thigh over her dark green pants. She had a knife strapped to her black, steel toed boots and the standard utility belt. She held a blue flare in her left hand.

"I don't have a flare," I said.

"I don't need one," the woman replied, twirling hers in her fingers. "I *do* need to lower the competition."

"Jade!" a man's voice called. "I got the girl."

I looked in that direction. Andresha was struggling in the grip of a tall, heavily muscled man with dark skin and eyes. His head was shaved, and he had a long scar along his arm. He wore dark pants and a blue vest.

Jade. The man had called the woman Jade. If I hadn't had a gun to my head I would have snapped my fingers.

"Jade Hura?" I asked. The woman looked at me.

"Yes, that's my name," she said. Andresha grunted as she tried to break the man's grasp.

"Jade," she called. "My brother sent us, Seth Kanway!"

I blinked and the gun pressed to my head was gone. In the same instant, Jade's hand closed around my throat, making it impossible for me to breath. She pulled me towards her.

"What did she say?" She hissed. I coughed.

"Seth … Kanway," I managed to gasp. The woman looked at me, then at Andresha. Andresha had stopped fighting against the man's grip. Instead she looked Jade in the eyes.

"Let my friend go!" she demanded. Jade glanced between us again, then she released me and let me slump to the floor. I gasped for breath, then coughed.

Jade went over to the man. "Let her go," she said. The man obeyed and Jade pulled off her helmet. She had jet black hair that came down to her jaw and ice blue eyes that were almost white. Her pupils were diamond shaped instead of round. So she wasn't Rendarian, then. She had a streak of color in her hair that matched her eyes.

"Andresha?" She asked.

Andresha shot the man an annoyed glance than said, "Yes, it's me."

Jade laughed. "Look how tall you are! And your hair … you dyed it!" The two embraced.

Jade became serious. "We can talk later. Come on!"

Andresha helped me to my feet. "Are you all right?" She asked. I had a small cut on my forehead, but other than that, I was fine now that I could breathe again. I nodded. We ran to the doorway, followed by Jade and her teammate. We stopped outside.

"You can't come through," Andresha said. "You don't have the same color flare."

Jade grinned. "You'll see. Go on through."

We did as she said, then she hit the light above the door with her flare. The light flickered, then changed to match the color of her flare. She and her companion ran through the door, which vanished behind us.

It was a room like before, with square columns throughout the room. I leaned against one, closing my eyes for a moment and sliding down to the floor. Jade held Andresha at arm's length.

"You're all grown up now," she said.

Andresha grinned. "Thanks to you."

I glanced between the two of them. "And you know each other how?"

Andresha turned to me. "Jade helped Seth and me when we were in a tight spot. We've been friends ever since."

Jade nodded. "That is correct." She motioned to the tall man. "This is my teammate, Garrick."

Garrick nodded, but said nothing. We all turned solemn as a screen appeared in front of us again.

"Another fine job, Hunters," Thanos said. "The field has been narrowed by four. Hunters Joelean and Eric Harrick, Trobar Ingvus, Hannah Rey, and Vulvim Liss have been eliminated. And now for our decision."

The screen showed the Hammer go up. We all held our breath. It came down. This time, two were victims of the hammer. Fenz Tip and Lyta Garrison fell and did not get back up.

There were now only twelve of us left, but for the first time since we entered, I began to feel just the tiniest bit of hope.

39

(Andresha)

The four of us sat around the heating lantern from Edrix's pack. Edrix was sketching quietly and Garrick was cleaning his weapons. That left Jade and I room to talk. I forced a bite of ration stick down my throat and washed it down with a sip of water. I replaced my canteen in my pack.

"So," Jade said, "What have you been up to since you got off Ten?"

I knew she wasn't talking about when we came here. I brushed hair out of my face.

"We went with Jess," I said. "We found this ... I'm not sure how to describe it. I'm in the resistance now."

Jade chewed a piece of ration. "Resistance, huh? Is that why you dyed your hair?"

I smiled. "Yes. And it reminded me of you," I said. Jade smiled a little. She looked over at Edrix, and I followed her gaze. He'd fallen asleep, his pencil on the floor.

"What's his story?" Jade asked.

I raised an eyebrow. "You mean you don't know?"

She shook her head. This surprised me. I assumed Edrix would be all over the place, with the bounty he had on his head.

I took a deep breath. "He was a REGS Higher One. Fastest and youngest one to graduate the Program. He tried to stop them from killing ... a lot of people." I hesitated, then continued.

"They were going to sentence him to the Surface for it. He escaped and found the resistance. REGS put out an apprehension order and a bounty even higher than mine. Seventy-thousand credits alive."

Jade whistled softly. "That's almost as much as the winner of this thing gets," she stopped.

"Speaking of which, what brings you here in the first place?"

I explained the situation to her. About the Core and REGS closing in on us. Jade listened quietly. When I'd finished we sat in silence for a moment. I tugged my braid and Jade smiled. "You

184

still do that." She didn't say anything else but I heard the unspoken comment. *Just like your mom.*

I changed the subject. "How did you get away with that thing back there with the door?"

Jade shrugged. "I didn't *get away* with anything. You could have gone out any door you wanted. The Anvil just wanted to trap you into thinking that you couldn't." She smiled wryly. "Besides, Hunters make their own rules."

I stared into the glow of the lantern. If only it was that easy. Only two of us could come out of here, if we started as a team we ended as a team. That's what Thanos had said, but Jade's statement gave me some new hope.

Jade nodded to Edrix. "So you know about him. Does he know about you?"

I shook my head. "No. We just started to be friends and …" I stopped.

Jade gave me a sympathetic look. "Just say it."

I looked down at my hands. "I'm afraid of what he'll think of me. I … I'm the very thing that everyone I work with hates. I'm afraid that *they'll* all hate me."

Jade didn't say anything at first, then her head snapped up. "Wait a second. Solan … he isn't related to *that* Solan, is he?" she said to herself.

I looked at her, confused. "What are you talking about?" I asked her.

She shook her head. "Never mind. It's not important." She tossed the rest of her ration aside.

"Get some sleep. Garrick and I will keep watch."

I wasn't tired but I knew it was pointless to try and argue. I folded my blanket into a pillow and curled up by the fire. I stared at the wall for a while, telling myself to sleep. I listened as Jade and Garrick talked quietly. Jade had been by herself when we'd first met. She hadn't said anything about Garrick to me. I was just glad she had a friend.

"Andresha?"

I looked over at Edrix. His eyes were open, but he didn't move.

"What is it?" I asked him. He blinked once.

"You trust them, right?"

I nodded. "With my life."

He nodded ever so slightly. "Just checking." He closed his eyes again.

"Edrix?" I whispered. His eyes opened again. I was still amazed at how green they were.

"You can call me Dresha. It's easier."

He looked a little stunned for a moment, then he just said, "Thanks."

He closed his eyes again.

I didn't really sleep, I just dozed for a while, then Edrix and I switched with Jade and Garrick. We'd been on watch for an hour when the next doorway appeared. I went over to Jade and shook her shoulder.

"Jade, wake up!" I said. She was instantly awake.

"What is it?" She asked. I motioned to the door.

"It's time for the next round."

40

(Edrix)

We walked through the door to a large balcony that overlooked something that looked like an arena. The four of us walked over to the railing and looked down. The only other person in the room was Fara Emrick. She stood in the arena below us. She looked up as we approached her face emotionless. Thanos' voice came to us through the speakers.

"Greetings, Hunters. I think it's time for something different, don't you?"

The screen appeared up on the wall across from me. I was *really* getting tired of Thanos popping up everywhere.

He continued, "So far, Fara Emrick has been first in every trial, with your team coming very close, Edrix Solan. So, I propose a duel, to change things up a bit."

He continued. "Don't look so shocked. Other contestants are going through something similar. Now," he stopped dramatically, then he said, "Fara Emrick, which will you fight? Edrix Solan, or Andresha Kath?"

I could hear my heart beating in my ears. Fara's gaze swept over both of us.

"Solan," she said, "I'll fight Edrix Solan."

I felt my throat tighten as a staircase appeared in front of me. I'd seen Fara during the other trials. There was a reason she was always first: She was terrifyingly skilled and didn't think twice about killing to get what she wanted. I looked over at Andresha. She shook her head, her eyes wide.

"You can't, Edrix," she said. "She'll kill you."

Jade folded her arms. "I have to agree. Fara is all over the Hunter world. She's known for her ruthless tactics and incredible combat ability." She shook her head. "You won't live through it."

Garrick hadn't said a word to me since we'd met, but now he shook his head. I knew they were right. Andresha was extremely

187

observant and was excellent at spotting dangerous adversaries. Jade and Garrick were the veterans here. They knew this girl and what she was capable of. Thanos now held up a finger.

"You could listen to them, Edrix, but if you refuse, there will be a price to pay." The screen split in half and cut to the Hammer rising above us.

"If you refuse, your team will be eliminated, and Fara will pick an opponent from the remaining two Hunters."

So my options were to die at Fara's hands, or die from the hammer and take Andresha with me, while leaving Jade or Garrick to face Fara instead of me. I couldn't do that. I wouldn't make them die just to save myself. Andresha shook her head.

"No, don't."

I spread my hands, palms upward. "What else am I supposed to do? Refuse and let you die too? I can't do that, Andresha, not when we've gotten this far."

Andresha set her jaw and lifted her chin. "I'd rather die than have you go down there for their amusement."

I looked at Jade and she nodded, just the tiniest bit. I pursed my lips and started down the steps.

"No!" Andresha yelled and lunged after me, but Jade held her back. I forced myself not to look back as I marched down to the arena floor.

"A wise choice, I should think," Thanos said.

I looked up at the screen, my jaw set. I was angry. I didn't like being forced into things.

"One condition," I said. Thanos spread his arms.

"Name it."

I thought before I spoke. I had to word this carefully, so that they couldn't turn this around. I lifted my chin.

"If I lose, you let Andresha join Jade Hura's team and continue the tournament," I said.

Thanos stroked his beard in thought. "Hmm, does Jade Hura agree to this?" He asked.

I looked back at Jade, who was still holding on to Andresha's arm. She nodded grimly.

188

"Yes, I agree."

Thanos clapped his hands. "Splendid! Now, shall we get to the fighting? I think it's been long enough."

Fara and I turned to face each other. We stood about six paces apart.

"Oh!" Thanos exclaimed, "One more thing. No guns. You may begin … now!"

My heart hammered behind my ribs. I drew one of the knives on my wrists and held it in my right hand. Fara laughed.

"So, that's how it's going to go." She drew her own knife. We both crouched in a stance and slowly circled each other. Fara's eyes met mine steadily. My heart beat thrice and she lunged at me, her knife blurring in a series of strikes.

I ducked and dodged most of them, only deflecting two on my knife. One slash caught my jaw and felt hot blood run down my neck.

Fara growled and rolled behind me. Before I could turn to face her, she was on her feet. She grabbed my head with one arm and pulled it down towards my shoulders while swinging her knife around towards my neck. I dropped my knife and put my hands up to catch her wrist. I stopped the knife centimeters from my neck. She pushed down, and I struggled to keep the knife away from my skin. She was strong, incredibly strong.

The knife came closer to my neck. I could feel the blade on my skin. I pushed back, but the knife didn't move. I let my legs buckle underneath me and fell to the ground, Fara's grip breaking. I rolled clear, picking up my knife as I did so.

Fara stepped back and our circling continued. She wasn't even breathing hard. I lunged forward and locked our knives together. I quickly drew the knife on my thigh and I went for her neck, but she grabbed my arm and stopped my knife in its arc, then she twisted my wrist. I felt a sharp pain in my arm and heard something snap. I yelled and Fara kicked me in the ribs, sending me flying backwards … without my glove.

I hit the ground on my back, and it hurt to breath. I hugged my arm close to my chest, as fear rose in my throat. My glove was gone.

Fara marched over to me and kicked me in the side. I yelled again, then I rolled away and came up on my feet.

Then flames erupted on my arm.

Fara stopped, her fist poised for a blow. She cocked her head to the side.

"Well, well, well, what have we here?" She said, a half smile playing on her lips. She opened her fist and put her hand towards me. At first, nothing happened, then all the fire on my arm started to go towards her open hand. It was the oddest sensation. My entire arm tingled.

As I watched, all the fire left my arm and gathered in front of her hand. The flames reflected in her eyes, giving her an insane expression.

"You hide it," she whispered moving her hand around the fireball. Then she scowled.

"You're *ashamed* of it!" she hissed, then she chuckled quietly. "I don't blame you."

Then she thrust her hand towards the ground, and the fireball smashed into the floor, where it extinguished. I struggled to swallow past the lump of fear in my throat. Fara brought her hands up level with her head, fire surrounding her hands.

"Let me give you a lesson, Agent Solan." She growled. She thrust her hands towards me. Ropes of fire snaked from her hands across the room. They slammed into me and threw me against the wall. My head hit the wall hard, and my ears rang, the fire holding me against the wall. Fara raised her knife, holding it by the blade in preparation to throw it.

This is it, I thought, *I'm going to die*. And that thought made me annoyed and angry. Angry that I'd come so far only to die here. At least Andresha could keep going and finish the mission.

Fara brought her arm back. I forced myself to keep my eyes open, determined not to flinch, when a voice rang over the arena.

"STOP!"

Fara froze. It was not Thanos who had spoken. This voice was deeper, colder, like knife rasping on stone. Fara stopped and lowered her arm. We both looked towards the screen on the wall.

"I have seen enough." The Client said. "We will continue to the next trial."

Fara sheathed her knife and left the arena. I thought I was seeing things because it looked like she walked right through the wall.

The fire that had been holding me to the wall disappeared and I slumped to the floor with a groan. Something had happened when she'd taken the fire from my arm. I felt dizzy and my ribs hurt where she'd kicked me.

Andresha was at the railing now. The staircase had disappeared, but that didn't stop her. She wrapped her cable around the rail and leapt over the side. Jade and Garrick followed suit. When her feet hit the floor, Andresha didn't bother to release the top and reel it in. She simply ejected the cable from her belt. She ran over to me and pulled me up, then grasped my shoulders and shook me.

"Don't you *ever*, emphasis, do that to me, *again!*" She shouted. "Do you hear me?"

Then she pulled me into an embrace, her tears wet on my neck.

"I was so scared!" She sobbed.

I wrapped my gloved hand around her. "I'm fine." I assured her, my voice a bit raspy.

She pulled back. "No, you're not. You're bleeding!" She started to open her pack, but I stopped her.

"I need my glove first." I said. "Do you see it?" Flames were starting to sputter along my arm again. Andresha wiped her eyes and nodded. "I'll look." She got up and moved over to where Fara had been standing.

"Here!" She shouted triumphantly, then her face fell as she turned towards me. She held my glove in her hand, but the silver band was gone, and it was torn in half.

41

(Andresha)

I stared in horror at the ripped glove in my hand. Edrix's face mirrored my expression. What would we do without it? The flames on Edrix's arms were already multiplying and getting bigger and hotter. Jade stood behind me.

"What's wrong with him?" She asked. I waved her off.

"I can't explain right now," I said.

I forced myself to stay calm. I needed to think through this, and panicking wouldn't help with that. I didn't know what the band was supposed to do, but maybe I could just stitch the glove together quickly and it would still work, but I was severely lacking in the thread and needle department. Maybe there was one in the med-pac?

I suddenly remembered Nelvin's hair pins and what he'd said. *If you need something, just ask for it.* I pulled a pin out of my hair. I was either crazy, desperate, or both, but I held that hair pin in front of my face and I told it, "I need a left-hand fire glove for Edrix."

Nothing happened. Jade and Garrick were staring at me. I really was crazy.

Then, a glow of light ran up the pin. Before my eyes it expanded and turned soft like ... fabric! I blinked and I was holding a roll of black fabric. I let go of one end, and it unrolled into a brand new, black glove, complete with silver band.

I stared at it in astonishment. "It worked," I said to myself.

"Great, can you hand it to me?" Edrix asked, his tone urgent. Those ears of his again.

"Right!" I shouted and hurried over. I held the glove out to Edrix and he snatched it and pulled it on, smothering the flames.

"How did you do that?" He asked.

I shook my head. "I have no idea," I said.

"Well, thank you, no matter how you did it," he said.

I smiled a little, then took my scanner out of my pocket. I scanned the wrist Fara had broken. It was a clean break, thankfully. I put my scanner away and gently took his wrist in my hands. Edrix grimaced as I touched it.

"I'm sorry," I said. He shrugged.

I pursed my lips. "I'm going to have to set it," I told him.

He took a deep breath and set his jaw. "Let's get it over with," he said through gritted teeth. I bit my lip, then quickly set the bone. Edrix yelled out and flinched.

"All done," I said.

Edrix nodded. "Thanks." He muttered. I was wondering what to use as a splint when I felt his glove's fabric stiffen around the break, creating a splint.

"Nelvin thought of everything," I said to myself.

Edrix nodded in agreement. "He's good at that," he said. I opened my pack and got out the med-pack. I remembered that I'd left Edrix's bag on the balcony. Too late now.

First, I gave him a shot of painkillers for his arm, then I dug out some gauze and started to press it to the cut on his jaw, but I stopped. I couldn't suppress a gasp of surprise.

Edrix knit his eyebrows together. "What is it?" He asked.

I wasn't entirely sure. "Your … your blood …" My voice died away.

I'm not sure how to describe it. It was like the cut on his jaw was glowing, along with the blood that had run down his neck. I got my scanner again and ran it over the wound, trying to make sense of it.

I took a deep breath and tried again.

"Edrix, your blood is on *fire*," I said quietly. "Look." I handed him the scanner.

He stared at the screen for a moment, then his hand reached up to the cut on his jaw. He brought his hand in front of his face and stared at the blood on his fingertips. He was silent for a full minute.

"Maybe that's why I'm fireproof," he whispered. I sat back on my haunches.

"I just hope it doesn't burn the gauze," I said. I cautiously pressed it to the cut and counted to five. The gauze quickly turned red, but it did not burst into flames. I let out a breath I didn't know I was holding.

193

"Hold that there," I instructed him. He put his hand on the pad.

I found a sterilizing pad and an adhesive bandage in the pack. No cauterizer, but we'd make do. I ripped the packaging off the pad and cleaned the cut, then put the bandage over it.

Again, I counted to five. The bandage didn't spontaneously combust. So far so good.

I opened my scanner again. It wouldn't be nearly as detailed as a medical scanner, but it would show if there was anything serious.

"Your ribs look fine," I told Edrix.

He smiled wryly. "They don't feel fine."

"Well, they're not broken, let's put it that way," I said.

Jade put a hand on my shoulder and I turned to face her. She motioned for me to move off a ways.

"Be right back. Try to clean your neck up a bit," I said to Edrix, handing him another piece of gauze.

He nodded and I got up and followed Jade over to the corner of the room.

"What is he?" She asked, nodding to Edrix.

I shrugged. "I don't know, Jade. His arms light on fire without the gloves, and he's fire proof." I shook my head. "If I knew more ... I don't know."

Silence stretched between us for a moment. I looked down and scuffed my boot against the ground. "If you're not comfortable with him, I understand. We can make it."

Jade didn't say anything, she just went over to Garrick and the two of them went to one side to talk.

I went back to Edrix and helped him to his feet.

"I'm still mad at you," I said.

He held up his hands in surrender. "And I would be too, if I was in your place."

I brushed hair out of my face. Satisfied that he was alright, my mind went back to when the Client had stopped the duel, when he'd spoken.

I knew that voice.

Jade stopped me from thinking about it further as she approached me. "We'll stay," she said.

I breathed an internal sigh of relief. After witnessing Fara's combat ability, I knew that we didn't have a chance on our own.

"I'm sorry I didn't tell you earlier," I said.

She waved me off. "No matter. I understand why you wanted to keep it quiet."

Edrix ran a hand through his hair. "She can summon fire, like I can," he said.

I assumed he was referring to Fara. I didn't know what to say, but Jade did. "I've heard rumors that she could, but ..." She stopped and turned to Edrix. "Why did she call you 'Agent Solan'?"

I shrugged. "He used to be in REGS," I said, but Edrix shook his head.

"No, no one outside of REGS would call me 'Agent'. I was a Higher One."

He turned to me. "She knows who we are."

The words hit me like a bucket of ice water.

"If she knows who we work for ..." I started, but Jade held up her hands.

"That doesn't matter right now. We need to keep moving."

She was right. I zipped up my pack and put it on my shoulders. "I forgot yours," I said to Edrix.

He shrugged. "Whatever." He retrieved his knives from the ground and replaced them in their sheaths.

Jade was examining the wall, looking for a doorway. "Honestly, I'm surprised she's here," she said.

"Surprised who's here?" I asked.

Jade continued to examine the wall. "Fara. Her invitation was revoked four weeks ago after her tech bailed out on her." She knocked on the wall, then opened her own scanner and ran it up and down the wall.

"I was happy for her, the tech, I mean. She seemed nice enough. She didn't fit in this business."

She shook her head and looked at Garrick. "Tasha did always have a knack for getting into places she didn't fit."

I stopped walking, a chill running down my spine.

"What did you say?" I asked.

Jade turned to me. "Tasha. That was her name." She came over to me.

"Are you all right?" She asked. "You look pale."

I was about to reply when I heard a grinding sound from behind us. I turned towards the sound.

The floor was shredding behind us.

"Run!" I shouted. My friends needed no second urging. We ran across the room just ahead of the splintering floor.

"Where are we going?" Edrix yelled. "There's no door!"

He was right. I looked up at the balcony.

"Maybe we could—"

As if it had read my thoughts, there was a loud groaning sound, then a deafening *CRACK*!

The balcony tore off the wall and came crashing to the floor. I covered my head and cried out in alarm. My foot caught on something and I started to trip, then Edrix had me by the arm, keeping me up.

"Go for the wall!" he shouted. The wall?

"Are you crazy?" I screamed back. The gaping chasm was gaining on us.

"Trust me!" Edrix called back, and we ran head-long into the wall.

42

Jess sat silently in Chief's office and listened to Nelvin's report. Tasha and Patrisha were with him.

"We have the virus seventy-five percent completed," he finished.

Chief nodded absently. "Good, good."

He sighed. "You're dismissed."

The three of them didn't move. Chief raised an eyebrow, an expression he shared with his younger sister.

"Is there something else?" He asked.

Tasha nodded. "I was thinking, we should have an extraction team ready for Solan and Kanway, just in case," she said.

Chief nodded. "I'm ahead of you on that one. I have Jim and Short on standby. If Edrix or Andresha activates their emergency signal, they'll go immediately."

"You have a ship?" Tasha asked.

"We got one this morning. REGS was going to scrap it, but Nelvin assures me that it will be in flying condition by tomorrow," Chief replied.

Nelvin nodded enthusiastically, grinning broadly.

Patrisha spoke up now. "Speaking of Edrix, I've been doing some more research."

Jess looked up. "What have you found?" She asked.

Patrisha pursed her lips and wrung her hands. "Well, I took some blood samples before he left, and I've been studying them." She paced the room once, thinking, then she said, "It's the strangest thing, but I *think* I know why he's fire proof."

Jess straightened in her chair. "What is it?"

Patrisha put a pad on Chief's desk. He picked it up and Jess peered over his shoulder.

Patrisha continued to explain. "I think … I think it's because … he has fire *inside* of him."

Chief looked up. "What do you mean?"

Patrisha motioned to the pad. "See for yourself. His blood cells, plasma, internal organs, bones … They're all on fire."

Chief put the pad down on the desk. "How is that possible? He shouldn't be alive."

Patrisha nodded. "Exactly what I thought, so there has to be *something* that's keeping the fire from burning the tissue, so I went deeper."

She tapped the data-pad and an elemental table came up.

"I found Nexus in his DNA make-up. I'm not sure, but I *think* it might have something to do with his being invulnerable to fire."

Tasha looked like she'd seen a ghost. Nelvin was staring at the wall, something he did when he was thinking.

Chief glanced at Jess, then said, "What are you saying?"

"I'm saying that whatever happened to Edrix did not happen naturally," Patricia answered.

Jess fought to stay calm. She had been right all along.

Nelvin tapped his chin. "Why would someone want to make a fire-resistant person?" He wondered aloud. Before anyone could answer him, the buzzer outside the door sounded.

Chief looked up. "Come in."

Jinx burst into the room.

"What is it, Agent?" Chief asked. Jinx nodded to Jess, then spoke to Chief. "It's Andresha, Chief," he said. "She's activated her signal."

43

(Edrix)

If I ever got to meet the creator of this "Anvil," I was either going to congratulate their genius, or punch them.

I hadn't decided which.

The wall had indeed been a doorway, as I had suspected. When the floor had begun to shred behind us, I had remembered that there hadn't been a visible doorway when Fara left the Arena. She'd simply disappeared. So I had taken a chance and tried to follow her. We had gone right through the wall, directly into the next trial.

Now, since I'd fought Fara, we'd been through two more trials. One was to test our code breaking skills. We were locked in a room and given three minutes to unlock the door, then we had to fight our way through another maze of sorts, but we often had rewire or disconnect something to continue forward. The other had been a room full of armed bombs. We had soon discovered that most of them were fake, and we had to find the real bombs and disarm them before five minutes were up.

Five Hunters had been eliminated in duals while Fara and I had been fighting. Three more were eliminated in the code-breaker, and five after the bomb-room. The Hammer had fallen after both. There were now only ten Hunters left.

Now we came to small room, just big enough for the four of us to fit. There was a closed door on the other side of the room, with the Rendarian rune for *I*.

We went towards it, but nothing happened. After a quick examination, we discovered that there was no way to open it ourselves.

"I guess we have to wait," Andresha said. But as she walked away with Jade and Garrick, the door opened. I was the only one standing in front of it.

Andresha stopped and turned around. "Never mind," she said.

They came towards me, but the door closed again. I studied the rune, *I*, but it was also commonly used as a symbol for *alone* or *lost*.

199

Alone …

I held up a hand. "Wait a minute. The three of you step back again," I said. They did as I asked, and the door opened again.

I turned to look at them. "I think we have to go through alone," I said.

Andresha folded her arms. "We are not splitting up again," she said.

I shrugged. "I don't think we have a choice, Dresha," I said. "The door only opens if one of us is near it. When everyone else comes, it closes."

"It makes sense," Jade said. "This way, they can assess how well each Hunter does individually, though I don't think there are many teams left."

Andresha shook her head. "I'm not letting you go alone, not after what happened last time."

And here we had a stalemate, because I knew Andresha wasn't going to change her mind, but if we wanted to win this thing, then going alone was the only option.

It was Garrick who solved the problem.

"I will go first," he said, the first words he'd spoken since we'd met him. He had a surprisingly deep voice.

Jade looked at him. "You're sure?" she asked and he nodded.

Jade waved towards the door. "After you then. If you can, signal us when you get through."

Garrick nodded, then went through the door. It shut ominously behind him.

I spent the next hour pacing the room, fiddling with the bands on my gloves.

"He should be through by now," I said apprehensively.

Jade looked up from where she sat, her gun in her hand. "Be patient. We don't know what the trial is. This could be normal."

I didn't stop pacing. "I hope you're right," I said.

Five minutes later, Jade's communicator finally beeped.

"He made it," she said.

I stopped my worried pacing.

Jade stood up and holstered her gun. "I'll go next."

Andresha and I both knew it would be pointless to argue. Jade put on her helmet, then walked through the door, which once again shut tightly after her.

I put my head back against the wall, and I think I actually went to sleep. I woke up to Andresha's scanner beeping. She motioned to the door.

"She made it through," she said.

Neither of us moved. We simply stared at each other.

Finally, I said. "I guess I'll go next."

"No!" Andresha exclaimed. "I'm not going through that again!"

I didn't answer right away. I stared at the floor, hands on my hips. I'd lost my jacket in the last trial, and I could feel the chill in the room.

"Think of it this way," I said finally. "You're going to be right behind me. No one's holding you back this time."

Andresha pursed her lips and looked at her boots. Then she looked up.

"Please be careful," she whispered.

I mustered a confident grin. "I will."

I turned to the door and took a deep breath. It slid open without a sound, hiding the rune from view, but it was burned into my mind.

That was the rune on Fara's necklace, I realized, then I walked through the doorway.

The room on the other side was pitch black. If I waved my hand in front of my face, I couldn't see it. I looked around, but the room was completely silent. Then a spotlight turned on above me. It didn't illuminate anything else, but it would keep my eyes from adjusting to the intense darkness.

I walked forward slowly, sliding my feet across the floor to avoid tripping on anything I couldn't see. I put one hand forward at what I judged was head height, in hopes of feeling anything low before I smacked my head against it.

The floor sounded and felt like metal, and there was a distinctly metallic scent in the air. There was low *boom, boom*, like a heartbeat, and what sounded like breathing. The air moved around me, like there was a breeze, but that was impossible, since I was inside. A fan maybe? Perhaps that was what was making the breathing sound.

Then the voices started. I couldn't understand them at first; they were just a jumble of sounds that blended together. I stopped walking and concentrated, hoping I could single them out. I began to pick them out one by one. My mother, Zaren, Andresha, Jai, Jess. I couldn't pick out individual words, but I could tell that they were all in trouble.

"Where are you?" I called back, but they wouldn't answer.

My ears saved me. I heard the dart whistle through the air and I reared back as it flew past my nose, missing it by a hair's breadth.

I spun around and drew my gun, holding it ready. There was someone—or *something*—else in this room. I closed my eyes. I couldn't see anything anyways. Then, I held my breath and just listened.

There! I could hear someone breathing to my left, about four feet away. I opened my eyes and spun towards them. A gun cocked, but I fired mine first. Glowing holo-cubes scattered across the floor by my feet, then disappeared. Holograms, just like the ones I practiced with.

I held my breath again. There was another hologram behind me now, but it was much closer than the first. I spun around and grabbed it by the arm. I pulled it forward and off balance, then punched it in what would have been its jaw, had it had an actual face. The hologram melted into blocks and disappeared.

Then they were all around me. I pulled out my knives and cut them down as they struck towards me. I had a feeling that these, unlike those back at Red Star, would do more than just shock me. I had to keep moving forwards. I fought through the sea of holograms, cutting down those in my way.

A small square of light appeared in front of me. I was getting close. I was running now, just keeping the holograms off me. Now, instead of calling for help, the voices were mocking me, telling me I was a traitor, Jai's voice in particular. I tried to cover my ears, but then the holograms would grab me, and I was forced to fight them off. The voices got so loud, I couldn't hear any of them individually. It just became a roar of noise in my ears, all of them saying the same thing. I'd betrayed my people, my friends, my planet, and my family. I was disgrace to my father's memory. The holograms grabbed my clothes and my arms, anything, trying to stop me, and they were no longer holograms. They were the people from Eight, all around me telling me that I'd killed them. I screamed and fell ...

Then I was out of the room. The voices were gone. I felt a strong arm catch me before I hit the floor. I thrashed, breaking its hold and scrambling away from it, striking with my knife.

Jade caught my arm by my wrist and held it there, making eye contact with me.

"Calm down," she said. "You're out."

Wait, Jade was here? Slowly, the fog of fear in my mind dissipated and I realized where I was.

I looked behind me, but there was a solid wall where I'd come from.

I put my back to the wall and slid down to the floor, dropping my knives and putting my head in my hands. I was soaked in sweat and shaking.

"Did you signal Andresha?" Jade asked. I'd completely forgotten. I fumbled with my scanner and sent a signal, then dropped it. I was exhausted, both physically and emotionally. The voices still rang in my head.

"That was awful," I said, mostly to myself. Jade handed me a canteen of water. I took a drink, then gave it back to her. She looked as tired as I did. And worried.

"Let me guess," she said, "everyone you know saying things you don't want to hear?"

"More like things I'm afraid are true," I muttered, then I looked at her. "How do you know?"

She tightened her mouth in a grim line. "Because that's what I heard." She looked at the wall where I'd come through. "I'm worried about Andresha."

"Why?" I asked.

And that's when we heard her scream.

44

(Andresha)

My scanner beeped. Edrix had made it. I breathed a sigh of relief as I folded it up and put it away.

Now it was my turn.

I took a deep breath and got to my feet. I didn't know how long it had been since Edrix had left, but it had seemed like forever. I'd lost my pack in the last trial, so I only had my canteen and the spare cable. I'd lost my poncho as well, thanks to a fire-breathing plant with *no* perception of personal space … long story.

"Let's just get this over with," I said to myself. I steeled my nerves and walked into the foreboding doorway. How bad could it be?

Very, very, *very*, emphasis, bad.

The door slid shut behind me, leaving me in total darkness. I couldn't see anything. I reached my hand up and started in surprise when it touched my face. The darkness seemed to compress around me, making it hard to breathe. I forced myself to take a deep breath in spite of the feeling of panic rising in my chest. *It's all in your head*, I thought, *you're fine.*

A bright, white spotlight beamed down on me, but nothing else. I could hear my heart hammering in my ears. I was starting to hyperventilate.

"Stay calm, stay calm, stay calm," I muttered to myself as I tugged my braid.

"Andresha."

I gasped as the name hit my ears like cold water. That voice … it couldn't be him. It *couldn't*.

Then I heard her voice, my mom's voice. Then Seth's and Jade's. Lar's scream as … as …

My hands started to shake. They were all there. I held my head in my hands, trying to shut them out. Jess, Nelvin, Short, Jim, they all started screaming, begging me to help them, but then *his* voice would come back, berating me. It was all my fault.

204

I collapsed onto the floor, clamping my hands over my ears. It wasn't real, it wasn't real …

Then the holograms grabbed me, and I screamed in alarm. I managed to focus enough to pull out my gun. I fired randomly, driving the holograms back, but then I had to stop because it hurt them … the voices, I was hurting them.

Somewhere in the back of my mind, I knew this wasn't possible, but that part of my brain was buried by the horror of everything else. Especially with *him* there. I could hear the disappointment in his voice, the sharp bark of anger that followed. I dropped my gun and ran, not caring where I was going. Tears streamed down my face and I struggled to keep my legs moving. I couldn't breathe, I couldn't see. I fell. I got back up, then I fell again.

A hologram grabbed me by the ankle. I screamed and kicked it off. I couldn't get my feet underneath me, so I crawled, the voices pressing in on me like a noose around my neck. They got louder and closer, and I couldn't do it anymore. I stopped and curled up in a ball, my arms over my head, trying to shut them out. The holograms swarmed me, but I didn't see them as such. I saw Lars with the bloody cut above his eye, his lips curled in a sneer, my mother, Jim, Short, my teachers, my guards, Seth, Jade. I couldn't do it. Right there on the floor, I gave up.

The rune on the door was right. I was going to die in here, alone.

Then, the holograms disappeared. The voices were still there, filling my thoughts, but the holograms were gone. Someone grabbed me and pulled me to my feet.

"Keep moving," she said. "You're almost there!"

I shook my head, my legs buckling. "I can't!"

She held me up. "Yes you can! Remember the song!"

The song that my mother had sung me to sleep with, that almost every mother on Rendaria sung their children to sleep with. The one that had made me feel safe.

I began to hum it to myself, the melody was simple and sweet, but the voices got louder. I shook my head.

"I can't do it!" I shouted.

She held me steady. "Yes you can, Andresha. You have to tell yourself that, or you won't!"

I took a deep breath and started to hum again. This time, she hummed with me. I took one step forward, then another.

"That's it," she said softly.

I continued to hum. The voices got louder again, and I faltered.

"Keep going." She whispered, and I did. Her humming softly faded, until I was humming on my own, mostly in my head. I turned back to thank my rescuer, but she was gone. I only caught a glimpse of her white hair.

I made my way forward. Humming the song had given me a breath of air, but now all of my fear was back. I closed my eyes and pushed forward, running as fast as I could. Everything seemed to fold in on me and the spotlight went out.

Then there was light all around me. I was screaming and scrambling backwards away from the wall. There were no voices, no holograms ... I had to be dead.

Then Edrix put his arms around me.

"You're out, you're out," he whispered.

I was trembling as I opened my eyes, afraid of what I'd see.

It took a moment for my eyes to adjust to the dim lights of the room, but then I made out Jade and Garrick standing behind Edrix. They weren't holograms. I threw my arms around Edrix's neck and began to sob. Edrix just held me while I cried. Jade put a hand on my shoulder.

"I'm so sorry," she said. I couldn't answer. I buried my face in my hands. All the walls I'd built up over the years to protect myself were gone in an instant as the voices still echoed in my head. I felt raw and vulnerable, exposed.

I started to hyperventilate again, my head beginning to spin.

Edrix brushed my hair out of my face, his arms still wrapped around me.

"Take a deep breath, Dresha," he said softly. "It's all right."

Tears still pouring down my face, I did as he said, taking a deep breath and beginning to breathe normally. My head stopped feeling like it was about to float off my shoulders. I finally stopped trembling, and my heartbeat more-or-less returned to normal.

"Are you feeling better?" Edrix asked softly. I tried for a confident smile and prepared to tell him that I was fine, thank you, but the smile never made it to my lips. Instead of a confident reply, another sob came out of my mouth.

Edrix hugged me again. I buried my face in his shoulder, my arms around his neck. A month ago, I didn't want anything to do with him. Now, I don't know what I would have done without him.

45

(Edrix)

We didn't have our next trial for twelve hours, which was a smart move for Thanos. I had a knife with his name on it.

As was to be expected, a screen had appeared after the last trial. Thanos had congratulated those of us who had lived, and told us that three Hunters had been eliminated. The Hammer had struck the anvil, and one more Hunter had been eliminated.

Only six of us remained, Fara among them.

Andresha had calmed down a few hours ago, but she was quiet and reserved. We'd lost all of our supplies over the last four trials, so we all just tried to catch up on some much needed sleep, but no one really wanted that.

I was on watch now, taking the opportunity to sharpen my knives. They were already wickedly sharp, but I didn't know when I'd get another opportunity to do it again. Plus, there was something reassuring about the *zzzing!* sound the sharpener made on the blade. It also gave me something to do with my hands.

I was finishing one up when Andresha came over to me.

"Hey," I said. She didn't say anything.

She sat down next to me. "Sorry for breaking down like that," she said.

I put my knife away and drew the next one. "You don't have anything to be sorry for. I was a mess when I came out of there, even Jade and Garrick looked shaken."

She shrugged. "It makes me feel better though."

We sat silently for a few minutes with only the sound of the sharpener on my blade between us. I couldn't think of anything to say.

Andresha wiped her eyes again. "Thank you," she whispered.

She didn't need to explain for what. I looked at her for a moment, then back at my knife.

"You're welcome."

We sat in silence for the next hour, then Jade and Garrick woke up.

Jade brushed hair out of her face. "I think they're ready for us," she said, pointing across the room. There was another doorway now.

I looked at Andresha. "Are you ready?" I asked her. She bit her lip, then nodded.

"Yes," she said softly.

We all got to our feet. Jade put on her helmet and Garrick picked up his rifle. Andresha and I didn't have anything but what we had on our belts and in our pockets. The only thing we'd managed to save from Andresha's pack was the med-pack, which I now had on my belt. Andresha had lost her gun in the last trial, so I unholstered mine and handed it to her.

"Here," I said.

She looked at me uncertainly. "Are you sure?" She asked.

I nodded. "Positive."

She took the gun from me and put it in her own holster. Then I looked around at everyone. Jade waved us forward.

"Come on," she said, "let's get this done."

We all walked through the door.

We were again in a spacious room. I could see Fara on the other side of the room in one corner, Gerris was in the corner opposite from her. I heard the soft hum in front of us.

"There's a force-field," I said.

Jade examined the wall behind us.

"Where's the generator?" She asked.

I shrugged. "I think it might be ..." I trailed off and we all looked up as we heard a hiss coming from the ceiling. There was a greenish-yellow gas flowing from vents in the ceiling. Within seconds, my eyes started to sting.

"Agh!" I groaned and doubled over, covering my eyes. Andresha and Garrick were doing the same. The only one of us not effected was Jade with her helmet.

"What is it?" She asked. I motioned to the fog around us.

"It's burning our eyes!" I exclaimed.

There was a sharp *snap!* as the force-fields went down. I forced myself to open my eyes, tears filled them as they continued to sting. Fara and Garris were running towards us. Obstacles rose from the floor creating hallways like ... like the Core.

Thanos' voice boomed down to us. "You have ten minutes to find the lift before security converges on the area."

Ten minutes? To get through this? I wiped my eyes, trying to see clearly.

"Come on!" I shouted. I turned to Jade. "You're the only one who can see clearly." I told her. "You're going to have to go ahead."

She nodded. "Right. This way!" She started out of our alcove, the rest of us following as close as we could.

It was nigh unto impossible. I tripped dozens of times, and I could hardly see. Thanos said we had ten minutes before security "converged" on the area, but there were "guards" all over the place. It wouldn't have been a problem if I could have seen them.

"We're almost there," Jade called over to us. "Stay close."

I wiped my eyes again, but this time, to my relief, the stinging was beginning to subside. I blinked a few more times and my vision cleared. I looked over at Andresha.

"Can you see now?" I asked her. She blinked furiously, then nodded.

"Yes."

The haze had faded, and I could now see the almost perfect replicas of the Core around us. White, reflective walls were all around us.

"How ...?" I muttered to myself, then started after the others.

I could see a lift door just twenty feet from us. We were going to make it!

"Hunter Garris has been eliminated." Thanos' voice echoed down to us. Five of us left. We were ten feet from the door. Just a few more steps ...

A gun fired. Jade stiffened and cried out, then fell.

"Jade!" Andresha shouted, running to her side. Garrick and I were right behind her. I looked back and saw Fara with one of her guns in her hands. She was preparing to fire again, but Garrick was

210

faster. He brought his rifle up to his shoulder and fired. Fara cried out and grabbed her arm. She holstered her weapon and disappeared behind a bend in the hall.

Satisfied that she was gone, I nodded to Garrick and we turned back to the girls.

Andresha had rolled Jade onto her back. The bullet had hit her shoulder. Not life-threatening if she got proper medical attention in time.

Jade gritted her teeth. "Is it bad?" She asked. Andresha shook her head, ripping her shirt sleeve and pressing the fabric over the wound. Jade gasped with pain.

"Looks like you're both on your own," she said, her face pale.

Andresha shook her head. "It's not that bad," she said, but Jade shook her head.

"If I was on a mission and got hit like this, I wouldn't be able to finish. I'm out."

As if to confirm her words, Thanos spoke again. "Hunters Jade Hura and Garrick have been eliminated."

Jade grasped Andresha's hand. "You can do this, alright?"

Andresha bit her lip and nodded. "Okay," she whispered, a tear running down her cheek.

Jade smiled a little. "Tell Seth hello for me when you get back," she said as Garrick helped her to her feet.

"Now get going!" she shouted.

Andresha got to her feet, and together we raced through the door.

Part Three

The Traitor

46

(Andresha)

I sat with my back to the wall, my head in my hands, my knees drawn up to my chest. Three of us left. Just three. So close to winning, but at the same time, impossibly far away.

Fara. The only thing that stood between Edrix, me, and victory. No simple task.

I wished Jade was still in, but at the same time, I was glad she wasn't. It would be foolish to believe that Thanos would let us both win. This way, I didn't have to worry about it.

On the bright side, we now knew that being "eliminated" didn't necessarily mean "dead." Maybe this thing hadn't been as bloody as it seemed.

I tugged my braid. I looked up at the ceiling of the dark room we were now in. There was nothing but four walls and the bare floor. I angrily wiped a tear off my cheek. I didn't have time to cry.

Edrix, who had been pacing the room, came over and sat down next to me.

"I'm sorry about Jade," he said quietly. I shrugged.

"She's alive," I said, my voice trembling a little, "that's all that matters."

I blinked back my tears. I needed to stop being such a watering pot! Crying was fine in its proper time and place, but I'd done enough for now.

I hadn't cried this much since I was thirteen. Since before that, actually. I rested my forehead on my knees. I hated this place! I hated Thanos!

I had spent years building emotional walls, and this ... *Anvil* had knocked them down in ten minutes. Ten minutes of pure terror.

I looked up. "Three of us left," I whispered. For once, the Hammer hadn't struck. Three Hunters had been eliminated during the trial, including Jade and Garrick.

Edrix breathed out slowly. "Which means were almost at the end." He turned to looked at me. "I don't think we can just charge in there and work out a plan then," he said. "We need to figure something out now."

I lifted my head from against the wall. "How? We don't know what the trial will be until we get in there," I said. Edrix nodded. "We won't know *for sure," he said.* "But I think I have an idea of what they'll do, and if it's what I think it is, I might have a plan that will make us win."

47

(Edrix)

Andresha and I stood before the newly opened doorway. We'd spent the last two hours making our plan, going over alternatives and things that could go wrong. It was relatively simple, since simple plans were less likely to go wrong, but as Jess always said; if something *can* go wrong, it will.

I gave my gloves one last tug, to make sure they were on firmly. I looked over at Andresha.

"Are you ready?" I asked her.

She bit her lip. "Are you?" She countered.

I smiled a little. "Nope. Never will be."

Now she smiled as well. "I guess we'd better go then," she said. I held out my hand, and she shook it.

"Nice knowing you," I said.

"You, too," she replied. Then, after a moment's hesitation, she threw her arms around me. I returned her embrace.

Andresha stepped back. "I hope that makes up for all the awful things I said to you when we first met," she said.

I smiled. That seemed like years ago. "Consider them forgotten," I said.

She grinned and motioned to the door. "Good. Now we'd better go before I lose my nerve."

Together, we walked through the doorway.

As I suspected, we were in a large empty room. On the other side, I could see Fara, her arms folded. She smirked smugly as we entered. There was no sign of the wound from Garrick's rifle. Thanos' screen came down between us.

"Here we are at last," he said, clasping his hands together in apparent delight. "The final trial!"

216

He looked at us, a smile on his lips. "I won't waste any more time talking," he said, his face becoming serious. I noticed that his robe was red today. Fitting, I thought. Thanos raised his hands.

"Let the final trial commence!" he proclaimed. The screen disappeared.

Fara walked towards us. Andresha and I walked forward as well. Fara smiled coldly.

"Shall we get started?" She asked. She unhooked a coiled whip from her belt. She gripped the handle loosely and let it uncoil, revealing its length of almost two meters. She flicked her wrist and the whip made a crisp *snap!* in the air. I glanced at Andresha. She nodded, and we launched our plan into action.

I drew two of my knives and kept moving forward, but Andresha kept back. I had to make sure that Fara's attention stayed on me, not her.

Just because it wasn't hard enough already, Fara flicked her wrist again, and as the whip snapped, fire ran down the length of the whip, starting at the handle and ending at the tip.

I bit the inside of my lip. A whip would have a delayed response, giving me an advantage, but I didn't doubt that Fara was an expert with it. My best chance would be to try to get inside of its reach.

I surged forward, my knives ready. Fara flicked the whip towards my shoulder. I swerved out of the way. I had to be wary of deflecting it with my knives. I didn't know what material the whip was made of. If it was something my knife couldn't cut through, the whip might wrap around the blade and wrench it from my grasp. I had more knives, but it could also injure my hand or wrist.

I got inside the reach of the whip, forcing Fara to draw her knife. Our blades rang together as she blocked my strike. I thrust towards her ribs with my second knife, but she blocked it with the whip's handle.

Behind me, Andresha was making her way behind Fara, un-holstering her gun as she did so. Almost there. I just had to keep Fara distracted for a few more seconds ...

She began to twist her knife around mine. I reversed the action and twisted my knife around hers. The knife fell out of her hand as something cracked in her arm. She growled in rage and sent a punch towards my face. I evaded it and stepped back.

Fara flicked her whip towards me again. When the handle had been locked around my knife, I had gotten a look at the whip's material. It was made of braided leather, not the fine metal of some whips I'd seen.

This time, I deflected the whip with my knife. I did this twice more. Fara growled in frustration. Andresha should be in position by now …

There was the sound of a gunshot and Fara cried out in pain. She dropped both her knife and her whip as her hands flew to her left shoulder, covering the red spot that had begun to spread across her shirt. It wasn't a fatal wound, but she collapsed, revealing Andresha standing behind her, the gun still raised. She lowered it now.

"That was the last bullet," she said.

I'd known that neither Andresha nor I could beat Fara, but Jade's elimination had opened my eyes. We simply had to make it so Fara couldn't continue to compete.

Andresha stepped over to me. "We did it," she said hollowly. I looked around. We had, hadn't we? We had won. So why hadn't Thanos said something?

Fara gasped like she'd been deprived of air.

Andresha and I backed away from her. I heard her wrist snap again as the bone set itself, then Fara slowly got to her knees and took her hand away from her shoulder. Andresha and I watched as the wound closed on its own. In a moment, there was no sign that she had ever been injured except for the bloodied hole in her shirt. She got to her feet, her face shining with sweat and her breathing heavy.

That was why there had been no sign of the wound on her arm from Garrick's rifle. She could heal herself. That's why she won every trial, why she was never eliminated.

It was because she *couldn't* lose. She was the winner by default. No injury would stop her on a Hunt.

This tournament had been rigged.

"Jess was right, something always goes wrong," I muttered as Fara regained her feet. Her gaze snapped over to me.

"What did you say?" She hissed. I stayed silent.

Fara scowled, her lips curling in a sneer. "*What did you* say?!" she screamed. Her entire frame was shaking with anger. Her breathing got heavier, and she growled continually. Andresha and I backed away from her. She shook harder, and she grabbed her head in her hands. I heard what she'd said to Thanos in the dining room in the Hub rotations ago:

"And that made me horribly angry, and you know *what happens when I get angry."*

Something told me that I was about to find out.

Fara let loose a bloodcurdling scream. She went ridged, her arms at her sides. Fire shot from her fingertips into the floor, beginning to melt it. She lifted her hands and focused it towards us.

I acted completely out of instinct. I raised my hands, willing the fire not to touch Andresha or me. The fire bent around us and dissipated. Before I could comprehend what had just happened, Fara had retrieved her whip and her knife.

"Scatter!" I said to Andresha. We dove in opposite directions as Fara lashed out with the whip. I thought Fara had been incredibly skilled before. She now made her past efforts look worthless.

She never stayed in one place for more than a second. It took all my concentration to keep the whip from striking me. She alternately used her whip and fire from her hands.

My knives were worthless, so I managed to slip them back in their sheaths. The whip caught me on the arm, tearing my sleeve. I felt a sting as a cut began to bleed. A blur of movement came from my right and I bent back under a cut from Fara's knife. I swung with my own knife again, desperately. I was aiming for her hand, but she moved at the last moment. Instead, I cut the whip from the handle.

Fara tossed the handle away and grabbed my throat. I couldn't breathe. I grasped her wrist, trying to make her loosen her hold, but it only got tighter. She lifted me off the ground, my feet leaving the floor as spots began to dance before my eyes.

Something knocked Fara over, making her release her grip. I collapsed on the ground, coughing and gasping as I tried to regain my breath.

Andresha had come to my aid. Fara was on her feet now, but so was Andresha. She grabbed Fara's arm and kicked her legs out from beneath her. As Fara fell, Andresha retained her grip on her arm. There was an awful snapping sound as Fara's shoulder came out of its socket. Fara cried out in pain and twisted her arm from Andresha's grasp. She rolled clear and got to her feet. Andresha was already running towards her. She launched herself into the air and back flipped over Fara's shoulder. As she landed, she grabbed Fara's neck in her arms and wrapped her legs around her. Then she went completely limp, bringing Fara down with her.

I was on my feet again, my knives out of their sheaths and in my hands. Both Andresha and Fara were on their feet as well. Fara bent down and picked up the severed whip and before I could react, she had lashed it towards me. I didn't have time to dodge and it hit my face.

I felt a sharp stinging pain as the whip cut my face on my right eyebrow. Blood ran down my face. Andresha looked like she'd seen a ghost. She went pale and stumbled backwards.

"Are you all right?" I asked her, but she couldn't answer. I looked over at Fara. None of the training or weapons we had would be enough to beat her. Unless …

There was *one* weapon I had that I hadn't used, not unless you count my deflecting the fire, but it was our only chance. The question was, would it work?

Why not? I said to myself. I had deflected the fire, somehow, so I *should* be able to do other things with it as well.

Besides, we were dead anyways.

I turned to face Fara and slowly pulled off my gloves. We both stared at each other. I counted to five and the flames appeared on my arms. I took a deep breath.

Stop. I thought, and the fire obeyed. The flames disappeared from my arms and hands. I slowly reached out my hand.

Fire leapt from my palm and shot towards Fara. She lifted her hand and caught it. We circled each other, a stream of fire between our hands.

Fara smirked. "Found out you can control it?" She said mockingly.

"Couldn't think of a better thing to use it on." I said back in a strained voice. It took an enormous amount of concentration to keep the fire in my hand. Perspiration beaded on my forehead.

"Realizing what a burden it can be?" Fara said. More tendrils of fire split off from the main stream, shooting across the room. The fire reflected in her mirror-like eyes, making it seem like they had become the flames.

"You don't know how to use it," she continued. She did not smile as she pushed her hand forward.

The stream of fire burst into a shockwave that made me fly backwards. I fell on the floor hard, all the air leaving my lungs. My vision swam and I managed to turn on my side. Andresha had been knocked back as well. She wasn't moving, and she didn't appear to be breathing.

Fara hadn't moved. She slowly lowered her hand as the screen reappeared on the wall above us.

"Well done, Fara Emrick." Thanos said, his voice devoid of any emotion. "The Client has proclaimed you the victor of the tournament. Congratulations."

Fara turned to the screen and bowed, but there seemed to be something almost ... mocking about it.

"Thank you," she said. She glanced at me, then continued. "I want something added to my reward."

Thanos raised an eyebrow. "And what would that be?"

Fara pointed behind her, to me. "I want them," she said. Thanos glanced at someone off-screen, then asked, "What do you mean?"

Fara folded her arms. "Solan has a bounty on him –"

Thanos held up a hand and cut her off. "The Hunter code forbids the collection of a bounty on a fellow Hunter. Any bounty on him is void."

Fara laughed. "He's no Hunter, Thanos. He was a REGS Higher One, yes, but not anymore." She looked him in the eyes. "They are both a part of Red Star, a rebel faction on Rendaria. I want them."

There was a quiet conversation off screen. Finally, Thanos made a decision.

"Fine. They are yours."

I had crawled over to Andresha while Thanos had been making his decision. The floor had seemed to roll and pitch beneath me, but I had made it. To my relief, Andresha was breathing.

"Andresha," I whispered, shaking her gently. She didn't move.

Fara had thanked Thanos and the screen had disappeared. She marched towards us as a door appeared in the wall, then the world fell into darkness.

48

(Andresha)

We'd seen the best the Hub had to offer. Now we saw the worst.

After Fara's victory, Edrix and I had been dragged back to the Hub and taken down to the bottom floor, which we found was where the containment cells were. We sat in one now, across from each other. I listened to the hum of the blue force-field.

It was all my fault. I knew that Edrix would deny it if I said it aloud, but it was the truth. If I hadn't let myself freeze up because of the cut Fara had given Edrix. If this had been any other mission, I wouldn't have, I would have been fine, but ever since that trial with the holograms, I hadn't been myself. Lar's whipping was all too fresh in my mind.

Of course, that had been my fault, too, which didn't help things.

Edrix fiddled with his sleeve. I'd grown used to seeing his gloves; I kept doing a double-take now that he didn't have them.

He met my eyes.

"What happened to you back in the Anvil?" He asked. I sighed inwardly. He really wasn't one to beat around the bush. I still wasn't ready to tell him everything.

"You getting that cut, it ... it reminded me of something," I said hesitantly.

He folded his arms and sat back against the wall. "Can I ask you something?" He said.

I shrugged. Why not?

He stared at me in silence for a moment, then he said, "Why don't you like to talk about yourself? Every time I ask something, you either change the subject or are really vague."

I froze, our eyes locked. He wanted an answer, and he deserved one, but I wasn't going to give it; at least not all of it.

I pursed my lips. "I don't like talking about it because A, it's hard for me to do so, and B, I don't want people to hate me." I pulled my knees up and wrapped my arms around them, clearly ending the conversation in my mind, but apparently not in his.

"Why don't you just say so?" He said, almost in a whisper.

I rested my chin on my knees. "Because people usually just ask anyways," I whispered back. There was a long silence between us. It was Edrix who broke it again.

"I'm sorry," he said.

I cocked my head to one side. "For what?" I asked him.

He shrugged. "For asking. I didn't know that it bothered you so much."

I honestly wasn't sure what to say to that, so I just said, "Thanks."

I wondered how long the victory celebration would last. The thought of celebrating this tournament made me sick. All the people who had died, just because they'd gotten in the way, or not met the Client's expectations. It didn't seem like something to celebrate.

After it was over, Fara would drag us to her ship, lock us up, and take us to REGS Command on Rendaria. I wondered how much time had passed, since we had entered the Anvil. Was Red Star still hidden, or had it been discovered?

How had Fara known who we were? We'd gone through all the trouble of changing my name, and my hair. We'd never said anything about Red Star in the Hub or the Anvil until we'd known that she already knew, so how did she know? I remembered Jade talking about Fara's tech assistant.

"Tasha always did have a knack for getting into places she didn't belong."

Tasha, who had told us about the tournament. Tasha, who informed us about the Hunters we might have faced.

Tasha, who made up our Hunter's licenses.

Tasha, the traitor.

Maybe I was jumping to conclusions, but how else would Fara have known? I had never really trusted Tasha in the first place, but her news had been our only option, or had it?

Edrix's voice drew me out of my pondering. "Why would someone else want to break into the Core?" He said softly.

I looked up. "What?"

He shrugged. "I was trying to figure out why someone would try to get into the Core. I mean, we wanted to so that Red Star wouldn't be discovered, but I can't think why someone else would."

I shrugged. "Maybe for a set of codes for a bank, or something," I muttered.

He shook his head. "It would be easier—and much cheaper—to just hire a Hunter to break into the bank directly. Why go through all this trouble?"

Neither of us had the answer, so we continued our silence. All our weapons had been confiscated, but they'd let Edrix keep his sketchbook and pencil. At least *he* had something to do.

He was sketching now, the sound of his pencil strokes filling the air.

I *did* have four more hair pins left, but I didn't know what to ask them for, or what I *could* ask them for.

Edrix spoke again without looking up from his drawing.

"Can I ask you another question?" He asked.

I shrugged. "Sure."

He still didn't look up. "If it falls under your past, you don't have to answer," he said.

I made a *go ahead* gesture with my hand. He paused, then looked up.

"Why were you so upset with Chief?" He asked.

I considered his question, then countered with one of my own.

"What makes you think I was upset with him?" I asked. He raised an eyebrow.

"Back at the base, before we left, you'd always tense up when he came in, like you were expecting a fight."

I sat back against the wall. REGS Higher Order training at its finest. I decided to answer his question.

"When we first found Red Star, it was great. We were off the streets, and somewhere safe. Seth started out just like you did. It wasn't until the Chief at that time disappeared that he was voted in as Chief."

Edrix stopped me. "You—I mean, we—get to vote on who the next Chief will be?"

I nodded. "Yes. Sometimes, the current Chief, if they just step down will name someone they want to see succeed them, but even then we vote on it. If we say 'no,' then we vote for whoever we want," I smiled a little. "Actually, Seth lost to Jess, but she denied the promotion."

Edrix smiled as well. "That sounds like Jess," he said. "Please continue."

I nodded. "Well, after he was promoted, I was old enough to join officially." I looked down at my hands. "At first, I only had small missions because I was new and because there wasn't much to do. Then, as Red Star started getting bolder, I expected my missions to get bigger and more important, but they didn't. Seth didn't want me going into something dangerous, so he'd put me on in-base assignments or the smallest missions possible.

"I didn't want special treatment, and he of all people should have known that. I finally confronted him about it." I smiled wryly. "You've seen me like that."

Edrix nodded with a small smile and motioned for me to go on.

"Well, with Jess's help I managed to convince him to stop coddling me, but then everything changed. After he'd been promoted, I saw him less because he was busy, but after my first *real* mission," I shook my head, "it was like he stopped talking to me unless it was official. Even off duty he still acted like my commanding officer. I couldn't confide in him anymore because he wouldn't let me.

"When your apprehension order came out and Chief ordered you brought in, I thought he was crazy. I asked ... okay, I sort-of demanded, to go with Jess to find you. When he refused, I thought he was letting the fact that I was his sister get in the way again, but ..." I trailed off.

Edrix had stopped sketching. "But ...?" He repeated.

I sighed inwardly again. He didn't give up, did he?

"He thought I couldn't keep my head if I went after you," I said and brushed hair out my face.

Edrix was silent for a moment, the said simply, "Why?"

I looked up at the ceiling. Might as well tell him.

"Last year, we got a message from a REGS Peacekeeper that wanted to defect, but he couldn't get out on his own. He needed our help. Jim and I went with Jess and three other agents to get him out.

"Long story short, we got him, but as we were getting out, we were stopped by a squad of REGS soldiers. They were being commanded by … someone I knew. I panicked and I started firing at them."

I looked down at my hands again. "If I hadn't started firing, we would have gotten out, but I started a fire fight. We lost two agents and the Peacekeeper," I whispered. "That's why."

Edrix didn't say anything, which I was grateful for. I didn't want to talk for a while.

Three more people had been dead that day because of me. Three added to the already too-long list. I bit my lip and shut my eyes tight, not willing to let a single tear spill onto my cheeks.

After a few minutes, I motioned to his pencil.

"What are you drawing?" I asked him. He handed me the sketchbook. A tree with a swing hanging from the branches, a garden filled with flowers. I handed the sketchbook back to him.

"It's beautiful," I said. It really was, even without color. "Are there flowers like that on Five?" I asked him.

He nodded. "Yes." He watched me carefully. "It's a sketch of a picture someone left me while I was in the Med-center," he said. "I never found out who."

I scuffed my boot along the floor, avoiding his gaze. I didn't think he'd remembered, plus the way he was looking at me suggested that he had his suspicions. "Umm … I actually left that there," I said quietly. His eyebrows shot up in surprise.

"Really?" He asked in disbelief. I nodded sheepishly.

"Even though you pretty much hated me at the time?" He continued. I looked down at the floor and nodded again.

Edrix grinned and shook his head. "Where did you get it from?"

I shrugged. "I brought it with me when I went to Red Star. Why do you ask?" I said.

He bit his lip, the smile suddenly gone from his face. I couldn't tell in the dim light, but there might have been tears in his eyes.

227

"Because my mom painted it," he said quietly. "That's the garden I grew up playing in." There was silence between us for a moment, then Edrix said, "Thank you."

Before I could reply, the lights outside our cell flickered uncertainly, then switched off altogether.

Edrix and I were instantly on our feet as blue emergency lights came on. They cast an eerie glow around us. There was the sound of something metal hitting the floor, then someone jumping down from something. Someone followed behind them.

"There's footsteps coming this way," Edrix whispered. I hadn't heard anything, but nodded once in acknowledgement. I knew I could trust his ears.

I saw a silhouette of a man coming towards the force-field, the emergency lights weren't bright enough to illuminate his features.

"Who's there?" I called out as the man came closer.

Then, as he stepped up to the force-field, I could see his familiar grin.

"I'm Happy to see you," Jim said. "Now why don't we get you out of there?"

49

(Edrix)

Alarms were blaring as Jim deactivated the force-field. The blue wall of energy shut off with a *snap!* and Andresha and I stepped out of the cell. Andresha and Jim hugged each other briefly.

"How did you find us?" She asked.

Jim shook his head. "Later." He looked behind him. "Sunrise, over here!"

Short emerged from the shadows. "We've got guards in our entrance tunnel, we'll have to head out another way," he said. He opened a bag hanging from his shoulder and handed guns to Andresha and me.

"Let's move. Code names only." He lifted his gun as we headed for the lift.

"Can't they control that by remote?" I asked. Short nodded.

"That's why we're not taking the lift," he said. He opened the doors, then reached inside and pressed a button for the top level.

Jim said, "Do you have cables?" Andresha and I nodded.

The Lift doors closed and we heard it start to ascend. Short silently counted town from five with his fingers. Then he motioned to Jim. They both stepped over to the doors and pried them open. Jim quickly threw his cable at the bottom of the lift as it raced upwards. The rest of us hurried to do the same. Then we pressed the controls on the reels to reel the cable back in. We zipped up the lift shaft. Jim stopped us at the second floor.

"We'll go up from here," he whispered. We all locked our cables. Short and Jim swung over to the doors. They braced themselves against the wall. Short did his silent count down again, and Andresha and I held our guns ready, aimed at the door in case there was someone on the other side.

Jim and Short pried open the doors, but only a small crack. Short rolled a small ball through it, then let the door slide shut again. After a moment, there was a quiet snap from the other side of the door. Short nodded to Jim and they pried the doors open completely. It was dark on the other side now, only the blue emergence lights glowing from the ceiling. Short and Jim climbed through and detached their cables. Andresha followed them next, I came last.

We stalked silently through the eerily empty hallways. Jim stopped under a grate and consulted a small screen on his wrist. He nodded to the grate.

"Here," he said. Short nodded. Jim reached up to the grate and pushed it aside. Jim climbed up first, then pulled Andresha up behind him. I followed them with Short coming behind me. We crawled about six feet to a shaft that went upwards. We all climbed up, then crawled ten more feet to another grate. Jim held up a hand for us to wait. He dropped another ball, which I figured had to be some kind of EMP device, through the grate. We waited for the soft snap, and the lights below us went out.

Jim pulled off the grate and we all dropped down into a large room. After a moment, I realized that it was the dining room. Already, I could hear hushed conversations. Asking each other what was happening. Some were wondering if the power was out. I heard Thanos' voice, talking to a security guard.

If Fara was in here…

I closed my eyes as I concentrated. I had to find out if she was here. I sifted through the conversations around me, listening for her voice, or for someone to say her name. Jim started to whisper something, but I grabbed his arm. He stopped. I continued to listen, but the only thing I heard was the door closing softly. So softly that I could barely hear it. Then guns slid from holsters …

My eyes snapped open. "Scatter!" I shouted. Bullets ripped through the air as the four of us scrambled to find cover. I ducked behind a toppled chair and snapped off three shots in rapid succession. All three found their mark. I heard Jim and Short firing as well. To our luck, the room wasn't packed with hunters, like it had been when Andresha and I had been here the first time. Thanos was gone, as were his guards. There had been seven Hunters in the room. Now,

230

four of them were nursing wounds and one was ominously still on the ground. Those that could fled the room.

"Come on." I waved everyone forward. "This way to the ship yard."

Jim and Short got to their feet. Andresha came out from behind a pillar. Ever the sensible one, she'd found decent cover.

"Isn't that where most of them just went?" Jim asked. I shrugged. "Do you know another way out?"

He shook his head.

"Nope, I guess we'll go out that way," he said.

"That's what I just said!" I muttered under my breath. Jim ignored me.

Andresha and I put our backs to the doors.

"On three," I said. She nodded.

"One," I started, "two ..." I took a deep breath. "Three!"

We pushed the doors open and came around to face the room, our guns held ready. Jim and Short were right behind us. I heard a gun cock behind us. I spun and fired. The security guard grabbed his arm and ran. I could see the hallway that led to the door. It was just five paces away. More gunshots echoed through the air.

"Take cover!" Short yelled. Jim knocked over a table and we all ducked behind it. I peeked around the side of our make-shift barricade. There were ten of them, a mix of Hunters and security personnel, but Fara was nowhere in sight. I turned to Andresha.

"Lay cover fire for me. I'm tired of this." She nodded and I started to rise.

"Wait!" Jim called. "Edrix, where are your gloves?" I turned to him and grinned.

"You'll see." I nodded to Andresha. Jim still wasn't satisfied.

"Where are his gloves?" He said to Andresha.

She waved him off. "Stop talking and help me lay down fire," she said. She rose up just enough to be able to see over the table and began to fire at whatever moved. I dashed out from behind the table. I heard Short call after me, then Andresha said something back, but I wasn't listening to them. Everything seemed to slow down as I looked around the room. I could hear my heart beating in my ears.

Three Hunters to my left, two more Hunters and three guards in front of me, and two more guards to my right.

The three Hunters rushed me. I shot one, then ducked under a punch from the other. I hit him in the jaw with my gun handle. His eyes glazed and he fell. I didn't have to worry about the third Hunter, he'd run off. The other guards and Hunters were coming towards me now. I took a deep breath. I let the fire appear on my hands. Then, I gathered it into a ball in my hands, and slammed it into the floor. A shockwave rippled over the floor, knocking the guards and Hunters back. Those that weren't unconscious fled the room.

Andresha, Jim, and Short came out from behind the table. Jim's eyes were wide and his mouth was open in surprise. Short was grinning.

Andresha folded her arms and turned to Jim.

"Close your mouth, Happy," she said.

Jim obeyed, then cocked his head slightly, a confused look on his face. "So … you don't need the gloves anymore?" He asked.

I shook my head. "Nope."

Andresha cleared her throat. "Yes, that's nice, but we have a route to the door, I suggest we take it," she said and started in that direction.

Short nodded. "She's right. We're not out yet."

He turned to me. "Dragon, take point with Happy." I nodded. Jim pressed the control to open the door. Nothing happened.

"We blew the power, remember?" Short said.

Jim grinned sheepishly. "Evidently, I didn't," he said. We pushed the doors open manually. A sharp, cold wind bit my cheeks. I wished I still had my jacket.

"I forgot about this part," I said as I looked over the ship yard blanketed with thick snow.

We kept our weapons ready. The ship yard was dark, only lit by an occasional light post. Flakes of snow gently drifted to the ground.

"Can you hear it?" Andresha asked me quietly.

"Hear what?" I replied.

She shrugged. "The snow falling."

I nodded and she smiled.

232

I stopped and turned to Short. "Which ship should we take?" I asked. "There's the one we have and ... whatever you came in."

Short considered the question for a moment. "We'll take yours. Nelvin did his best, but I don't think our ship would survive another flight."

"Nelvin had to salvage it from a REGS junkyard," Jim clarified. "Plus, it's about six miles from here."

I nodded. "Our ship then. This way!"

We ran through the rows of ships, the snow crunching beneath our feet. Alarms were still blaring around us. I saw the *Triumph* ahead of us.

"There!" I shouted. Its hull was coated in a thin layer of frost and snow. We all ran up to it. Andresha opened a small compartment next to the entry ramp and retrieved a small remote. She closed the compartment, then pressed a control on the remote. The ramp came down, and the four of us hurried inside. Andresha flipped a switch near the end of the ramp. There was a soft hum as the power came back on. Jim and Short were already in the cockpit. The ship rumbled as it began to ascend.

"So how did you find us?" Andresha asked Jim again, standing in the back of the cockpit.

"We followed your signal after you activated it. Chief had us on standby, he said. Andresha furrowed her brow and went over to one of the consoles by the small brig.

"What are you doing?" I asked her. She didn't look up as she started tapped controls.

"I'm contacting the base," she said.

"What were you guys doing in jail?" Jim called back to us.

I sat on one of the bunks. "One of the contestants knew we were in Red Star. After she won, she added us to her reward. She wanted my bounty."

Short shook his head. "I don't think I'll ever understand some people," he said. Then the cockpit door slid closed.

"I think Fara was tipped off." Andresha said.

I looked back at her. "What do you mean?"

She turned away from the console to look at me. "You heard Jade. Tasha used to work with Fara. What if she told her? I mean, she is the one who told us about this whole tournament thing in the first place; *and* she got our licenses and got my name changed. You have to admit it looks suspicious."

I folded my arms. "Yes, it looks suspicious, but I don't think Fara let her go. She was pretty beat up when she found us," I said.

Andresha folded her own arms. "Maybe they did it to get our guard down. You'd be surprised at the lengths people will go to get something they want," she said.

I shook my head. "It still doesn't make sense. Why even tell us about the tournament then? If Tasha wanted REGS to find us, all she would have had to do was keep her mouth shut."

Andresha nodded. "Fair point." She thought about it for a moment, then continued. "Do you think she knew Fara was going to be there?"

I shrugged. "Not if she's been telling the truth. Jade said that Fara's invitation had been revoked, and Thanos was pretty surprised when she showed up." I said.

Andresha started to reply, but was cut off as the ship started to rumble again.

"Do you think we're through the atmosphere?" I asked her.

She scowled in thought. "I'm pretty sure we reached orbit already," she said.

"Then why ..." I started, but Andresha ran back to the console. After tapping a few controls, she said, "We're being pulled inside another ship."

I stood up. "What kind of ship?"

Andresha shook her head. "I don't know. The sensors just went dead!" We did nothing for moment, then Andresha came over to me.

"Edrix, did you activate your signal in the Anvil?" She asked me, her tone low and urgent. I shook my head.

"No. I thought you had activated yours," I said.

Andresha pursed her lips. "I lost my signal pack after the voices, Edrix. I couldn't have activated it if I wanted to," she said.

I tried to understand what she was hinting at.

"So, if neither of us activated our signals …" I started.

"Then how did they find us?" Andresha finished. We both jumped as the door from the cockpit opened. Short came running out. He was starting to shout something, but it never made it past his lips. A gun fired, and Short fell.

Andresha and I ran to his side.

"Short? Look at me!" Andresha said urgently. He didn't answer. There was lots of blood. Too much …

Short whispered something that only I could hear.

"Don't … trust … him."

Then he went completely still.

Andresha checked his neck for a pulse, her hands shaking.

"Short? No. No, no, no, no, no. Short!" she shouted, tears running down her face. I already knew that he was gone. He wasn't breathing. My hands were shaking as well.

"What did he say, Edrix?" Andresha whispered.

"'Don't trust him,'" I said hollowly. Don't trust who? There were only four—three—of us on this ship. Either there was an intruder, or …

"I'm afraid Tasha isn't the traitor, Andresha," Jim said as he came out of the cockpit, his gun barrel still smoking.

"You are."

50

*F*ive minutes earlier …

Short quickly sat in the pilot seat of the *Triumph*. Jim sat in the co-pilots seat beside him.

"Let's get this bird in the air," Jim nodded.

"I couldn't agree more."

Short started the engines and grabbed the steering yolk. After the ignition sequence was complete, he brought the ship up towards the dark sky.

"So how did you guys find us?" Andresha asked from the back.

"We followed your signal after you activated it. Chief had us on standby," he replied. He checked the controls as the ship headed for the atmosphere. He tapped a few controls, then waited as static filled the cockpit. After a moment, the static cleared.

"Base, this is Sunrise, we have Dragon and Water Bird and are en-route back," Short said.

There was another burst of static, then Jess's voice came over the transmission. "What's their status?"

"A few cuts and bruises. Dragon's got a broken wrist, but that's the worst of it." Short replied.

"Excellent. We'll debrief you once you get back here."

Short nodded. "Sunrise out."

He shut off the transmission and sat back in his seat. The last, minor turbulence cleared as the ship broke orbit from the planet.

"It'll be good to get back," Short said. "I hate to tell Nelvin that we left the ship behind, though."

The salvaged Transport-class REGS ship had been Nelvin's pride and joy, and he'd fixed it up the best he could with the limited parts he had. It wasn't his fault it hadn't stayed together, Short thought.

Jim remained silent. Short glanced over at him. He was flipping switches and controls almost non-stop.

"Something wrong?" Short asked. Jim shook his head.

236

"No, just getting myself familiar with the ship," he said. Short shrugged. It made sense. He turned his attention back to the view port. His brow furrowed as a display caught his interest.

"Where did the signal go?" He asked.

Jim looked up. "Pardon?" He said.

Short motioned to the display. "The signal we were following. It's gone."

Jim shrugged. "Andresha or Edrix probably turned it off," he said. Short turned to face him.

"You can't turn off the signal packs. Once they're on, they can't be turned off unless they're destroyed."

Jim still didn't seem concerned. "Then maybe that Thanos guy destroyed them after he locked up Edrix and Andresha."

Short narrowed his eyes. "Who's Thanos?" He asked. Jim calmly took his hands off the co-pilot's steering yolk.

"I asked Tasha about the tournament," he said. "She said it was run by Thanos Albanathy. I assumed that he's the one that locked them"—he jerked his thumb towards the back of the ship to indicate their friends—"in a cell so they could be this Fara person's prize."

Short was no fool. Like Edrix, he'd been a part of the Higher Order. He was an expert at telling when someone was lying, even someone good at it."

"I asked Tasha the same thing. She said she didn't know," Short said evenly. An alarm started to blare. The proximity alarm. Short checked his display and pursed his lips.

There was a REGS battle ship coming in behind them. He also noticed the homing signal that the *Triumph* was sending out.

He didn't want to believe it, so he gave him one more chance.

"We have a REGS ship behind us. Charge the weapons," he said. Jim didn't move.

"Jim?" Short said. Jim didn't look up. Short looked down. "You called them, didn't you?" He muttered.

Jim looked up. To him, it looked like Short was defeated by this realization, but in reality, Short was planning how to get out of the room. Jim had closed the cockpit door and the control was where he now rested his hand on the console. His chair was already partially turned towards the door. He had to warn Edrix and Andresha. Jim spoke now.

"I'm sorry, Short," he said.

Short's gaze met his. "No you're not!" he snapped.

It had the desired effect. Jim flinched away from him at his harsh tone. In an instant, Short had pressed the control for the door and had launched out of his seat. He saw Andresha and Edrix standing by one of the consoles, both of them looking at the door.

Short began to shout a warning to them, but it came out as a yell of pain. He heard the gun fire, and the bullet hit him in the back. His vision was already starting to dim when he hit the floor. Someone knelt beside him and said his name. He forced himself to take another breath. It was Andresha. Oh, how this would hurt her, but he had to warn her.

"Don't ... trust ... him." His warning was barely audible, but Edrix would hear it.

A tear fell on his cheek. How it pained him to see her so sad. She'd had enough sorrow in her life, Short thought. Then his vision went black and he saw no more.

51

(Andresha)

I couldn't believe it. I didn't *want* to believe it; but Short was lying dead at my feet, the bullet from Jim's gun in his heart, so how could I deny it?

"How?" The question exploded out of me, mixed with a sob. "How?" I repeated, unable to comprehend how my best friend had just shot Short in the back. The ship rumbled again as it was pulled inside the bigger ship. Edrix was on his feet, glaring at Jim with his hands ablaze.

At that moment, the boarding ramp lowered. Armed soldiers came pouring aboard, surrounding Edrix and me. All of them had the blue star symbol on their sleeves, marking them as REGS agents. One of them shot some kind of dart at Edrix. It hit him in the neck, and he collapsed on the ground.

I bitterly put my hands up in surrender. I'd never fight my way out of this, not by myself. My grief was rapidly turning into anger and betrayal. One of the soldiers cuffed my hands behind my back and dragged me to my feet. Another soldier did the same with Edrix.

"Put them in the brig," Jim said, holstering his gun. I was speechless as the soldiers dragged me off the *Triumph*. I hated the name of the ship now. First, it had almost been a mockery, since we'd lost the tournament, then a dim ray of hope as we were rescued. Now, it seemed that the only triumph was Jim's.

I fixed my face into a cold, unfeeling mask. I was too numb for tears.

We were in a huge hangar bustling with people and filled with smaller ships like the *Triumph*. We took a lift that seemed to go sideways as well as up and down. We exited the lift into a dark detention deck, and the guards un-cuffed my hands. Then, I was thrown—quite literally—into an empty cell. I tried to catch myself with my hands, but my head hit the floor.

The guard that had been dragging Edrix threw him in with me. At least they hadn't split us up … yet. The soldier that had thrown me in activated a force-field. A moment later, a set of metal bars slid down in front of it. So much for shorting out the force-field's power and escaping.

After determining that Edrix was only unconscious and pulling the dart from his neck, I huddled in a corner and stared at the floor. We'd been captured, escaped, and been captured again in less than an hour. And Short was dead. It left a hole in my heart, but I was too angry to cry. How could Jim do this? Short had been a father to me. He'd been one to Jim, too. And Jim! He'd been like another brother.

I put my head in my hands and felt something wet and sticky. I put my hands down and saw blood on my fingers. I carefully felt around my face until I found the gash on my forehead. I must have cut it when the soldier threw me in.

I jumped as Edrix started to stir. He slowly sat up and rubbed his neck.

"That stuff is nasty, whatever it was," he said bitterly. He looked over at me, his face becoming concerned.

"You're bleeding," he said.

"Happens when you get thrown in a prison cell," I said with a shrug. I let him examine the cut on my forehead.

"It doesn't look serious," he said. "We just need to stop the bleeding." He started to tear his shirt sleeve, but stopped as the bars rattled upwards again. We both looked up as the force-field snapped off and Jim stepped through the door way. If it weren't for the armed guards at his side, I would have lunged for him. He was wearing a REGS uniform now, and the very sight of it on him made my blood boil.

Jim pursed his lips angrily as he came towards me. I flinched as he pushed the hair back from my forehead. He turned towards the guards at the door.

"Why is she bleeding?" He shouted, fury evident in his voice. "You didn't *throw* her in here, did you?" One of the guards shuffled his feet sheepishly. Jim jerked his head towards the guard.

"Get him out of here, and get me a med-pack," he ordered. The other guard nodded and the two slinked off.

I pushed Jim's hand away from my face. "Don't pretend like you care about me," I snarled.

Jim looked back at me, looking genuinely hurt. "I'm not pretending, Andresha," he insisted.

I folded my arms in contempt. "Just like you weren't *pretending* to be in Red Star?"

Jim waved my remark away. "That's not—"

I cut him off, my fists clenched. "Don't you *dare* say it's not the same thing, because it is, Jim Hummer!" I shouted. "If you cared about me, you wouldn't have killed Short, and you wouldn't have called your REGS friends!"

Jim started to take a step towards me, but I stepped away from him. "Don't come near me again!" I said.

A guard stepped into the cell. "The med-pack, sir."

Jim opened it and found some kind of tool that I'd never seen before. It was about the size of my finger, and slightly curved at one end. Jim turned it on, and the curved end glowed blue.

"Here," he said, reaching for my cut. Edrix stepped in front of me blocking his path.

"Get out of here," he said. He held Jim's gaze, and I could have sworn there was actual fire in his eyes.

Jim bit his lip, then said. "Fine." He handed the tool to Edrix. "Just fix that up before it gets infected," he mumbled. He turned and left the cell, the force-field flickering back on and the bars falling into place. I put my back to the wall and slid down until I was sitting. *Now* I started crying. Edrix knelt beside me and put the tool down, then put his arms around me. I buried my face in his shoulder.

"I hate him!" I exclaimed. "I hate him!"

Edrix let me cry for a good half hour. Then I pulled back and wiped my eyes.

"I've got to stop doing this to you," I said.

He picked the tool back up and ran it over my cut, closing it completely. "Let's talk about something happy," he said.

I stared at him. "Something happy?" I repeated dully.

He nodded and thought for a moment.

"What's your favorite memory?" He asked. My favorite memory. Three hours ago, I would have picked when Jim and I had stopped fighting with each other, but now that memory was shrouded in a black cloud. So I went back further.

"When I finally joined Red Star," I said quietly. "And Seth could finally stop worrying about me."

I looked over at him. "That's my favorite memory," I said, looking down at my hands. "What's yours?"

He didn't hesitate. "When my mom taught me how to finger paint when I was five," he said as he grinned broadly. "I turned it into a paint fight."

I smiled too. "That sounds …" I trailed off. Nice, I thought, but I couldn't say it past the lump in my throat.

"Most of my favorite memories are about home," he said. "What about you?"

I bit my lip. "Red Star is the only home I've ever really had," I said in a hoarse whisper. I kept ruining all of Edrix's attempts to cheer me up.

"Will you tell me what Five is like?" I asked him. "I've never been there before."

He leaned his back against the wall and sighed. "Well, to start, it's one of the only levels besides Four that has plant life, like trees, and grass, and flowers. There's some birds, too."

I sat back and listened as he described it, trying to picture it in my mind. He talked about how kind everyone was, and about how closely knit the community was.

"You kind of had to be, when you have that profession," he said. "Unless you're lucky, you don't make a very big living. Most barely have enough to get by."

Which was the complete opposite of where I grew up. It was rare to see financial struggle. Who am I kidding? It was practically non-existent!

"How did you celebrate things?" I asked Edrix. "Where I'm from, it usually involved a lot of boring speeches."

Edrix closed his eyes and smiled.

"They're always outside," he said. "And everyone who plays an instrument will bring it, and everyone else dances." He got a faraway look in his eyes. "Sometimes half a district will show up for the smallest thing." I closed my eyes and imagined the scene as he described it. All the people dancing and laughing. According to him, he could dance before he could walk, but it wasn't like the dancing I knew. I was used to dances that were slow, and calm. The dances Edrix described had people clapping and twirling along to fast-paced jigs.

He was smiling broadly now. "People really didn't care what you were celebrating. They just liked to make it special," he said. "When I painted my first bush, my mom showed it to a neighbor, and before we knew it there were fifty people outside our house. They'd always be there when I came back on leave."

We were silent for a while, then I looked up at him. "I think that's sounds much more fun than speeches," I said.

He smiled. "One day, I'll show you one," he said.

Which was terribly optimistic of him seeing as we were now in REGS clutches, but I appreciated his optimism.

"Get some rest," he said, but I was already falling asleep.

I think I ended up with my head on his shoulder.

52

(Andresha)

I nudged Edrix as the footsteps came closer.

"Someone's coming," I whispered. He was instantly awake. As we usually did, one of us would sleep while the other kept watch. We both got to our feet as the force-field snapped off again. Four guards entered our cell.

"Let's go," one of them said. They cuffed our hands behind our backs and led us to the lift. No one talked, but I was glad Jim hadn't shown his face.

The lift stopped in the enormous hangar. The guards escorted us onto a small craft that looked like little more than a metal box. The door, or hatch, more like, closed behind us and the small craft rumbled as it lifted into the air. As usual, there were no windows. I didn't really know why, but I reached out and took Edrix's hand. He gave it a reassuring squeeze. I took a deep breath, sure that everyone on the ship could hear my heart hammering in my chest. Maybe just Edrix could, because he squeezed my hand again.

"Take a deep breath, Dresha," he whispered, the same words he'd said back in the Anvil. The guards told him to be quiet, but I smiled a little when they weren't looking.

Just a few minutes later, the ship lurched and the hatch opened. The guards pushed us out into another hangar, the scent of fuel burning my nose. I saw Edrix stiffen out of the corner of my eye. He must have recognized where we were.

We were escorted to another lift that seemed to go down forever. We must have landed on One, I thought. Why else would it take so long?

After about twenty minutes, the lift finally opened to a crisp, white hallway. It must have been part of the Med-center. The guards led us down the hallway to a door marked M-18 and brought us inside.

244

The room was as white as the hallway outside. Medical equipment was placed around the room, with a table in the middle. I noticed the straps attached to its sides. *Why did they bring us to the Med-center?* I asked myself.

I noticed that we were not the only ones in the room. Jim was there—cue internal growling—standing beside two doctors. There was a man with graying hair and impressive cheekbones that I recognized as Supreme Authority Fisk. Standing near the door, and flanked by two Higher Ones was a tall man with brown hair and blue eyes. Next to him, was the Grand Commandant, Nero Jackal, judging from the pins and medals on his lapel. Edrix stiffened, and I placed the brown-haired man. He was his older brother, Jai Solan.

Jackal did not smile as he walked over to me.

"Well, we meet at last, Miss Kanway. I must admit, I didn't believe it when you and your brother ran off, but here we are."

I stared across the room, not meeting his gaze. He didn't comment; instead he turned to Edrix.

"And you, Edrix Solan, our rogue Higher One."

Edrix didn't answer either.

Jackal nodded to the guards. Two of them pushed me over to where Jim was standing, the other two brought Edrix to the table. Jackal paced in front of him.

"I must say, a mission well done, Edrix," he said. Edrix looked around, confused.

"What do you mean?" He asked. His eyes flicked to Jai, but his were fixed on his boots.

Jackal took a deep breath. "It was the only way to get you inside Red Star's ranks," he said. "When we found out you knew one of the suspects personally, I knew you'd be welcomed with open arms." He must have meant Jess. She was the only one who had known Edrix when he showed up. Edrix tried to break his guard's grip on his arm, but to no avail.

"You didn't send me on a mission. You sentenced me to life on the Surface!" he shouted.

Jackal nodded. "Yes, that's what I said, but the best way to make sure you weren't caught was to have you, well, commit treason," he said. I could feel Edrix's confusion from across the room. Jackal continued.

"You see, Edrix, we … let's say, programmed, you to believe that what REGS had done on Eight was wrong. We then let you believe that you had escaped our custody and let you find the Red Star base."

Edrix lunged towards him.

"LIAR!" he shouted. Jackal made a conciliatory gesture with his hands.

"All will be made clear in a moment." He nodded to the doctors. One of them took a large syringe from a tray. He started towards Edrix, but didn't get very far. Edrix knocked the syringe from his hand and lunged for the door. The guards caught him and pushed him back onto the table. He kept fighting, kicking and punching. My guards had gone to assist now. I winced as they pushed Edrix down again, making his head slam painfully on the metal surface.

"Stop it!" I shouted and started towards him, but Jim grabbed my arms and held me back.

"Let go of me!" I tried to fight my way out of his grasp. Jai and Fisk had gone to hold Edrix down. The guards had gotten the straps on his hands and feet, and Jai was holding his head, leaving his neck exposed.

The doctor had retrieved his syringe and moved forward again. The straps around Edrix's arms creaked and groaned as he strained against them. The needle was almost to his neck when they snapped off.

He grabbed the doctor's wrist in his hands, pushing it back. Fisk muttered something under his breath. He motioned the doctor back and took the syringe himself. Edrix repeated his action, pushing against Fisk with all his strength.

"Edrix, we're trying to help you!" Jai yelled above the chaos. Edrix answered with a yell as he pushed harder, trying to stop the needle from inching closer to his neck.

Then, I gasped as something strange happened. Usually, Rendarians can only sense emotions if they're strong enough, but I heard a thought as clearly as if it had been spoken aloud.

Don't let it touch me.

246

I had heard what Edrix was thinking. I didn't know how, but I had. It made me fight all the harder, but it was in vain.

The needle stabbed into Edrix's neck, and Fisk pushed the fluid it contained into his veins. Almost immediately, Edrix started to scream.

"Don't fight it, Edrix," Jai said.

"Stop!" I cried, but no one listened. The guards had to continue to hold Edrix down as he thrashed and screamed. Jackal stood by, his face emotionless.

"What is your rank and specialty?" He asked calmly. Edrix stopped for a moment, his face beaded with sweat.

"Higher One Solan, specialty…" He shook his head violently.

"No!" he howled. Jackal didn't flinch. He repeated his question. Edrix shook his head, refusing to answer, his teeth clenched so hard, I was afraid they would break.

I had stopped fighting now, just wishing for it to end. Jackal repeated his question again. This time, Edrix stopped fighting and went silent. He was soaked in sweat and trembling, his chest heaving.

"Higher One Solan, specialty: knife combat."

Jackal nodded. "Excellent. Who do you serve?"

I watched in horror as Edrix responded almost robotically.

"I serve the Chairman and the protection of order," he said.

Jackal raised his head, looking down his nose. "And do you swear to abide by that oath?" He asked softly.

Edrix nodded. "I swear on my life and my freewill, to uphold the oath that I have taken."

"No," I whispered, letting my head hang in defeat.

Jackal nodded. "Wonderful," He turned to Jai. "Take him to his room, and let him rest." He turned to me.

"As for her," he paused. "Put her in 36-A."

Jim let go of me and handed me over to the guards. I didn't resist. I let them lead me back to the lift. I didn't know what they'd done to Edrix, but I did know this:

There was no way that I would *ever*, emphasis, trust the word of Nero Jackal over that of Edrix Solan.

53

"What's the problem?" Jess asked as she walked into the Command Center. Tasha came in behind her. Nelvin and Jinx were hovering over a console. Chief was beside them. He looked up as she spoke.

"We lost contact with the retrieval team. We've paged them twice with no reply," he said.

"Did they take the ship Harris gave them?" Tasha asked.

Nelvin nodded. "Yes. Short contacted us about six hours ago, but there's been no contact since."

Jess rubbed her forehead. "This *is* a problem. If something's happened, we don't have another ship to go after them."

Chief ran a hand through his hair. "I guess we'll have to wait for now," he said. "If they don't respond in another hour, I want options ready," he said. A console began to beep. Jess went over and checked it.

"There's a REGS battle cruiser heading to the space port," she said.

Chief came over to the console. "Can you pull up a file?"

There was silence as Jess tapped several controls, then flicked a holo-file into the air.

"The *Majesty*, designation number: 15784395. Crew compliment of forty-six, and can carry two hundred and twelve soldiers, *and* can carry up to twenty prisoners, she said.

Chief held up hand to pause her. "Jinx, are they transmitting anything?" He asked. Jinx didn't respond right away. He was listening intently to information in an earpiece he was wearing.

"They're sending down a landing craft." Another pause. He looked up in surprise. "They say they have two rebel prisoners."

Nelvin folded his arms. "Two? What about Jim and Short?"

Jess, who had continued to scan the ship's file, gave a gasp of surprise.

"No," she whispered. Chief was by her side in a moment.

248

"What is it?" He asked quietly. For a moment, she was at a loss for words, then she recovered her voice.

"Look at the mission leader," she said quietly. Nelvin and Jinx came over with Tasha as Chief scanned the document.

"What is it, Chief?" Nelvin asked. Chief set his jaw. It was a full minute before he spoke.

"Jim Hummer is a REGS agent," he said grimly, "and he's on board that ship."

54

(Edrix)

The mess hall was bustling with activity when I walked in with Jai. We grabbed two plates of food and found an empty table towards the back of the busy room. It had been three rotations since I'd returned.

Fisk and Nero had explained everything. I had been selected to infiltrate Red Star. Jim was already inside, but when Jess became a suspected conspirator, it had been decided that if I appeared to be a traitor, she would help me find them. In order to prevent my being discovered, my memories had been altered. Though I felt fine, I had not yet been debriefed.

I ran a hand through my hair. "I can't believe Jess," I said quietly. Jai shrugged.

"I couldn't either, but I guess she's made her choice," he replied. He was right, I supposed. I nodded to the blue ribbon on his lapel.

"Promotion, huh?" I asked. He smiled and nodded. "Yep. Commandant."

I almost dropped my fork.

"*Commandant?*" I repeated in disbelief. Commandant was the rank higher than Supreme Authority. Whomever held the position was second only to the Grand Commandant himself. It was the position our father had held before the accident.

Jai shrugged. "It's actually not new. It happened two months ago. I was waiting to tell you."

That meant that it had happened before my mission to Eight.

I smiled. "A late congratulations then," I said. Jai shrugged it off.

"Did you tell Mom?" I asked him.

Jai's smile faltered for a moment, then he recovered. "Yeah. She says we're going to celebrate next time we go home."

Jai had been able to move our leave dates so that we could both be home at the same time. I nodded.

"I can't wait." I said.

Jai motioned to my plate. "That's going to get cold, and you've got duty in thirty minutes," he said.

I rolled my eyes. "Yes, sir," I said. Jai shook his head, but he was still smiling. I picked up my fork and took a bite of food.

"So you run away and you suddenly can't find food to eat?"

The phrase echoed through my head. I ignored it and took another bite.

"Or are you just used to a wonderful feast and can't stand the sight of civilian food?"

I dropped the fork and leaned on the table. There was a sudden, spiking pain behind my eyes.

"Agh!" I put my hands to my temples.

Jai looked up, concern in his eyes.

"Are you all right?" he asked, starting to rise from his seat.

I waved him off. "I'm fine, just a headache," I said. Already, it was beginning to subside, but Jai was persistent.

"Come on. Let's go to the med-center," he said, taking my arm. I shrugged him off.

"I'm fine!" I protested, but in truth, more memories kept bombarding my mind. Nelvin's lab, teaching someone how to throw a knife, a damaged plane …

I shook my head to clear it. To my relief, the memories stopped.

Jai still looked unconvinced. "Edrix, we need to check this!" He insisted. I started to agree when we were interrupted by an alarm beginning to blare. We looked up as red lights began to flash.

"Later," I said. We both got to our feet.

Jai checked his wrist communicator. "They want me up in command," he said, then gripped my arm with sudden intensity.

"Promise me that you'll go in if it gets worse," he said.

I nodded. "I promise," I said, confused at his concern. His mouth was a tight line, but he released my arm and left the mess hall.

Turns out I'd never get that far.

55

(Andresha)

Three rotations. I think it had been three, but I couldn't be sure. All I had to mark the passage of time was when I would get one of my bi-daily IVs. Those were my meals. Something weird happened the first two rotations. It was like I was in a daze. I couldn't remember much. I must have slept a lot. There wasn't much else to do, but something was different.

I'd seen specs for this building. I was not in the standard cell block where they would usually put someone like me, and I'm pretty sure normal prisoners don't have a cardiac and neural monitor.

But then again, most members of Red Star were not like me at all. Maybe that was it.

My trial was most likely happening at this very moment. If the court was feeling merciful today, I'd be sentenced to death by firing squad. If they were in their usual mood, I could look forward to a slow and painful death via freezing, heat stroke, or starvation on the Surface. Joy and happiness.

Anyways, my cell was barely large enough to walk around in. No furniture, just bare floor. I was secured to the wall by electric cables that were attached to cuffs around my wrists. I could move around if they were unlocked. When someone came in, they would pull me back against the wall until they left. I'd given up trying to get the cuffs off. There wasn't a keypad or lock on them that I could see.

That left me with so much time to think about things I didn't want. Short lying dead on the ship, Jim with the gun in his hand, and Edrix ... Oh, Edrix!

What had they done to him? One minute, he's the Edrix I knew, and the next, he's a REGS puppet again. A month ago I'd be shouting "I told you so!" at everyone I came across, but not now. Now I knew the boy who'd run away, and it was not because Jackal told him to. I would never believe that in a million years. Not after all we'd been through. I wasn't going to let him go without a fight. I'd find a way to get him out of here, but first, I had to figure out what they'd done to him.

Okay, technically, *I* had to get out this cell first, but there was *no*, emphasis, way that was going to happen anytime soon.

I started with when Edrix had escaped REGS in the first place.

He'd said that he'd started to feel dizzy when he was on Eight, whatever that meant. Then, when Jai had confronted him, Edrix had said that his mind had felt "shattered," like his thoughts were arguing with themselves.

So ... according to Jackal, Edrix had been assigned to infiltrate Red Star and had his memories changed so he would commit treason, or "treason."

I didn't think Jim had been a spy either, but he hadn't been bleeding when he came to us, *and* he didn't have a historically sized bounty on his head.

Why the bounty in the first place? I thought. Why was Edrix so important? He was a Higher One, probably headed for high places in the REGS command chain. That would make him important, but seventy *thousand* credits important?

I'd been in line for something *a lot* more important than that, and I'd only been worth fifty thousand alive.

Alive ... Edrix's bounty was higher if he was brought in *alive* ... That couldn't be a coincidence.

"Why would they want him alive?" I whispered aloud. I sat in the corner of my cell, my back to the wall and my knees drawn up to my chest. I put my arms over my knees and rested my chin on them. Why not let a Hunter do their dirty work for them?

What if ... what if there was something they needed from him.

I got up and began to pace the room. I'd hit a wall in my thinking. I needed to do something else. Escaping would be good. I decided to focus on that for a while.

The door was obviously locked, with a force-field on both sides of it, and bars outside the door. No good chance of getting out that way. I'd already examined the floor and ceiling. The ventilation shafts were the size of my hand. Couldn't get out that way either. I turned back to the door. That was my only way out, but *how?*

I looked around the cell again. There were security cameras of course. My hands reached up to my forehead and brushed the neuro-sensor stuck there. It was only slightly larger than my fingernail.

When I'd first woken up this morning, I'd ripped both sensors off and thrown them across the room. I had blinked and there were guards, doctors, nurses, all rushing to and fro until they realized that I'd just taken the sensors off.

So, removing the sensors wasn't going to work, but maybe I could pretend to be dying or something, to manipulate the guard into thinking ...

The word *manipulate* stayed in my mind, stopping my thoughts in their tracks.

Had Edrix been manipulated? No, the word was changing in my mind now. Instead of *manipulate*, I saw *control*.

Edrix was being controlled. His mind...

My hands began to shake as those two words came together: *mind control.*

Was that even possible? I mean, I know that mind control was possible. It's a lot more common than one might think. But it happens gradually, over months or even years. If you hear something often enough, you believe it. That you're not pretty enough, not strong enough. If someone tells you you're crazy enough times, you start to wonder if they're right.

But that wasn't what happened to Edrix. He'd been injected with something. Something that wasn't pleasant. It had taken a mere three minutes. Three *horrible* minutes. If his mind was being controlled, then it had been done technologically.

It was the only logical answer either way you spun it. If Jackal was telling the truth, then there would have had to be a way to make Edrix think like a traitor. If I was right—and I hoped I was—then that was how REGS kept their troops in line. Why no Higher One had a mark on their record. Why Edrix Solan would be worth seventy thousand Credits alive. If he'd broken free ...

My shaking hands covered my mouth as I gasped in silent disbelief. I hadn't realized that I'd been thinking aloud until this moment. The words of Edrix's oath rang through my head.

"I swear on my life and free will..."

It was no idle promise, because no Higher One—possibly any REGS agent—was free to choose.

56

(Andresha)

I looked up as I heard the bars outside the door clattering open, then both force-fields deactivated with a crisp *snap!* I stood up straighter as the door opened.

Anger boiled inside me as Jim Hummer entered the room.

"You!" I growled. If it wasn't for the cables, I would have lunged at him.

He held up his hands. "Calm down, Dresha," he said quietly as the door closed behind him.

I tossed my head in contempt. "Don't call me that!" I spat.

Jim didn't flinch. Instead, he held out a hand. "Let me see your wrists," he said.

I hesitated, then slowly did as he asked. He took a small tag from his pocket and waved it over a hidden sensor in each cuff, then pulled them off. He tossed them to one side while I rubbed my wrists.

"Thank you," I whispered. He waved it aside. I *was* grateful. That was one less thing I had to worry about before escaping. I brushed hair out of my face.

"What do you want, Jim?" I asked.

He folded his arms. "I came to see if you were all right," he said.

I stared at him in disbelief. "'All right,' Jim?" I snapped, my own arms folded. "I've seen my friend turned into a robot, and I've been locked in a cell, and you've probably sent a force of REGS agents to Red Star to wipe them out. No, I'm not 'all right!'" I shouted. He held up his hands.

"I'm sorry! It was a dumb question," he said.

"Well, I'm glad we agree on something," I said flatly.

He still hadn't left so I said, "You have your answer. Why are you still here?"

Jim didn't say anything for a moment. We stood in silence, staring at each other.

"They're trying figure out what to do with you," he said. I had gingerly removed my monitors. No alarms were going off, so I tossed them aside.

"I would think it was obvious," I replied. "Give me a token trial, then ship me off to the surface to die a slow and painful death."

Jim bit his lip. "Jackal isn't blind, Andresha. No one here is. Everyone knows who you are—"

"Was," I interrupted, "and that has to be a bluff. Edrix didn't know who I was."

Jim ran a hand through his hair. "Of course he didn't, Andresha. You'd never let him stay if he did."

I put my head back against the wall. "I'm not stupid, Jim! You never sent Edrix on a mission, he broke through your mind control!" I shouted.

There was a quick flash of fear behind Jim's eyes. He hastily concealed it, but I caught it. I was right.

Wait! What if ... what if Jim was under mind control as well? I could hear my heart beating in my ears as I considered it. I stared at Jim. Was my best friend still in there? The one that I could always confide in, who'd be there when I needed someone to listen, the one who'd always have my back.

Jim was talking again. "The entire planet's a bomb without a timer, Andresha. One wrong move, and it will blow up beneath our feet. Your death would do that."

Thoughts of redeeming Jim vanished now. I looked at Jim in disbelief.

"The people are starting to stand up, aren't they?" I whispered.

Jim looked down at his boots and nodded. "We've already had three riots since Eight."

Eight. All my sympathy was gone. Hatred had replaced it.

"That's what we've wanted, Jim. That's why we did the raids and attacked caravans. Why we sent out the messages on the comm channels. It was so that people would stand up!"

"To what end, Andresha?" Jim shot back, marching towards me. "What good will it do? REGS will shut down the lifts and cut off their supplies, trapping them. The people here will never stand up, and you know why. The fire will die before it even catches! Hundreds, maybe even thousands, of people will die. Is that what you want?"

I looked away as he stopped in front of me.

"You know it isn't," I muttered.

"You could stop it, Dresha," he said quietly. I still didn't look up. I knew what he was leading up to.

"If you spoke to the people, they'd follow. They *chose* you to lead them, Andresha."

He lifted my chin with his finger so that I was looking at him, our eyes meeting. I was surprised at how close he'd come.

"Please," he whispered. I didn't move. If he knew me at all, then he'd know that I'd never do what he said.

Our eyes were locked, and he was still touching my face, but I'd never felt so distant from someone. He was moving closer still, and our lips touched for a fraction of a second.

I pushed him violently away, repulsed. Jim stumbled, off balance.

"NO!" I shouted. There was a vile taste in my mouth, and a deep despair in my heart.

"I will *never* tell them to go home, or to stop fighting, because that's why Red Star was started, Jim Hummer, to make sure that those Lifts would keep working, and that this fire would get so hot, even everyone up here will turn against their masters. I broke free, so can they!"

Jim held up his hands. "Andresha, please—" he started, but I didn't let him finish.

"No, Jim." I shook my head and pointed to the exit. "Open the door!"

He said my name again, but I didn't listen. I moved forward and grabbed his gun from its holster. In one fluid movement, I had hit him in the jaw, his eyes glazing as he fell to the floor.

It turns out I didn't even need a pin. The door was opened from the outside as a guard came in.

"What's going on?" He said. I shot him in the shoulder and snatched the communicator from his ear and wrist. I crushed the ear piece, but kept the wrist band. Alarms had already begun to blare.

I'd done it. I'd escaped. So why were there tears on my cheeks?

57

(Edrix)

It hadn't been ten minutes when the alarms stopped. I hadn't even left the mess hall. I shrugged to myself.

"I suppose I should go to the Med-Center now," I muttered under my breath. I left the mess hall and headed for a lift. There were agents bustling to-and-fro around me, but they stayed out of my way, saluting when I passed them. I would nod in return and continue on my way.

I got on the lift and stated my destination. The lift started to move and I leaned back against the wall. My headache was back full force. I put my hands to my temples as a flood of voices filled my thoughts. There were so many, I couldn't tell what they were saying, or who they belonged to.

I lowered my hands and raised my head as the lift doors opened. I recognized Higher One Lars. His face was set in a grim line.

"The Grand Commandant wants you," he said shortly. I nodded once. No words were needed. Lars did not redirect the lift vocally. Instead, he typed a code into the keypad near the door. The lift lurched and began to ascend. Neither one of us spoke.

A few minutes later, the lift doors opened into a large, circular room. Above me, I could see an observation deck where Fisk, Jai, and Jackal stood. Their faces were all impassive. I bit the inside of my cheek and stepped out of the lift. Lars stood to one side as I took another step forward.

"Edrix Solan," Jackal said quietly. "Do you remember your oath?"

I swallowed and took a deep breath. "Yes, sir," I said, staring straight ahead.

The Grand Commandant nodded. "It is now your duty to rid Rendaria of one who would see her fall."

I lifted my chin as I stood at attention. Lars looked down at his boots.

260

"I'm ready, sir!" I said.

Jackal nodded again. "I'm glad to hear it," he said, then snapped his fingers, the sound echoing crisply around the room.

A door across the room from me slid open and three figures came out.

One was a Peacekeeper, his face hidden by his helmet. The other guard was Higher One Sanders, a chain in his fists. The chain attached to a collar around her neck. Black hair falling around her face, and keen purple eyes staring at me.

Andresha Kanway, the enemy of Rendaria.

58

(Andresha)

I flinched as Sanders yanked my chain. I felt like a dog on a leash. My escape had—quite obviously—been short lived. I hadn't even made it to the lift when I was surrounded and disarmed. After I was restrained, I had been dragged down here, apparently to my execution. No, not my execution. That would be all over the channels. This was for Edrix, both a test of loyalty, and an assurance that he would never rebel again.

Even if he was able to break free of the mind control, he would never forgive himself for killing me. I know, because he blamed himself for letting those people on Eight die. I know because I haven't forgiven myself, and it's been three years.

Looking at Edrix now, there was no sign of the Edrix I knew. Instead of a bright, warm glow in his green eyes, they were cold and empty. They had been empty when I first met him, but that had been from sadness. This ... this was a lack of any kind of emotion. Just blind obedience. No ability to think. It was like he had ceased to be a living being. It is the ability to think, choose, and act for themselves that makes someone into a person. Take that away, and they may walk and talk, but they would be like the walls around me, gray and featureless.

I did not cry. My heart was far too broken for tears.

Sanders dragged me into the center of the room. I couldn't suppress a cry of pain as the collar dug into my skin. Edrix met my eyes.

There! Just for a moment, there had been a flicker of Edrix's old self in his eyes ... and confusion.

He had broken free before, maybe it was happening again? It was my only chance.

He began to walk towards me as Sanders forced me to my knees.

"Edrix, listen to me," I said, trying to keep my voice even and calm in spite of my desperation. "This isn't you. We're friends, you must remember that!"

Edrix didn't react, he just calmly drew his knife. I tried again.

"They're controlling you, Edrix! You've broken it before, do it again!" I pleaded. My desperation was creeping into my voice. Edrix stopped, his knife still raised. A small glow of hope glowed in my heart. The confusion in his eyes was back. He could do it!

Jackal scowled above us. "Remember your oath, Higher One," he said it calmly, but I could hear the hidden anger behind his words.

Edrix bit his lip and nodded to himself, but I wasn't going to give up.

"You're oath is empty!" I protested. "They made you say the words. It's not a promise if you don't decide to make it!"

It was something Jess said, and it had my desired effect. Edrix stopped again, his head held to one side like he had a headache.

Sanders was getting angry, I could sense it without even trying.

"Kill her, Edrix. Do as Jackal says!" he growled.

"Don't listen to them!" I retorted. Edrix grabbed his forehead.

"STOP!" he shouted. Before I could understand what was happening, he rushed towards me.

Then his knife, glowing red hot, was slashing towards me.

I ducked and raised my hands in a vain attempt to block his blow, but it never came. Instead, I felt the chain around my neck go slack. I flinched away in surprised and spun around.

Sanders was holding the broken chain in his hands uncomprehendingly, and the room erupted into chaos.

Fisk was yelling out orders that no one could hear, and Jai was shouting something to Edrix. Edrix was currently battling off Lars, who had come up behind him. The other guard who had brought me in was nowhere to be found. Jackal stood silently, an angry gleam in his eyes. He said something to Fisk and Jai as he turned to leave, the latter following him reluctantly. An alarm began to blare as the door closed behind them.

I had not been idle. I'd pulled all the remaining pins from my hair. I slipped them all together and hoped that this would work.

A transmitter wouldn't be enough. REGS had most likely set up a jamming signal, not to mention that we were in the heart of REGS headquarters. There was no way we would be able to get out on our own. We were going to need help.

"I need to contact Nelvin," I said quietly, hoping the pins could hear me.

Before they could react to my command, I suddenly felt a hand close around my throat, and I was unable to breath. I found myself looking into the scarred face of Higher One Sanders.

"If he won't do it, then I will!" he shouted.

Edrix, who had knocked Lars unconscious, turned towards us, his gun in hand.

"Put her down!" he shouted, raising his weapon towards Sanders.

Sanders released my throat, but wrapped one arm around my shoulders, still trapping me. His other hand drew his own gun and pushed it against my head.

"Make a move, and she dies, Solan," he shouted. Edrix didn't make a move to come closer or lower his weapon.

"Let her go, Sanders," he said.

Sanders' finger tensed on the trigger. "Why should I? So you can escape?" He shook his head. "Not if I can help it!"

Neither of them moved. It was a stalemate. If Edrix shot him, he'd shoot me. If Sanders shot me, Edrix would shoot him. There had to be some way out of this ...

I had an idea, but I needed a small distraction. I raised my eyebrows twice to get Edrix's attention, then looked down at my boots. A look of understanding dawned in his eyes, but only for a moment.

"So we can make something better," Edrix said defiantly. Sanders shook his head in apparent disgust.

"Don't do this again, Edrix," he growled.

Edrix cocked his head to one side. "Do what again? I thought you made me commit treason last time, right?"

Sanders was speechless, but I was ready.

While Edrix had started talking, I'd been able to twist the heel of one boot against the toe of the other, revealing the small hidden blade inside.

Now, I grabbed Sanders' wrist and shoved it towards the ceiling. At the same time, I kicked my heel back into his leg.

He yelled, firing his gun and let go of me. I pushed back into him, causing him to stumble, and swept my other foot from behind him, and knocking his feet from beneath him. As he fell, Edrix stepped forward and punched him in the jaw, knocking him out cold.

Edrix ran over to me and unlocked my collar, then the cuffs. He put his hands on my shoulders.

"Are you alright?" He asked.

I nodded. "I am now," I said, my voice full of relief. We embraced briefly.

"I never believed them," I whispered.

Edrix was silent for long moment, then he finally said, "I'm glad you didn't."

My chance to reply was cut short by the sound of footsteps outside both doors, and there were a lot of them.

"We need to lock the doors," I said. Edrix nodded, turning to the one he came in.

"Press the yellow button after it's closed," he called back to me. I ran to the other door and did as he said, then we both went back to the middle of the room.

"Now what?" Edrix said, looking around. "I guess we could try to hold this room, but we'd be overrun pretty quickly." He looked up at the empty observation platform. "We could try and find a way to go out that way, he said, mostly to himself. We both jumped as there was loud *BANG!* from one of the doors.

"Let's see if my pins worked," I said, dropping to my hands and knees to look for them. I must have kicked them with my foot when Sanders grabbed me.

After a few moments of searching, a found a small, square device that fit in the palm of my hand. There were four metal spokes that extended from each corner and met in the center. A thin antenna poked up from the spokes with a pulsing blue light at the tip.

"What is it?" Edrix asked. I stared at the strange device in my hand.

"I have no clue. I just asked them for a way to contact Nelvin," I replied.

The doors rattled again.

"Those aren't going to hold for much longer," Edrix said. I stared at the device, trying to decipher its use, but it came up as a blank.

We both stood up. We'd have to either hold them back, or fight our way out.

"I guess this is probably where it ends," I said quietly. Edrix shrugged.

"Maybe. We said that in the Anvil and we're still alive."

Short also died and Jim revealed himself to be traitor, but I decided not to mention that.

The door shuddered again. Edrix handed me his gun, then set his hands ablaze.

The door burst open, followed immediately by a frantic cry of, "Don't shoot!"

I lowered my weapon and Edrix extinguished his hands as we stared at the unexpected intruders.

"*Nelvin?*" I gasped in amazement.

Nelvin, his hands still held above his head as a signal of peace, grinned broadly. "Who else?"

59

A soft breeze swirled around her as she waited in the shadows. She checked her equipment again, just to be sure. Then she loaded a full magazine into her hand gun and locked it into place, and turned her head to look at the tall building twenty yards away from her.

Here, on level Eight, the Core looked like a prison. Three walls surrounded it, topped with turrets and patrolled constantly by guards. After that, there was a ground-force of fifty agents and three tanks.

Usually, she would go to Level Six, where it was virtually unguarded, and *sneak* in, but those were not her orders.

Make sure they see you. Fara Emrick thought silently. It didn't matter to her. She stared at the fortifications through the dim lights. It was no hindrance to her mirror-like eyes as they studied every detail of the guard's movements, their rotations, which ones got bored the quickest. There weren't many, but there were a few. That was all she needed.

She streaked over to the first wall with almost impossible speed and crouched in its shadow. Now was the time to make her move.

Fara checked her weapons one more time, then brushed hair away from her face. She closed her eyes and took a deep breath.

Then, she was on her feet, a cable shot from her wrist as she twisted around to face the wall. The cable magnetized itself near the top, then it lifted her into the air, the cable making a loud *zzzzing!* sound.

Then she was on top of the wall. The unfortunate guard that was nearby was shoved over the side. Fara did not stay to see his fate. She drew both her hand guns and shot down two more guards. She heard someone behind her. She spun on her heel, her elbow slamming into the guard's temple. He fell with a grunt.

Alarms were screaming now, as red lights flashed on guard towers and buildings. Shouts of alarm came from all around her. She was already moving to one of guard towers on her wall. She unclipped a thick leather strap from around her ankle, then slid it over one of the cables that connected the guard towers to one another. Searchlights were following her, bathing her in bright lights, but she didn't care. She pushed off the edge of the wall, zip lining across the huge gap.

Her feet hit the ground on the second wall, but only for a moment. She transferred her strap to the next cable and was off again.

When she dropped down to the last wall, guards who had been waiting behind the towers instantly swarmed her. She fought through them, clearing the way to the edge of the wall, then, as she perched on the edge, continuing to fire at her assailants, she let herself fall backwards over the edge.

Fara flicked two small switches on her guns, revealing cable launchers beneath the barrels. Both fired into the wall above her, then went taunt, slowing her momentum, then snapped. She tucked herself into a roll, and came up firing at the fifty soldiers ahead of her. They were in a stretch of empty courtyard, with sparse cover. There were no tanks in this area; they were guarding the main entrances.

Fara growled as she ducked behind a stack of crates. There were too many guards for her to shoot, so she listened. She listened for their footsteps to come closer, she could hear them clearly. She silently reached into one of the pouches on her belt and retrieved a small hand grenade. She waited one moment more, then she pressed the activation control. The grenade began to emit a shrill beep that rapidly increased in speed and pitch. She turned and rose from behind her cover as she threw it into the midst of the soldiers closing in on her.

As soon as it hit the ground, it exploded. There were startles cries of pain and confusion as the darkness was briefly illuminated by the blast.

Fara vaulted over her crates and ran through the newly emptied stretch of land, her boots making no sound on the hard ground.

She reached the wall of the building, then holstered her weapons and retrieved another grenade. This time, it was a flat disc that she attached to the metal wall. She stepped back two paces and turned away, covering her ears with her hands.

The grenade exploded, taking half the wall with it. Fara lowered her hands and turned around. She ducked through the charred opening, emptying the empty magazines from her guns and reloading them with full ones.

The inside of the facility was much different than the outside. Inside, the walls were spotless white, and polished so she could see her face in them. She glared at her reflection.

Be quiet. She ordered herself, then she moved on.

She turned the corner, coming face to face with two Peacekeepers. One she dispatched with a lighting fast punch to the jaw, the other was run through with her knife.

Fara neatly sheathed the blade and quickly walked over to a ventilation shaft in the ceiling and pulled off the vent covering. She glanced up and, seeing that the shaft had a vertical junction, quickly attached a cable to the launcher on one of her guns. She raised it into the shaft and fired the cable through the upward passage. After a moment, the cable went taunt. She clipped it to her belt and let it pull her into the shaft.

60

(Edrix)

Two hours earlier...

Nelvin was not alone. Behind him, I could see Jinx, Tompson, and Jess. Jess came up to me, holstering her gun.

"Are you all right?" She asked, concern in her voice. I wasn't sure what to say, but she must have felt that, because she gave me hug instead of waiting for a reply. She pulled away as Andresha spoke to Nelvin.

"What exactly *is* this?" She said, holding up the device her pins had made. Nelvin's eyes got the slightly-crazed gleam that they always did when he was going to explain something.

"That, my friend, is a beacon design I've been working on," he said. "It emits a sub-axellating frequency that is lower than most jamming signals and shielding, making it untraceable and it can transmit almost anywhere. It's how we found you."

As he finished speaking, the device let out a soft squeal, and the pulsing light sparked and popped, then let out a small wisp of smoke.

Nelvin blinked a few times, his lips pursed.

"Unfortunately, I'm still trying to stabilize the power source for long-term use," he finished.

Jinx cleared his throat to get our attention. "We should get going," he said gruffly. Jess nodded.

"He's right, we need to go."

Nelvin opened the backpack he was carrying and handed Andresha a gun. I already had my REGS equipment. Jinx and Tompson led us through the hallways, the alarms still shrieking loudly. I brought up the rear of the group.

In front of me, I heard Jess say softly to Andresha, "I'm sorry about Jim."

I glanced at Andresha. Her emotions weren't quite strong enough for me to sense, but her face held a mixture of hurt, sadness, and disgust.

"I think we all are," she said back. Jinx held up a hand to stop us and turned to Andresha.

"Where's Short at? We didn't detect his Pill," he asked.

Andresha bit her lip and looked at her shoes, her eyes filling with tears. I spoke for her.

"Jim shot him after he discovered his true loyalties. He didn't make it."

There was silence throughout our group. Everyone else had known him much longer than I had. Finally, Jess broke the silence.

"Let's make sure it wasn't for nothing," she said, and the group started moving again. I stopped as we came across a console. I hesitated, then quickly crossed over to it and powered it up. Andresha stopped and turned back to me.

"Edrix, what are you doing?" She said. Jess had stopped and turned around as well, staring at me. I focused on the console, quickly typing in the password to activate it.

"I need to know where they put my family," I said quickly. Andresha and Jess glanced at each other, then came over to me. My hands were shaking as I typed in my mother's name. A blue circle appeared on the screen as the computer searched files. Jinx, Tompson, and Nelvin had been waiting for us, now Jinx spoke.

"We don't have a lot of time!" he said urgently. He was right. I could hear the rumble of footsteps coming towards us.

The console beeped as it pulled up a file. I quickly tapped it open and scanned it until I came to the section titled: **LOCATION**. I froze, my eyes fixated on the words. I couldn't move. It didn't make sense. The footsteps got closer. Someone was yelling at me, but I couldn't hear them.

Why would they be on Eleven? I thought. Then someone pulled me away from the console, its power shutting off.

"—we've got to go!" Andresha shouted. I nodded and followed her back to where the others were waiting. We were running, but

I didn't know where we were going it until I realized that we'd stopped. We'd come to one of the few windows in the building. Jinx listened to something on his ear comm, then waved us forward.

"He's in position," he said to Jess. She nodded and he carefully opened the window. Jinx then jumped out, followed by Tompson and Andresha. I glanced at Nelvin.

"After you," he said, waving me forward. I stepped forward and ducked through the opening. I didn't have far to fall; there was a sky-sailor just four feet below me. I dropped down through the hatch in the roof and moved out of the way.

A few moments later, a silent, but thoroughly frightened Nelvin dropped through and scrambled away from the hatch.

"That is the most terrifying thing I have ever done!" he said as Jess dropped through the opening. She smiled at him. "You get used to it."

The hatch closed and the ship veered away from REGS command. I dropped onto a bench, my head in my hands, while everyone else was busy checking each other for injuries.

Physically, I was fine, but I wasn't sure about my mind. I couldn't remember anything after the needle had touched my skin, except for pure agony, then when I'd realized that my knife was heading for Andresha's neck, barely changing the stroke in time for it to cut her chain instead.

What if I hadn't? What if I hadn't woken up in time to save her? These thoughts all echoed through my head as everyone was talking to each other.

Nelvin came over to me with a medical scanner in his hand. He took the scanning wand out of its slot on the side and waved it around me.

"Nothing but a few cuts and scrapes," he said after a moment. He turned to walk away, but I called out, "Nelvin!"

He stopped and turned around. "What is it?" He asked.

I hesitated, then said, "When we get back to the base, do you think you could run a more detailed scan?"

Nelvin shrugged. "I don't see why not. Is something wrong?" He asked.

I shook my head. "I'll tell you when we get there."

Nelvin, though he looked confused, nodded. "All right," he said and walked over to Andresha, taking the wand from its slot again, but she waved him off.

"I'm fine, Nelvin," she said softly. Nelvin put the wand away and closed the scanner.

"Alright," he said, replacing the scanner in the med-pack he'd opened.

Andresha turned to Jess. "Who's flying?" She asked.

Jess smiled and nodded towards the door to the cockpit. "Maybe you should see for yourself."

Andresha turned around to where Jess had motioned and stopped for a moment. I think everyone in the room could feel her excitement, but now I saw just how disciplined she was. Seth was standing not six feet away from her, but she did not run to him, for it might reveal his identity. Jess, seeing this dilemma, motioned for Tompson, Jinx, and Nelvin over to her.

"Take a look at this," she said, turning on a console.

Chief went over to Andresha and caught her in an embrace. I looked down at my boots, guilt crashing over me.

Everyone turned to look at me.

I bit my lip as Jess came over to me.

"What is it, Edrix?" She asked me quietly, so only I could hear. I wished she could hear like I did, so I didn't have to tell the others. One tear escaped my eyes. I couldn't find my voice. Jinx, seemingly for the first time, noticed my uniform.

"Why are you wearing that?" He asked me. I didn't think it could, but my guilt increased. How was I going to explain this? I wasn't even sure what had happened.

Andresha leapt to my defense as silence began to fill the sailor. She came over to me and sat on the bench.

"It's not what it looks like. I think REGS is using mind-control to keep their agents loyal, she said. Mind control? What was that supposed to mean? Jinx folded his arms.

"How? You've been in there for three rotations, that's it. How could they do something like that in such a short amount of time?" He said.

Andresha looked at him. "I saw them do it, Jinx. They injected him with something."

I looked over at her. "He made you watch?" I asked quietly. She nodded.

"Yeah."

Nelvin broke the silence that had ensued.

"Is that why you wanted me to run a more detailed scan?" He asked. I nodded.

Chief finally nodded and turned to Nelvin. "Run the scan as soon as we get back to base," he said. Nelvin nodded.

Chief opened the cockpit door, and said something to someone in the cockpit, who replied, then I heard footsteps coming towards us. Andresha and I looked at each other as Tasha entered the room. To my surprise, she was wearing a Red Star uniform. Her blonde hair had been gathered into a short ponytail, and she wore some kind of transparent visor over her eyes. Glancing at Jess and Jinx, I saw that they had similar visors over their eyes as well.

Andresha stood up slowly and went over to Tasha. "I just have one question for you." She said calmly. Tasha looked slightly confused.

"What is it?" She asked.

Andresha stayed calm. "Did you tell her who we were?" She said softly. Tasha knit her eyebrows.

"What are you talking about?" She said.

Andresha sighed. "You used to work with Fara, didn't you?"

Jess held up a hand. "Andresha, she already told us her story. That's how she learned about the tournament. She didn't reveal your identities."

Andresha didn't look thoroughly convinced, but I trusted Jess. Tasha looked down at the floor, then back at us.

"I'm just glad we got you out ... safely," she said. "I'm sorry Fara showed up. If I'd known she was going to be there I never would have suggested the tournament."

I waved her off. "Don't worry about it. Thanos didn't know she'd be there either."

We were all silent for a moment, then I asked her, "Why did you leave?"

Tasha folded her arms. "You met Harris. I don't know why but there was a bounty on him from someone. Fara took the offer. We'd met Harris a few years back, we were friends. I helped him get off the planet.

"When Fara found out, she was furious. She wouldn't listen to me, going on about him betraying us, or something like that. It didn't make sense. If I hadn't run away..." She hesitated, her eyes fixed on the floor. "I don't think I'd be alive right now," she finished quietly.

I didn't know what to say about that.

Another sound caught my attention and I cocked my head towards the outer hull of the sailor. I could almost hear something through the thick plating, but I couldn't make it out. Like a soft chirping sound. I held up a hand, my attention still on the wall.

"Shh! Quiet a minute!" I said urgently to the others. Their voices slowly drifted into silence. I listened intently, my eyes closed in concentration.

"What is it?" Andresha asked quietly. I could hear the sound clearly now, even though it was muffled by the ship's hull. A loud, electronic *CLANG!*

"It's the planetary alarms," I said, turning to the others.

"Someone's attacked the Core!"

61

Fara dropped from the vent shaft into the hallway below in a crouch, and arm slightly raised behind her. She paused, listening for the sound of footsteps. She heard them in the distance, then she raised an eyebrow and looked in front of her.

There were five REGS agents waiting just ten feet away, their weapons raised. Two knelt, the others stood. She slowly rose to her full height as she recognized the fifth Higher One, the blue ribbon pinned to his chest.

"Well, well, well," she said, slowly walking towards him, "if it isn't Jai Solan, the new Commandant. Here to do some of your dirty work yourself?"

She spoke softly, but her voice carried over the agents clearly; it was filled with contempt and mockery.

Jai was unperturbed. "Put down your weapons and put your hands in the air," he said calmly. Fara didn't move.

"If you couldn't stop your brother and his revolutionary friends from escaping your clutches, what makes you think you can stop me?" She said.

Jai set his jaw. "I won't ask again," he said.

Fara raised her hand and examined her nails. "Did you know about his … what did she call them?" she paused, waving her hand in the air, "… *talents*?" She asked.

Jai's confidence wavered, and she saw it in his eyes. She shrugged.

"Hmm. I guess not," she said, staring at her nails again. She looked at him, only with her eyes, and raised an eyebrow, an awful smirk playing on her lips.

"I suppose I'll have to show you then," she said.

She opened her hand, and tendrils of fire shot away from her palm. They started gently, then the tendrils began to multiply, becoming a wide strip of red-hot flames roaring towards the five agents before her.

276

"Cover!" Jai shouted, and the REGS agents dove to the side. He rolled behind one of the consoles near the side of the hall. There were cries of pain as the wave of fire rolled past him, but he didn't dare look.

The heat became so intense, he had to raise his arm to shield his face to avoid being burned. Then, as quickly as the fire had come, the heat dissipated.

An iron grip grasped his collar, yanking him to his feet. Fara was an inch shorter than him, but she still lifted him off the ground. He found himself staring into her cold, emotionless eyes. No, not emotionless; there was rage there; barely controlled rage. They were like mirrors, he realized; he could almost see his reflection in them.

Fara let out a savage yell as she shoved him away. He flew back and hit the floor, absorbing his momentum by rolling to his feet. This had taken less than five seconds, but Fara was already upon him. She ran towards him at top speed. Jai drew his gun as she came within three feet. Then, she reached up and grabbed one of the vents in the ceiling, and delivered a two-footed kick to his chest.

Jai grunted as the gun was knocked from his grasp and he stumbled back. Fara let go of the vent and landed on her feet. She walked over to him quickly. Jai raised his arms and fists in a defensive stance. Fara sighed.

"I don't have time for this," she said.

Jai, thinking that she was distracted, aimed a punch for her jaw. Fara simply swayed back, evading his strike, then grabbed one of the many bracelets that hung on her wrist. This one, made of a thick, metal material, concealed a small reel of metal cord. She pulled out the end of the cord now, a small hook on the end. Before Jai could pull his hand back from his punch, she grabbed his wrist, wrapping the end of the cord around it. The small hook secured it in place. She pressed a hidden control on the bracelet that locked the reel in place, then she yanked her arm back, pulling Jai off balance. As he stumbled forward, she grabbed his other wrist, unlocked the cable, and rapidly wound it around both hands, binding them together. She ejected the end of the reel from the bracelet. This end had a hook as well, and she used it to fasten the cord. Still holding Jai's bound hands, she swept his feet from beneath him, then released her grip on his hands.

She had done it in five seconds.

Jai let out a cry of pain as he hit the floor, feeling bones crack in his ribs and shoulders.

Fara paused, studying him. "You're really Kane's son?" She said, almost to herself. "Edrix is more like him than you are."

She studied him for one more second, then she kicked him in the side of the head, knocking him unconscious.

62

(Andresha)

E drix's announcement sent the passengers of the Sailor into chaos.

Jinx and Tompson wanted to know how he knew that the Core was under attack. Nelvin and Tasha were talking different hacking techniques, and Jess was calling Chief out of the cockpit.

Edrix and I were completely silent. I spoke quietly to Edrix.

"Can you hear the sirens?" I said. He nodded. His head was still cocked to the side, listening. I was worried about him. He'd been relatively silent ever since he'd looked up his family. I was afraid of what he'd found.

"It's not a hack," he whispered. "The sirens wouldn't be going off for that." He met my eyes. We both knew what it was.

I looked up as Seth entered the room.

"What's the problem?" He asked, the whole room going silent. Jess informed him of Edrix's announcement. Seth remained perfectly calm.

"Do we know what's causing it?" He asked. Nelvin started talking.

"Well, it *could* be a micro-hack aimed at a high-priority file, like the Chairman's schedule or weapon plans."

Edrix shook his head. "It's not a hack. Jackal would never let an embarrassment like that be public. Those sirens would be silent."

We glanced at each other, then I said, "It's Fara. She's in the Core. She must be on the mission the Client gave her."

Nelvin was already working at a console. After a moment, he flicked his display into the air so we could all see.

"I hacked their security feed," he said. Everyone was silent as we stared at the holographic screen. I could see a smoking hole in a building, and the white walls inside. REGS soldiers were everywhere, making it look like a disturbed insect nest.

"What are we looking at, Nelvin," Seth said quietly. Nelvin consulted his console, but before he could say anything, Edrix answered.

"That's the east side of the Core on Level Eight."

I looked over at him. "You knew that just from looking?"

He nodded. I blinked a few times. "Okay."

Seth ran a hand through his hair. "What kind of security is down there?" He asked. Edrix thought for a moment.

"There's three walls, each thirty feet high, ten guard towers on each one and a sentry change every two hours. At the foot of the building, there's a squad of fifty soldiers, and three tanks."

Jinx gave a low whistle. "That's a lot of fire power for one building."

Edrix shrugged. "The lower you go, the heavier security gets."

Jess shook her head, examining the image before us. "I don't get it. Why not go to one of the upper levels and break in there? Wouldn't that be easier?"

Edrix nodded. "If you had the right equipment, you could just cut through the glass walls."

I held up a hand. "Wait a second. If this *is* Fara, then why go through all the trouble to break in this way? Tasha said that we were going to get everything we needed to get inside."

Tasha, who had been silent until now, looked up.

"If you had won, you would have gotten the equipment you asked for. Edrix knew the building and what you would have needed to get inside. Fara doesn't need them."

Jinx looked over at her. "If I remember correctly, Edrix said that twenty percent of REGS forces are stationed there. That's like, what, two *thousand* guards?" He said.

Nelvin cleared his throat. "Two thousand-seven hundred and five, to be precise."

Edrix didn't look up from his hands. "It was thirty percent, actually."

Nelvin paused, then amended his statement. "So, that would actually be four thousand and fifty-six guards."

Jinx folded his arms. "That's not better," he said.

280

Tasha held up her hands. "She'll avoid them, and if she can't, she'll take them out."

"All four thousand and fifty-six of them?" Jinx scoffed.

Tasha looked over at him, completely serious. "She could kill everyone in that building if she wanted to."

She looked over at Edrix. "I'm guessing she showed you her trick." Edrix nodded.

I glanced around as the Sailor went silent. "Well we have to stop her!" I said.

Seth looked over at me. "What are we supposed to do, Andresha?" He asked.

"Why even stop her?" Jinx put in. "If she's taking down the Core, I say good luck to her, and thank you!"

I folded my arms. "We don't know what her mission is, Jinx. It might be to expose us!"

Jinx shrugged. "That's going to happen anyways," he said.

"You don't know that!" I protested.

Jinx shook his head. "Everyone does! We got another report today. They've already gone through fifty percent of the Core's military files. At this rate, they'll find the base in a matter of days!"

Tasha stood up. "We can stop that!" she almost shouted.

Tompson looked at her sympathetically. "Your idea was good, Tasha, but Edrix and Andresha aren't the ones in the Core. That mission, quite frankly, failed."

Tasha spread her hands. "That's my point! This is our way in!"

"Our way in?" Jinx exclaimed. "All those guards are going to be on high alert!"

Edrix spoke now. "Don't you see?" He said, motioning to the image of the Core. "Fara's gotten us inside. All the guards will be looking for her." He moved over to Nelvin. "Punch 'Therris forty-eight' in for me." Nelvin did as he asked, and the image of Fara's attack was replaced a holographic model of the Core.

Edrix moved over to it, manipulating it with his hands. "The middle levels, Six and Five, will be relatively empty." He enlarged the

281

map in those sections. "We can go in there, and be to the Information Hub in twenty minutes."

Nelvin nodded enthusiastically. "Then we could plug in the virus!" he exclaimed.

I looked over at him. "Virus?"

"He means the computer virus we made." Tasha said. "It will wipe anything about Red Star from the Core, as well as anything that's on our Core portion."

Seth nodded. "I agree. This is our way in."

I stared at the map in front of us. "Great. You can drop us off," I said.

Seth looked over at me. "No one said you were going," he said.

"I did." I retorted.

"I'm going with her." Edrix said. "I know the layout, and we've both faced Fara before. We know what we're up against."

Seth sighed. "You just got back from a mission *and* we just rescued you from REGS headquarters. You've been in there for three rotations and …" He trailed off, but we all heard the unspoken comment.

We don't know if Edrix can be trusted.

I lifted my chin. "I trust him. We can do this!"

Seth wasn't convinced. "You'd have to take Nelvin with you. He has to install and activate the virus."

"He did pretty well just now," I said. "If we wait, we won't have time."

Seth sighed. "You know I don't like this," he said quietly.

"I don't like it either, but I think it's our only chance," I replied.

"I'll go with them," Tasha said. We all turned to look at her. She smiled wryly.

"I was tech-support for Fara; I know how she works, and I know how to fight."

Seth started to say something, but she cut him off.

"*And* I can help Nelvin install the virus. It will go faster that way."

I could tell Seth didn't like it, but there was no way he could logically refuse. Jess stood and went over to him.

"It's our only chance," she said quietly. They seemed to have a silent conversation with their eyes.

Seth bit his lip, a look in his eyes that I'd only seen twice, when he was barely keeping his emotions in check, because there would be consequences if he didn't.

He looked at me, his eyes brimming full of emotions. When he finally spoke, there was strain in it that only I could hear. It brought back a flood of memories that came all too quickly since the Anvil. I pushed them aside and listened.

"She beat you last time," he said, his voice almost inaudible.

Edrix took a deep breath. "Yes, but I think I can fix that," he said confidently as he rubbed his hands.

Nelvin held up a finger. "Um, yeah, one question: where are your gloves?"

Edrix looked confused for a moment. "Oh, those gloves. I kind-of … well … lost them."

Nelvin blinked three times. "You … lost them."

Edrix nodded. "I don't need them anymore," he said and held up his hand and a small flame flickered to life. The look on Nelvin's face was priceless.

63

Nelvin came over to Tasha.

"Mind if I sit here?" He asked, motioning to the seat beside her. She looked up and shook her head.

"Not at all."

Nelvin sat down and buckled his safety straps. They both tensed as the sky-sailor turned tightly towards the Stream.

"Are you …" Nelvin started, then he stopped. Tasha looked over at him.

"Am I … what?" She asked.

Nelvin hesitated for a moment, then he said, "Are you, you know, afraid?"

She considered his question. "I suppose I am," she said. "This is the first time I've actually been on a mission. All the other times, I've just been on the comms."

Nelvin adjusted one of his straps. "I'm glad I'm not the only one," he muttered.

Tasha smiled. "Well, Jess told me you did great in the REGS building," she said, hoping to settle his nerves.

Nelvin laughed a little as he set is backpack on the floor in front of him. "I just hope we aren't jumping out of windows this time," he said. They both laughed.

"That bad, huh?" Tasha asked him. He nodded, his eyes wide and eyebrows raised.

"Worse than the plant!" he exclaimed, and they both laughed again as they remembered the plant in his lab that grabbed those careless enough to come too close.

"Compared to that, this will be easy," Tasha said.

They both fell into silence. The ship began to shake and lurch as it entered the Stream. The silence stretched between them. Tasha glanced at Nelvin.

284

"May I ask you a question?" She asked, making sure her grammar was correct. Over the past few weeks, she had discovered that Nelvin was a bit fanatic about correct grammar usage. He had been rummaging through his backpack, but now he sat up and looked at her.

"I congratulate you on your proper grammar, and yes, you may ask me a question," he said.

Tasha looked down and fiddled with her hands for a moment. "How did you get mixed up in this?" She said, motioning to their surroundings. He raised an eye brow.

She shrugged. "I don't know. You just don't seem like the kind of person to join a rebel uprising."

Nelvin looked back at his backpack. "Long story short, I grew up on Three. My sister wanted to be a nurse, talked about it all the time growing up." He stopped and smiled a little. "She had this stuffed animal that she was always patching up."

"Was she younger than you?" She asked.

He shook his head. "Older by three years." He sighed. "Our parents told her that it wasn't an option, since medical science was the Level above us. She wouldn't take no for an answer. She started trying to find ways to go up.

"They took her the next day, REGS agents. I don't know where or why, they just did. I left home the next day. I didn't know where I was going to go, I was just ... upset. All she wanted was a different career, and they arrested her for it. I just kept thinking, 'what if I'm not the only one?' you know? That had lost someone like that. I ran into Short, and, to make it brief, he brought me back here."

Tasha hesitated, trying to think of something to say. Finally, she said, "I'm sorry about your sister."

He shrugged, obviously not wanting to talk about it. After a moment, he said, "So, you never told me about your dream."

Tasha knit her eyebrows in confusion. "Pardon?" She asked. Nelvin gave her a half shrug.

"You know, a week ago, when we were working on the virus."

Tasha sighed inwardly. "It's silly, really."

Nelvin stared at her expectantly. It's only fair, she thought. You *did* just ask him a difficult question.

She shrugged. "Well, I don't remember a lot of it, but for some reason, I was running from something, and I tripped and hit the wall. Instead of just getting up, or getting a bruise or cut on my head, my skin cracked, like glass, and there were gears, or something under my skin."

She forced a laugh and shook her head. "I guess all the machinery I'd been working with got to my head."

She looked over at Nelvin and he nodded. "Thanks for telling me," he said. Tasha just shrugged.

They both looked up as Jess came over to them.

"It's time in three minutes, get ready," she ordered. Both Nelvin and Tasha nodded.

"Yes, ma'am," they answered in unison. Jess nodded and walked back over to Jinx and Chief. Tompson had taken over piloting the ship. Tasha and Nelvin unbuckled their safety straps and got to their feet. Nelvin shouldered his backpack while Tasha strapped a gun and its holster to her thigh. Edrix and Andresha were already up. Edrix had been able to find a spare Red Star jacket to replace his REGS one. They both had their weapons checked and ready. They nodded to Nelvin and Tasha, who nodded back, then they got in position near the sailor's exit hatch.

Tasha took a deep breath and held her gun ready as the light above the hatch blinked yellow. The ship had descended and the hatch was ready to open.

She looked over at Nelvin.

"What was your sister's name?" She asked. Nelvin met her gaze.

"Tasha," he whispered.

64

(Andresha)

I rubbed my hands nervously as the sailor sped through the Stream.

Five minutes ago, we had all gathered by the Sailor's ramp to get our gear together. Edrix and I had been able to find some spare uniforms in the sailor's cargo hold. These uniforms were designed specifically for missions, with a built in harness, and a tough material that Nelvin had designed to protect the wearers from knife blades. It would only protect against a glancing strike, but every little bit helped.

There were also the standard black combat boots, and some black, half-fingered and reinforced gloves.

I had looked over at Edrix as he walked up to the rest of us and nodded.

"You look better in red," I had said, referring to the symbol on his jacket's shoulders.

He had smiled a little. I'd managed to towel out most of the purple and teal dye from my hair, leaving only my original red streak behind.

Seth and Jess had joined us. "You know the plan?" Seth had asked. All four of us had nodded. Seth hadn't quizzed us. We wouldn't have said yes if we hadn't remembered.

"All right, Nelvin," he'd said, "show them what you've got."

Nelvin had clapped his hands and then rubbed them together.

"First things first," he'd said, reaching into one of two backpacks at his feet. He had pulled out two pairs of the visors that Tasha and he were already wearing. He had handed them to Edrix and me.

"These are … well, visors, obviously," he'd said as we put them on. "You activate them with the control on the side."

He had motioned to a small button on the frame. I had pressed mine, and immediately lines and scanning readings had begun to display before my eyes.

"Whoa," Edrix had said. Nelvin had nodded.

"I know, right? The night-vision setting will activate automatically if you enter a dark area. The switch next to the activation button controls the binocular settings. Forward zooms in, backward zooms out.

"The visors will scan automatically, but if you need a more detailed scan, there are two buttons on the other frame. The first one will activate an infrared scanner, the other can link to your scanner, or scan by its self."

I had repeated the controls to myself until I was sure I'd had them memorized. Nelvin had reached into his pack again.

"All right. Last thing for now," he'd said as he withdrew several magazines of ammo from the backpack. He had handed three to each of us. Edrix had looked one over.

"Umm, what are they?" He'd asked. "We already have ammo."

Nelvin had held up a finger. "You have more bullets. These are stun charges," he'd opened the back of the magazine and took out a "stun charge"

It had looked about the same as a bullet, but it had had two small prongs in the front.

"Inside this little beauty is a contained electric current," he'd said.

"Like a battery," Tasha had translated. Nelvin had nodded distractedly.

"Yes, yes, like a battery. Now," he'd motioned to the prongs on the end, "when the charge hits something, the current is released through these prongs."

I had studied the charge. "And this will do … what exactly?"

Nelvin had replaced the charge in the mag, then he had replied, "The currant is strong enough to render someone unconscious without permanent or serious injury."

"Handy," Tasha had said, placing one of her magazines in her gun. I had followed her example, then placed the other two mags in the loops in my belt.

"How many shots in each mag?" Edrix had asked, locking a magazine in his gun.

"There are twelve shots in each one," Nelvin had replied.

Tasha had holstered her gun. "Against over four thousand guards? Three mags are thirty-six shots each."

She'd had a point. If things went according to plan, we wouldn't need any more than that—hopefully even less—but as Edrix and I had learned before, things would always go wrong. Four thousand and fifty-six guards could make a *lot* of things go wrong.

"If we run out of charges, switch back to bullets, but shoot to disable," I had decided. The rest of them had nodded, including Seth.

"We'll be entering the stream in just a few minutes. Strap in," he'd said, then gone to the cockpit while the rest of us had hurried to find a seat.

Now, Edrix looked over at me. "What's eating you?" He asked, and I smiled a little myself. He could read me like a book now. I guess spending a week in a death-trap did that.

I kept my eyes on the floor, aware that he was looking at me.

"Do you really think this plan will work?" I whispered.

He didn't answer right away. There was a stretch of silence between us, then he said, "It has to."

I folded my arms and leaned back in my seat, my gaze now focused on the ceiling. "It had to work in the Anvil too, and we lost." I said flatly.

Edrix nodded. "That's true, but we were on our own then, and we didn't know what we were up against."

Also a fair point. I looked over at him.

"I just hope you're right," I whispered.

65

(Edrix)

I stared at the ramp hatch with my eyes slightly narrowed. I took deep breaths, and stood with knees slightly bent, ready to launch out of the hatch. I could hear my heart beating in my ears.

Tompson was setting down on Six. We wouldn't have time to land and take off again, so the sailor would hover a few feet above the ground.

The light above the hatch now began to flash yellow.

I ran through a checklist in my head, making sure I had all my equipment. Then I thought through the plan, on last time. I clenched my hands into fists, then relaxed them, my gaze fixed on the hatch, waiting for the signal.

The light came on green.

The hatch opened, and the four of us raced out, jumping the three-foot distance to the ground. We hit the ground running, headed for the huge glass-paneled building looming in front of us. I stopped when I reached it. The others were only a few steps behind me and Tasha shot the panel in front of me, creating a web of cracks across the thick glass. I raised my arm to shield my face, then I threw myself into the panel. It shattered on impact, and I crashed to the floor. I quickly got to my feet as the rest of them came through.

"This way," I said, as we headed down the hallway. We could hear the alarms shrieking throughout the facility. We stopped at one of the vents in the ceiling. I reached up and pulled the vent off, carefully setting it aside.

"Cables ready," Andresha ordered.

Back on the sailor, when we were planning our assault, Tasha had recommended using the shafts instead of the lifts.

"Two reasons:" she had said, "one, lifts can be controlled by remote—as you all well know—and they have security cameras and DNA scanners. REGS may be preoccupied with Fara right now, but if *four* rebels walk onto that lift, I can almost guarantee that they'll forget all about her.

"Secondly, Fara will most likely have gotten a detailed map of the building. She knows the fastest way to where she wants to go. It's obvious that she wants to be noticed, so if the lift was the fastest way, she could have disabled the remote and taken it, but Nelvin says that their lift security feed is still up and running. That means that there's another way that's faster."

The only other way up on our map was through the shafts.

Now, I clipped a cable launcher to the barrel of my gun and shot it up through the shaft. After a moment, the cable went taunt, telling me that it had found an anchor. I tested it by giving it a firm tug. The cable didn't give, so I nodded to Andresha.

"It's good."

Since she was the highest ranking agent on the mission, she was in charge. She took a deep breath.

"You go up first, then Nelvin. Tasha will go after him, and I'll come up last," she said. The shaft was too narrow for all of to go up at once, so we had decided to up single-file.

There was a ladder, but we would be going up several Levels. Climbing would take far too long.

I nodded, then I released the cable from the launcher and clipped it onto a loop on my harness. I looked over at Nelvin.

"Are you sure that remote reel will work?" I asked him. He nodded confidently.

"Yes," he said simply. That alone bolstered my confidence. Nelvin didn't rattle off about all the reasons why it *should* work. If he wasn't sure, he would say so.

The reel was the same tech that Nelvin had put into Andresha's hairpins. If we had simply attached the reel to the cable, it would have been too heavy to shoot up the shaft. Instead, Nelvin had attached a small metal square to the end of the cable. Supposedly, after the cable had found an anchor, it would unfold into the reel. I looked up the shaft and took a deep breath. Then, I pressed the control on the remote that I had strapped to my wrist.

I hope this works, I thought. Suddenly, I began to move rapidly upwards. I practically flew up the shaft. In twenty seconds, I had reached the end of the cable. I looked in amazement at the reel.

It had indeed worked as Nelvin had predicted. The metal square had become a large, square block attached firmly to the side of the shaft. There was a glowing green circle on the front, indicating that its anchor was secure.

I looked around. I was in the middle of a junction with four tunnels branching off from my position.

"What's it look like up there?" Andresha's voice crackled in my ear.

"I'm in a four way junction," I said, looking around me again.

"Nelvin's reel worked. The tunnels are marked as L-3—Level Three. According to the chatter Nelvin's been monitoring, Fara was headed this way."

There was silence for a moment, then Nelvin's voice came to my ear.

"Take the tunnel to the left of the reel."

I braced my feet on the wall of the shaft below me, then I turned to face the tunnel Nelvin had referred to. I grabbed the sides of the tunnel and pulled myself inside. I turned around and unclipped the cable from my harness loop. Then, I reached into my pocket and withdrew a small weight that Nelvin had given me, and attached it to the end of the cable.

"Cable coming," I whispered, and dropped the cable back down the dark shaft.

"Cable received," Andresha said. I sat back away from the tunnel mouth and waited.

After a moment, the reel began to whirr quietly. Then Nelvin came up, coming to a stop just a few inches below the reel.

"I'm up. Prepare for cable," he said shortly. It was slightly disconcerting to hear his voice in front of me while hearing in my ear at the same time.

Nelvin pulled himself into the tunnel, and repeated the actions that I had taken. Attach the weight to the cable, send it down the shaft and report that it's on its way. Andresha confirmed it again.

Two minutes later, Tasha was in the tunnel and sending the cable down one last time.

"Cable coming," she said.

A moment later, we all heard Andresha say "Cable received." There was a moment of deafening silence, then she said, "I'm on my way up."

The reel began to spin again, confirming her words. Nelvin was studying the reel.

"She's halfway up," he said. How he knew that from looking at a flashing green light, I didn't know, but I thought it best not to ask. We were a bit short on time.

A few seconds later, Andresha had reached the top of the shaft and climbing into the tunnel.

"Nice work, Nelvin," she said. Nelvin simply nodded.

Andresha brushed hair from her face. "How far?" She asked.

Nelvin thought for a moment—he'd memorized the map I'd found before we left—then said, "About twenty feet down this tunnel, then there should be a hatch above us that leads into the Information Hub."

Andresha nodded. "Edrix and I will take point. Tasha, you take up the rear."

Tasha nodded, then we started to move. No one spoke, fearing that we would be heard. Our boots made only the slightest sounds as we moved. There was crouching-room only, making our progress slow.

Nelvin tapped my arm. "We should be there," he said in a hoarse whisper. I nodded, then relayed the message to Andresha. We both looked up as we examined the hatch.

I held up three fingers, meaning that we would open the hatch and go up on the count of three. Andresha nodded her understanding. Then she turned to Tasha and Nelvin, and motioned with one finger, then pointed to them with two. This meant that we would go first and secure the immediate area, and they would wait for the all-clear.

They both nodded back to us.

Andresha turned back to me. I took a deep breath, then slowly counted up with my fingers.

One…two…three…

I threw the hatch open and we burst out. There were three agents that never saw us coming. We'd shot them down in two seconds. Andresha glanced over at me.

"Well, we know the stun charges work," she said. I nodded silently. We still had our weapons raised as we carefully checked the area.

The walls, floors, and ceiling were spotless white and covered with a reflective glaze. The hatch had opened into the middle of a large, empty circular hallway.

"It's clear," I said after I'd activated my ear comm.

"Be right there," Nelvin replied. A moment later, both of them were out of the hatch. Nelvin looked around.

"There should be a door around here somewhere …" he muttered to himself. Tasha headed down the hall. Andresha looked over at me.

"Should we split up?" She asked.

Before I could reply, a cold voice rang across to me. "You should've stayed with REGS, since you seem to keep coming back."

The three of us spun towards the sound.

Fara was standing by the hatch behind us. She looked almost exactly the same as when we'd been in the Anvil, except for the two long, carved cylinders that hung from her belt. Her hands were empty at the moment. She slowly walked towards us, kicking the hatch closed on her way over. She opened her hand and a stream of fire swirled around it, melting it shut. So much for our exit.

"Did you bring your lab rat this time?" She said, looking at Nelvin. She raised an eyebrow in disdain. "I think you need some better friends."

Andresha didn't flinch. "Like you?" She said and Fara laughed. The sound reminded me of metal scraping against metal.

"I don't have friends. Everyone I knew who gave themselves that title crushed it under their feet," she said acidly.

"Maybe they couldn't handle your dazzling personality," Nelvin said sarcastically. Fara didn't react. "Like I told the Commandant, I don't have time for this."

"What did you do to him?" I asked. Fara cocked her head to the side.

"Who? Your ... brother? He's alive, if that's what you wanted to know," she said. Why had she hesitated? The fact that Jai and I were brothers was common knowledge to REGS, even though we shared almost no similarities.

"Just shoot her!" Nelvin whispered behind me.

Fara smirked.

"Listen to your *friend*, Edrix," she taunted.

"Please stop talking!" Andresha shouted.

Fara switched her attention from me. "Don't tell me what to do, girl! If you wanted to do that, you should have stayed home."

Andresha bit her lip, but she didn't waver. "I got bored," she said finally.

Fara laughed again. "Like I'm going to believe that," she snapped. There was a dangerous look on her face—the one in the Anvil when I'd mentioned Jess's name.

"Andresha—" I started, but Fara cut me off.

"You know what he did when you left?" She asked, her voice dangerously low, still slowly walking towards us. I could have felt her fury four levels down.

"He made me!" she barked.

"Andresha!" I said again, my voice rising in urgency. Her face was whiter than the walls around us.

"What do you mean?" She gasped, her voice shaking.

Fara never got a chance to answer. REGS agents flooded the room, surrounding Fara and ordering her to drop her weapons. I bit back my anger as I recognized Jim's voice. I realized that we'd soon be targeted as well.

"Raise your guns and don't look at anyone!" I hissed to Andresha and Nelvin. Andresha understood first, raising her gun towards Fara. The rest of the agents were equipped with rifles, but I hoped that we wouldn't be around long enough for that to be a problem. Nelvin followed Andresha's lead.

"What now?" He whispered. Only I could hear him.

"When I start to back away, follow me," I said back. I *really* hoped that Tasha had found the door. Otherwise we'd be caught in the middle of an army.

"Move!" I began to step back slowly. Andresha waited for a count of five, then followed me, and Nelvin after her.

We were moving backwards, the tension in the room so thick I could have cut with one of my knives. Fara was completely silent. She simply stared at the agents around her, as silent as a stone. I could hear my heart beating in my ears, along with fifty others. It was then that I realized that she was glowing; a thin aura of fire surrounding her and gradually getting thicker. Fara drew her arms in, her head bowed and knees bent.

"GET AWAY!" she shouted, then thrust her arms out and head back. The fire around her exploded into a spherical shock wave.

"Go! Go! Go!" I shouted, forcing myself to shut out the chaos behind me.

I glanced back, only to see the edge of the wave just three feet behind us.

"We're not gonna make it!" Nelvin cried. He was right, we weren't. Not by running. I wasn't sure if Fara's fire could hurt me, but I didn't want to find out. I'd have to try something I had never done before and hope it would work.

"Stay close to me!" I shouted to the others, then I raised my hands, imagining a bubble around us. My hands started to tingle, like they always did when the fire came, but this time, it didn't stay in my hands. It shifted into a disc above my head, then expanded above Nelvin and Andresha. The edges then seemed to melt down until we were in a dome of fire, almost exactly like the one I'd imagined.

Nelvin, still running, stared at the dome, his mouth agape in awe.

"That. Is. Awesome!" he exclaimed. Andresha simply smiled. I hoped that the dome would hold. The last time I'd tried to use my fire, it had drastically drained my energy, and I'd only been able to sustain it for a few seconds. And that attack hadn't been *nearly* as powerful as this one.

Fara's shockwave hit my dome ... and passed over it. It wasn't effortless. I had to work to keep my fire sustained enough to protect us from the shockwave, but it didn't take nearly as much energy as it had in the Anvil.

I breathed a sigh of relief as I let the dome disappear.

296

Andresha nodded. "Nice work, let's find that door," she said.

"Already done."

All three of us jumped as Tasha seemed to appear in front of us. She seemed to not have noticed.

"I found the door." She continued. "It's this way."

She led the way down the hall to a plain white door that blended into the surrounding wall.

"I walked past it three times." She said. "I'm not sure how to open it though."

Nelvin was already digging through his backpack. He brought out a small, round device and placed it on the door, then pushed a button in the center. It made a series of beeps, then the door slid open.

"Nice," I said to Nelvin as he retrieved the device, stuffing it back into his pack.

"Thanks," he said. We heard shouts back the way we'd come.

"We need to hurry," Andresha said. "We're almost out of time."

Then she led us through the door into the Information Hub.

66

Tasha caught her breath as she walked through the door. The Information Hub spread before the four of them, and to her surprise, it was beautiful.

The door led to a narrow platform that ran around the perimeter of the vast, circular room. It was darker than the hallway, and the walls and floors were no longer white. Instead, they were a deep gray, almost black. In the center of the room, there were thousands of tiny, twinkling lights. Each one, she knew, represented a data file. There were so many, it seemed that she was looking out into space. The lights expanded both upward and downward until she couldn't see them anymore. As she looked down at her feet, there was a transparent walkway that started at the platform and led to the information. It seemed so thin and delicate, she was sure it would shatter if she stepped on it. As she looked, she could see similar walkways weaving through the lights.

"Wow," Nelvin whispered. Tasha could only nod in agreement.

Edrix, who had been locking the door, looked around. "Where do we install the virus?" He asked. Nelvin sighed, then rubbed the back of his neck.

"That is an excellent question," he replied.

Andresha checked her gun, then started forward. "It has to be up there somewhere," she said motioning to the lights. "We might as well get moving."

She hesitated when she came to the walkway, then gingerly stepped onto it.

"Seems stable enough," she said. There was only room to go single file. Andresha looked around, then said, "I'll go first, Nelvin behind me. Then Edrix and Tasha." She started up the walkway.

Nelvin stared at the walkway like it had teeth. "Did I mention that I don't like heights?" He grumbled, then edged onto the walkway. Edrix stepped on after him.

"Just don't look down," he said.

"Hard to do when the walkway is clear," Nelvin called back.

Tasha stepped onto the walkway next. "Just follow Andresha," she called up to Nelvin, her voice echoing off the walls. "Then you won't have to look at the ground."

"This is not ground," Nelvin stated, "but I will try your suggestion."

Tasha smiled, then glanced behind them. So far, no one had pursued them, but Tasha didn't want to think about why.

It didn't take them long to reach the first data files. Now that they were closer, Tasha could see that they were enclosed in small, dark boxes, almost like consoles.

Andresha motioned to the closest ones. "Work your magic, Nelvin," she said. Nelvin moved over to one of the files, examining its box, then he looked up towards a non-existent ceiling.

"I wonder," he whispered, then he said, more loudly, "Computer, show me to an access port in the Information Hub."

There was silence for a moment, then an electronic voice said, "Please follow the blue line on the walkway."

Tasha looked down at her feet. A thin, glowing blue line had appeared on the walkway. No, not on—*in* the walkway. That must have been why it was transparent.

Nelvin nodded. "Right, shall I lead or shall you?" He said to Andresha.

She considered his question for a moment, trying to see through all the files to the line's end.

"Edrix and I will both lead. Tasha will take up the rear," she said finally.

They began to move again. Tasha was enthralled by the sights around her. She couldn't help but occasionally glance through a file. There were so many, most of them on the daily activities of citizens on the various levels.

"Why go through all this trouble?" She muttered aloud.

Edrix glanced back at her. "Trouble for what?" He asked. Tasha, who had forgotten about his hearing, jumped a little. Finally, she said, "I mean, make all this," she motioned to her surroundings, "to see what people eat for breakfast?"

Edrix didn't answer, but Andresha did.

"If you ask them, they'll say it's for security; to stop threats before they become a real danger, and that's true, if you're a threat to *them*. To the system. If you dare to think that things could be different. It's just another way to take our freedom from us, to make sure we're doing as they say, even in our homes."

This quieted the group. Tasha hadn't lived on Rendaria for very long; a year at the most. As such, she didn't know what kind of oppression these people had been through to cause them to rise up. But she did know REGS, and she knew what they did. Based on her own experience, she could at least imagine what it was like here.

She could see it in the way Andresha spoke. How she was defensive of herself and those close to her. Her distrust of those who worked under the REGS insignia.

Nelvin had told her his story, and it was close to hers, but at least she knew what had happened to her family. Nelvin didn't. He may never get an answer.

Edrix had seen something horrible. It was written in his eyes. It was hidden deep now, like an old wound, but the scar was there, and it came out whenever someone mentioned Level Eight. Whatever it was, it had been enough for him to turn his back on his own family.

She amended the statement. His brother had turned his back on *him*, and it had hurt him all the more.

She was pulled out of her pondering as the rest of the party stopped. They had reached the end of the blue line, and there was no access port in sight.

"Umm, Nelvin?" Edrix asked as he examined the files.

"I know," he muttered, his scanner whirring quietly. He let out an exasperated sigh and shut the scanner.

"The computer lied to me," he said, sounding genuinely insulted. "There's no access port here."

"In this area?" Andresha asked. Nelvin shook his head.

"In the *entire building*!" He said, a frustration in his voice.

Tasha's mind raced. If there wasn't an access port, they wouldn't be able to install the virus. All this effort would be for nothing. Finding the files individually and deleting them manually wasn't an option either. With all the information she'd seen, it would take *rotations* to find them all. There had to be some way ...

"Nelvin," she said finally, "what if we put the virus *in* a file?"

Nelvin turned to look at her. "What do you mean?"

She pointed to a file next to her. "Like one of those? They have to be adding them all the time, they wouldn't even notice it!"

Nelvin, considering her idea, began to nod. "All the files are linked as a security precaution, and that will just spread the virus through the system!"

Andresha brushed hair out of her face. "But where do we make the file?" She asked. Nelvin looked around for a moment. He turned to Edrix.

"Do you hear a soft humming noise?" He asked. Edrix nodded. "Ever since we came in the room. Why do you ask?"

Nelvin didn't answer right away. Instead, he asked another question. "Can you tell where it's coming from?"

Edrix paused for moment, listening intently. "Yes," he said finally, wisely waiting for Nelvin to answer on his own.

Nelvin paused, then said, "That's what we're looking for. The computer probably has an automatic program to create and install the new files. Considering the number of people on the planet and the amount of nonsense that the Chairman and his officials are spouting all the time, it would be working overtime, making that humming noise."

Andresha nodded. "Lead the way then," she said to Edrix.

Tasha began to follow them, when she suddenly tensed.

"Tasha? What is it?" Nelvin asked, his voice sounding far away.

Tasha turned towards them. "Go! Get the virus installed. I'll try to hold her off as long as I can!" she shouted.

Nelvin shook his head uncomprehendingly. "Tasha what are you talking about?"

"She's talking about me," Fara said as she came into view. "And I suggest you take her advice."

67

Tasha could hear her heart beating as she stared into her eyes. Her former best friend stood before, completely different from the girl she'd known.

She heard her friends leaving, or trying to. Nelvin wasn't having any of it.

"Tasha, come on!" he shouted. She didn't dare look behind her. That would give Fara her opening.

"So, the traitor decides to show her face," Fara said, her voice low and menacing. "And you're hanging out with *this* group?"

Tasha didn't speak, she simply nodded. Fara glanced behind her, at Nelvin.

"It sounds like the lab rat's attached to you."

Tasha ignored her. "What happened to you?" She asked simply. Her friends needed to go … and they needed to go *now*!

"I realized that the nightmare we were living wasn't a dream," Fara said acidly. "And what did you do? You saved the man who sold us out!"

"It was an accident!" Tasha exclaimed. "Harris never wanted any of that to happen—"

Fara held up her hand to stop her. "Stop defending him! He knew full well who he was talking to!" She turned away from her.

Tasha shook her head angrily. "The only person who knew who that was, was you!" she said. "You never told anyone, not even me! Harris said he was sorry *so* many times!"

Fara wheeled back around. "He said he was *sorry*?" She said mockingly. "Tell that to his son, who's lying buried with all the rest!" Her voice caught with unexpected emotion.

Tasha lowered her voice. "Do think that this is what he would have wanted? What would he think if he saw you now?"

And then she realized the mistake she had made. She'd gone too far, said too much, but maybe she could fix it.

"I'm your friend. I always have been."

302

Fara's breathing increased and she was growling almost continually. One tear slid down her cheek.

"You are not my *friend*!" She lashed out as she said the last word. It was so fast that Tasha didn't have any time to react.

The blow caught her cheek, receiving the full force of the blow.

She cried out in pain as she lost her balance—and fell off the walkway.

"NO!"

Nelvin broke free Edrix's grasp. He'd had to drag him up the walkway while Tasha had been talking, Nelvin struggling all the while.

Fara had disappeared from the walkway—off to complete her mission, maybe, he didn't care—and now he ran to where Tasha had stood, kneeling to try and see her.

He found her, on a lower walkway, and she didn't seem to be moving.

He looked around frantically. She couldn't be, she couldn't be! His visor found where his walkway connected with hers. He was on his feet in an instant, running towards it. His feet could have had wings, for he seemed to never touch the ground.

"Nelvin, wait!" Andresha called after him, but he couldn't hear her. All he could see was the unconscious girl on the walkway.

He slid to a stop as he reached her, dropping to his knees beside her.

"Tasha!" he shouted. "Come on! Come on!" He shook her urgently. His friends came to a stop behind him, but he barely noticed. His had went to his scanner, opening it, his heart pounding, and his hands trembling in fear.

She stirred and her eyes fluttered open.

Nelvin's heart soared with relief. She was alive!

"Tasha?" He whispered urgently. She didn't answer, but she started to sit up, and stopped.

She stared at her hand, then she felt her face.

"Nelvin," she whispered, her voice choked with tears.

"What is it?" He asked softly, and she turned to look at him.

Her nightmare had come true.

Her face had cracked, like his mother's glass doll that he had accidently knocked to the floor as a child. Not just her face, but her hand and arm that she had fallen on.

But instead of gears beneath her skin, there were blinking lights, wires, and innumerable tiny buttons.

"What am I?" She cried out in fear. Nelvin knew, but he thought it was only theoretical.

"Like, you walk around, and you have thoughts and feelings, but there's just something ... missing?"

There had been something missing.

With tears in his eyes, Nelvin pulled Tasha into his embrace.

"You're Tasha. You're my friend and that's all that matters."

He could feel how hard she was shaking, her gaze fixated on her hand. She was starting to hyperventilate, tears running down her face.

"Hey, don't look at that," he said, cupping her cheek in his hand and gently turning her face away from her hand, so he could meet her eyes.

"You're going to be fine," he said, trying to fill his voice with confidence. Tasha smiled a little.

"Don't let the plant get you," she whispered. The lights were beginning to flash and blink rapidly.

Nelvin smiled through his tears. "I won't."

Tasha reached up and brushed a tear off his cheek.

"Nelvin," she started. She took a shuddering breath, then tried again.

"Nelvin, I ... I lo—"

Her body went stiff, then completely limp. The lights went dark.

Nelvin collapsed, sobbing, his arms still around her. He didn't want to let go. He knew what she was going to say, and it broke his heart in half.

Still weeping, he gingerly closed her eyes, those beautiful brown eyes. He couldn't stay here forever. He wished he could, but Tasha wouldn't have wanted him too. She'd want everyone to be safe.

"For you, Tasha," he whispered. "For you."

68

(Edrix)

Tasha toppled from the walkway, while Fara leapt nimbly to the one above us. Nelvin wrenched himself out of my grasp, an anguished cry escaping his lips.

"Nelvin, wait!" Andresha called after him, but he wasn't listening. Everything had seemed to happen in slow-motion at first, now time seemed to have sped up around me.

And Fara was getting away.

"Follow Nelvin," I said. "Find Tasha, then get that virus installed!"

Andresha grabbed my arm. "Where are you going?" She shouted.

I stared at the walkway Fara had jumped to.

"I'm following her."

Andresha was in command, but I was the only one who would stand a chance against Fara.

"And here, take these," I added, quickly handing her my other magazines of stun charges. Andresha shook her head.

"No, keep them," she protested, trying to give them back. I pushed them into her hands.

"Go!" I shouted. She hesitated a second more, then headed after Nelvin.

I looked at the walkway again, then at the wall of data files across from me, the hollow boxes they were stored in.

I approached the boxes at a run, then I pushed off with my foot, finding a foothold. I immediately leapt from there to the walkway. I paused briefly, listening. I placed a hand on the walkway, keeping myself perfectly still. I felt the slight vibrations of someone moving quickly across its surface, and heard her soft footsteps. I was headed in the right direction.

I was on my feet in an instant, heading off at a run. I had to watch my footing, since the surface was not only narrow, but transparent as well. I nearly fell twice, causing my heart to pound.

My thoughts briefly went to Tasha. I hoped she was alright. I hoped she hadn't missed the walkway below the one we'd been on. Then, she might be injured, but she would be more likely to have survived the fall.

I was pulled from my pondering by three bullets whizzing over my head. I ducked my head down, drawing my own weapon and dashing behind a stack of data files. I could see two REGS agents up the walkway, coming towards me. I reached around and snapped off two shots. There was a sharp snap of electricity, and a cry of pain.

I peeked out cautiously. I'd stunned one of the agents, but the other was still coming towards me. Two more bullets clipped the boxes by my face. I waited a moment more, then dashed out onto the walkway and shot twice more. One of my charges found their mark. There was another *snap*, and the REGS agent crumpled to the ground, unconscious. I quickly counted in my head. I had six more shots in this magazine. I'd have to conserve them as much as I could.

I continued after Fara, moving as quickly as I dared. Looking around me, I wondered where she had gone. For all I knew, she'd gone to another walkway.

My question was answered when fire shot towards me.

I was too surprised to catch it, so I deflected it. It slammed into the data files next to me, completely obliterating them. An alarm began to shriek. I winced at its intensity.

Quickly looking around me, I saw Fara twenty feet away from me. The alarm must have affected her more than it had me; her hands were pressed over her ears, and her eyes were screwed shut.

Now was my chance.

I rushed forward, my hands ablaze. Fire shot from both my hands, snaking towards her. At the last second, her hand shot out and caught it, then threw it into the abyss below the walkway.

"You're really starting to annoy me," she said, straightening from her hunched position. She flicked her hand towards the direction of the alarm. Fire shot away from it, and a moment later, there was an explosion, then the alarm stopped.

"That usually means I'm winning," I replied. Fara smirked.

"*Usually,*" she repeated. then lunged towards me, her knife appearing in her hand.

I leaned back, away and under her strike, drawing two of my own knives. She sliced towards my head, I parried her blow. Then I thrust for her ribs, she stopped my knife with hers.

We continued like this for a few minutes; I couldn't tell you how long. It all seemed to blur together. Adrenaline does that.

I caught a slash from Fara's knife with mine, just inches from my face. She had me backed up against the data files.

My arm shook as I kept the blade away from my neck. Andresha's voice sounded in my ear quietly.

"She's gone."

Gone ... Tasha was dead.

I felt the flames in my hands intensify as my anger grew. How many friends was I going to lose? My hands were shaking from anger now, not fatigue. In fact, they felt stronger. I drew my feet up, then, with a yell, kicked her away from me.

Fara stumbled back, almost falling from the walkway. Unfortunately, she recovered her balance.

"Congratulations. She's dead," I said, my voice ominously low. Fara touched a bleeding cut on her lip, then spat blood from her mouth.

"She was never alive," she snapped. I knit my brow in confusion.

"What's that supposed to mean?" I shot back. Fara scowled.

"It means that the girl you knew as Tasha, was an android from the start."

Android? As far as I knew, androids existed only in theory. I didn't care.

"She was my friend, and that's all I care about!" I shouted. Fara growled and started towards me, but stopped as a rain of bullets appeared in the air. We both ducked behind the data files, bullets peppering the walls and consoles around us.

Peeking around, I saw five agents on one walkway, and five on the other.

I had six charges left. I could clear one walkway, and have one shot to spare, counting that I didn't miss. I'd broken records in training with my hand-eye coordination, but that was with stationary targets.

But which walkway? I had no idea where I needed to go, plus the other agents would probably shoot me on my way over.

I touched the communicator in my ear.

"Andresha, I'm pinned down," I said. There was a brief silence, then she said, "We're in the same situation over here." She paused. "Send the signal."

I nodded, even though she couldn't see me.

"Got it."

I quickly swiped a control on my wrist comm. It beeped twice, telling me that the signal had gone through.

Fara fired her hand guns four times, and four agents went down, two on each walkway.

I didn't hesitate. While the remaining guards were focused on Fara, I snapped off three shots at the walkway leading to the left. Electricity snapped, and three more guards went down.

The agents turned to me, and Fara shot again. This time, only one guard fell, leaving two more. One walkway was completely clear.

I shot twice. One guard gave a cry and fell, the other glanced at his comrade, then continued firing.

I'd missed.

Fara's gun fired, and the last guard fell. She looked over at me and smirked.

"Sorry, but I don't have any more time to play."

She moved lightning fast and kicked me in the stomach. I fell to the walkway, all the air forced out my lungs.

"We're at the central controls," Andresha said.

"That's great," I said, rolling onto my knees and grabbing my gun. "You're doing better than I am."

69

(Andresha)

I tried to help Nelvin, but I soon discovered that my attempts to were only slowing him down so I set myself on watch instead. I patrolled around the control console, my eyes alert for any sign of trouble.

"How's Edrix doing?" Nelvin called over to me. I checked down one walkway, then headed over to another one.

"He got pinned down by some guards, then Fara got away. He's been better." I called back.

"I think we've all been better," he muttered. I didn't know what to say to that.

To say I was shocked by Tasha's death would have been an understatement, but I didn't have time to grieve right now. I had to stay on top of things for the rest of my team.

"Time?" I asked Nelvin, keeping my eyes on the walkway. There was a pause, then he answered, "Maybe … ten minutes?"

I nodded to myself. It was pushing it, but it was do-able.

"Fine." I called back to him.

I continued around the control station Nelvin was working at, alert for anything that moved. I actually jumped when Edrix's voice sounded in my ear.

"I've found her again." I guessed he meant Fara. His voice was hushed to a whisper. I could barely hear it, it was so soft.

Fara must have been in earshot … for them.

"What's your status?" I asked him.

He didn't answer right away. It was a good minute before he spoke again.

"She's sixty feet away from me. She hasn't spotted me yet, and she's looking at a file."

Sixty feet? He could hear a whisper from sixty feet away? *That's beside the point!* I chastised myself. Her mission must have been to retrieve a data file; but then why all this noise? According to Tasha, she could have gotten in and out without tripping a single alarm. Edrix was talking again.

"I was wondering if Nelvin could see what she was accessing."

I turned and looked over at Nelvin. The comm channel was open, so he'd heard Edrix's question as well.

He was nodding. "Do you know the file number?" He asked. Another pause, then Edrix replied, "Seven-seven-four-eight-two-nine-dash-four-four-three-verith-five."

I walked up to the panel while Nelvin typed the number in. After a moment, the computer pinged, and a file came up on the screen.

"We've got it," I said.

"Better hurry," he said, still whispering. "I think she's downloading it."

I bit my lip, then looked at Nelvin.

"Keep working on the virus. I'll look at this."

Nelvin nodded and went back to another screen. I began to quickly scan the document. When I was younger, I'd loved reading, I still did, but I'd never had a large amount of time to do so. As a result, I had become an incredibly fast reader.

The file looked to be a collection of reports of some kind, labeled, "PROJECT PHOENIX." I had no idea what a phoenix was. Maybe it was a code for something. I selected the first report.

DAY ONE: SUBJECT NORMAL. NO EVIDENCE OF CHANGE.

It continued like this for several lines, until I reached "Day Thirty-seven."

DAY THIRTY-SEVEN: SUBJECT POSITIVE. NEXUS LEVELS AT NINETY-FOUR PERCENT.

Nexus levels? Nexus was an elemental substance found most commonly in specific rock deposits, and was *extremely* rare. What was the "subject" the file was talking about?

I switched to the next report. It was full of scan results for this mystery "subject," but they were medical scans. Blood pressure, brain waves, everything you'd find on a medical report, except for another Nexus Level. It too, read "ninety-four percent."

"What in the world?" I muttered under my breath. Nelvin stopped working and came over to me.

"What is it?" He asked. I motioned to the screen.

"These reports. I can't make any sense of them," I said.

"Let me have a look," he said. I moved aside, but looked over his shoulder.

His eyes scanned the report, his lips moving wordlessly as he read. As he reached the end, he suddenly grew pale. At the same time, Jess spoke to me in my comms.

"We're in. Location and status?" She said. It was Edrix who answered, but he was no longer whispering.

"Water Bird and Lizard are in the main control center, I'm following Fara, further in the Hub." Then he added, "Runner's dead."

"Runner" had been Tasha's code name. Jess started to reply but, to my surprise, Nelvin stopped her.

"Blizzard, Sandstorm. We've recovered information that we believe Fara was sent to retrieve," he said quickly.

"Lizard, what is it?" Seth was speaking now. When outside of the base, he was called "Sandstorm."

Nelvin didn't answer them, instead turning to me. "Find the subject name, hurry!" he shouted, his fingers flying over the controls.

"What are you doing?" I asked, looking at the screen. He didn't look up.

"Downloading it," he said shortly.

"Water Bird, what is going on?" Seth said again. *I wish I knew,* I thought to myself.

"Stand by!" I shouted. I swiped to the last report, searching the top of it.

PROJECT PHOENIX: WEAPONS DEVELOPMENT
PROJECT ORDERED BY: NERO JACKAL AND CHAIRMAN ORMUS

311

PROJECT ADMINISTRATOR: **NAME RESTRICTED**
SUBJECT NAME:—

"Edrix Solan?" I gasped.

"Water Bird, report!" Seth shouted. My hands were trembling, and my blood ran cold. I was unable to speak, so Nelvin spoke for me.

"Edrix ... Edrix is a REGS experiment."

"*What?!*" Edrix exclaimed. Seth began talking rapidly.

"Lizard, get those files and anything else on Project Phoenix, then get that virus installed. Now!"

Nelvin typed so fast, I expected smoke to come pouring out of the console. Then he slapped a control on his screen and all chaos broke loose.

A high-pitched scream erupted from all around us. At the same time, a bright flash appeared across the Hub. I looked in its direction, then used my visor. I used the binocular setting, letting me see across to the area. Edrix and Fara were locked in combat, fire swirling around them. Then, above me, a door blew open. Jinx, Jess, and Seth raced through the smoking opening onto the walkway right above us.

"Andresha, where's Edrix?" Seth shouted. I pointed across the Hub, and saw them activating their visors. I heard a gun fire, and Edrix shout in pain.

"Edrix!" I shouted, running down the walkway.

"Andresha!" Seth yelled after me. I ignored him. I practically flew down the walkway, changing the stun charges in my gun with bullets.

I didn't know how long it took me to get over there, but it felt like forever. Would I get there in time? Would I get there in time? The thought repeated over and over again. I tripped over something. It was a guard's arm. I got up and kept going. I was getting close!

I could see them now, about a hundred feet away. Edrix was lying on the walkway, his gun kicked away from him. He was holding his leg, and there was red seeping from beneath his fingers. The scanner in my visor showed that it wasn't serious; the bullet had only grazed his leg. Fara was just a few steps away from him.

"You're a weapon. We're all a weapon. That's the only thing we were all made for!" she shouted. She grabbed fistfuls of her hair, then she pressed a control on one of the bracelets on her wrist.

"Open it!" she shouted, then she raised her gun to Edrix.

"Shame to lose the original," she said, her finger tensing on the trigger.

I emptied my magazine. Some of the shots missed, since I was rushed, but I spent hours in the gun range, and I was an expert shot.

Fara staggered back, red stains blossoming on her shirt. Wounds on her arms and face closed almost immediately. I let my fingers release the empty mag from my gun and replace it with another.

I blinked and she was over to me, fire wreathing her hands, but I was ready. I kicked her back, then snapped off four more shots.

These were stun charges, and I'd shot her point blank. There was no way I could miss.

Electricity snapped and Fara screamed, falling to the walkway, smoke curling from her body.

"This ... This isn't over," she said, her voice strained. Then she laughed, but it turned quickly into a cough. She curled her lip in a sneer.

"You've only begun,"

She rolled off the walkway, and I rushed to the edge, peering over after her.

Suddenly, a flash lighted the empty passage in the center of the Hub so bright, I had to close my eyes. The entire building shook, and I lost my balance, toppling from the walkway, and into the light.

70

(Edrix)

Fara slipped the device she had been using on the data file into a pouch on her belt and turned away from the console. I didn't have time to wait for Andresha to look at the file, otherwise I'd lose Fara again. It had been sheer luck that I'd found her this time. I'd been on my way to the control center when I'd walked past the station she was at.

Now, I started to follow her noiselessly. She was tapping something on her wrist.

"I have the info. Stand by for exit," she said. She must have been on comms with someone.

No way was I letting her get away.

I silently drew one of my knives. All of the ones I was carrying were weighted for throwing, but this one was made for that specific purpose. I brought my arm up and back slowly, still matching her pace and her footsteps. I was barely breathing, not wanting her to hear me. Then I brought my arm forward in one fluid motion.

Fara's hand snapped the knife out the air, just and inch from her head. She spun around. She let out a wordless shout, then took off running. I took off after her, watching my footing on the twisting walkways.

Jess's voice came over the comm. "We're in. What's your status?"

I swiped a hand across my ear. "Water Bird and Lizard are in the main control center. I'm following Fara, deeper in the Hub." I hesitated, then added, "Runner's dead."

Before Jess could reply, Nelvin began to speak quickly, concern in his voice.

"Water, Sandstorm, we've obtained information we believe Fara was sent to retrieve."

"Lizard, what is it?" Chief was speaking now. Nelvin didn't reply.

"Water Bird, what's going on?" Chief shouted now.

314

"Stand by!" Andresha shouted back. What were they all worried about? Two REGS agents came onto the walkway. Since it was narrow, their shoulders were touching. Their mistake.

I shot my last stun charge. Electricity snapped and they both went down without a sound.

"*Edrix Solan?*" Andresha gasped. What was she doing? We weren't supposed to use our names on the comms.

"Water Bird, report!" Chief shouted. It was Nelvin who answered him.

"Edrix … Edrix is a REGS experiment."

"*What?!*" I exclaimed. Everything seemed to stop as his words echoed through my head. That couldn't be right. I didn't remember anything. But then again, I didn't remember the last three rotations, either. I stopped in my tracks, my brain trying to work out what Nelvin was saying. It was a mistake.

Fara stopped running and spun around, delivering a lightning-fast punch just below my eye. It had all the weight of her shoulder and arm behind it, along with the speed and power from her spin. I was lucky I didn't black out. I had to stagger back several steps in order to stay on my feet. I felt blood running down my face. Following her advantage, she drew her knife and aimed a thrust for my ribs. I stepped to the side, then grabbed her wrist. She wrenched it from my grasp and aimed a kick for my ribs. I caught it in my hands and threw it aside.

We continued like this for several minutes. Finally, we both let our hands blaze white hot. They collided together, creating a blinding flash. Then we played a deadly game of catch; shooting fire and catching it, then tossing it back.

"You don't know when to give up, do you?" She said.

"No, not really," I replied, letting a wave of fire leave my hands. Fara simply lifted her hand, and it parted around her.

"Still learning, I see." She thrust both hands forward, fire streaking towards me. I caught it, but I was surprised at its force. It felt like it was pushing against me. Then, she abruptly let go, then pushed her hands forward again, this time, just a short burst, but I was distracted by her first attack. The second one hit me and sent me staggering back. Fara already had her gun in her hand and fired.

I yelled as I felt pain flare in my leg as it buckled from beneath me. I had been reaching for my own weapon, and now it clattered away from me. Fara kicked it farther away.

"You're a weapon. We're all weapons. It was what we were made for!" Fara shouted. She spoke as if there were more of us … people with powers. I tried to pull myself backwards, frantically looking for something, anything that I could use to get away. Fara growled and grabbed fistfuls of her hair. Then she activated the bracelet on her wrist she had been using earlier.

"Open it!" she shouted. She turned back towards me, anger evident in her every move. She raised her gun.

"Shame to lose the original," she said, not a hint of regret in her voice. Her finger tensed on the trigger, and the sound of gunfire erupted around me.

But I was still alive.

Fara screamed and stumbled back, ominous red stains appearing on her shirt. Then she was running down the walkway. I looked behind me, trying to see who had come. Everyone else was on the other side of the Hub.

I heard four shots, then a loud crackle of electricity. Fara screamed again. I'd gotten to my knees, and could now see what was going on.

Fara was collapsed on the walkway. Andresha stood over her, gun in hand.

"This isn't over," Fara said in a strained voice. She laughed, then coughed. I couldn't see her face from here, but Andresha was perfectly calm.

"You've only begun." Fara said, then she rolled off the walkway, and Andresha rushed over to the edge, peering into the dark abyss.

"Andresha!" I shouted, but she couldn't hear me, because at that moment, there was a loud *BOOM!*

The entire building shook and a blinding light flared from where Fara had fallen. I raised a hand to shield my eyes, my gaze still locked on Andresha.

Then, with a cry of alarm, she fell into the light.

316

71

Seth rushed into the room, Jess and Jinx behind him.

"Go get Tasha," he said to Jinx. He nodded and headed down the walkway at a run. Then Seth looked down into the control center.

"Andresha, where's Edrix?" He called down to her urgently. She pointed across the Hub. Seth and Jess both activated their visors looking in the direction she had indicated. Seth could see Edrix locked in combat with a girl who couldn't have been older than seventeen, maybe even eighteen. Her skin was pale, and her hair was white. It contrasted her grey clothing. Dark pants and boots, and a lighter grey shirt. Her belt was loaded with weapons, and there was fire in her hands.

Seth looked over at Jess.

"That's her?" He asked quietly. She nodded, her face expressionless to everyone but him. He could see the tears brimming in her eyes. She was probably biting her cheek, he thought. Fear and concern were her strongest emotions … and regret.

Suddenly, they heard a gun fire and Edrix cried out in pain.

"Edrix!" Andresha shouted, taking off down the walkway.

"Andresha!" Seth shouted after her, but she ignored him.

"Every time," he muttered under his breath. He jogged down to the control center, Jess behind him.

"Status?" He asked Nelvin. Smoke was pouring out of the sparking console. Nelvin raised a hand in front his face to shield it from another shower of sparks.

"The virus is working. That's that shrieking noise. It's overloading the system. I don't think anything has ever been erased from this thing." He motioned to the Hub as he spoke. He had to shout to be heard over the alarms.

"I've got Runner, and I'm at the extraction site," Jinx said over the comms.

317

"Stand by," Seth replied. Nelvin had his backpack on his shoulders once more. More gunshots rang over to them from Edrix's location. Seth turned that direction, counting silently.

Twelve. There had been twelve shots. An entire magazine. His visor focused on their source.

There was Edrix, and Fara had run up the walkway towards Andresha. Seth gripped his gun, knowing he was too far away to help if something went wrong.

But she didn't need him. As Fara reached her, Andresha kicked her away, then fired four more shots. Fara screamed as electricity flared briefly around her, then collapsed to the walkway.

Seth felt mixed emotions. He was proud of her, that she'd handled the situation calmly and by herself, but he also felt guilt and sadness for the same reason.

"She grew up too fast." He whispered. Only Jess heard him.

"You both did," she replied.

"All of us did."

Fara rolled from the walkway and Andresha rushed over. Edrix shouted something just as the building shook violently, knocking him and the others to their knees. There was a deafening *boom*, and the Hub was illuminated with a blinding light. Data files storage unites tumbled into it. The walkways began to shatter, and lights exploded and fell into the light, almost as if they were being sucked in.

Andresha cried out in alarm, as the building's rumblings shook her from the walkway.

"No!" Seth howled, his hand reaching towards her, but he knew that he'd never get there in time.

"Dresha!" Edrix screamed. Seth could barely see him through the light, but he'd gotten to his feet and run over to where she had been standing. Jess understood what was happening before Seth did.

"Edrix, don't!" she yelled, but it was too late. Edrix leapt from the walkway after Andresha, and disappeared.

318

72

Nero Jackal sat at his desk and stared at a hologram of the Core. The smoldering hole where the Hunter had entered, and the two shattered windows where the rebels had gone in; one on Six, the other on Five.

His office was sparsely decorated, with only the desk and three chairs. He didn't have guards, not inside the office anyways. He was more than capable of taking care of himself, and he smiled. He'd received the highest scores in the Higher Program. The smile faded. Until the Solans had applied, he thought to himself.

He didn't look up as the door opened. He knew the footsteps of everyone authorized to enter that room.

"What is it, Fisk?" He said, still looking at the hologram.

Supreme Authority Fisk saluted briefly, a data pad in his hands. Only then did Jackal look up.

"What did they find?" He asked. Fisk handed him the data pad.

"Doctor Kevis has come to the conclusion that he cannot be controlled, not with our current methods."

Jackal took the pad. "How did he come to this conclusion?"

Fisk motioned to the data pad. "As designed, the Nexus improved his immune responses, killing any microbe, bacteria, or virus that it detects. Apparently, it has begun to target more than germs.

"Anything injected into his bloodstream is instantly attacked by the Nexus, and that includes the compound."

Jackal frowned as he looked at the pad. He did not respond, his brow furrowed in thought. Finally, he came to a decision. He turned to Fisk, then flicked his eyes to the cameras placed throughout the room. One didn't know who had access to what information now. He waited until Fisk slightly raised an eyebrow, then he said carefully,

"Inform the Client. He'll know what to do."

73

(Andresha)

White and red snow beneath me. Strange trees. Hot sticky blood running down my numb face and hands. Trying to get up, falling back down. Calling Edrix's name. Receiving no answer. People finding me, then everything going dark. My promise ...

I replayed the memory over and over again in my head as I walked through the snow. My head was tucked down against the icy wind that seemed to go right through my coat. That had been a month ago. When the light had dumped me in the middle of the forest with strange trees. They didn't have leaves, just bare branches. Others had green needles. The people here called them spruce trees. I didn't know exactly where I was. I knew that the nearest city was over ten hours away by car—a car with wheels that drove on the ground. The town where I was currently staying is small, with barely a hundred people, and it's in the middle of nowhere, in someplace called Alaska.

There were a lot of things I don't know. I didn't know if Red Star was still hidden. I didn't know if Seth and rest of my friends were still alive. I don't know if Fara was here with me. I didn't even know if Edrix was alive. And above all ...

I didn't know how I was going to get home.